An Obsidian Sky: Part One

Joel Thomas Cooke

ISBN: 978-0-6488094-0-1

DEDICATION

To Carol, the love my life and my ultimate source of inspiration.

I couldn't have done this without you

ACKNOWLEDGMENTS

Brendan, you were the first person I ever spoke to about the story, back when we talked for hours about stories in general. Clichés, characters, settings and my plans for the book; you helped with the groundwork for this story, and after many years of blood, sweat and tears, it's finally on paper.

Ryan, getting the feedback about the pacing, setting, and bouncing ideas off you has been tremendously helpful, and you've always been there to ground me when I get too carried away!

Carol, my dear wife. I've made more progress on these words and pages these last few years I've known you, compared to the combined six years that I previously worked on it. You are my muse, my daily inspiration, and my reason. I pray that you enjoy this story, and can readily identify how much you mean to me with each word, as you've helped with each one in your own way. With you by my side, I feel as though I could write a thousand novels, as you consistently energize my creativity, and challenge me to deliver my best work.

And to the rest of my family and friends, I thank you as well. For listening to me carry on about the book, the characters, the events. For hearing me babble on about the minutia of fiction in general, and about how long I've spent on this project. But most of all, I thank you for being there for me, through the good times, and the other ones.

Last but not least, I thank you, reader. At the end of the day my goal here is to entertain, and I hope you're pleased with your stay on Vale.

⌘

By my speculation, our fate appears to be linked to our act of extraordinary evil as it all began after that night, however many days ago it's been now. It cannot be a coincidence; for after the night of our most heinous moment, we were plunged into this nightmare.

We all share responsibility for what we did to those people, but I feel that I am held responsible for the actions that took place in my home for one significant reason. I can perceive the world around me with no discernible signs of madness, while the minds of those around me wither and descend into lunacy. If this is not some eternal punishment, then why is it that my mind is the only one spared from madness? The fact that my wits are still intact, it cannot be a coincidence.

It was all done under my supervision and ignorance. I was steadfast in my belief that we were above reprimand from anyone, fulfilling the will of the Pioneers that left us behind. The blessings given to me were ill-spent, to be sure, but how was I to know what fate had in store for us?

What we did was monstrous—I do not deny this—but do we deserve to be here? In this place?

We are forever damned in a prison of our own hopes and dreams, devoid of logic, time, and meaning. Surely no one deserves such a horrible fate?

It is not that we cannot leave our cursed home, but rather, a far greater threat looms patiently beyond the entrance, keeping us locked away in the house I raised my family in.

I have seen it, in a way, though I do not fully understand the method I stumbled upon many years ago.

One cannot see it when staring directly at it as it is simply imperceptible this way. Rather, it can be seen with one's peripheral vision, a phenomenon that I do not wish to make empirical. The being that I have glimpsed, I do not ever wish to see it again, so let it be an observation, not a fact, at this time.

When my son ventured beyond the doorway, I watched him from the second floor, begging him to see reason. I knew as I watched him open the door to our home that I wouldn't be able to get down to stop him in time, not with my limp the way it was. Instead, I clutched the worn, wooden railing as he disappeared into the endless sea of darkness that seemed to consume him.

By the time I did manage to shuffle down the stairwell, I had raced to the entrance as quickly as my old bones would carry me. As I gazed into the endless and unbroken obsidian sea, I saw nothing. My voice did not carry in that place, nor did I hear a sound of any kind. It felt cold as if the space outside the doorway was draining the heat from my flesh. As I breathed short, panicked breaths, the warmth of my air came out as fog, another

5

chilling reminder of the fate I'd unleashed upon my family and home.

I screamed and cried out for my son until my loving daughter tried to tear me away from the endless nothingness that had claimed him. I remember stubbornly clinging to the sides of the door with my trembling, white-knuckled hands for hours, and as I held my head beyond the portal yelling for my son to return to me, it had seemed as if nothing existed at all in the space beyond the doorway, only darkness. After a time, my daughter convinced me to turn away, my heart consumed with sorrow and remorse thinking of the pain and torture I had brought upon my family.

It was then that I saw it. As I turned my head to leave, I glimpsed it in my peripheral vision . . .

A presence reaching out with thousands of crimson appendages, each a different size, and yet all of them snaking towards me, wishing to consume us, enslave us.

I slammed the door as hard as I could. The terror that followed was enough for me to understand, so I would never let anyone else go near that doorway ever again. Throughout my entire life, I have never felt terror such as this. My daughter escorted me to my bedroom, wiped the beading sweat from my face, and sat me down to rest, where my insides felt cold for weeks on end.

So here we remain.

The home that I built with my bare hands now engulfed by an ancient, malevolent power, and our souls at the mercy of this unseen, whispering presence. I can still feel it there, yawing at the edges of our perception and our waning sanities. All of these things I have detailed here raise alarming questions for us. What happens to us at the end of our journey?

Is an ending even in the realms of possibility?

Death is not possible. We have tried.

All that we have now is time and torment. Endless, torturous, self-inflicted suffering.

Should my mind fail me before I can pour my soul into this book, know that I am sorry, endlessly, helplessly sorry, for the fate of my family, and my patients.

My name is Mosferul, and this is my confession.

⌘   ⌘

Excerpt from the book of Mosferul EST. 193 BGF

PROLOGUE

⌘

"Trauma has a way of changing the way you see things."

Therapy was never an area she thought necessary in days past, but the Inquisitor had encouraged Janus to focus on the future, not history.

"With enough time behind you, I promise that you'll make it through all of this far stronger than you were before. It is the traumatic times that allow us to grow the most, after all. And when it seems as though nothing will ever be the same as it once was, remember that time is the great mender of all things. What I want you to do now is to continue working on your mindset, to challenge those negative, intrusive thoughts of yours. And don't forget your family. Lean on them; let them and friends support you in your dark moments."

These words never left her. Each syllable spooling through her mind repetitively. The session with the Inquisitor left her reeling with anxiety, an effect she'd thought therapy would reduce, not increase.

Words aren't going to get me through this, neither is my family. I'm on my own.

Putting her faith in the Inquisition was a mistake. With the internalised reflective skills they'd instilled in her, Janus felt as though she'd been worse off than before. She now felt imprisoned within her own mind, unable to hold the line against the incessant negativity any longer. Whether it was self-analysis, talking to her mother, or even sharing herself with the colleagues and superiors within STARCOV, no matter what she did, it always led to more anguish. She should've done something about it sooner, but at least she was doing something about it now.

Better late than never, I suppose.

Janus trudged through each day as if moving through a mire, labouring under the crushing burden of her new reality. Her will, once unbreakable, had been completely obliterated, slowly worn away by time and negativity. Once looking forward to her weekends and holidays, Janus could no longer see past the hour she was stuck in, anxiously marking time until she could make it home and drink herself to sleep. Her obsession had consumed her, evident in her wandering gaze as she drove across the connecting bridge.

The fact that she was operating a vehicle at high speed among hundreds of others had somehow pushed its way to the back of her consciousness. Janus stared blankly through the windscreen into the darkness, her weary mind sifting through the session with the Inquisitor, tearing apart each word in an attempt to uncover a hidden meaning as if the solution to her trauma lay hidden within the experience. The repetition of her analysis was exhausting, and as she yawned, her muscles trembled from weariness as she rubbed her irritated, bloodshot eyes.

The dull yellow street lamps on the side of the road mingled with the blue moonlight, sending her mind into a trance-like state. The red bulbs of the cars travelling ahead of her streaked across her vision, melding with the lights, forming a surreal spectrum that danced playfully in front of her. Fixated by the display, Janus failed to notice her vehicle drifting to the other side of the road. A car horn rang out on the bridge, then another, snapping her back to reality as she clenched the leather steering wheel, heaving her SUV back into her lane and cursing herself as she steadied the wheel with her trembling fingertips. The person driving next to her gestured obscenely before speeding away as her heart pounded against the wall of her chest like a drum. Janus exhaled, the heavy rain pattering ceaselessly against the windscreen as she tried to calm her tattered nerves.

You're better than this. Get it together.

Shifting her rattled focus, Janus peered into the night sky through the rain-smeared windshield.

The obsidian expanse stretched over Menilax, flecked with intermittent cloud cover and glowing from the many buildings and monuments resting quietly underneath.

The journey to her parents' home was overshadowed with dark, ink-like clouds splotched along the skyline like a cancerous growth, refusing the usual splendid view of the night sky. The thick smog was a growing concern for Menilax, the city infamous for the worst weather patterns on the planet, yet some people did not seem concerned. The extreme climate that punished Menilax had the scientific community troubled, and yet the information surrounding the cause of the change was skewed with many parties disputing those who made it their life's work.

The world doesn't make sense to me anymore . . .

Janus smiled faintly. At least she could see parts of the sky behind the clouds.

The moonlit luminescence peering in between the clouds served to soothe her fatigue, and the rare sight of stars burning brightly behind helped ease her troubles if only for a moment.

Something about the display awakened her confidence, a boon she desperately needed on this night above others.

Tonight's the night.

Glancing to the clock on the dash, Janus sighed.

It's almost ten o'clock. I hope they're still awake.

Thinking on her parents and the conversation she was about to have with them, Janus felt as if she didn't want to proceed with her plan after all. All because she didn't want to participate in the conversation she needed to have.

Before her brother's disappearance, a few cold drinks would work wonders for her burdened mind after a taxing day, soothing her frayed emotions, relaxing her stress-ridden body. Shaking her head, Janus knew she'd been leaning on the crutch far too much of late. What was once an occasional tool had become a habit, growing dangerously close to an addiction. An obsession that her mother had gone in and out of for most of her life.

As the stray thought pierced her fragile calm, her palm began to tremble, doubling in intensity as the traumatic memories of her mother resurfaced.

Don't think about that. Pioneers deliver me, haven't I got enough to worry about?

Janus was positive that her binge drinking had only served to fuel her nightmares, which had become malicious and vivid. But a drunken stupor was preferable to not sleeping at all, she'd justified.

For every lousy behaviour Janus had developed since losing Oscar, there was a half-baked justification behind it. It was her reality now, a framework constructed by grief, preventing her from processing the truth of her situation.

Don't think about it; focus on the road.

Her knuckles began to whiten from exertion. Releasing them, Janus gasped as she realised her arm had been clenched since her near miss on the road a few minutes ago. Letting out a muscle-quivering sigh, Janus turned the wheel gently to get into the right-hand lane, pressing the brake down with her foot as she came to a stop before the car ahead of her.

Resting her back into the chair, Janus tapped her hand on the dash, waiting impatiently for the light to change. She gently flexed each of her fingers, using her wrists to hold onto the wheel as tingles scuttled across her skin like spiders, slowly restoring sensation to her extremities with a wave of sensation.

At first, Janus believed that moving away from fieldwork would've helped settle her nerves, but after three weeks, she felt worse. The time she was allocated to sit at her desk was spent rigorously over-thinking the ways she could rescue her brother rather than completing her assigned work.

I wonder if I'd have come to the same conclusions if I were still in the field . . . Didn't have a lot of time to think then . . .

The grain pattern of the steering wheel made her feel at ease. It brought back memories of driving with Oscar. She remembered him jumping inside the passenger seat, bursting with excitement as he told her about his first kiss, delivering him safely to school or to his group of friends. They had discussed practically everything, a result of spending such a great deal of time together over the years. Life was simply not the same without her little brother.

What if I never see you again . . .?

The thought brought with it feelings of rage and powerlessness. Janus reacted to the burning hatred flooding her senses by raising her fist, ready to pummel the wheel. Instead, she exhaled, grasping the steering wheel firmly as she concentrated on her breathing to calm herself. Janus sat there in silence, panting and sweating as her eyes ached on the inside. After another minute of focused breathing, Janus managed to quell her rising anger, pushing it away like she'd done so many times before. In its place came the muscular tremors in her hand, returning worse than they were before.

No more stalling. Tonight's duty is happening.

Janus nodded with her jaw clenched tightly. She was done feeling powerless.

I get him back, or I die trying.

⌘

Pulling the steering wheel to the left, Janus pulled into the driveway of her parent's home, switching the engine off quickly with the press of a button. She sat in the cabin for a few moments listening to the familiar ticking of the engine's internal components cooling down. Janus found herself frozen in place, the sudden silence jarring and unsettling.

Taking a deep breath, Janus went over the conversation she would have with her parents for what felt like the hundredth time.

Dad will understand.

She sighed.

But I doubt he's not going to let me go without a scolding first . . .

She had to be firm and harden herself emotionally to shield her conviction from her mother's passionate nature. Janus ran her fingers through her hair before pushing her head back into the headrest, tapping the steering wheel in a half-remembered rhythm.

Get it over and done with. Be blunt. Be honest.

Janus nodded to herself, reaching for the door handle.

If you don't come back from this . . . at least they'll know why . . .

Janus left the car promptly, pushing her body against the frosty, metal door gently so as not to bring any attention to her arrival. She closed her eyes as the gentle rainfall sprinkled over her face, making her shiver with anticipation while the tall grass tickled her ankles as she moved briskly across the lawn.

Opening her eyes, Janus stood before the door to her family home. Resting her hand on the copper handle, a sudden realisation stilled her.

Maybe they've been through enough heartache. I should leave them be.

Janus pulled her hand away, contracting her fingers as she visualised the look on her father's face after sharing the details of her plan.

They'd only try to talk me out of it.

She gasped, her hands trembling uncontrollably as she rubbed them together nervously, clenching her jaw as she grew furious with her apparent weakness. It felt as if her hands kept disobeying her, revealing her insecurity to the world. Turning around and eyeing the car longingly, she wanted to get back inside and leave, venture to the National Park without a second thought. But she couldn't.

Janus felt frozen in place, unable to make a decision either way.

Go and tell them.

"You okay, honey?"

Startled, she turned to her left, finding her father sitting quietly in a chair a few feet away from the door. The dull light of the cigarette in his mouth illuminating his greying facial hair, middle-aged features, and the Scitilliant snub nose the family was known for. She smiled thinly at him, and he smiled knowingly in return.

He had aged gracefully, despite a few scars from a career in the unit. No one got out of STARCOV without injuries. She hadn't realised until that moment that Nathan was in good shape for his age, looking at him as if it was the last time. His black t-shirt hid strong, lean muscles that did not seem to match his wrinkled face.

Her mind took her to a place where they would both be storming the National Park together, a hurtful fantasy that she ached for all the same. Two STARCOV legends taking matters into their own hands. But he'd retired a long time ago and would never yield to lawlessness, not even for her.

Tell him now. You can gauge his reaction and adjust your approach for Mother.

As she looked into his eyes, she felt the words catch in her throat. Janus had always loved her father more than her introverted mother, and after seeing his gentle features and easy smile, Janus felt calmer than she'd felt all day. Yet, it only made her hesitate. She was about to break his old heart. He seemed to sense her hesitation.

"I see you've got your old combat uniform on," he said, "are you back on field duty?"

She eyed him curiously, tucking the collar of her thick black shirt underneath her navy jacket. The move made Nathan chuckle.

"I've found Oscar," she spewed out.

Janus let the words hang in the air for a few moments.

"I know," he replied.

He had smile wrinkles, a feature that made him seem friendly, approachable, even if it was a smile meant to mock her attempt at secrecy.

Of course he knows . . .

The smile reminded her that it was possible for someone who'd lived through a career as a STARCOV operative, who had seen the things that he'd seen, to still let his guard down and express happiness like an undamaged individual. It was hard to imagine Nathan as a retiree sometimes as it'd been over a decade since he was considered an active operator, after all.

How could I be so naïve that he wouldn't find out?

"Davis has been keeping me up to date for the last few weeks," he said, breathing in smoke. "He also told me what you're thinking . . ."

She nodded thoughtfully, leaning on the bricks of their home as he eyed her curiously.

"I have to go," she said after a few moments of silence, shrugging like she had no choice. "I can't keep waiting around like this . . ."

The report contained sensitive information about the crew that had taken Oscar. A few members of the cell were on the STARCOV blacklist, and apparently, they had augurs in their ranks, a chilling fact that changed the equation completely. Every duty she'd ever been on where augurs were involved had been catastrophic.

As was typical for her mind lately, she burrowed into the roots of her psyche, yanking the most troubling memory that was on topic. The first time she'd encountered an augur was during her first duty with STARCOV. She remembered Captain Logan's face, the man who was to be her mentor. Images of the Clarenton Hotel and Darius Malaroth, the boy whose abilities haunted her to this very day, refused to leave her be. The details made Janus rub her forehead as if doing so would remove the trauma from her mind.

That bastard threw us around like we were toys . . . And he was only a boy . . .

Apparently, those involved with this cell were older, more senior augurs, which added another complication to the duty at hand. They would be well versed in their abilities, not to mention any other training that they had on top of their natural skill.

"Are you sure you're up for this?" he asked, smoking quietly.

Janus shrugged. "I know the topography, the Centre itself, and I've seen what these 'augurs' can do firsthand . . ." Gesturing firmly, she continued, "If you read Davis's notes, then you know these guys don't keep hostages for long. Soon enough, they become victims, even *if* the ransom's paid."

Information regarding the cell responsible was scarce; however, their operating procedures were discerned through an examination of their previous work. Her mother had paid the ransom immediately despite the advice from STARCOV command. Unfortunately, the syndicate had not been in touch afterwards, leaving the family to gestate with fear for over three arduous months. Adalia had claimed that the money had never been an issue for the family, and what they were asking for was a spec against the family fortune. Being the CEO of one of the largest weapons manufacturers on Vale was public knowledge, something Janus noted may have been a factor in the asking price of Oscar's captors.

Janus crossed her arms and gazed into her father's eyes. "I have to do this . . ."

He looked away, weighing her words carefully.

The wind whispered over the silence of the neighbourhood, the subtle rustling of trees and the chirping of mate-seeking insects accentuating the stillness of her father's position. After a few minutes of deliberation, Nathan took a deep breath before putting out the cigarette.

"I know that I can't stop you from going," he said, getting up from his chair and pacing over to the front door beside her. He opened it without any hesitation.

Before closing the door, he turned to Janus, who watched him apprehensively.

I thought you would've at least tried to talk me down . . .

"I can see it in your eyes," said Nathan, nodding in agreement. "You've already made up your mind." He swallowed dryly before continuing. "Don't worry about your mother . . . I'll talk to her."

Closing the door behind him, Janus was left alone under the night sky, speechless.

As the muffled discussion between her mother and father bled through the door, Janus tucked her hair behind her ears as her hand started to tremble again, albeit more violently than it had before.

I'm such a mess . . .

Nathan's words echoed through her skull as she clenched her fists.

"Are you sure you're up for this?"

Janus held her face in her hands, rubbing her damp cheeks restlessly.

Perhaps this is a mistake . . .

Releasing a heavy sigh, Janus stepped back onto the lawn, looking wistfully at the exterior of her family home. As her gaze wavered over the two-story home, her eyes drifted towards Oscar's bedroom window on the second floor near the left-hand side of the house. She began to feel a wave of terrible emotions bubbling in her chest. Uncertainty, anxiety, and dread began to overwhelm her as tears welled up in her eyes.

Looking down at her clenched fists, Janus decided then and there that she was done living like this. Of course she did not wish to die, and she'd be risking everything, but the thought of losing her brother while she sat on her backside as her emotions controlled her all day was intolerable, giving her the final nudge to take the leap.

Rather than indulge her anxiety any further, she decided to focus on preparation. The boot of the car popped open with a stern grip, and it didn't take her long to unzip her bag and visually confirm that she hadn't forgotten anything.

Janus zipped the bag up, closed the boot, and returned to the driver's seat of the SUV.

Switching the engine on, Janus inhaled a nervous breath as the car rumbled to life.

I've put this off for far too long. It's time to get it done.

The porch lights of the house came to life, causing Janus to squint as she used her hand to protect her eyes from the sudden bright beam. The motorised garage door thrummed and creaked, bringing the thick wooden slats into the roof with a slow slide as they collapsed into each other. The raising panels slowly revealed Nathan, who stood before the opening with a duffel bag draped over one shoulder, dressed in black and smirking at her playfully.

She watched him with her mouth open as he casually stepped around the SUV and opened the boot to drop his bag inside. Janus turned around to watch him through the gap as he smiled at her before closing the boot firmly. She turned to face the front, squinting her eyes in confusion as her mind struggled to grasp his intentions. Within a moment, he opened the passenger door and slid into the seat with a grunt.

Nathan turned to face her and nodded.

Janus nodded to him with a smile on her lips and a tear in her eye, quietly reversing the car into the street without a second thought. She couldn't find the words to express how she felt, and as her eyes took one last glance over the house she grew up in, she saw her mother watching them from the lounge room window.

"What did you say to her?" asked Janus.

She turned to face the road as they began the journey through the quiet suburban streets.

"I told her that we're going out for a few drinks," he said without looking away from the windscreen. "She doesn't need to know what we're up to."

Janus sighed. "And if we don't come back?"

"She'll figure it out," said Nathan. "I'll bet the farm her sister and mother will move in after a time. She won't be alone for long; don't you worry."

You've put some thought into this . . .

Janus exhaled, releasing the tension in her throat. "She needs you."

He chuckled. "You and your brother need me more." Nathan pointed towards a side street up on the right. "Turn there. We can make the freeway quicker this way."

⌘

"This is the place," said her father.

Janus was already driving slowly, a wise allowance for the dirt road they'd found themselves trekking across. Gently applying the brake, Janus pulled the vehicle to a gradual, complete stop.

"I'll need a few minutes to get ready," said Nathan, promptly leaving the vehicle and ejecting the boot.

Janus looked further up the hill as she turned the engine off, regarding the National Park's Information Centre with a warm familiarity. The last time she was here, she was merely a child, visiting the open expanse with her family. It'd seemed like a world of its own then, a place so large she could barely comprehend it.

After zipping open his bag, Nathan lifted the frame of his rifle out, holding it before him with a quiet awe. "This'll be the first time I use this rifle," he said, exhaling as he regarded it. "For practical purposes, at least."

Her chest tightened. Up until now, she hadn't considered how her father felt about wet work after such a long time without participation, not to mention he was about to return to the field with a rifle he had an emotional connection with.

Janus hopped out of the car and rounded the corner where she found Nathan working expediently on putting the components together. She placed her hand on his shoulder.

"Are you sure *you're* ready for this?" she asked delicately.

He didn't even glance up at her, handling the polished silver barrel as he gestured with it.

"Well, not yet," he said with a warm smile. Nathan chortled as he worked away, sliding the bolt into the chamber before attaching the combined piece to the weapon platform.

The rifle quickly became his pride and joy since retirement, and although he hadn't been a sharpshooter during his time in the service, civilian life came with an abundance of spare time. Nathan spent the majority of his customising, practising, and perfecting the piece. He'd always idealised the sharpshooter but was never good enough to take on the role full time. At least, that's what he told Janus.

You were better than most, you humble old fool . . .

She'd seen him at the range; he had a natural talent for it. It wasn't unusual for a retired operator to spend so much time with weapons; in fact, most veterans from STARCOV carried a few hobbies over from their time in the service, and Nathan had thought ever highly of this particular model during his particular stint.

After putting the rifle together, Nathan slung it over his shoulder, the leather strap resting neatly over his chest. They shared a look of recognition and respect before he gestured sharply towards her bag.

"Do you need some help putting your kit together?"

She tilted her head to the rifle, ignoring his question.

"Is *that* all you're taking?" she asked. "I hope you have a backup plan if that relic of yours doesn't work . . . ?"

Nathan chuckled, lifting his jacket up to reveal a pistol strapped to his midsection. "I got my Lugar right here," said Nathan with a knowing smile.

"My bad," she said with a smirk. "You've got *two* relics. Now I feel *much* better . . ."

Nathan stared into her eyes with a jarring tonal shift. "Last chance now," he said, pulling his jumper back over his belt and placing his hand on her shoulder. "Are you good?"

Janus took a deep breath before nodding. "As good as I'll ever be."

"Good girl," he said gruffly. "Good luck, honey."

Janus watched Nathan joylessly as he turned around and sprinted across the dirt road. As he dashed through the tall, unkempt grass, Janus went over the plan again in her mind.

Nathan's going to roost on top of the radio tower nearby while I move in on these bastards, engaging them in close quarters while he covers me from the tower. The schematics show plenty of visibility on the first two floors, but the attic's going to be a tricky one, so I'll be on my own up there.

After a minute of running, he reached the tree line and vanished amongst branch and shadow.

Relieved of conscience, reactions remain, remain limber.

She took a few quick breaths.

Hopefully, this isn't the last time I see you, old man . . .

Janus had a moment of panic, as the all too familiar intrusive thoughts returned, spurning her overzealous plans to retrieve her abducted brother.

What if this is the last time you see your father?

What if you get him killed?

What happens if—

Janus clenched her jaw, snarling at her own neurosis as she reached down to her bag.

Enough!

She unzipped it forcefully, refusing to entertain the thoughts any further.

Janus slipped out her own pride and joy, the ST-31s, also known as "the Viper." The compact machine gun was capable of firing all eighty rounds within the space of three seconds, an incredible amount of firepower for any weapon platform.

During her first duty with Captain Logan, she'd carried the same model into the duty. It had served her well then, and it would serve her well now.

Most of the sensible operators in the field had moved on to the newer models, but she preferred this one.

Janus Scitilliant, using the Scitilliant Model 31s.

She chuckled, slipping the weapon strap over her shoulder.

Mother would be so proud . . .

Judging by the blueprints and heat maps of the building, Janus felt confident with the Viper as her weapon of choice as she reached back into the bag for the next piece of equipment, her gloves. Fitting them snugly over each hand, she fished out the next one, the black leather holsters for her handgun, and knife. Next came her beanie and facemask, and finally, her earpiece.

Before closing the boot, Janus strapped her handgun and knife into each compartment, confident that she was now ready for the task at hand. Locking the car with her remote, she slipped it into one of her belt pockets before launching into a run towards the tree line.

Janus repeated the words drilled into her mind during the STARCOV cadet program.

Relieved of conscience, reactions remain, remain limber.

The words brought on the focused mindset of the operator.

Relieved of conscience, reactions remain, remain limber.

Countless years of conditioning soaked through the fragile state of mind she inhabited, melting away her hesitation, transforming the worried, anxious woman she was into the weapon her superiors had spent decades developing.

You are a scalpel. You act with precision, diligence, purpose.

Janus slowed down upon reaching the tree line. Before she began weaving between the trees, she spotted a large stone tablet rising from the damp soil to her left. The tablet described the age of the site through a metal plaque scrawled with words. Before she had a chance to review it, her father's voice crackled through her earpiece.

"I've reached the tower. I'm beginning my ascent."

No time for inspirational quotes.

She dashed between the trees like a wolf, staying low, moving with agility, and watching her surroundings vigilantly. Every step she took was considerate, avoiding branches and thickets of leaves on the forest floor to prevent her presence from being telegraphed.

Approaching the Information Centre directly, by moving up the hill would've been quicker, but skirting the Centre through the tree line offered her a cleaner approach. They didn't have any other support out here, making her current route the safer choice.

Stalking her way through the forest, Janus kept checking her position in relation to the Information Centre, the lamps around it lighting the building like a beacon in the darkness. Nathan reported through the radio that he was now on top of the radio tower, signalling that he was ready to cover her approach.

"I can see two on the balcony," he reported soon after.

Janus now stood as close as she was going to get by tracing the tree line, so she started approaching the overgrown field carefully in a low crouch.

It's a straight shot from here. It'd probably take me two minutes of sprinting to get me there.

"Can you take them out?" she asked, wiping the cold sweat from her forehead.

"Hard to say," he replied. "Looks like there are five targets inside the Centre. If they look out the window, they might see their buddies go down."

After a time, he continued, "I suppose it is possible if I time it right, but you'll be out of position if I do it now."

"The two on the balcony," said Janus. "What are they sporting?"

"Standby . . ."

Janus took a deep breath, attempting to restore her stamina while she had a moment to rest.

"Looks like they have automatic rifles with standard sights."

She shook her head. "Can you make out the model of the weapon?"

Nathan chuckled. "We're not all gun nuts, honey."

Janus slipped the facemask over her nose and mouth, squinting as she watched the two men on the balcony talking to each other.

"Hmm," mused Nathan, "I can't see any thermal optics . . . or night spotters around their necks."

"So," said Janus, "might be time to get on my stomach and crawl . . . ?"

"It could work," said Nathan. "The lighting around the Centre isn't the best, so it'll keep you hidden until you get close."

"I'll get into position," said Janus. "If I'm spotted, I'll make a run for it."

"Crawling through the grass, hmm?" he said, grunting to himself. "A tried and true method of infiltration. I love it."

Janus chuckled, moving into the grass as she lay on her stomach. "Going old school."

Nathan scoffed. "Come now, old school is the best school. Besides, it's good for your spine. You'll thank me when you're older."

Janus shook her head with a smile as she tightened the strap of the ST-31s before crawling. Moving slowly through the dew-soaked grass of the forest, Janus kept her eyes peeled on the two men on the balcony, squinting through the blades of green grass.

"Keep me covered, old school," she said mockingly.

"School's out, kid, get your game face on."

"See you on the other side," replied Janus.

The crawl went relatively quick for Janus, mostly because she was focusing so intently on whether or not the men were making any sudden moves. Her instincts reminded her that she could unsheathe her pistol in a split second, so if they did spot her, she would be ready to return fire before they had a chance to react.

Janus eyed the wooden support slats supporting the building, which looked climbable. The balcony could be accessed from a stairwell on the left-hand side, but Janus didn't like the visibility it presented.

"So far, so good. They have no idea you're there," said Nathan.

"Not far now," she whispered into the headset.

"So, second floor . . ." After a few moments of mumbling to himself, Nathan continued, "I can see three more, looks like they're playing cards—of all things—and it looks as if there are three more in the attic, although I can't be sure; the angle's pretty bad . . ."

She tallied the total at thirteen, although the two immediate threats above her were the priority. Ahead of her, Janus could see the L-shaped staircase winding around to the balcony. The cover that the staircase presented was inadequate, so Janus placed her hands on the wooden slats, and began the slow climb.

Because the Centre was constructed on the slope of the mountain, these frameworks were designed to make the floors of the building level, going against the naturally sloped environment. They were, of course, not intended for climbing, so Janus had to be patient as she ascended. If she made any noise whatsoever, it would place the entire duty at risk, not to mention their lives.

The two gunmen stood above her talking in hushed voices.

She looked up at the man resting over the edge of the balcony, catching the scent of tobacco wafting down as she gripped the next handhold. Testing each pillar with a delicate wiggle, Janus took no chances, ensuring each hold was structurally sound before committing to it. She didn't want to force her weight on a creaky joint after all.

When she came closer to the ledge, Janus overheard the two men conversing about a sport of some kind. She never found the time to watch television, so it sounded more like nonsense to her. The smoke continued to waft down, and at least now she was close enough to take a good whiff.

Old Port Premiums. Pretty expensive brand . . .

As she got as close as she wanted to be to the top, Janus delicately placed the weapon barrel through one of the slats on the floor. The unbraced recoil wouldn't do her wrist favours, so she hooked the handle over the slats and waited for the men to make a move. If they looked down, they would see the muzzle of her weapon poking through the floor. So she watched them, quietly and carefully, ready to fire at a moment's notice.

Janus lifted her right hand to her earpiece and hit the talk button on her radio two times, confirming she was in position. Glancing to the right, Janus took a moment to locate the metal tower where Nathan would be positioned, barely visible in the darkness, apart from a faint red light, blinking intermittently every few seconds. Within a few quiet moments, a distant cracking noise echoed through the valley. The non-smoking man's head blew apart in the space of a second, sending his twitching body to the ground to writhe, as gore spattered across his colleague and the floorboards behind him. As the smoker gasped in terror, she gently squeezed the trigger, sending a quiet stream of lead into his chin and through the top of his skull, killing him instantly as he fell back, the balcony rumbling from his fall.

She pulled herself up and over the railing, sprinting to the windowsill as she crouched down as low as she could. Resting underneath, Janus listened in to the next room, ready to assess any potential signs of distress. After a few moments of patient listening, she heard a man talking inside.

"I used to love that stupid lizard as a kid."

Lizard . . . ?

Janus moved towards the door, allowing her a better position to hear the conversation.

"Mascots give me the creeps . . . You know it's just some old alcoholic playing nice for the kids," said the voice of another man.

"Hey, my daughter's a mascot, and she's studying to be an inquisitor!" The woman was incredulous.

"Yeah, but I'll bet the guy who does the night shift is a drug addict . . ."

Most of the people in the room laughed, but not the woman.

Janus could make out the sounds of an old advertisement playing inside.

They must've found the television on that rusty cart.

She shook her head with a smirk.

Can't believe that thing still works . . .

Peeking over the windowsill, Janus observed their blatant ignorance to their dead comrades. She exhaled, releasing the tension building in her muscles.

"We're clear," she whispered into her headset.

She assessed the room quickly.

Three lights, one television, five threats with pistols strapped to their waists.

Raising her right fist, Janus made a blinking motion with her palm.

If Dad takes out the lights, I can sneak inside and get behind the television.

After three seconds, two gunshots rang out from the darkness of the forest.

Janus opened the creaky door as two slugs pelted the wooden wall, smashing the lightbulbs to pieces. Nathan had placed his shots precisely, slowing the bullets enough to break the lightbulbs but not travel much further.

Janus closed the door quickly as the third shot took out the last light in the room, blanketing her entrance in shadow and covering the noise of the door latch closing with the exploding lightbulb. Janus crept around the lounge to her right, noticing one of the large bullets from Nathan's rifle rolling around next to her.

Good shooting, old man.

"Damn!" said one of the younger men. "That scared me to death! Did you hear that?"

One of the women stood up, gesturing to the light bulb closest to the TV.

"They all exploded . . . !"

One of the men stood up and walked towards the entrance, flicking the light switch on and off.

"Weren't you listening to me?" said the woman. "The light bulb *exploded.* Why are you flicking the light switch?"

The man shrugged.

"You never know."

She looked at him like the fool he was, gesturing with confusion.

During the commotion, Janus crept around the room, using the furniture to relocate without detection. Crouching low behind the television—which still blared old advertisements at the squabbling terrorists—Janus waited patiently.

She heard them fumble in the dark, cursing and grunting to themselves in frustration, all the while biding her time. With a careful hand, she reached over to the side of the television, fumbling with the controls as she winced and prayed that she would remain undetected.

"What's going on down there!?" said one of the soldiers upstairs.

"The bulbs blew or somethin'. It's okay, though; we'll figure it out!"

The woman was beginning to lose her cool. "We need new bulbs you *idiot*; go upstairs and find some spares."

Janus turned the volume to its maximum before rotating the dial controlling the channels. The hissing static of the new channel reverberated through the cabin, causing the insurgents to cover their ears. The sudden racket gave her a clear advantage, but what Janus was really taking advantage of was the obfuscating white light blinding them all from her presence as they squinted and averted their eyes.

Janus rose up from behind the TV, standing in plain sight with her ST-31s shouldered and ready. They were all looking around; one of them even scanned the darkness behind the TV where she stood with her weapon.

They can't see me at all. The light's too bright.

Exhaling slowly, Janus depressed the cold metal trigger as she lined up her first victim. He fell under the whispering chatter of gunfire, barely audible over the hissing TV. Snapping the weapon to her next victim, she depressed the trigger again before moving onto the next one. Within a few seconds, they were all dead.

"They're onto you," said Nathan. "You've got five seconds."

Janus clicked the button in the middle of the weapon, ejecting the spent magazine as it fell to the floor. She crouched down behind the television and inserted another magazine into the gun as three insurgents came downstairs with their automatic weapons raised.

The rear guard clicked on a torch, angling the bright beam of light through the darkness behind the TV, sweeping over her head as she waited patiently for her moment.

A young man yelled over the hissing static; the only words she could make out were "alert" and "upstairs."

Now!

She stood up and squeezed the trigger.

A barrage of bullets peppered the stairwell, killing all three men in the space of a second as they collapsed and lay still. Janus raced around the lounge and dashed up the stairwell, ascending to the second floor in a matter of seconds. As she reached the top, she moved carefully with her ST-31s held forward, sweeping the area for any threats that may have come down from the attic.

Three more . . .

To her left, she could see the attic atop the stairwell, which she'd have to clear next. To the right was a bolted-in, steel table with pamphlets strewn messily around it. It looked to her as if the insurgents had cleared the table to make way for their card game, among other things. She found wads of cash, bottles of alcohol, and a variety of weaponry scattered across it. Scanning the rest of the room, Janus found a large fridge in the corner standing adjacent to a small desk with souvenirs and a rustic cash register. Some of the stuffed toys had been placed in provocative positions, serving as a curiosity to her.

She chortled.

Well, after the discussion I heard downstairs . . . it's not that out of character . . .

Satisfied that the remaining threats were in the attic, Janus placed her boot on the first step to the next floor, not wishing to waste any time.

I need to get to them before they have a chance to prepare.

As she reached the middle of the staircase, Janus believed it far too quiet upstairs for her liking. Pausing for a moment, she exhaled gently before pressing the talk button on her earpiece.

"Do you have eyes on the attic?" she whispered.

"I can see two men standing there," said Nathan. "Looks like they know you're coming, although they're not armed. Can't see the third anywhere . . . but visibility is poor from my side," continued Nathan. "I'll make my way down to you. Can you wait until I make it over?"

Where's the third one?

Janus took a single step up.

A large sword came down from the top of the staircase. The unseen attacker thrust it toward the side of her head, but her instincts kicked in before it connected. Janus dashed back down the stairs, but the blade punched into her weapon, pinning her machine gun to the wall. Clenching her jaw, she unsheathed her pistol, but as she raised it to the top of the stairwell, an invisible force pushed her down the stairs. Before Janus could understand what was happening, the back of her head cracked against the ceiling of the stairwell. Spinning out of control, she landed on her chest, feeling a rib fracture against the dust-coated floor as her head slammed into the wooden floorboards.

She cried out in agony.

"Janus! What happened?" barked Nathan. "Pioneers save us . . . are you okay!?"

Janus had never heard her father's tone sound so panicked.

Her chest flashed with pain as she tried to stand.

Ears ringing, vision swimming, and eyes watering, Janus stood up despite it all. The blinding pain prevented her from thinking clearly as a harrowing panic swelled in her gut while she clutched her side and gasped for air.

"Need to . . . get to cover . . ." she croaked out, still breathless from the tumble.

"Are you still alive, *girl?*" said a voice from the stairwell. Glancing up to the stairs, Janus looked around the room for somewhere to recover, snatching up her pistol before moving towards the other side of the room. Janus wheezed as she shuffled behind the refrigerator in the corner, cursing her situation as she leant up against the cold metal of the appliance. She grimaced as a wave of nausea took hold, it felt as if a white-hot fire poker had impaled her side.

Shit . . . Shit!

"Janus!? Please answer me . . . Are you okay!?" crackled her earpiece.

She closed her eyes, trying to catch her breath to talk to Nathan, to tell him she needed help.

Her breathing was slow and pained, her voice raspy and jittery.

"I . . . need . . . help . . ." she managed to mutter in between breaths.

There was no reply.

She peeked around the corner and watched the man who'd almost killed her come down the stairs. Coming into view, Janus managed to catch a glimpse of him and his smug grin before she pulled herself back behind the refrigerator.

He was a tall, dark-skinned man, and he strolled over to her position seemingly unfazed that he was standing out in the open. Janus peeked around the refrigerator with her pistol raised and fired off four rounds, hoping to put down the arrogant fool quickly. Raising his hand, he stopped the bullets before they collided with his flesh, holding the projectiles in suspended animation before him. The man waved his wrist about, carrying the ammunition in mid-air as he moved closer to Janus.

"Janus!?" boomed Nathan's voice. "Please . . . You have to talk to me here!"

"I . . . can't . . ." She gasped for air, still physically unable to catch her breath.

Pioneers . . . what am I going to do . . . ?

"You have given me curiosity, girl," said the man in a foreign tongue.

You've been through worse than this, focus up!

She pressed the talk button on her radio four times.

Peeking out at the man again turned out to be a mistake as he flicked his wrist towards her, dispatching the bullets her way with ferocious velocity. Janus pulled back to avoid them, but she was too late. They pelted the fridge and peppered her body before she could hide completely. Janus gasped, feeling a stab of pain in her side as her fingers naturally touched the impact point, nursing the wound as the mounting pain and anxiety threatened to overwhelm her. Her trembling hand came away bloody.

They're only surface wounds; the vest would've taken away most of the impact. Focus.

She closed for eyes for a brief moment.

Relieved of conscience, reactions remain, remain limber . . .

Had her mindset been different, she would've thought it impossible that this man had just thrown her own bullets back at her. But she was in the middle of a fight, and with it came an adrenaline-fueled clarity that refused to validate any fear-based emotion.

It was the place a soldier inhabited, but she was beyond even that.

STARCOV operators are the best of the best.

Captain Logan's voice spoke to her, coming to her aid and reminding her of the values of the unit.

You are resourceful, undying, your conviction is not to your country or your duty, but to yourself. You've been given the ultimate set of tools to deal with every possible situation, developed from the wisdom of those who have chosen armed combat as their life's work, forged through centuries of warfare. Trust yourself, believe in your instincts, and remember our words . . .

Janus took a deep, pain-filled breath, reciting the words once more.

Relieved of conscience, reactions remain, remain limber . . .

"*Okay, time to kill this fool,*" she said under her breath.

"Come again, girl?" he queried, confused at her overheard words.

He must have some kind of kinesis, or telepathy . . .

Her mind raced with possibilities.

This is the augur we'd been warned about.

"It would please me to know your name," said the man. "Perhaps it doesn't have to end this way for you," he chortled.

Does the ability surround him? Is it constantly active?

"You're an impressive woman, to be sure, and it would be a shame to kill you without at least knowing your name." He chuckled confidently. "And cowering behind a fridge, of all things."

Was it like a shield? Could the ability be neutralised somehow?

She needed to buy some time.

"I'm here for Oscar," she said.

Janus felt around her wound to discover that the bullets were lodged shallowly in her side; the bulletproof vest she wore had indeed kept them from penetrating, which allowed her a sigh of relief. She picked them out one at a time, clenching her jaw, accepting the pain that thrummed through her body.

That kinetic ability he has . . . It can toss those bullets pretty quick.

She continued to breathe as she felt her mind return to the mindset of the operator.

Do not underestimate him again.

"I know the boy well," he replied smoothly. "Why is he important to you?"

"The why is irrelevant," said Janus. "I'm a mercenary. I don't make it a habit of asking questions. If you're willing to negotiate, then perhaps I can tell my team outside to back off. We need him alive, so it benefits us both if you're willing to talk this out . . ."

"Tell me your name first, and then we shall talk," said the man.

Janus felt the fridge she rested against begin to rumble against her.

Is he . . . controlling the fridge . . . ?

"My name doesn't matter," she said confidently, visualising her next move. "The rest of my team is nearby, ready to fire on my command," she bluffed. "I can call them off, but only if you're willing to work with me here."

She let her words sink in for a moment. "Let me speak to the person in charge, and we can work something out. We want the boy, that's all . . ."

"Very well," he said. "You speak words of truth; I can see it. Come out from there, and I'll take you to the boss."

The fridge began to rumble considerably.

His shadow started to appear beside her, which meant he was very close now.

"If you won't come out, then I shall force you out!" he yelled.

She felt the fridge lurch towards her as she dived out from behind it.

Rolling across the room, she fired her pistol at him. She managed to squeeze off six bullets in quick succession before rolling to her feet.

Five bullets left.

He recovered from his attempt to crush her with the kitchen appliance, catching the rounds in mid-air before sending them back towards her. They missed Janus by millimetres as she dropped on her stomach. Firing three more shots, Janus watched the man twitch and yelp as two of the bullets pelted his stomach, knocking him off balance as he stumbled back. Her manoeuvre had cost her as a wave of nauseating pain pulsated through her body, making her scream out in agony.

"You *shot* me . . . ?"

The man was incredulous, his shocked state giving her time to stand up despite the searing pain flaring across her chest.

"You . . . !" he bellowed. The augur clenched his teeth in anger as he extended his arms. Within a second, a massive wall of energy came to life before him as he continued to stumble away. Staring him down, she unsheathed her knife, flicking the hilt between her fingers as she began marching towards him.

His eyes seemed to gaze through her, completely consumed with rage.

"Do you know who I am? Girl!?"

He threw his arms forward, sending the blue energy roaring towards her. As the blast wave engulfed the room, howling toward her like a monsoon, she took off into a sprint.

Janus's timing was impeccable.

As the wall of power picked up everything that wasn't nailed down, Janus was sliding underneath the table where the card game had been. Saved from the destructive rage of the augur's ability, she stood up on the other side of the table before he could recover. As he lowered his tired arms, Janus threw the knife at his throat. The blade plunged into his neck, causing him to gurgle as he clutched the wound with a grimace. Within a moment, he fell to his knees, staring at her weakly as she approached him to finish the job.

She clutched the knife by its handle before yanking it free as the blood bubbling from the wound became a free-flowing pump, spewing crimson over his chest and clothing.

His eyes widened in horror as his neck pulsated, his hands clasping and squeezing, trying to seal it as he gasped like a fish out of water.

Janus watched the light from his eyes fade away before the body fell forwards.

Using her shirt, she wiped the bloody knife clean before sheathing it calmly.

"He's down," she said into the radio, panting heavily as she rubbed the sweat from her face with the back of her hand.

A great many questions lingered after silence enveloped the room.

Questions can wait . . .

She took a deep breath. "Dad . . . are you there?"

"Your skills are impressive, surrogate." Looking up to the top of the stairwell, she saw a man standing before the precipice. She raised her pistol.

You have two bullets left. Make them count.

"Identify yourself!" she demanded.

The man began walking down the stairs, his hands clasped behind his back.

"I won't ask again!" she yelled, clicking the hammer back on her handgun.

"My name is Keynan," said the man. "May I ask yours? You never did give it to my—"

he gestured to the dead augur, "—associate."

His tone was too casual, too relaxed for someone who had a gun in their face. She was about to assert control, but she made the mistake of looking into his eyes.

White eyes . . .

She shook her head as a cold shiver danced along her spine.

"You're . . . a Pioneer . . . ?"

He chuckled warmly.

"No one has called me a Pioneer in a very long time."

The longer she looked at him, the more her nerves began to fray. His salt-and-pepper hair, short beard, and austere features gave her the impression that he was an average person, but the eyes were nothing close to normal. He wore a black overcoat with a dark purple chest plate underneath it which reflected the stale yellow lights beaming down from the ceiling.

She stepped away from him, giving his presence a wide berth as she became lost in a sea of anxiety and nerves. It was like witnessing God in flesh form, his presence captivating her and terrifying her at once.

"You killed Desiriah quickly," he said, flicking his chin toward the body as he joined her on the second floor. "He was a gifted augur . . . and you took him down, on your own?"

He nodded, gesturing confidently. "I am impressed."

Her arms were trembling from the cocktail of pain, nerves, and fear swirling like a storm inside her skull. The handgun in her hands rattled as she willed her body to relax.

You're in control . . . Stay focused.

"Sinew, will you join us please?" he said, craning his neck towards the attic.

"As you wish," said an old man. She heard footsteps cross the attic.

Another man walked down the stairwell, his appearance far more unsettling than the Pioneer. He had a broad, sinister smile as he came into view, the cowl he wore masking the rest of his face. Sinew wore an elaborate purple and black cloak with gold runes embroidered over it. It made him look like a zealot, but from what religion, she did not know.

His grin widened at the sight of her; a clean-shaven, wrinkled chin was the only thing that she could make out in the low light, along with his blackened teeth.

Pioneers never age . . . So this "Sinew" can't be one . . .

She shook her head, unable to comprehend what was happening before her eyes.

"Unfortunately, we don't have a lot of time to spend with you, surrogate," said the Pioneer. "You're interrupting a business discussion, one that involved the man you killed, in fact."

The white-eyed man sighed impatiently as he moved closer to her. "I'd have you state your intentions sooner rather than later."

She cleared her throat, her hands trembling more and more with each passing second.

"My team and I . . ."

She cleared her throat, wincing as she gasped. Speaking made her chest ache, so she tried to get out the words as quickly as she could. "We've been sent to recover . . . an asset," she said, holding her weapon as tight as she could. "We know you've abducted Oscar Scitilliant."

The Pioneer chuckled. It was a noble, pompous chuckle, which caused her anxiety to flare up even further.

"Where is he . . . ?" she asked, losing her composure as she began to lose feeling in her hands.

Keynan nodded. "You are his sister, are you not?"

Her neck twitched violently, causing her to yelp as she dropped her weapon.

She crouched down immediately, picking it up and aiming it at Keynan, her eyes wide with shock. The two of them chuckled at her display, glancing to each other fondly.

"She's so . . . jumpy!" said Sinew, shaking his head.

They were close now.

Moments passed in silence as Keynan inspected her with his eyes, his expression remaining neutral.

"He's in a safe place," he finally said, nodding to her.

His nonchalant attitude was starting to bug her. She wanted to fire a bullet into his leg, but her fingers refused to squeeze the trigger as she grunted in frustration, repeatedly trying to fire her weapon.

"I can't—" was all she could say as she started to lose sensation in her arms.

Like a fast-acting poison, the numbness spread along her arms, slithering through her flesh like a serpent. Soon enough, she lost feeling in her extremities as she dropped the pistol again, but this time, she was unable to pick it back up. Her limbs now refused to obey her.

She clenched her teeth together, breathing heavily as her body felt swarmed by a thousand tiny stings. Her heart pounded in her chest as the numbness quickly took hold of everything inside of her. Watching on in horror, her limbs began moving on their own as if someone else was controlling her. Janus took out her knife and tossed it away limply.

"No . . ." she muttered.

Piece by piece, her arms tossed her equipment away, surrendering to the unseen force that was controlling her like a puppet, panting and sweating as she tried to resist the malicious effect.

"She's easy to control . . ." said Sinew, slurring his words slightly as if he were drunk.

"Forgive my associate," said Keynan. "He can be quite uncouth at the best of times."

A thunderous roar echoed through the room. A gunshot outside the window, shattering the glass like rain as it sprinkled across the area. Janus watched as a giant slug pelted Sinew, sending his body across the room as blood splashed over the walls.

His withered body fell to the floor as the Pioneer turned to face the window where the shot had rung out. Another round smashed through the window, and then another, and yet the Pioneer stood defiantly, completely unaffected as the slugs battered into his chest. The bullets simply bounced off him as he looked out of the window with frustration.

"You didn't mention you had a friend," he said as he extended his hand.

Janus regained control of her body for a moment as she turned to look out the window.

She saw Nathan hanging outside with a harness, his Lugar raised towards Keynan as he ejected the empty magazine. Then, he was flying through it, sending more shards of glass throughout the room. Keynan grunted with displeasure as he lifted his hand into the air, bringing Nathan before him. Her father hovered a meter off the ground, serving at the mercy of the Pioneer.

Janus took off into a sprint, picking up her knife from the ground along the way, but Keynan was ready for her too. Snapping his hand out and picking her up off her feet, he brought her next to her father, suspending the both of them as he grimaced. The overwhelming numbness returned in an instant this time; she couldn't resist at all as he overpowered both of them easily.

"It's rare that I'm caught off guard, primal," said Keynan, observing Nathan with curiosity.

"You are both part of a Special Forces unit; of that, I am sure."

Janus felt as if she was being crushed, and by the sound of Nathan's scream, so did he.

"But which one, I wonder?"

Nathan began raising the large pistol in his hand, trying to levy it towards the Pioneer.

"Go to hell, you bastard!" he screamed.

"You've got quite a lot of fight in you, it seems." Keynan nodded towards the window. "Are there more of you out there?"

Janus saw Sinew's body writhe on the floor, wiggling around in his own blood as he tried to find his feet. Within a few moments, the old man rose up and dusted himself off.

"I cannot sense any others . . ." said the old man, who joined Keynan.

He seemed unaffected by the rounds Nathan had knocked him down with, fixing his cloak as he rubbed his receding hairline with wrinkled hands. Before the old man could slip the hood over his face, Janus got a good look at him, estimating him to be in his sixties. He watched her with a wicked, yet curious smirk.

"Forgive me," said Keynan, "but I cannot allow you two to leave this place alive."

Keynan sighed, looking each of them in the eye before continuing.

"You have seen my face, and that . . ." he brought his arm close to his face, clenching his fist, the action pulling Nathan even closer to him, "cannot be abided . . ."

Janus's heart stopped.

Keynan extended his arm, throwing Nathan out the window so quick she would've missed it if she blinked. Raising his arm high into the air, the Pioneer closed his eyes, holding his limb outstretched for a moment before releasing his clenched fist.

She listened intently, her eyes wide with horror as she heard her father scream into the lonely night. Then he stopped, and there was nothing more.

Janus wanted to shriek, to express her grief, but she couldn't move or speak. Janus clenched her jaw, trying desperately to move any part of her body that she could, but all she felt was icy cold numbness, which continued to restrict her movements, holding her in place, leaving her unable to express the agony that was tearing her insides into pieces.

Keynan walked over to her, his hands returning to the small of his back.

"Your eyes . . ." he said, caressing her face as she snarled at his touch. "You share similarities with him . . ."

"He—" said Keynan gesturing out the window, "was your father . . . Which means you've come to save your little brother . . ."

She screamed in his face through a clenched jaw. Janus wanted nothing more than to slam her head into his face.

He sighed.

"I am sorry," said Keynan, "but your brother cannot be released. We need him for something larger than all of us, surrogate. The work we are doing, it is far too important to discard based on sentiment alone."

"Take me . . ." she managed to say. "Let . . . him go . . ."

Janus grunted as the force brought her to her knees, crushing her against the floor as she tried desperately to resist.

"That's enough!" said Keynan, dismissing Sinew with a sharp gesture.

Janus's head started pounding as she clenched her eyes, trying to will away the pain as she felt control return to her. Adrenaline surged through her body like a tidal wave, wiping away her nerves and anxiety like a cold snap. Then, as if on cue, the intense sorrow and grief of listening to her father suffer and die obliterated her renewed control.

She cried.

Janus became completely immobilised by her emotions as her throat tightened and her heart ached like it'd caved in on itself. It was a paralysing, overwhelming feeling, one that she had never experienced throughout her entire life.

Keynan walked towards her slowly. The fearful realisation of her impending death shot through her spine like a bolt of lightning, and yet, she could not move a muscle.

"Tell me, Sinew," said Keynan sorrowfully. "Is she augmented?"

Sinew shook his head as he turned to face him.

"She doesn't appear to be . . ."

"Well then," said Keynan, sighing heavily, "I'm afraid we won't be able to proceed with your suggestion."

Keynan touched her shoulder as she lay on her hands and knees.

"I am . . . sorry, for what we have done to your family. Despite your obvious, extraordinary skill, you do not possess the gift that your sibling does, which is why we cannot accept your proposal. We need him, not you . . ."

He helped her up to her feet. Janus watched him, completely empty inside as tears rolled across her face, staring into his godly eyes with an empty expression.

"I think it's honourable of you to volunteer in his stead, especially considering you lack the knowledge on why we've detained him in the first place."

She tried her hardest to process what was happening, but her mind was broken and refused to cooperate. She wanted to kill him.

Fury and hatred engulfed her.

She wanted to tear him apart with her bare hands.

Keynan patted her shoulder a few times, opening his mouth to say something.

Janus screamed as loud as she could as a mindless frenzy took hold of her. Screaming louder and louder until her lungs burned like forges within her chest, Janus threw furious fists into the man's body and face. The trained killer was nowhere to be seen, replaced with the embodiment of unbridled wrath. Janus gave herself freely to the feral, primal nature of her spirit, screaming a blood curdling, grief-stricken battle cry as she unleashed everything her body had left.

Janus continued to pummel into the man who had flicked his wrist and killed her father, ignoring the blinding pain that radiated across her ruined, spent body. In the blink of an eye, Keynan clutched her wrists, pressuring her ligaments and bones and bringing her to her knees with irresistible strength. She screamed in agony, but she did not stop, kneeing his chest as she continued to spend the little amount of energy she had left.

Keynan released his grip from her wrists and brought his palm behind him, preparing to strike her down once and for all. Janus knelt before him, panting, sweating, and completely exhausted. She met his white eyes confidently, struggling to keep them open as she felt an overwhelming fatigue sweep over her muscles.

Keynan seemed almost sorrowful.

With a quick jab to her chest, Janus was flung across the room, rolling and slamming into the corner as she felt her body and bones crumble against the rear wall.

After what seemed like an eternity of blinding pain, she lay still. The grief became background noise as her eyelids grew heavy. Janus knew she didn't have much time now.

She heard a ringing in her ears which grew louder and louder as she closed her eyes. She could feel her heartbeat in her chest pounding more than it ever had in her life, but then it slowed, the moments between beats growing wider.

I . . . can't . . . breathe . . .

Then she felt it.

Peace.

Darkness.

Then nothing at all.

⌘

1: MOONLIGHTING

⌘

Jone mused on the nature of mortality.

When examining his own biological makeup, he felt a twinge of pity for himself, specifically for the way his body dealt with adrenaline and uncertainty. When his nervous system became distressed and overactive, his body became flooded with adrenaline and cortisol, resulting in a mixture of symptoms. Trembling hands, heart palpitations, intrusive thoughts, vivid perception, and enhanced problem solving were some results. Certainly a mixed bag of affects.

This could serve as a new project for our research division. We can try to remove the adverse effects of such chemical reactions.

Jone had always treasured his apathetic composure, it helped him see the world with logic and was the main reason he'd been blessed with the position he currently retained at Lornan Futuristics. Once he'd begun to undertake his true calling, however, he'd found that this mental state malformed, revealing a new dimension of his personality.

The dormant beast had awoken, exposing traits he'd always had but had never truly realised. The loss of control had frightened Jone initially, forcing him to confront his own mortality and imperfections. If only he could experiment without such weakness. Fear and excitement, pure joy and terrible anxiety; these afflictions of the mind were inconsistent, although he was quite content with what he'd uncovered about himself throughout the process. Jone had quickly discarded the goals of his past life, dedicating his mental resources to explore this newfound obsession.

What I'm doing now is my real purpose. All I need to do now is keep everything afloat, enough so that no one asks any questions.

Driving his sports car through the quiet, industrial streets of Sector Five, Jone reflected on his place in life, as the car speakers whispered violins and piano medleys to his overstimulated mind. The pacing of his old life had been monotonous, resulting in a bland emotional spectrum from life's many occurrences. During the rare moments when Jone's genuine self rose beyond the imitation he presented the world, he found himself unable to control himself. Such episodes were intense and overwhelming. The fragments of sensation were so powerful, that they would quickly override his logic-driven mindset. Despite some learning difficulties at a young age, he'd learned to suppress these outbursts, forming an emotional veil of intellect and social engineering to shield his true nature from outside curiosity. This veil was his last line of defence, and it had protected him from the piercing eyes of the populace more times than he could count.

With his latest indulgences, Jone finally found an outlet, a pure form of expression that resonated with every cell in his body. Such luxuries were dangerous, but he was meticulous, patient, and careful. Menacing traits indeed when paired with his social status.

The quiet hum of the engine settled his nerves, gently encouraging introspection as he brushed his hand through his balding scalp.

Jone spent the ride from the Broken Sector revising every detail of the night, sifting through each detail carefully. His smile grew wide with satisfaction the deeper he delved, confirming that he hadn't made any glaring mistakes. These "nights out" gave him ample enjoyment, and it was exciting to revisit the events in his mind after it was all done.

Pushing his foot on the brake, Jone slowed the vehicle down, quietly coming to a complete stop in front of the building. Amongst the many skyscrapers in this sector, there was only one that stood as tall as his did. Lornan Futuristics was listed as one of the most massive manmade structures on the planet, serving to boost his reputation and renown.

With so many impressive structures littered across the landscape, there would always be a need for one man to have the grandest. Jone happily accepted this distinguished accomplishment.

Once he'd finished construction, he'd met with thousands of people from all over the globe, all of which had come to see the fruits of his labour. It had single-handedly turned the Industrial Sector of Menilax into a tourist attraction as the weapon manufacturers, car dealerships, and new business ventures demonstrated their latest endeavours and technologies to society.

With the insane amount of foot traffic Sector Five saw, many businesses clamoured for any piece of real estate they could get their hands on. Relocating from Sector Four, such companies spread themselves throughout the sector, sprinkling their presence between food and beverage outlets. Not to mention the restaurants, which provided Menilax with a splice of many cuisines across Vale. Lornan Futuristics served as a boon to Jone's fame and power, and with each passing day, he would be suspected less and less of guilt now that he'd begun his dark career of self expression.

It was early in the morning now, so there would be no tourists floating around the streets. Sector security would be keeping a close eye on the comings and goings of those who chose to walk the streets at this hour, but it was always staff working late.

Gripping the steering wheel, he rotated it to the right as he pushed the accelerator pedal under his shoe, driving the luxury car down the ramp. Jone pulled up to the garage doors, winding down his window to swipe his identification card across the scanner, which activated the metal sliding doors of the garage, sending them up into the ceiling.

With the handbrake on, he impatiently pushed the accelerator down as the mechanism brought the gate up, smirking in pleasure at the roaring of the engine. Once there was enough clearance for the car, he released the brake and floored it, barely clearing the gap as the tires squealed through the concrete parking structure. As his vehicle soared through the empty lot, he pulled into his personal parking spot near the elevators with a screech from his tires.

The executive left the luxury of his vehicle as the car door began to close automatically. Jone continued to feel rather pleased with himself as he whistled, the noise echoing throughout the lonely, polished corners of the parking lot. It wasn't until he began to walk away from the vehicle that he realised how exhausted he was. Dragging himself over to the elevators, Jone yawned and stretched, his full-grain leather shoes tapping on the polished cement, sending a clapping echo throughout the winding tunnels of the complex.

Once he reached the elevator, Jone pressed the call button to summon one of three lifts while his foot continued to tap away impatiently. Grumbling to himself, he fished out his car remote, turning his head to lock his car as it whistled back to him. Jone turned his neck around too quickly, sending a twinge of pain across his muscles. He twisted his head around, massaging the sore spots with his chubby fingers as he winced, quietly groaning while the massage relieved the distress.

A quiet hum emanated from the doors as they slid open, revealing the dark timber interior and plush carpet embroidered with the company logo; a gold crown with the company initials below it, encapsulated with the outline of a diamond. Jone stepped inside, swiping his ID once more in front of the scanner before tapping the button labelled "G." Within a few moments, the elevator doors closed, sealing him inside.

He couldn't help but notice the dim red light of the elevator interior. Usually it was so bright that he could check his reflection in the mirror, but the weak, crimson bulb didn't reveal much of anything in the cramped cabin.

Must be the bloody power again . . .

The building had suffered random power outages over the last few weeks, and despite how hard he pressed the council to resolve it, the power kept failing, and it always occurred around this time.

Someone needs to lose his or her job after this is resolved . . . !

It frustrated him immensely, but thankfully, he had a separate power phase for his office upstairs, which utilised a localised battery compartment that few people knew about. This would ensure that his appliances would still run properly, at least for forty-eight hours or so. It was incredibly expensive to install, and even more to maintain, but he could spare the money.

My investments are paying off in dividends, and now that the circuits in this old city are going to hell, I might need to invest in a better battery system to give me more time.

Staring at himself in the poor lighting, he smiled as he took a brief moment to fix up his tie and shirt, slipping the white cotton fabric back underneath his belt. Even at such late hours, he still had to look the part.

Remember: You are here to review paperwork, nothing more . . .

Jone's face was dark and satisfied, but as the doors slid open, he slipped on his mask of humanity, smiling warmly at the security guard on duty as he left the elevator.

Cris smiled and waved as he tapped away on his keyboard, opening the sliding glass doors that divided the parking elevators to the rest of the lobby. The marble floors must've been polished today, Jone observed, the scent of the cleaning cream unmistakable as it wafted pleasantly around his nostrils. Cris looked up expectantly as Jone approached the desk, and although he despised small talk, he did have appearances to keep up.

Approaching the desk, Jone leaned in casually and started a conversation with the humble security guard. Jone asked about the man's wife and child, which seemed to satiate the man. Simple folk enjoyed discussing the trivialities of their meaningless existence.

"And how's Maria?" asked Cris.

Unfaithful, addicted to wine, passive-aggressive . . .

He smiled, hiding the contempt that wanted to steal the spotlight of his fraudulent expression.

"She is well. I haven't seen much of her lately because of the new contract . . ." Jone feigned a wistful look before continuing. "Oh well, not to worry. She knew what she was getting into, marrying me."

Jone was never interested in a family, but having one around had kept curious eyes at bay. It was expected of a man his age to have a family and partner. People rarely asked questions about the family man, but the loners, they were the ones people kept their eyes on.

Keeping up appearances . . . takes up far too much of my life!

Jone placed his elbow on the counter, his eyes growing heavy from exhaustion.

"It must be challenging, working late all of the time," asked Cris while his eyes returned to the computer screen.

"Yes," said Jone smiling politely.

Don't you take your eyes off me . . . !

After a moment of disdain forming quickly at the corner of his mouth, Jone continued, quelling his desire to reach over and demand the peasant pay attention to him.

"Yes, you are challenging," he said under his breath.

The security guard looked up to him, squinting at Jone curiously.

"Pardon me, sir?"

Jone snatched Cris by the collar, lifting him across the desk and slamming him into the marble floor beneath him.

"Sir?"

Hovering his shoe over the man's face — the leather of which would've cost more than this scum's monthly salary— Jone grunted and slammed the sole into his face.

"Sir?"

Jone roared as he crushed Cris's face, stomping his head over and over, his face becoming so bloodied that his features quickly became unrecognisable.

"Sir?"

Jone gasped, opening his eyes as he almost hit his head on the counter.

"Are you okay?" asked Cris.

Jone flinched as he blinked repeatedly, glaring at Cris with confusion as he backed away from the counter with a start. The humble security guard looked up at him with concern in his dark brown eyes.

"Yes, sorry," said Jone. "I must've drifted off for a moment..." He shook his head before smiling with his perfect teeth.

Cris nodded and began tapping on the keyboard, but his concerned eyes lingered over him, nodding again after a moment of uncomfortable silence. Jone cleared his throat, moving the conversation along.

"What's going on with this bloody power, eh?" said Jone more aggressively than he had intended. "How much longer do we have to wait until they sort out this mess? I swear, our taxes go straight into the council's pockets!"

"Sorry about the outage, sir. I've been told that they're looking into it, but, well, you know how it is . . ."

Nodding to himself, Jone decided to move the conversation along. "Is there anyone else in the building tonight?" asked Jone, tilting his head slightly.

Cris smiled. "Just you, sir. Would you like some coffee?" he asked, gesturing to the coffee machine behind him. "You look like you could use some."

Jone shook his head. "I'll pass. I think, tonight, I'll be needing something a *little* stronger."

Jone winked to the humble security guard, who laughed genuinely at his appeared honesty.

"Try not to stay up too late, sir."

I do need to get some sleep; I've been up for three days straight . . .

These nights out required a lot of planning before he was able to execute them. The chances of being caught in the Broken Sector were reasonably slim, but precautions and proper routes needed to be planned ahead of time.

Councilman Greyson's little pack of dogs are growing by the minute . . .

Clearing his throat, Jone passed the desk and walked briskly to the executive elevators.

By the time he'd reached the glass gates, Cris had tapped away on the computer to allow him entry. They slid aside with a quick whisk, and once he was through and inside the elevator, Jone pressed the button for the top floor, Jone's private level.

He had to swipe his ID again before the elevator began to move, shaking his head at the effort required to get to his office. As he watched the elevator screen built into the door come to life, it began to display the usual advertisements from his partner companies. Jone's eyes drifted to the floor numbers, nodding in agreement with the simple white font of the characters he'd insisted they change them to.

Thank god my backup's working. I would probably have a heart attack walking up the stairs.

When drafting the designs for the building, he'd envisioned the elegance of each floor gradually increasing the higher you went. Moreover, spending decades working out of a shoebox in his early career selling his weapons and shipping them from a separate storage facility had afforded him plenty of time to iron out every little detail before he finally signed the construction contract. Jone's office was, of course, the peak of luxury. And when he grew tired of seeing the same design, he'd demolish it and redesign it. Settling only for designs that stirred feelings of pride within his greasy heart. Jone spent the majority of his life inside his office, so the investment was worth it in his eyes.

His stomach fat jiggled slightly as the elevator carried him through the belly of Lornan Futuristics, the reaction causing him to sigh as he looked down with shame on his own body.

Now that I've acquired these abilities, I really should get in shape . . .

He clicked his tongue as he squeezed the fat around his waist, shaking his head.

Maria will take credit for it, as always. She incessantly hounds me to lose weight . . .

The steel elevator doors slid open, revealing his private floor. Leaving the cabin, Jone's polished shoes clapped against the black marble as he stepped across the lobby, his presence causing the room to illuminate thanks to the sensors linked to the lighting system. To his right rested a reception desk where his assistant would work during office hours. To his left was a sizeable shatterproof window and a hallway splitting off into a bathroom with the boardroom on the opposite side.

Jone leant into the double doors of his office to push them open, but he stopped short, gasping aloud as he winced and clenched his eyes. He lurched forward in discomfort as his bladder tightened, feeling full and on the verge of popping like a balloon under stress. Gritting his teeth, he dashed down the hallway and darted to the left and into the men's bathroom with haste as the lights blinked on. He pushed the doors open, dashing over to the urinal and unzipping his pants.

After relieving himself, Jone sighed with relief before dragging himself to the basin, inspecting himself in the mirror as he washed his hands.

Jone chuckled at his reflection.

"You're a dangerous man . . ."

Nodding confidently, he reflected on his overall performance for the night.

Keep practising. You still have a lot to learn . . .

Jone washed his hands repeatedly.

He would inspect them for a few moments before scoffing and rinsing them again with soap, doing so several times, satisfying his ambition for perfection. Drying his hands, Jone absconded to his office, feeling as though he'd wasted enough time as it was.

Stepping through the double doors, he felt a warm, nourishing feeling as the high pile rug crumpled beneath his shoes. The lights in here didn't come to life, much to his surprise, and after flicking the light switch next to the entrance a few times, he shook his head in defeat.

Maybe they've shorted out. Can this night get any worse?

As he marched through the quiet office, Jone took pride in his possessions, eyeing them all as his smile stretched broadly across his face. On the left wall stood his handmade timber bookcase, built as high as the ceiling, the fresh lacquer applied by the maintenance team serving as further inspiration for his grin. It was stacked to the brim with media collected throughout a privileged life. Nested in the middle of the books and video cases was a network of television screens, nine to be exact. Each one was capable of independent play and controllable from his desk at the rear. Seeing the displays made him think of the surveillance systems he had running throughout the building, and more specifically, the cost involved for keeping them running and recording at all hours.

I hope those stupid things still work if the power is out . . .

Sighing heavily, he moved over to his liquor cabinet in the rear corner, seizing a crystal glass along with a lavish bottle of black spirits. Jone threw in a few ice cubes from the freezing drawer in his desk and fell into his overpriced leather chair, groaning in pleasure at how cool it felt through his suit. Jone wiggled his way in between the arms of the chair, breathing a sigh of relief, satisfied that he could finally relax after a long night. Closing his eyes momentarily, he took a moment to savour the small luxuries he'd become accustomed to.

My drink, my office, my building . . .

He sniggered.

The perfect method for relaxation . . .

Jone rubbed his fingers over the engraving on the crystal.

"To Jone Patrick Lornan, a man who has given thousands of peoples the chance to rise

above the turmoil of our world and provide a better one for the next generation. Through your tireless work, you gave birth to an industry, gave our community a framework to build from, and provided peace of mind to millions of people around the world with your reliable weapon platforms. Your charity and kindness will never be forgotten."

Gordon Frazer had given him the engraved mug during the grand opening of Lornan Futuristics. He'd given a speech, accepted awards, and bowed graciously at the time. All it served to do, however, was remind him of the shitty office he used to work from before ascending to the monument of his success. Those were bitter memories, but the experiences were worth their weight in gold for his career.

Not a complete waste. I had to start somewhere . . .

Gordon was a volunteer, a senior man who was far too trusting for his own good. He'd believed all of Jone's lies, eating them up with a certain naiveté, which was bewildering to Jone. Still, taking advantage of his trust was necessary to secure an excellent reputation within the community—and as with most of his good-natured work—adding more fabric to the veil he wore to protect his true nature. It was unusual of a man Gordon's age to be so gullible, especially one who spent most of his volunteering time in the Broken Sector.

Those peasants are paid a tenth of an employee from any other sector. If it weren't for the rebates given to me from the council, I would've refused to have their pestilent kind in my building.

He detested interactions with people from the Broken Sector, but he knew better than to make a scene when they confronted him.

Filthy little cretins. Always whining about how adverse the conditions are . . .

Rolling his eyes, Jone reached into his desk drawer, pulling out a small silver case housing his most prized possessions. Depressing the little switch at the top of the case released the latch, popping the front panel open, displaying the imported Kendelli Cigars. He lifted one free from the case, eyeing it as if it were solid gold as he rolled it between his fingertips.

Jone lit the cigar with a lighter from the drawer and puffed on it leisurely, feeling content at his place in life as he leant back into his high chair. There was an herb inside the cigar that incited euphoria for brief moments, encouraging calm in his overstimulated mind. Jone took off his gloves, laying them on his desk along with his tired feet, leaning back into the chair as he exhaled.

When shall we go again? It must be sooner than last time; I simply won't be able to resist!

He shook his head; it might be another few days before he could go back. There was work to do, contracts to sign. All he could do was dwell on the next outing, the next kill. To witness a young soul vanish before his eyes was intoxicating, exciting his every cell throughout his body. The experience terrified him and thrilled him at the same time.

An insidious facet of his soul was awakened, and with each kill, it grew stronger. The influence reached out to him like bloody tendrils, snaking out and grasping at other parts of his mind for bloody purchase. It revelled in the carnage he'd created, demanding more of him with each task.

It had begun to challenge him, demanding he plunge deeper and deeper into the pit of horror he'd been responsible for. The challenge itself made him anxious, and yet he was dying to see what happened when he'd perfected the art form. All of his old desires had been replaced with this one ambition. Nothing else mattered to him now.

Rolling his tongue around his teeth, he savoured the aniseed flavour of the cigar smoke. The fat man let out a groan as he stretched back even further, leaning against the weight of the chair, his face smiling with pride.

Laughter boomed from his chest. In fifteen years, his company had flourished. Lornan Futuristics had no shortage of interested parties because there simply was no other manufacturer around who could meet the demands of hungry investors. This, along with everything else that was going his way, encouraged him to laugh more and more.

"All my hard work, all my sacrifices . . ." he whispered to himself, *"It's paid off, after all this time."*

A warm delight rose up from his chest, making him take his feet off the table, and spin around in the chair, rotating until he was staring out the window. As he watched over the city from the safety of his office, he smirked as his own faint reflection grinned back at him coolly.

"I have an empire; I have the contracts, the money, the power . . ."

He tittered joyfully.

"This city is mine . . . !"

"This city ain't yours," whispered the shadows.

Startled, he dropped his delicacies onto the carpet and stood up from his chair, his eyes darting around in a panic as he desperately searched for the source of the voice.

The silence that came next was interrupted only by his heart throbbing painfully in his chest, the wet fleshy beating somehow audible inside his office.

The door at the opposite end of the office was sealed shut, granting him a brief reprieve. As he scanned the area around his desk, Jone couldn't notice much beyond the blueish hue of the moonlight carving a slice of light out from the darkness.

I could've sworn . . .

Jone swallowed the bile building up quickly at the back of his throat.

The silence was suffocating.

You're hearing things . . .

He sighed, tittering to himself nervously.

Might need to lay off the cigars . . .

He felt his straining heart skip a beat when he heard a gun hammer click down, slowly.

"Do I have your attention?" murmured the man's voice from the shadows.

Jone couldn't find the perpetrator despite the manic scanning his eyes did on their own accord.

"Y—, Yes . . ."

Instinct demanded he flee, to bolt for the exit, but he was too frightened to move.

He swallowed dryly. "Please don't shoot me . . . Let's talk about this."

Jone raised his hands, his tense muscles giving away his inner fear. Then he heard footsteps in the middle of the room approaching slowly, confidently. The muffled crumpling of boots pressing into the rug was all that he could discern in the dark. Each step the intruder made sent a shiver down his spine as his body's trembling grew worse and worse until his neck began to spasm, causing pangs of pain and panic to overwhelm him.

Jone was in complete shock now. He couldn't think, move, or even breathe.

He stepped away from the chair, feeling the cold safety glass behind his back as he pressed into it.

Suddenly, the executive's network of displays powered on.

Blaring to life, Jone squinted against the sudden lighting change and the crackling static of the loud speakers around the office.

The man was visible now, standing just beyond the desk, and yet, Jone could only make out his silhouette against the white light of the displays. The man was shorter than Jone but only slightly. He was broad-shouldered, and his muscled neck was hunched over. The frightening, metallic finish of the gun eerily reflected the static of the television screens like a mirror.

Suddenly, the loud static on the TV dissipated, replaced by a darkened image. It seemed to be from a security feed, the black and white image and fixed camera positions a dead giveaway. All nine of the monitors now displayed this single image, stretching across each one as if it were a single video feed. Jone rubbed a shaking hand across his sweating face, making out what looked to be a woman and a man arguing outside of a convenience store on the video. The store was dilapidated, and the people were poorly dressed.

"I don't understand," he said as he watched the displays intently, glancing to the man with the gun.

The couple were arguing about something, completely distracted by their own conflict. So much so that they failed to notice a shadow materialise from the alley, sprinting over with its hands extended toward them. The man from the dark appeared as though he was holding something towards them. It was a large man dressed in black, and despite his size, he managed to close the distance between them in a few seconds, quick enough to catch them off guard before they could turn to face him. Then, a flash of light, then another; the video didn't seem to have any audio, so the series of flashes were somewhat underwhelming, but it was evident that the man was using a gun by how the people fell down quickly after each flash.

The shooter put two more rounds into each body to ensure his work was done.

As he kicked the mother in the head to double check that she was dead, a child ran from the interior of the store, screaming and crying as she ran over to her mother who wasn't moving a muscle.

Oh no . . .

Jone now understood.

So there was a camera there . . .

He finally managed to take a breather. This man was here to exact vengeance even though there'd been many more victims since that night all those weeks ago.

Feign ignorance, the footage doesn't show your face . . .

"Please . . ." he sputtered, trying to sound convincing, "Why are you showing me this? I don't—"

"Marianne was her name," boomed the man's voice.

"Why are you showing me this!?" he screamed a second time. "I don't understand what's happening. Who—"

The man began to jog.

"Please! I don't—"

The man sheathed the pistol, an odd move for someone looking to threaten Jone. Then he grunted before launching into a sprint, scaling the desk and sliding across it before walking up to Jone's face with an aggressive gait. Jone wailed, reeling his head back and hitting the glass with an awkward thump, surprised at the assailant's speed. He held his arms up defensively, expecting an attack.

Pioneers deliver me from this! Why is this happening to me!?

"Why me!?" exclaimed Jone.

"You're asking *me* why?"

The man punched Jone in the ribs, causing him to reel forward, then he jabbed him in the kidney. Jone yelped pitifully as he tried to protect himself. It was a pathetic attempt; after all, he'd never been in a fight. Not a fair one at least.

As he raised his hands and pleaded for mercy, the man stopped his assault, standing over him with a grimace.

Use your power! What are you doing!?

He tried to summon forth the energy that allowed him to manipulate gravity, which would've helped Jone deal with this threat. But he was too fearful and weak to focus.

Shaking and twitching, Jone looked up at the man. He wore black cargo pants, a black t-shirt and gloves, and black boots. He had a short, unkempt beard, a tanned-Caucasian complexion, and villainous features with an ugly scar running across his slightly wrinkled cheek.

A photograph glided through the air toward him, settling down next to him on the carpet.

"Look at it," said the man, backhanding him viciously as Jone fell to the floor next to the photo.

"Doesn't resemble a girl anymore, does it?"

The photo was taken after he'd dumped the body. This man had obviously found it somehow.

"Oh, so that's why you're here . . ." said Jone with a wicked grin. "It's a shame, really. And here I thought I was being careful . . ."

He stared at what was left of the little girl in the picture, unaware that he had just spoken aloud. The video was still playing in the background as he lost himself in the memory. The tape now showed the man clamouring at the girl, who attempted to scurry away from him, although the attempt to flee was in vain. He clutched her little arm and clubbed her with his pistol, carrying her into the night.

"Why do you wear that mask?" asked the man.

The mask he wore that night was of a pale woman, painted white and embroidered with gold and green flowers. Jone knew right away when his wife gave it to him all those years ago that despite the fact it was crafted as a collection piece, he wanted to wear it, although perhaps not in public. He was an artist after all, so he needed to look the part.

The man knelt down; his blue eyes seemed almost ghostly when combined with the bright beam of the moonlit area around the desk. He got a closer look at his scar too, which looked like someone had cut his eyebrow and cheek open. The man had a thick brow, and as he craned his neck down, his eyes resubmerged into the dark shroud as he looked to the photo.

Jone was terrified, and yet the creature inside of him was not.

The man turned his head and reached over to the bottom desk drawer—which was locked—and yanked it open with a strong pull, ripping it free from its housing and sending the rails and lock bursting across the carpet. Holding the drawer in his hand, he tipped it upside down, spilling the contents out across the floor.

"You display yourself in such an effeminate way . . ." said the man picking up the mask to scrutinise it. "I'd wager that's how you'd picture yourself too. Graceful, delicate . . ."

The man looked at him with murderous eyes before crushing the mask between a clenched palm. "Truth is, you're a monster, a plague . . ." The man put his head down for a moment, his brow crinkled. "You're sick . . ." he said. "So takin' you down is a mercy."

He took out the handgun from his holster, pushing the barrel against

Jone's face, who began to whimper pitifully.

"Putting you out of your misery . . . It'll keep people safe . . ."

As Jone began to look up to plead for mercy, he recognised the man.

"Councilman . . . Greyson . . . ?"

The Councillor lifted his head, scoffing at him as if he were a dog begging for scraps.

"That's right. Who else would it be? Coming out all this way to—"

He slammed his boot into Jone's gut.

"—put you in the ground you—"

The Councillor brought his knee into Jone's chin.

"—piece of shit!"

Jone's head cracked into the safety glass, as he whimpered and pleaded for mercy.

"Please!" he said in between sobs, "No more!"

"Yeah, you're right . . ."

The man slid his pistol into the holster on his hip, strapping it in securely before reaching down and lifting Jone up by the neck.

"I don't want to make this easy for you," said the man, growling with disgust as held up more photos, "because *these* children deserve *some* sort of retribution."

There were at least six photos, each with a different child, all illustrating their remains. Greyson flicked them at his face; the sweat making some of the photos stick to his skin.

As the photos began to slip away, the creature inside him took hold.

It was in control now.

It bellowed at the man, "You have no idea who you are dealing with . . ."

"Is that right?" The Councillor was not intimidated. He smiled, tilting his head up so Jone could see his eyes. This blue-eyed apparition was here to punish him for his sins. Fitting that it would be the leader of the Broken Sector, where all of his victims had been taken.

I can't let him just kill me here, not like this . . . !

Jone had so much left to do. So much experience and effort would be wasted if he were to die here and now. It would be a crime to let his potential be destroyed so early before he could perfect his craft and bring the beast to life in its glorious, luminous, complete form.

The pain from his wounds was excruciating, but it faded into the background of his mind as the cold, piercing realisation that it might all over washed across his flesh.

"I'm going to enjoy . . . killing you!" screamed Jone as he flailed around.

"You wanna throw down, fat boy?" said Greyson.

The Councillor stepped away from him and walked behind the desk, chuckling as he did so. The move perplexed Jone, but he didn't question it further. The man had given away easy ground, allowing Jone to stand without interference.

"Let's see what you got," said Greyson.

That'll be your last mistake, you worm!

Rising to his feet and grinning all the while, Jone cackled as he leapt on top of his desk. Once he did, he smiled as wide as his mouth would allow, showing the man that he no longer felt fearful. Flexing his arms, Jone extended his palms towards Greyson, a low growl forming in his throat as he clenched his teeth, grinding them together as he focused, channelling the power to his hands. All sensation in his body dissipated. His muscles trembled and tore, and sweat spilled from his pores like miniature faucets. Waves of heat began to exude from his arms and hands.

Jone forced the power into his extremities, his body crying out for mercy as he pushed his potential to the limit. Screaming a terrible and bloodthirsty scream, Jone unleashed a wall of bone-shattering energy towards the man, shimmering blue like a tidal wave. Greyson stood with his arms crossed, unbothered by Jone's display of power as it roared closer, destroying everything not nailed down.

Furniture, booklets, and documents were swept away amidst the marching energy wall covering the entirety of the room, as it decimated everything in its path. Office clutter tumbled and thrashed around as the wave carried it towards the entrance. The collective rubble smashed into the wall at the far end of the room, sending shards of wood, plastic, and metal across the carpet. With one move, Jone had turned the elaborate workspace into a garbage heap.

The only thing that remained was the insurgent, smiling confidently, standing in the exact same spot he was a moment ago.

"Impossible . . ." muttered Jone as he slumped forward, falling to his knees from exhaustion.

"Makes sense, I suppose," said the man as he rubbed his chin. "I'd wondered how a fat mess like you could suddenly be so confident against a man who's come to kill you."

Before the power dissipated from his chest, Jone snatched it back, wishing to summon it once more as he rose up and readied his arms again. "We'll . . . see . . . who's killing who!"

Greyson shrugged, "all right, I'll give you one more I suppose," he said, scratching his scalp before crossing his arms again.

Jone brought forth as much of his energy as he possibly could, pushing every single ounce of strength he had into another volley of power. It only took a few moments before he was ready this time. Jone threw out smaller waves of gravity-defying energy at his foe, lobbing them furiously as he screamed and bellowed at the expense the ability had on his body. And as before, the assassin stood silently, utterly unaffected as the small waves of energy that dissipated on contact with him. The energy waves would knock an average person out cold if it impacted them in the skull; he'd seen it many times before.

"Just die!" he screamed.

Lobbing a final wave at the Councillor with his remaining energy, Jone ensured this one was double the size compared to the others, as he knelt down and launched it across the floor.

The man stood against the wave, his short hair settling quickly like grass swaying amidst a gentle breeze. Everything else in the office lay destroyed, the once tidy office now completely dishevelled and broken.

"Impossible . . ." said Jone, panting and wheezing.

Greyson scoffed, "You done?"

The man's voice bounced through the office, encircling him, engulfing his senses.

Jone heard the words clatter around his mind repeatedly.

These words . . . are the last I'll ever hear . . .

"You . . . aren't . . ." he began to say, realising too late what this man truly was.

This creature was not human. He was like Jone.

Jone chuckled to himself, dusting himself free of the small debris that was on his person as he leant back and sat on his desk, his eyelids heavy.

The man leapt forward so quickly he thought he was hallucinating. He was in front of him before he could blink, those blue eyes of his burning insidiously.

He lifted his hand behind his head in a raised fist, ready to bury it into Jone's skull.

⌘

The human body was a marvellous thing, that much was certain.

Knowing the intricacies of the human body, such as organ placement, bone structure, and muscle density, was a unique talent. Such knowledge translated into an understanding of the body's pressure points, where discomfort could be maximised; advantageous insights for delivering excruciating pain to those who he deemed deserving. A personal favourite was the space between the ribs guarding the heart. If one was to jab this spot hard enough, it would cause a twinge of pain and panic so intense, the victim felt as though their heart had stopped for a moment.

Grey brought raised his index finger before Jone, as if were a blade.

"You know somethin'? I could butcher you *so* easily—" he said confidently, bringing the finger in front of him and smiling. Regarding his finger in such a way had its intended effect, as Jone's eyes grew wide with fear and concern, unsure of what he was about to do.

"Might be worth showing you what *real* power looks like before you die."

The display caused more fear and confusion than a weapon ever could.

He jabbed his finger into Jone's chest with enhanced power. The frightened executive yelped and stumbled back, crying and screaming pitifully. After some more yelling and toppling, he managed to crawl underneath his desk, raising his hands as he continued to pant and wheeze from exhaustion.

"Please!" he whimpered, "Stop!"

"You want mercy . . . ?" Grey's lip twitched.

The mocking smile faded, his expression now formed into a snarl, moulded from hate and disgust.

"Did you show *them* mercy!?" He barked, gesturing towards the picture. Grey kicked him in the face, hard, sending Jone's head into the desk before he fell forward, pitifully holding his hands up as they trembled uncontrollably.

Jone started to cry.

Clutching at the CEO's throat as he reached under the desk, Grey threw him behind towards the shatterproof glass, which cracked against the force of the fat man's back as he smashed against it.

"Confess. Before I tear you to pieces."

The glass began to crack and split as Grey kicked him in the chest, pushing him against the glass as he snarled at the executive.

"I had to do it!" he finally said. "I hear voices . . . They gave me no choice!"

"Confess!" Grey screamed as loud as he could, his face almost touching Jone's as he picked him up by the scruff, lifting him up against the glass, and fighting the urge to crush his throat like a vice.

"I killed them!" screamed Jone.

Grey kneed him in the chest. "Who did you kill? I want names!"

Jone agonised aloud as Grey held him up with one hand and punched him in the ribs with the other, striking him repeatedly and breaking the bones under his mighty blows.

"Say it!" He kneed Jone again.

Jone cried out the names of his victims. It took longer than expected, and he heard names that he didn't know of before, but once he was done, he continued sobbing and crying like the broken man that he was.

"I hurt them! I tortured them! The voice didn't give me a choice! You don't understand!"

Holding him up with one hand, Grey gave him a brutal backhand with the other, knocking him out cold as he slid against the glass and fell to the floor silently.

Then Grey was holding him down. He'd unsheathed his dagger, holding it tightly in his gloved hand, pushing it against Jone's throat with trembling palms. The hairs along Grey's flesh held blobs of sweat, his skin forming bumps against the cold air and the fear of his own instincts. He'd already been mentally prepared for the kill, shocking himself as he pulled the knife away and stood above Jone with a grimace.

It's not worth it . . . He'd be getting off way too easy.

The world would be better off without Jone Lornan and his festering corruption, but over the last few years, Grey had made a persistent effort to avoid taking lives, unless it was absolutely necessary. The haste of his actions and complete lack of control over his impulsive habits frightened him as he watched the steel blade balanced in his hand, the involuntary trembling slowly coming to a calm rest within a moment of quiet meditation.

You are the master of your own mind.

"*I am . . .*" whispered Grey as he sheathed the blade quickly, "*and I don't kill people anymore . . .*"

With his eyes shut, he took a few deep breaths from his diaphragm, quickly releasing the intent from his mind like a flock of birds escaping a cage. Grey visualised the image in his mind repeatedly, slowly freeing himself from the murderous mindset. Such quiet moments of reflection helped him balance his frail thoughts in times of intense stress. He'd been conditioned to take lives for most of his life, and changing such habits was a challenge, one that he'd spent the last few years fighting to counter.

Before leaving, Grey took one last look at the screens, which had been tossed around the room in Jone's pathetic attempt to dispatch him. He sighed, remembering the many weeks of research it had taken to put a name to the shadow in the video.

Shaking his head, Grey felt satisfied that this was now over, taking his leave immediately without a second thought. As he stepped through the alcove where the double doors had been, he thought about his plan to seal Jone's fate. Having a parcel of relevant photographs, call logs, and digital messages would look like someone had framed Jone, but the evidence was substantial and wouldn't be ignored by Enforcement regardless of where it came from. As Grey opened the double doors and passed the reception area, he took a minor detour to investigate the parcel which he'd placed behind the reception desk.

Still there . . . Good . . .

Grey picked up the phone receiver, calling Enforcement by entering one, two, and three on the keypad.

"Location?" asked the voice.

Grey closed his eyes for a moment, changing his voice to something a little less like his own.

"There's been a break in! Uh, I'm at, um. Oh man . . . !"

"Sir, please calm down. What is your location? Are you in a safe place?"

"I'm an employee at Lornan Futuristics; someone's broken into my boss's office, and I think he's been hurt! You need to come quick!"

"It's okay, sir; we already have units on their way. Are you safe?"

What . . . ?

Grey pondered this as the phone began to drift away from his face. If they'd already dispatched enforcers, someone must've called them a while ago. Unless he'd tripped some sort of silent alarm, no one should've been around to call them early. He shook his head.

Doesn't matter now, I suppose . . .

He was getting rusty.

"Sir? Are you still there?" said the voice. "Can you get to a safe location?"

Grey disconnected the call.

Dashing over to the elevator, he tapped on the button anxiously as his mind raced. The dim red lights in the reception hall went out completely, and the low hum of the elevator ceased entirely.

Damn it! Enforcement must've cut Jone's backup generator.

Grey was now bathed in darkness. Rubbing his jaw with an open palm, he weighed his options carefully.

⌘

2: FERVID MOVEMENT

⌘

Jamming his meaty hands in between the panels, Grey hauled the elevator doors apart with a grunt before peering inside the darkened shaft with apprehension in his heart.

Only one way out of this that doesn't involve beating into Enforcement . . .

Inhaling a lungful of musty air, Grey sighed as he leapt down to the first ledge. Descending the skyscraper this way would avoid suspicion as Enforcement would be remotely monitoring the building's systems. An Enforcement officer would have seen the elevator being summoned from the top floor before the emergency shutdown, which meant they'd be coming straight up to Jone's office.

Shouldn't have pressed that damn button so many times!

He didn't look forward to the climb down, especially considering how fast he'd have to descend to stay ahead of Enforcement. Lornan Futuristics, the tallest building in Menilax, stood at an incredible six hundred meters high, so to say that the climb down would be challenging was an understatement.

A constant torrential wind flooded the chamber, causing his hair and clothes to flap around as he leapt from ledge to ledge, the shallow platform in front of every floor providing a place for him to land. Dim red lights cut through the darkness along the walls every three floors, making the elevator seem like a tunnel down to hell.

To his right—against the wall—was a ladder. This would guarantee a safe but slow passage through the tube. All things considered, the ladder was out of the equation. Grey wouldn't make it down in time to escape without anyone noticing.

The building would be on lockdown, and the streets would be full of enforcers by the time he reached the ground floor. Grey knew that once Enforcement had secured the building, the power would be switched back on after they'd cleared it of danger. Once it was restored, he'd have a much stricter passage to leave unnoticed.

Need to speed this up. Maybe I can leap down six floors at a time . . .

Quickly stretching his arms and legs and honing in on the ledge six stories down, Grey leapt, reaching out with his arms as he fell through the dim red darkness. His jump arc was short, allowing him to land precisely where he wanted to. He hadn't considered his weight when he enhanced his muscles, however, as he landed with a mighty crash, crushing the metal door panels in with his bulk. His grip bent the metal door inwards as he fell, leaving indents in his wake.

Damn it! Need to go a little slower.

He took a few moments to regain his composure, deciding to jump four stories at a time instead of six. Mentally preparing himself, Grey leapt down, landing more gracefully this time with less force.

Slowly but inevitably, Grey descended through the elevator shaft.

Focusing on the task at hand and not wasting any time between jumps, he'd made considerable progress in a short period. Landing at the fourth-floor elevator entrance after twenty minutes of acrobatics, he finally saw a weighty elevator ascending slowly as he tucked himself into the small crevice of his chosen platform. The slow pulley system had to operate on low power, which explained why it was so sluggish.

Assuming the maximum weight of one thousand kilograms, the elevator would've had at least ten operators inside. Grey chuckled to himself; he could've leapt his way up and back by the time they had reached the top floor. The fact that ten enforcers were travelling up meant that there would be more outside, but what sort of call would've been made to warrant such a massive turnout, Grey wondered.

Did someone set me up?

Grey shook his head, holding his head against the cold doors of the fourth-floor exit while his eyes rolled up alongside the elevator as it creaked past him.

No one had known about the duty tonight, not even Ducard. Which begged the question, who had made the call to Enforcement?

I can find that out later. I need to focus on getting into the lobby for now.

Getting in the elevator shaft to begin with had turned out to be a matter of patience and timing. He'd stolen a master key from the guard at the front desk while he was distracted with his coffee machine. He couldn't have triggered an alarm by accident; Grey had made sure that the power outage that affected the street had affected the alarms and security systems.

Leaping down to the bottom of the shaft, he quickly moved against the elevator doors as he placed his ear against the cold metal. He could hear footsteps inside the lobby—large, clomping steps from numerous sources. Grey focused on the patterns a few quiet moments, discerning at least six sets of steps wandering the lobby. Enhancing his fingers for strength, Grey pushed them inside the gap between the doors, applying a delicate amount of force so he could peek through and get a better assessment without alerting those on the other side. He saw six enforcers patrolling, but none of them were close to the elevators, serendipitous positioning he was thankful for.

Looks like there are two more stationed at the front door.

Beyond the security gates was a waiting area, with a wall of glass separating the area from the outside world. Tracing the hundreds of window panes that made up the wall of glass, Grey's eyes locked onto his exit. He'd pushed one of the glass panels in to gain access, leaving it slightly ajar so he could slip back out in a pinch.

Good. That's my ticket out of here.

He slid the doors open a little more, glad to note that they made almost no noise with the small amount of strength he applied.

Need to make this quick, once they see that the elevator's been pried open, they might start searching the lobby more thoroughly.

Grey climbed into the lobby and kept his profile low as he dashed quietly to the security gates. With his back pressed against one of the middle gates, he listened to the footsteps once more. Waiting patiently, he felt relief when he concluded that he was, as of yet, undetected.

No cries of alarm, no hurried footsteps. So far, so good.

Peeking over the gate assembly, he looked to each of the enforcers attentively.

They were all wearing standard patrol equipment: bulletproof vests, navy shirt and pants, and handguns. Their gloved hands were clasped tightly around the black metal grips of the guns, scanning each area fervently. Grey concluded that it was a regular call out. If they were expecting an augur, they would've brought more serious firepower. But still, the sheer number of enforcers still didn't add up.

I can do some digging once I get the hell out of here . . .

Grey rose to his knees, and after a moment of adjusting his muscles for speed, he was ready to sprint at a moment's notice. His soft-soled shoes would ensure his short trek wouldn't give away his position, unlike the loud clapping of the Enforcement boots.

When he found his moment, Grey slid under the security gates and slipped inside the U-shaped reception desk, tucking himself into the centre crevice opposite the exit to the street. Leaning heavily against the polished wood, a pang of urgency surged through his spine as he tried to listen in on the positions of the patrollers.

"The elevator shaft is open," said one of them as Grey cursed under his breath. "Can you two take a look inside?"

"Why us?" asked one of the enforcers at the door.

"Because I *said* so."

Grey closed his eyes, using the sounds of the enforcers' footsteps to visualise where they were, planning his next move. He heard the two near the entrance begin to walk over to the elevators.

Leaning forward and peeking over the reception desk, Grey noted that they were patrolling in pairs. Two of them were shining their spotlights around the rows of chairs to the right, near his exit, while two more were through the security gates now, passing the other two who were heading that way from the entrance. Instead of going towards the doors to the street, they began to walk towards the reception desk. They were so close now that if they were to turn their heads and look under the counter, they would've spotted him.

He could already imagine the look on their face upon seeing an esteemed Councillor and prominent board member crouching underneath the desk of a private business.

It would be a hard one to explain.

"Howdy fellas, funny story . . ."

Eyeing them intently, Grey tensed his muscles, ready to move. As one of them began to turn towards his hiding place, he reached up with both arms and slid over the desk, landing quietly on the other side as the torchlight beamed over his head. The soft material of his T-shirt and pants meant the vault would be completely silent, allowing him to remain undetected. The two enforcers were utterly unaware of his presence as they began to check the cubby he'd been hiding in only moments ago.

Using enhanced speed, he darted next to the beverage machine across from the desk. The poor lighting conditions of the lobby made repositioning that much easier.

Grey had learned a long time ago when stalking his fellow man that he could move undetected if he were quick enough. So long as paranoid eyes were not looking directly at him as he moved, Grey was able to slip around like a shadow. Moreover, in low-light environments, one's presence would be undiscoverable when operating within a person's peripheral vision. The worst he'd seen was the occasional glance; most believed his movement to be a figment of their imagination. Everyone had these moments, especially when tired, stressed, or pumped full of stimulants, like coffee or tobacco.

In this day and age, who doesn't rely on something to take the edge off?

Seeing shadows shift and swim at the edge of your vision was frightening, but you could convince yourself you were seeing things. Grey glanced at the enforcers; none of them seemed to notice him, proving his movement theory accurate yet again.

Turning his head, he managed a glance outside to assess his next move.

Two enforcers were strolling between the vehicles that were parked outside, while another two leant against a large, reinforced van in the middle. One enforcer was lighting a cigarette while talking to the colleague beside him, expressing frustration at being called out so late, he assumed.

Looking to the right, he could see the two enforcers patrolling the waiting area turn away from him, walking along another row of chairs. Grey remained stationary until he saw the enforcer behind the desk open a drawer. Upon seeing his attention hone in on the drawer's contents, Grey sprinted along the wall of glass before reaching the opening, where he quickly displaced to the street.

The fresh night air nipped at his skin as he passed through, leaving him in the middle of the blockade. Not the ideal position for remaining unnoticed.

There were at least six enforcers that he could see from where he stood weaving in between the various vehicles on the road. Thankfully, most of them weren't paying much attention to their surroundings. He stepped around the cars, keeping his footsteps quiet and considerate as he skulked around the makeshift parking lot. He hastily moved to the other side of the road, ensuring he kept his head down as he navigated between the vehicles.

Once he made it across, Grey hid behind a garbage crate, peering over the top as he searched for signs of his potential discovery.

Free and clear. Time to get out of here.

Satisfied with his work, he searched the building behind him for a windowsill or a ladder, craning his neck up as he scanned the wall for purchase. Finding a good vantage point, he channelled his ability to his leg muscles for a few moments before jumping and reaching for the ledge. Gripping the window sill with his fingers, he began his ascent.

"Excuse me, sir," said one of the enforcers below him.

Grey's jaw hung loose as he stopped in his tracks, lowering his head in shame and frustration.

Tried to get away too hastily . . .

His heart began to pound in his chest as his mind began to race with a viable story to explain why he was here.

Damn it, I was so close . . .

He held on with his right hand, turning around with an embarrassed expression as he searched for the man who'd spoken. He'd have to play this one correctly if he was going to get away with his reputation intact.

As he turned around, he looked at the enforcer behind the car closest to him, who in fact wasn't facing Grey at all. He sighed and shook his head, realising that the enforcer was talking to someone else.

The enforcer was hailing a man in a purple robe with a hood covering his face.

Grey shook his head erratically.

No . . . No, it can't be . . . !

⌘

The robed man raised a trembling, wrinkled finger towards the entrance of Lornan Futuristics.

"I'm here to speak with Mister Lornan. Is he in today . . . ?"

Shaking his head, the enforcer raised his palm in protest.

"Sir, I suggest you move along. We've reason to suspect that—"

The man's head twisted around. The audible snap of bone and muscle sent a crippling terror through Grey's mind as he watched the enforcer fall to the ground, dead before his face hit the pavement.

"Holy shit!" yelled one of the enforcers at the door. "Officer down!"

The two enforcers at the door dashed over to confront him, their pistols held firmly towards the new threat.

It's Sinew! I have to do something!

Grey leapt from the ledge, landing on the robed man with an empowered fist, slamming him into the bitumen with a monstrous blow. All of the nearby enforcers converged on the scene, raising their weapons at Grey without a second thought as he stood and snarled at the man he'd landed on. Raising his hands as quick as he could, Grey stared at the enforcers apprehensively. Their eyes were wide with fear and uncertainty as he placed his boot over the robed man's back.

Shit! Don't have time for this!

"Wait!" he yelled. "Hold your fire!"

"Keep your hands where I can see 'em!" yelled the man without his helmet as he stepped forwards with his fellow enforcers at his side.

Grey took a breath, glancing down at the ruined pile of gore underneath his foot.

"Listen to me; we don't have time for this. You all need to leave, right now!"

"Councilman *Grey*!?" said the sergeant as she stepped forward. "What are *you* doing here?"

"You need to listen to me, darlin'; get your team and get the hell out of here, now! This man is—"

Grey felt a hand grip his ankle.

Within a moment, he was being swung around like a plank of wood as the robed man threw him into the group of enforcers, knocking them away and sending them into the vehicles lining the street. Unable to resist the powerful momentum that the old man had built up, Grey tried to reach for his handgun as the man kept swinging him around like a toy.

What the hell! What is Sinew doing here!?

Before he could slip out his gun, Sinew brought Grey down, slamming him into the road with a godlike swing. Grey's body crashed into the bitumen, sending black chunks of rock over the street.

Grey groaned as his entire body became lanced with white-hot pain. If he hadn't had his ability primed, it would've killed him.

"It's always a pleasure to see your face . . ." said Sinew, bending down to look him. He stared at Grey from underneath his hood with a wicked smile, appearing more like a frown considering Grey was looking at him upside down.

The robed man threw an empowered fist into his chest, sending Grey further into the ground as he wailed into the night, a horrible, grief-stricken howl. The blow left Grey winded and breathless as he tumbled over into the broken ground, now covered in dust and debris, as he coughed and wheezed, fresh pain searing through his chest and back.

I need to . . . get up . . . !

His heartbeat began to grow slower as his observation of time screeched to a crawl. Grey's breathing had become laboured and pained as he clenched his jaw.

"I see you haven't lost your edge," said Sinew, waggling his finger at Grey as he writhed on the ground.

Sinew's rattling voice sounded like he was a career smoker, and his speech sounded sluggish, more so than Grey remembered from their last encounter. He surmised that his age had finally caught up to him.

Sinew reached down and pinched his cheek.

"You've always had a knack for this sort of work . . . It's a shame your father can't see you now."

Grey slapped his hand away as he tried to stand. Sinew pushed his bare foot on top of Grey's face, pushing him deeper into the road with incredible strength.

"You!" barked the sergeant, standing before Sinew. "Raise your hands, now!"

"Excuse me . . . for one moment," said Sinew with a trembling finger raised to Grey as he tapped it on his nose. Sinew turned around sluggishly, tilting his head to speak with the enforcer as he smirked wickedly.

"I'm in the middle of a conversation, officer, *if* you don't mind."

The sergeant snarled at him, "You have exactly *five seconds* to cooperate, or you w*ill* be shot." She made a few gestures to her subordinates. They began to close in on the old man.

"Raise your hands! Now!"

Sinew crossed his arms. "You can shoot me if you like . . ." he said, shrugging with his lips pursed. "I've had worse, as this young man would happily tell you . . ."

The enforcers' limbs began to tremble. In the space of a second, the officers started to lose control of their bodies. Each enforcer wailed in terror and agony as their weapons fell away, leaving them to fall to their knees crying and screaming as loud as their lungs would allow.

"Leave them alone you . . . bastard . . . !" yelled Grey, groaning as he tried to rise amidst the pain. Sinew stomped on Grey's chest as he did so, knocking the air from his chest as he wheezed in pain, curling over and continuing to writhe.

Busting and popping noises could be heard over the screams as the enforcers' limbs broke and twisted in on themselves. Each of them looked to their disfigured forms in disbelief, engulfed in a reality of pain and terror as they watched joints and bones break, their bodies deforming before their eyes.

Grey screamed aloud as his heart continued to pound inside his chest as every part of his body pleaded for the strength to act, to help them. Nevertheless, he knew how this was going to end.

"Please!" yelled Grey, raising a hand to Sinew. "Take Jone, but leave them be. I *know* that's why you're *really* here."

Grey coughed and wheezed as he tried to catch his breath. "You don't need to kill these people . . ."

The man took the hood away from his head, slipping it behind his neck to reveal his wispy, white hair, a clean-shaven face, and jade-green eyes which watched Grey curiously. Seeing those eyes again made his skin crawl, instilling a disheartening sense of dread in his gut. Knowing that this man was alive placed a heavy burden on Grey's mind, a stressor he'd been cursed with for over half of his life.

Sinew looked Grey up and down, pursing his lips.

He chuckled, but it sounded more like he was choking on something.

"Their quality of life isn't going to be much of anything now, you know. You're a little late with your—" Sinew tittered, "pleas of mercy . . ." The corner of Sinew's mouth twitched. "Taking their lives would be the real mercy, at this point."

He spoke to Grey as one would talk to an infant, chiding him for his naiveté. Sinew smiled a toothy grin, revealing that more than half of his teeth had been removed, but the remaining teeth were sparkling white.

"These people can *identify* you. Have you not thought of that?"

Grey closed his eyes, shaking his head as he gasped for air.

"I don't care," said Grey, "Don't kill them . . . Please . . ."

Sinew tilted his head.

"And, what are you doing here, exactly?" he asked, pressing his foot into Grey's chest.

Grey winced, looking up at him with a scowl.

"And what happened to your face . . . ?" asked Sinew curiously. "You used to be such a handsome boy."

The screaming died down after what seemed an eternity. The officers had fallen unconscious.

He winked at Grey as if he was about to tell a joke.

Sinew kept his eyes on Grey, his features becoming deadly serious.

Grey smashed Sinew's legs out from under him with an empowered fist. Sinew toppled immediately, falling on his back as Grey leapt on top of him. He raised his arms behind his head, bringing them down into one formed fist to deliver the most potent attack he could muster from his tired, worn-out muscles. His knuckles hammered into Sinew's skull, splitting it open with an audible crack. Such an attack would've killed a normal man, although not

Sinew, so Grey was far from done.

Delivering monstrous blows to the old man's chest, Grey swung his arms as hard as he could, breaking flesh and bone apart like they were made from wet paper. Pummelling the old man into the pavement, driving him deeper and deeper into the ground as he screamed, his mind consumed with rage.

Once he stopped, Grey stood and stepped away, exhausted and breathless.

Stumbling and blinking sluggishly, Grey looked down at the remains. They did not resemble a man anymore.

I can't . . . keep going . . .

Sinew's victims were silent. Grey turned around to look at the poor, outclassed souls that lay still, their minds shut down, overloaded from excruciating pain. They would live, Grey quickly assessed, but would be horribly disfigured, not to mention traumatised from Sinew's malicious treatment. It would take a lot of work to mend their limbs, possibly even having to take on prosthetics to live as they once did.

Inevitably and predictably, Sinew began to reform his body. Grey winced, consumed by utter exhaustion as he fell back onto his backside, holding himself up with one trembling hand. He was totally drained, making it impossible to do anything more than sit and wait for his destruction as he wiped the sweat from his face.

He closed his eyes, not wishing to look at the disfigured body pull itself together as he'd seen far too many times. The rattles and creaks of bone reforming, the wet sound of meat rubbing together as muscles repaired themselves. Grey shook his head as he opened his eyes, looking on with tired eyes, unable to help himself as he tried to catch his breath.

Ignoring logic and reason, the old man regenerated his body to the way it was before his brutal beating.

"Oh, young man . . ." he said, snapping his own neck back into place with a distorted arm, which was still rebuilding. "How many times are we going to go through this?"

He reached down to push a rib back into his chest.

Blinking slowly, Grey stood up, trying to call on any energy still lingering from his overheated body. However, Sinew was ready this time.

Sinew began his offensive, attacking with blinding speed and power beyond what a man his age should be capable of, even while his body was still rebuilding itself.

Focusing on defence, Grey's momentum-based guard defended against the blows as he moved his hands and arms in the way of the attacks, hoping to stall Sinew's offence. Their limbs ploughed against each other with incredible speed and power, causing loud cracks of flesh and bone as the two augurs clashed in a display of violence and grace not often witnessed by many.

A rogue strike glanced off Grey's wrist and struck his temple, causing him to see white spots as he opened his eyes wide with fear and disbelief.

With the enhanced strength of his enemy, it was like being hit in the head with a hammer, sparking a streak of pain across his skull which radiated down his face and neck.

Shit . . . !

Sinew stepped away for a moment, placing his hands behind his back and smiling at Grey as he began to pace around him. Grey danced around, hoping to throw off his aim, but he was stumbling from the blow, trying to feign his waning defence. His arms were trembling intensely as he raised them, returning his stance to the flimsy guard he now held. With his vision obfuscated and his head swimming, Grey wouldn't be able to fight anymore. But he couldn't quit now; he had to try for the sake of the wounded officers. Holding up both hands, Grey stepped over to Sinew sluggishly, spitting a mouthful of blood in Sinew's face.

The old man screamed as the bloody spittle splashed over his cheek and eyes, causing him to reel in revulsion. Grey enhanced his fists as much as he could before thrusting it towards Sinew's sternum. The blow ploughed into the chest cavity of his foe as bones, organs, and flesh parted way for his hand without hesitation. Sinew gurgled and chortled as Grey's hand became stuck in his chest. Grey made a point of watching the light from Sinew's eyes fade away, taking less than six seconds to pass on with his arm impaling the old creature.

Grey tried to rip his hand out of the chest cavity, but it wouldn't give. He placed his foot on Sinew's chest, using the leverage to tear his arm free as he kicked the dead body to the shattered bitumen.

Need to do something . . . to finish him . . . before he wakes . . .

But what the hell am I supposed to do . . . ?

Grey placed a boot on his face, slowly pressing down.

"Yes . . . Kill him . . ."

Grey's heart skipped a beat as the whispering voice spoke to him.

"You . . . are . . . a killer . . ."

"No, not anymore," whispered Grey in rebuttal.

"Some . . . deserve death . . ."

He closed his eyes and unsheathed Sithaleir. Gripping the hilt of his blade, Grey knew that it was the only way.

"Still hearing those voices, eh?" said Sinew licking his lips.

Grey couldn't manoeuvre in time to defend himself against the monster in the robe suddenly returned to life quicker than last time. He held up his guard once more, but Sinew managed to attack before he was ready. The blow slid over his shoulder and smashed into his collarbone, knocking him to his knees. More strikes came with the same intensity and dexterity as Sinew's first. The old man's stamina seemed limitless as he punched Grey in so many places in such a short time that it felt as though he had ten limbs, striking him all at once. His body and mind began to fail him as his vision became bleached with white.

Within seconds, Grey was beaten and bloodied as he fell onto his back, barely conscious as he lay still, accepting his defeat with shame. Overwhelmed with agony and exhaustion, he stared at the sky, blinking slowly.

"Why are you . . . doing this . . . ?" Grey asked as he felt his vision darken.

Sinew looked down at his robe, sighing as he realigned it. With his trembling, old hands, he brushed the dust and bits of gore away from the fabric, clicking his tongue as he did so. When he was finished, Sinew smiled as he stared down at Grey.

Sinew laughed aloud. "One would think . . . after the time it's been since we last saw each other, that you would've come up with a *better* question than that . . . !?" Sinew shrugged. "One day soon, you'll see what it's all for . . ."

Grey stood up despite himself, wincing at every minor movement as his body demanded rest.

"Next time I see you, you're a dead man . . ." said Grey grimly. "No more games. I have the funding, and I have the resources now . . . You're as good as dead."

Sinew laughed. "Yes, my death is coming soon . . . but it won't be by your hands, young man . . ."

Grey winced as a stab of pain shot through his chest, causing him to groan and fall back into the crumbled bitumen. A low ringing in his ears began to pulsate through his brain, a death rattle overwhelming his mind with numbness and peace as he closed his eyes. His body was making him rest, too exhausted to stay awake.

No . . . Not yet!

Groaning and cursing, Grey leant up to watch Sinew walk towards the mass of enforcers not far from where he was. Sinew turned around, glancing at the broken bodies scattered around before him. Then, within the space of a second, all of their necks snapped at the same time. The sound of it made Grey throw up immediately.

Sinew turned around to bow before Grey, who was dry reaching onto the street.

"What the hell do you want from me!?" Grey screamed.

Grey could hear Sinew's voice in his head, yet another gift that the old man possessed. "*. . . You'll see . . .*"

Sinew stepped inside the building, prying open the doors as he walked towards the elevators.

What am I supposed to do now . . . ?

Grey tried to rise to his feet, but he fell on his face, pushing the wind from his chest.

I can't . . . beat him . . .

He coughed bloody spittle onto the road, immediately trying to stand once more.

"Need to go . . . I can't . . . be implicated here . . ." whispered Grey.

Closing his eyes, he managed to stand as a powerful ringing in his ears overwhelmed him again, his mind was trying to rest, to force sleep upon Grey. His vision began to grow dark in an instant, causing him to stumble forward. Holding out his hands in time prevented himself from falling any further as he clutched the side of a car door.

Stay awake . . . You sleep, you die.

Rising to his knees, Grey began to stumble along the street back towards his sector.

⌘

3: LORNAN STREET

⌘

Exhausted, battered, and defeated, Grey pushed onward.

The walk to the checkpoint would be a quiet one as the Industrial Sector became a lonely place at night. A fact he was thankful for in his current state.

Don't focus on the pain . . .

During the day, people from all over the city went there to work as the sector was responsible for 65 percent of Menilax's overall workforce. People from all over the world went there to see Vale's most significant buildings while companies marketed their latest and greatest technological marvels.

After the invasion, the economy had gone into overdrive. The once small industry of weapons manufacturing had transformed, becoming the most critical product in the city. City officials became paranoid of attacks from other nations, be they domestic, international, or interplanetary, which resulted in a significant boon for the economy. The boost sent investors into a frenzy, pouring their financial favour into defence and military projects.

Considering Sector Five's massive impact on the city's wealth, it made sense that it would have some exceptional security systems in place. A few small deposits of Enforcement officers were positioned in outposts around the sector, in addition to security cameras placed on every block. These systems had been the only reason Grey hadn't acted sooner as it had taken a lot of planning to neutralise them for long enough to get inside the building without being spotted.

The localised power outage he'd arranged had ensured the security cameras on Lornan Street wouldn't have recorded what really happened that night; his city-wide connections had proven fruitful for these sorts of operations. Having citizens from the Broken Sector employed throughout the city had given him the reach he needed to ensure that men like Jone were not above retribution. After explaining Jone's crimes to Quinten Price—one of the night shift engineers for the nearby power station—he'd agreed to tamper with the power for the sector for the last few weeks to set up Grey's alibi.

His nightly walks through Menilax would work in his favour, serving as an explanation to the inevitability of Enforcement checking the security footage. They would see Grey taking his nightly walk through the Industrial Sector—as he had hundreds of times before—before he ventured along

Lornan Street. Inventing a plausible story on how he'd returned a few hours later, bloodied and beaten within an inch of his life was now the priority, assuming he'd live long enough to tell the tale.

Can't lie my way through the encounter with Sinew. Too many enforcers are dead . . .

Grey went over the events of the night; he didn't have a great deal of time to get his story straight, so he had to do it quick. Knowing Enforcement would be asking a lot of questions encouraged him to come up with a concrete story, one that wouldn't implicate him too much nor reveal the truth as to why he'd been there so often. It would take him at least ten minutes to walk to the outpost on the corner of Lornan and Main, time he could use preparing a believable story.

I came across a bunch of enforcers who were fightin' with someone. He tore 'em apart with his bare hands . . .

Grey felt immense shame upon reviewing the slaughter he'd witnessed, trying to lie about his involvement with the entire situation only made him feel worse. He'd let them die by Sinew's hand, and despite knowing that he was powerless to prevent their passing, the knowledge did nothing to relieve his already burdened conscience.

Sinew would've claimed Jone by now, and no one would ever see the CEO again, a fate shared by the hundreds of others that the augur had taken from society. What Sinew did with those he took was a mystery, one that had plagued his mind for many years.

Wincing under a flash of pain in his chest, Grey found himself unable to catch his breath. He grimaced as the pinching sensation in his lungs brought him to his knees. Willing himself to find any remaining strength, Grey cursed his weakness, demanding his body to stand and keep going. After what seemed like hours of suffering through shallow, agony-filled wheezing, Grey rose shakily to his feet, forcing himself to limp down the dark road yet again to try and get help.

Shit . . . Need to . . . keep going . . .

Sinew was, without a doubt, the most dangerous person Grey had ever encountered, a creature that seemed invulnerable with goals and qualities only his worst nightmares could rival. Years of his life were spent trying to track him down, but every time they crossed paths, Grey fell short in every way when it came to blows. The old man never seemed interested in killing Grey; in fact, he'd always treated Grey like he was too insignificant to deal with, chastising him with quips and words rather than finishing him off. The sudden reappearance of Sinew after so many years had resurrected an abundance of questions and pain. Pain that he tried to bury along with his past.

Sinew has a lot to pay for . . .

As he walked through the street, Grey couldn't help but dwell on the demon that had haunted him for more than half of his life. Sinew's power was unlike any augur the world had ever seen, let alone a dredge like himself. Most dredges could manipulate individual components of their own bodies to make them faster or stronger, depending on the situation. A learned dredge could accomplish feats an average human could never achieve, like surviving a fall from a great height or moving faster than the human eye could keep track of. Sinew could not only do these things—on a considerably higher level than Grey—but he could also extend this manipulation to the bodies of other people, twisting their biological composition at will. No one else in the world had this power, at least not to Grey's knowledge.

Even the Pioneers—the original augurs—were nothing compared to the power this man wielded. He couldn't have been immortal because of his old age, nor could he be a Pioneer due to his eye colour.

This has to end . . . I need to find this bastard and put him in the ground . . .

In the present moment, Grey's augmentation was the only thing keeping him upright. If he lost focus for too long, he would be dead within minutes, having suffered too many wounds in such a short time. His head ached, his vision was swimming, and his chest burned from the inside as if a flame was roasting his organs.

Every step brought agony.

Every breath felt strained.

Falling to his hands and knees as he had done every few steps, Grey's body began to tremble. His ears began to ring, his eyes grew heavy, and his heart hammered like a drum.

No . . . Not now . . . I've too much left to do . . .

"If you make it through this . . ." said a familiar woman's voice, *"promise me you'll come home . . ."*

Grey threw up on the road for the second time that night, the discharge filled mostly with blood.

"God damn it . . . Get, up!" he whispered, shaking his head at his incessant weakness.

Breathing heavily, he gazed lazily at the road ahead. The road home was dark; the power had yet to come back online. At that moment, he felt as though he should've returned to Ciril Station when he'd had the chance.

"You've earned your rest. Come home to me," continued the woman.

He could see her ankles out of the corner of his eye. He reached out to gently touch her soft, caramel skin, feeling overwhelmed with sorrow at her presence.

"No . . ." he said aloud. "It's not you . . ."

Grunting in pain and overwhelmed with exhaustion, Grey forced himself upright despite his jelly like legs refusing to keep him that way, as he continued the trek along Lornan Street.

You've got so much more to do, so many wrongs to right; it can't end now . . .

Grey took a deep breath, causing a spike to pain to jolt through his chest as he yelped. It felt as though his lungs were being pinched by serrated blades.

I'm sorry, Ciril . . . The Broken Sector needs Grey more than ever . . .

"*Please . . . Come home . . .*"

He shook his head, ignoring the visage of her in the corner of his eye.

"Leave me be . . . Please . . ."

Stumbling along the street, Grey kept his mind busy so as not to pay her any mind, mentally grasping at stray thoughts in an attempt to remain focused and motivated, ignoring his clumsy sways and bloody coughs.

When he'd volunteered to be a Councillor for the Broken Sector, he'd initially despised the role and the social stigma that came along with it. Calling the Sector by another name misrepresented the reality of the place, so he'd come to terms with it after a while.

A Councillor . . . takes on the heat . . . so the sector . . . can flourish . . .

The ringing in his ears returned as his eyes closed of their own accord. Grey woke up moments later on the ground, clenching his jaw as he groaned and muttered.

"*Get, up!*" he grumbled through gritted teeth.

Standing up and marching forward, Grey held his side instinctively, breathing and moaning as if every step could be his last.

The sector . . . Think about the sector . . .

The sheer amount of work required to bring it back to its former glory was beyond imagination, with almost every layer of infrastructure eliminated during the invasion of the Strin, a group of humanoid insurgents that threatened to destroy Menilax all those years ago. Once their invasion was repelled, the sector became filled with poverty, crime, and the homeless, not to mention the constant threat of augurs that were hiding in plain sight. This prevented support from the rest of the sector, stifling it from growing due to fear and ignorance by the other sectors.

When Grey had come forward to volunteer, his notions on what was involved with such a role were misplaced. A long career of espionage and assassination taught him a great deal, but when it came to politics and discussion, he was woefully underequipped.

Shaking his head, he smirked despite himself.

Don't regret anything, but I underestimated every detail of the role . . .

The only thing he had going for him over his failed predecessors was his augmentation, which prevented his citizens from taking him down during his first month, the fate that all of the previous representatives had suffered. It had taken an augur to get things moving, it seemed, but for every problem he solved, three more would take its place. Despite the challenges, Grey would never stop working to rebuild the sector. It was the only thing helping to ease his weary conscience.

As he approached the end of the street, he could finally make out the small Enforcement outpost ahead, situated on the corner of Main Street and

Lornan Street. He'd never been happier to see the law in his life.

"Councilman!" yelled the man inside the structure. "Are you all right!?"

Three enforcers dashed out from the reinforced steel doors, sprinting over to him in a hurry. Grey saw one of them with a first-aid kit, making him so happy he almost wept.

"Sir?" yelled one of them as they approached. "What happened?"

Grey groaned as he tried to talk, dribbling blood over his chin.

"There was . . . an attack . . ." he said, trying to push the pain aside to concentrate on his choice of words. As they reached him, two of the three enforcers ducked under his arms, lifting him up before supporting his weight, while the third trailed anxiously in front of them, assessing Grey's body as he rifled through the green first-aid box.

"Please, sir, try to relax," said the young man with the box.

They carried Grey over to the outpost as he closed his eyes, fighting the urge to sleep as his head hung loosely.

The young man began to take off Grey's shirt before he gestured dismissively to him. Grey pulled his own shirt over his head while wincing and gasping as the movement flared up the myriad of biting pains across his body. The Enforcers reacted in shock at the state of his body, coated in crusted blood which covered too many wounds to assess at a glance. Some of the clots peeled away with the shirt, causing fresh blood to seep out as he hissed and cursed.

"You're going to be okay," said the medic.

An enforcer knelt down, taking off her helmet before looking Grey in the eyes. "We have a team deployed on the street you came down," she said. Sighing, she took a moment to weigh her words carefully. "Did you see anything down there?"

Grey nodded, spitting a mouthful of blood and saliva onto the pavement as he wiped his mouth and face with his crumpled shirt.

"Your team . . . they ran into someone . . . I was caught in the middle . . . barely made it out . . ."

They shared a look of concern, before the woman promptly stood up, catching the attention of the medic and the other enforcer.

"I'm sorry . . ." continued Grey, looking up into her eyes. "Your team . . . they didn't make it . . ."

I don't deserve your kindness . . . or your medical attention.

Grey shook his head, disgusted with himself.

The sergeant sighed, nodding solemnly before addressing her subordinates. "Make sure the councilman is escorted to Captain Wayne." She nodded to Grey before exhaling exhaustedly. "Please excuse me, Councillor. I have to report this . . ."

Grey gestured dismissively, "It's . . . all right, darlin'. You do what you have to do . . ."

She picked up a handset from the wall and promptly left, sealing the door behind her.

"I'm sorry about your team," he said. "I tried to stop the guy . . ." Grey shook his head. "Messed me up pretty bad . . ."

The medic had prepared two cloths, one soaked with a numbing agent that he applied quickly around the wounds on Grey's chest, which was practically everywhere. The second was an antiseptic, which followed soon after.

"Did you get a good look at him?" asked the other enforcer, who looked to be in his mid-twenties.

Grey gently swung his head.

"He was an older man. Didn't recognise him." He winced as the fluid scorched his wounds. "Damn. This shit burns."

"It'll make you feel better, sir," said the medic.

He sighed. "I knew going down Lornan Street was a bad idea, saw the power go out, should've known better . . ."

Grey coughed, covering his mouth to prevent spittle from landing on the enforcer cleaning his wounds, who had now begun scraping the dirt and crust away from his chest.

"Any idea on . . . what's causing the power outages?" asked Grey.

"No clue," replied the mid-twenties enforcer.

Sighing to himself, Grey stood up once the medic had finished bandaging the wound.

"Do you need help walking, sir?" asked the mid-twenties man.

Shaking his head, Grey pointed his arm towards Main Street. "I'll make it son, thanks; the checkpoint's not too far from 'ere."

Wicked and blinding pain had been replaced with a dull, burning ache. It made moving around a little easier, so his pace had quickened by a small degree as he left the outpost.

"I'll escort you," said the mid-twenties man as he stood up.

Grey chuckled. "Sounds good to me, kid. I hope you don't mind keeping your eyes on an old man for a little while . . ."

As he chuckled, his chest tightened, sending him into a coughing fit that he couldn't resist.

"It's no problem at all, sir. Come on, let's get you home."

"I'll let the sergeant know," said the medic as he gave Grey a crisp salute.

"Pioneers watch over you, sir. We all know how hard you're working to rebuild the sector behind that barricade. Please, take care of yourself."

Grey nodded.

Definitely don't deserve this . . .

"Thanks, son. If I make it through this, I'll make sure to pass on a word to your superiors."

"Not a problem, sir."

Leaving the outpost promptly, Grey eyed the massive concrete wall that rose into the sky. Fifty meters tall and encircling the entire Broken Sector, the concrete barricade was built after augurs began spilling into the other sectors post-invasion. The depth of the structure was impressive, taking up one hundred meters of space. Such a thick obstacle was impossible to penetrate, even for a dredge of Grey's calibre.

I'll bet Sinew could knock it all down over lunch . . .

"So . . ." said the enforcer, "no one in the team made it out?"

Grey turned to face the young man. He had short brown hair, dark skin, and dark brown eyes. It didn't take an Inquisitor to know that he must've had friends with that crew; Grey could tell by the concerned look in his eyes.

"I'm sorry, son . . ." said Grey, his tone filled with empathy. "Those people . . . Well, I barely got out in one piece; they . . ." He shook his head, grunting at his pathetic attempt at answering the question. "They didn't make it."

Grey nodded, exhaling as he felt a lump forming in his throat.

The enforcer sighed, turning his head away from Grey as they continued towards the checkpoint. After a few minutes of moving up Main Street in relative silence, Grey could finally see the entrance to the checkpoint offices.

Glancing up to the top of the barricade, he spotted a few heavily armed guards patrolling above, protected by bulletproof windows. Above the walkway were snipers observing Grey and their colleagues quietly. He'd come the same way a few hours ago, so it wouldn't be a surprise for the staff that he'd be coming back this way.

His wounded state would raise questions, which would likely spread fast through the enforcers across the city.

Hopefully the fallout from this isn't too vast . . .

He saw one of the snipers scoping them through binoculars before gesturing to the rest of them. Within a few moments, he saw Captain Wayne Pritchard step over to talk to one of the officers above before motioning for a few of them to follow him as they moved over to the nearby staircase, disappearing inside.

In between the two towers stood the steel gate, which separated Sector Five and the Broken Sector. As they approached the gate, Grey noticed the sliding doors on the tower to his left slide open, revealing Captain Wayne with an escort of four armed enforcers.

"Councilman," he said with a curt smile, "I hear you have had quite the night!"

His Silver City accent made each pronunciation come off as eloquent yet humble. His hooked nose, smile lines, and relaxed brow made him seem more like a politician than an enforcer, but he was good at what he did nonetheless.

Wayne's welcoming expression encouraged an opinion Grey had earlier of the man, that he appreciated Grey's work. He'd made a natural ally and friend with his political actions alone.

"Need . . . to get to the hospital." He grinned, showing a bloody smile as he struggled to remain standing.

"Pioneers have mercy . . ." said Wayne. "You look awful. Compatriots, please, assist the Councillor upstairs. We will get you checked out, and then we shall have my team escort you safely through your sector to the hospital."

"You know what'll happen to your boys when they realise who's escorting me," Grey shook his head. ". . . It's not worth the risk."

"Please, Greyson. Help *us* to help *you*," said Wayne, gesturing to his chest. "It will do you no good—nor any others in this city—if you do not come back from—" Wayne gestured to Grey's many injuries. "—whatever *this* is . . ."

Nodding his head, Grey accepted that he'd have to follow this through. Such hesitance was not unfounded; he knew the dangers involved with such a journey, and the last thing he needed was more dead enforcers on his conscience. But it was either stay here or make the journey.

Let's get this over with. Can't afford to stay out of action for more than a day or two . . .

Grey nodded his head after a few moments of deliberation.

"Thanks, Wayne. I appreciate it."

Wayne nodded with a warm smile. "Come then, let's have the medic take a look at you before we head off."

⌘

Standing quietly in the clinic, Grey was promptly sat down on an inspection table in the sterile room by the doctor. A middle-aged woman had been waiting inside the room with a row of medical instruments laid across the table. She'd been professional enough, thankfully avoiding questions about being an augur, which was a rarity for a doctor outside of the Broken Sector.

"So," said Wayne, "are you going to tell me what happened?"

The doctor sat down in front of Grey in an office chair, rolling over to him as she started to inspect him with her instruments.

Grey chuckled mockingly as he rubbed his chin. "Some old guy was hassling a team outside of the Lornan building."

He winced as the doctor snipped away the bandages the medic had wrapped around him.

"I tried to intervene, thinkin' I can handle the guy. Turns out he was an augur . . . Didn't end well for any of us . . ."

"The great Greyson taken down by an old man? I find that hard to believe." Wayne smiled faintly, but his eyes showed his distress.

"He looked to be in a hurry," said Grey. "Didn't stick around after he dealt with us . . ."

"Well," said Wayne, "you're alive; that is the main thing."

The captain sighed as he weighed Grey's words for a few moments.

"We did receive reports that line up with what you are saying, Greyson—" Wayne sighed heavily. "But a lot of officers lost their lives trying to take down this man, and those *blasted* blackouts prevented us from getting any security footage of what happened. I'm going to have to ask you a few questions before we can take you to the hospital."

Wayne gestured openly. "I know it's tough to put you under the spotlight so soon after your . . . ordeal. But I could lose my job if I do not follow procedure."

Grey yelped as the doctor injected something next to one of the more severe wounds on his chest.

"Damn it! Sorry . . ."

He shook his head, waving the doctor to continue with the injections. "It's okay, do what you need to do."

"Okay," Wayne rubbed his hands together. "I'm going to record our conversation; do I have your permission to do this?"

Okay, try not to give away any information unless directly asked . . .

"Suits me."

The doctor wiped the wounds on his chest, picking at the remaining contaminants from Grey's injuries using a thin pair of tweezers. It stung his skin on contact, but he knew it was for the best, so he tried to remain focused on the incoming questions instead of the pinching pain from the instrument.

"You mentioned earlier that you were attacked by an old man, an augur," stated Wayne. "Can you describe this man for the record?"

Grey went on to describe Sinew precisely as he was: wispy white hair, wrinkled skin, and green eyes. He even detailed the purple robe he wore with the strange runes embroidered across the shimmering fabric. Wayne was understandably taken aback by the description, but he quickly moved on as it was an official conversation after all.

"Doctor Alsetta, can you please state Grey's injuries for the record."

The doctor tossed the soiled bandages into the disposal shoot beside her before answering.

"Greyson Lorath has suffered three broken ribs, a punctured lung, internal haemorrhaging in multiple places, and excessive lacerations across the head and chest. He looks to have suffered a concussion, although it's hard to tell without a more thorough examination. By all accounts, he should be dead . . ."

Wayne smiled. "It would take a lot more than that to take down this man, I assure you."

Gesturing softly, Wayne weighed his next sentence carefully. "What sort of person could do something like this? I always thought *you* were on the higher end of the spectrum when it came to . . . enhanced individuals."

Grey chortled, the captain's politically correct language was a skill he envied.

"No idea. This guy didn't say much, just beat the hell out of me as I approached." A pang of guilt struck Grey as he reached up to scratch at his scar. "I tried to defend myself . . . but this guy was something else."

Sighing heavily, Grey added that he felt lucky to be alive after the encounter. "Like I said to you before, Wayne. This guy was in a hurry, not sure where he was off to, but he didn't seem to be too worried about me. I'm not even sure he knew who I was, to be honest."

Shouldn't have said that . . . Didn't need to commit to such a statement . . .

Wayne stopped the recording.

"Let's get you to the hospital," he said. "We can get a written statement from you once you are well."

Grey nodded as he put his shirt back on.

"Do you mind if we bring along some o' your food rations?" asked Grey, reaching over to his tattered black shirt.

"Rations? Whatever for?" asked Wayne.

Grey smiled. "Consider it a donation."

Wayne crossed his arms with a smirk.

"A donation? Perhaps I should do more than giving an old friend some crusty old bread and water, in that case?"

⌘

4: BROKEN

⌘

Four armed enforcers were all that stood between Councilman Grey and the frightening unknown of the Broken Sector. Being positioned at the gate for half of her career had instilled a reasonable level of respect for the ongoings of the sector, which was replicated across the entire Enforcement institution with good reason.

Oriana had never been inside the sector before. Her career had consisted of observing the sector from the safety of the checkpoint, but now she was venturing inside against her better judgment.

Before the invasion and subsequent riots, the checkpoint was merely a small concrete wall serving as more of a separator rather than a hard construct to keep people out. After the ensuing chaos, the concrete had been reinforced, building it up into the robust structure it was now. The concrete itself wouldn't do much on its own as a single determined augur would be able to leap over it, or even cleave through it with empowered fists.

It was a sobering thought to consider, making her question the equipment they'd been provided for this duty. The rifles and bulletproof uniforms would keep them safe from regular people, but if they ran into a competent augur, they would be in serious jeopardy.

The ground began to rumble, although no one in the vehicle reacted in any significant way. Soon enough, a large aircraft zoomed along the border, causing her teeth to chatter as she peeked at the space worthy craft through the front window.

Looks like an off-world cargo ship. Wonder where she's headed.

Being under the flight path for most domestic, international and interplanetary craft, the outpost saw a variety of airships coming and going. Oriana had learned most of the models by observation alone, becoming a bit of a fanatic through repetition.

Wonder what it's like to fly in space with one of those cargo ships. Must be nice.

"All right," barked the vehicle's radio deck, "we're going to open the gates. Are you ready, Sergeant?"

Oriana didn't hesitate to respond. "Confirmed, we're ready."

Using her index finger, she pushed on a plastic button on the right side of the steering wheel. Holding the button down, she used her left hand to pull two levers next to the steering wheel, which brought the engine to life.

After so many years of watching and observing, I have no idea what to expect in there . . .

The motors responsible for opening the gate whirred to life as her imagination ran wild with what awaited the team inside. Enforcement hadn't taken a step into the sector for approximately twenty years. Anyone brave enough to traverse the shattered landscape wearing a uniform wouldn't return, so eventually the unit stopped sending people in. Sector Eight was unpredictable at the best of times, but at night, this patch of Vale became the most dangerous place on the planet.

The nights of silence were a respite due to the general nature of chaos and unpredictability. Only in the Broken Sector were these things possible: where people were flung around like rag dolls, weapons were discharged with recklessness and without punishment, and vagrants would wander around aimlessly seeking trouble, drugs, or their next victim. Over sixty thousand people were living in this place, and no one had a clue how many of those were antisocial cretins, augurs, or regular citizens trying to get by. Those numbers were an estimate, of course, as the Broken Sector had no institutions or government in place to keep track of the population.

Apart from this dying man we have in the car . . .

After taking a good look at Grey sitting next to her on the passenger side, she felt pity for him. As strong as he may be, the man looked like death warmed over, hardly in fighting shape if they got into trouble.

A thousand questions burned in her mind.

How did he gain this power? This 'Augmentation'?

Why did he become a councillor? In such a place of constant turmoil?

How did he stay sane in such a chaotic landscape? How could one even sleep in such a place?

She shook her head.

This is hardly the time or place to question him . . .

"I'll take us through the back roads," said Grey suddenly, as the giant steel doors finally slid into place. "I doubt we'll run into any trouble this way. Keep in mind we'll be passing through the home of some good folks, so don't get too excited . . ."

"Lead the way," said Oriana, driving underneath the massive archway.

Looking through the windscreen, Oriana depressed the accelerator pedal with her foot, moving the vehicle forward quickly. The stark contrast between the smooth, clean, and organised Industrial Sector compared to the dilapidated ruin of the Broken Sector was jarring. Her tactical mind was overwhelmed with possible ambush points, as the street was littered with obstacles. Cement blocks, broken down cars, toppled building rubble, every square meter could've housed an augur or a gang member waiting for Enforcement to come in like the overeager fools that they were.

Stay positive. Stay focused. You're a lieutenant now, so act like it!

Oriana took a deep breath, slowly and quietly so as not to worry her subordinates.

She heard Alex take a jittery breath in the backseat.

Glancing in the mirror to look at the young enforcer, Oriana was disappointed that she was nervously glancing out of the windows, not following her confident example.

"*Welcome to Sector Eight . . .*" whispered Alex.

"Private," snapped Oriana, staring at Alex in the mirror, "focus on the duty at hand," she continued. "You're not here to sightsee."

"Yes, sir," she said curtly, sitting up straight against the hard leather seats.

"That includes you two—" said Oriana, gesturing to Paul and Bart. "Watch out for—" She stopped herself short.

For Pioneer's sake . . . Don't call the citizens hostiles.

She glanced over to Grey, who thankfully wasn't paying her much attention. He had his head in his hand, his eyes flittering restlessly as he tried to stay awake.

I should ask if he's okay.

"Sir?" asked Bart with a concerned tone.

She cleared her throat, realising she hadn't finished her sentence.

"Keep your eyes open," she said, "and let me know if you see anyone approaching the vehicle." Oriana glanced to the three of them in the backseat. "Any *sensible* citizens are going to notice that we're Enforcement, which means we just need to watch out for the insensible ones."

She stopped the vehicle, glancing to the wounded Councillor fighting for his life. "Greyson?"

He slowly turned his head to her, raising an eyebrow as his eyes seemed on the brink of closing.

"Are you okay?" she asked, despite her internal plea to leave the man in peace.

Don't forget, he's a VIP.

She sighed softly.

Well . . . he's more than that. Greyson is the best hope this sector has for restoration.

"I'll be just fine, darlin'." He smirked warmly before turning to address her colleagues. "You folks don't need to worry about me. I'll be all right."

Greyson turned back to Oriana with a relaxed smile. "We're takin' a left here; follow the road until I say otherwise . . ."

She knew that there was nothing to gain from pushing the point, so she followed his instructions. Oriana felt confident that he knew what he was doing; working in such a wasteland would've demanded dedication, something no sane person would fake for so many years. Greyson's predecessors hadn't lasted more than a few weeks, making his tenure of four years incredibly impressive.

Let's get you back in fighting shape, sir.

Her eyes returned ahead while her gloved hands stretched over the wheel as she analysed the environment of the Broken Sector at street level for a change.

Greyson had been working ceaselessly to rebuild it, but from the way things looked, progress had been slow. There weren't many people on Vale that could visualise how Sector Eight could possibly come back to form after so much pain; the cursed landscape had suffered much over the years.

Oriana's father had told her of the invasion during many a late night, and the riots that followed soon after. Some from stories he'd witnessed personally, and others from *his* father. The history of Sector Eight had been drummed into her head so much that gradually, she'd become obsessed with the history surrounding it.

There was still a great deal they didn't know about the Strin - a mysterious collective of humanoids from another world - but when they invaded Vale, they'd chosen Menilax as the initial incursion point. Within a few hours, they'd completely neutralised the city's defences, forcing citizens to either evacuate or perish amidst their ruthless offensive.

Oriana's grandfather, Ian, had been an enforcer at the time. He was on patrol while the first Strin soldiers had infiltrated the city walls, marching through and clearing the way for the bulk of their forces to land inside the borders. Menilax had not been the powerhouse of war that it turned into, meaning the Enforcement had to rely on small arms and fundamental tactics to try to defend the city. Ian had been on patrol at the time and had taken a few rounds in the abdomen during the retreat. He'd made it out of the sector alive, barely.

The Pioneers had retaliated immediately as the Menilax temple had emptied in haste, all forces striking at the heart of the alien force invading one of the cities the Pioneers had sworn to defend.

Her father told her stories about their holy broadcasts, citizens around the world watching pensively as the tone of each message worsened. The Pioneers were confident that their place on Vale was just and that the invaders were foolish to challenge them. As the days progressed, the messages became less hopeful as attempts to retake the sector had failed miserably.

Once Menilax fell, the Strin had gained all the information they needed on where the Pioneer temples were located around the globe, and within a few short days, the Pioneer Order had fallen. Without the protection of the Pioneers, Vale was utterly defenceless. Within a month, Menilax had been evacuated, but those still hiding in the rubble of Sector Eight remained. Frightened and desperate, the citizens remaining were wholly drained of hope. It was the perfect storm.

Ordinary citizens had begun to come out of hiding to face the Strin in various offensives. Some chose to fight head-on, while others preferred to employ guerrilla tactics, hiding and striking from the shadows using the Strins strategies they'd employed against the immortal defenders of Vale. Within the frenzied minds of those with nothing to lose, something had awakened within them: the dormant powers of the Pioneers. Augmentations.

Once relegated to the Pioneers, these abilities gave the wielder various inhuman strengths. It wasn't too uncommon to see Pioneers partnering with regular humans, however their offspring didn't seem to inherit their mysterious abilities, as most had assumed. The dormant augmentations within their genetic makeup were awoken by necessity, it seemed. With insurgent tactics, stolen Strin weapons, and scrappy augurs fighting back, the Strin were slowly vanquished, leaving them no choice but to retreat.

The only part of the sector's history that remained a mystery to Oriana was how Greyson had managed to squeeze his way into the role, or where he'd even come from. Regardless, he'd solved the problem that plagued the Broken Sector for so long. Ironically, it had taken an augur to stand up and take charge to get things moving in the sector. And as slow as the reconstruction process was, any progress at all was welcome. The entire city had their eyes on Greyson, sceptical, yet hopeful that this man could fix the unfixable.

"We'll be taking the route under the old Main Street bridge," said Greyson as he raised his hand to her. "Take it slow now; let's keep the engine as quiet as possible."

Oriana nodded, ignoring her inner voice; if an augur came to intercept them now, they were in serious trouble.

Put it out of your mind and become the leader the team needs you to be.

"Keep your headlights off," said Grey, gesturing softly.

Oriana complied, reaching over the steering wheel to depress the headlight button, disabling the lighting on the vehicle.

That's going to make things a little difficult . . .

There were no power stations in the Broken Sector, so without the headlights on, they would only have the moonlight above to light the way. The bright light was obfuscated by cloud cover, giving the sector an ominous, foreboding aspect.

The once mighty government structure that had been standing at the crossroads was now just a massive pile of rubble scattered across the sides of the road. Most vehicles would struggle to navigate through the sector, although their armoured cruiser would make the journey without much trouble.

I can't believe the captain gave the cruiser to Grey. This old girl has been at this outpost for years . . .

"Where is everyone?" asked Alex.

Grey chuckled to himself. "Most folks tend to sleep during the night, darlin'."

She nodded, scrunching her brow.

"*Makes sense*," she said under her breath.

"The only ones you'll see wandering this part of town are drug addicts or criminals. So keep your eyes peeled," reported Oriana.

"Greyson," said Bart.

"Please—" Grey raised his hand gently, "just Grey."

"Excuse me, Grey. I really respect what you are doing here with this sector," continued Bart. "It takes a hell of a person to take this sector head-on, trying to fix . . . all of this . . ."

"I appreciate that, son. Maybe one day, when we fix it, you can come back and work the beat." Grey nodded to himself. "But we still have a lot o' work to do before we get there."

The street turned into a tunnel leading under the remains of the highway, which encircled most of the sector.

"No matter what happens here," said Grey, "do *not* leave the cruiser."

As they descended into the tunnel, Oriana spotted a source of light ahead in a small alcove hiding on the right-hand side. With the cruiser rolling across the massive potholes in the bitumen, Oriana didn't have much time to concentrate on the collection of people that began to form near the light source. When the vehicle was clear, she looked up just before the cruiser went into the tunnel, noticing at least six people with rifles now lining up before the cruiser.

Damn it! This could be bad.

She exhaled quietly.

I hope Greyson knows what he's doing . . .

Grey seemed to notice her concern.

"Hold up," he said. "Follow behind me and keep those windows up." He touched her shoulder, catching her attention. "These folks are good people. They won't do anything to us unless we do something to them first, understand?"

She glanced over to him, nodding quickly before pushing her foot on the brake and coming to a complete stop. Grey promptly left the cruiser and began to walk down the tunnel.

It looked to be a small parking complex with a booth, some old service cars, and even a broken boom gate adjacent to the line of those holding guns towards them.

To the right, the tunnel opened into an old parking complex which had been retrofitted into a shanty town. At least twenty people were lining up behind the booth, watching Grey step into the dimly lit tunnel pensively. Upon seeing the Enforcement cruiser roll down into their space, everyone's attention turned immediately to it, a few of them raising their weapons.

You got this.

⌘

"Well now," said Grey as he walked towards the guns trained on him. "How are ya'll doin'?"

He attempted to mask his pain as best as he could, although the hearty wave he gave them served only to inflame his wounds. Grey heard the cruiser pull up to a stop behind him while a few of the citizens shuffled around nervously.

"Good to see you, Grey," said a young woman. "I'll let Lionel know you've come."

"We're actually just passing through," said Grey, gesturing softly. "No need to disturb him."

"Grey!" yelled Lionel as he gently pushed through the developing crowd. "Good to see you!"

Well . . . so much for passing through.

Lionel was quite tall, and his bulk was filled with muscle. He'd been through hell, Grey had no doubt. Not too long ago there would be a different leader each time he'd made the trip through the underpass.

The man had a short beard, light brown skin tone, and a simple t-shirt and shorts. The large, bearded man tilted his head towards the cruiser.

"Who are your friends?" asked Lionel.

Grey remained neutral, extending his arm to the cruiser.

"Enforcement were kind enough to donate one of their cruisers, so we're taking it for a spin."

He flicked his chin towards their makeshift home built from the ruins of the parking complex under the old government checkpoint. "How are things here? Y'all doin' okay?"

Lionel shrugged. "Could be better. We've had a few people showing flu symptoms, can't seem to shake this thing . . ."

"Well, you're in luck," said Grey. "We're on our way to the hospital . . ." Grey gestured to the road leading out of the tunnel. "Got a few folks who can give us an escort? In exchange for running alongside us, I'll make sure we get you stocked up with some antivirals."

Lionel smiled, nodding happily. "Sounds good to me. Let me round up a few guys n' gals."

As Lionel turned around, Grey glanced back to the Cruiser giving a thumbs up.

They must be freaking out . . . Hopefully, they can keep it together a little longer.

Josie stepped out from the growing crowd of people lined up. She was one of a handful of people who could lead but would likely say otherwise if asked directly. Her upbeat attitude and ceaseless work ethic helped pull these people together. She had her hair cut very short to try to lessen her increasingly greying fringe, but it suited her quite well.

"Greyson," she said curtly, "always a pleasure."

Turning to face her, he nodded respectfully.

The corner of her smile was curved like she knew something he didn't. Her tanned skin tone came from a life of working under the sun, giving her a salt-of-the-earth vibe.

I wish I'd spent more time in the sun when I was younger . . .

She was worldly, wise, and had been around the block more than once. Josie was one of the rare few who was still around after the invasion, even more unusual was a survivor who still retained their sanity.

"What brings you down *this* way?" she said, crossing her arms. "And tell me, dear Greyson, why are you driving one of *those* around here?"

She laughed. "I'm surprised you haven't been shot already."

Grey smiled, hiding his concern. "Well, ya'll need to get used to seeing this old thing driving around here. Enforcement was kind enough to donate it." He shrugged. "She's a little on the older side, but some things only get better with age."

Grey smirked at her, raising an eyebrow.

She laughed even harder.

"Oh boy, if you were twenty years younger . . ." she said as she eyed him over.

Grey laughed despite the irony, and the smile he wore stuck with him as he continued to speak. "This old girl'll help us transport people and supplies a little easier around here."

Grey placed his hand on her shoulder, causing pain to flare over his shoulder and chest. He hid the pain as best he could.

"How are you holdin' up?" he asked.

She looked at him quizzically then back to the cruiser. "I find it hard to believe that Enforcement would just give you one of their vehicles . . ." Josie crossed her arms. "Reckon I can take a look inside?"

Grey shook his head, lowering his voice. "Maybe on the way back . . . ?" he proposed. "I have a doctor being transferred from Sector Three." Grey opened his arms, gesturing to the area around him. "I'd rather not spook her too much on her first visit to our *fine* little piece o' the world."

Josie smiled broadly. "Pioneers bless you, Grey." She crossed her arms. "How in the hell do you manage to get these young doctors to come out our way, eh? Treat *our* sick." She shrugged. "We all know how the rest of the world sees us . . . You must have one hell of a 'silver tongue' on ya!" She slapped his shoulder in jest, causing the pain to flare up again.

Grey laughed, the tension melting away as quickly as it had come, which eased the pain. "With a few rotations under their belt, these kids will be able to work *any* hospital they want to. *That's* how *prestigious* we are." Grey gestured wildly.

Josie laughed out loud. "Well ain't you a natural born salesman."

Grey crossed his arms, smiling broadly as he continued to gesture softly. "Oh, I bet you'd've been a slick talker back when you were my age; it's a shame I'm too nice a fella to be corrupted by the likes of you."

She smiled a toothy smile. "Oh yes, I would've corrupted you all right . . ."

The two of them laughed boisterously.

I'm getting too paranoid; these people have good hearts, and more importantly, they trust you . . .

The thought sobered Grey.

It wasn't too long ago that I had to fight my way through the sector, even had a run in here, in this very place. I wish I had more experience with people earlier in my life, things would've been so different. Those early days were tough; It's hard to believe I made it out alive . . .

As he was about to change the subject, Lionel stepped out from the row of people who'd woken to see what the commotion was about. He had his rifle at his side, nodding to Grey as he began walking towards the other side of the complex. A few others came out with him, men and women with rifles hopping along to catch up with Lionel.

Six should be plenty. Hopefully, we won't run into any trouble the rest of the way.

Somehow, they'd managed to get their hands on bullet-proof vests. While their shirts covered most of it, the straps over their shoulders were a key sign, visible to those who were trained to look for such things. It struck him as odd to see civilians wearing such heavy plating, he mused as he scratched his scalp.

Well, it is the Broken Sector, so it's warranted I suppose. Wonder how they managed to get their hands on them . . .

"I have something for you, Josie," said Grey as he gestured towards the cruiser.

Grey stepped over to the vehicle, quickly approaching the trunk. He felt around for a few moments before finding and pressing the rubber button which released the latch and popped the trunk open. Inside was a box of rations, enough to feed at least eighty people. Grey lifted it with both arms, and walked back to the two of them, handing it to Josie, who raised it with one hand.

Everything I do hurts . . . Damn this, I need to get to the hospital right now . . .

Josie chuckled, shaking her head as she playfully jostled the box of rations. "Seriously, I don't know what we'd do without you."

Grey scoffed. "Well you wouldn't have an enforcement cruiser comin' at ya at two in the morning for one . . ."

Josie laughed. "If you keep bringing us food, you can drive around these parts with whatever you want!"

Joining in on the laughter, Grey felt his spirits lift as he pondered what she said about him.

What would they do without me . . . ?

He sighed. There was some truth to the statement, reaffirming his motivation to keep going.

"You take care of yourself, honey," said Josie, rubbing Grey's shoulder. She smiled warmly. "You hide your pain well, but it'll catch up with you if you keep pushing it away."

Story of my life . . .

Grey moved over to the bonnet of the cruiser, slapping his hand on it twice as he gestured ahead. He waved to Josie.

"Sound advice," said Grey. "See you around, Josie."

Taking his leave, Grey walked in between the row of those holding weapons as they parted way for the cruiser driving behind him. Lionel and the others were on the precipice, waiting patiently for Grey and the hidden enforcers in the cruiser.

As he approached the apex of the underpass, he glanced around to the various other roads branching out before them, snaking around the rubble and destroyed cars that were all too familiar to them all. As his eyes returned to the main road, Grey traced the faded lines in the broken bitumen all the way to the Farley Tunnel entrance, their next destination. Grey and Lionel walked ahead of the Cruiser, which rolled over the apex of the underpass with a creak. The others Lionel had brought along took defensive positions, forming a U-shape around the cruiser.

People are going to think twice about taking us on now that we have the numbers.

It was only a few more minutes before they reached the tunnel, but this sector was unpredictable.

"You look like shit," said Lionel, shaking his head with a smirk.

Grey chuckled. "Little Lion, always the gentleman."

"Seriously now, are you okay?" The smile he wore changed into a look of concern.

"Yeah, I'm doing just fine. Got into a tussle with a few idiots as I came into the sector, nothing to be worried about."

Lionel moved closer to Grey, his tone softening so the others couldn't hear. "Who was it?"

Grey shook his head. "Don't you worry now; they got theirs. Now—" smiling warmly, he jolted his head back towards the camp, "how're things goin' for you folk? Apart from the flu keepin' you down, of course."

"We have a lot of people coming and going, which is to be expected, I suppose."

Grey nodded.

"Saying that we've had a lot of addicts coming through willing to accept treatment. More than we'd initially planned for." Lionel gestured to one of the two women of the six ahead. "Rita's just come back from the rehab centre—" said Lionel. "She's making good progress, *and* she's already given a lot back to the community in exchange for ongoing treatment."

Grey patted Lionel on the shoulder, ignoring the punishing pain. "That's great news, Lion. You make sure to let me know if you need some more meds."

"Thanks, we really do appreciate what you're doing for us."

Grey shook his head. "All part of the job, son."

As they moved along the dilapidated road, Grey noticed a massive thicket of clouds forming over the horizon now covering the moonlight that had illuminated his path so far. Flecks of light sparked in the parts of the sky that had yet to be smothered by the inky clouds, the hopeful stars burning as bright as ever. It was a humbling display, which inspired reverence in Grey.

That storm will hit us soon. Might as well enjoy the bit of starlight I can see now.

Grey's eyes drifted to Rita. She was muscled, clean, nervous, and watchful. She had a youthful body, yet her face seemed wrinkled and aged, a jarring difference that told him the sort of addiction she must've struggled against. Her arms had plenty of scars from her past behaviour, and yet she didn't seem to cover them up as most others would have.

The strength of the woman was evident. An iron will born and bred from the Broken Sector. It made Grey happy to see someone recovering from addiction, the road to recovery was long and arduous after all. Plans were in place to open a proper recovery centre to help the denizens affected by drug and alcohol addiction, however the hospital would have to suffice for now. Most of his resources were placed into rebuilding the Enforcement building, which still needed considerable resources to complete. It was hard enough keeping the tunnel and the hospital secure, so he had to spread his resources across a few areas, rather than pouring everything he had to construction.

The hospital and the Enforcement station are easy to defend, can't imagine what it's like to secure Josie's place . . .

For Josie and the people living under the highway, there were far too many places where threats could emerge. The hospital had been built at the barrier of the sector towards the south-eastern side, so there was only one way in for ordinary folk, and that was the Farley Tunnel.

Back when we were barely a ten-person team, this tunnel kept us safe while we rebuilt it all with our bare hands . . .

Thinking on how the hospital had been rebuilt always made him nostalgic. Working with the other citizens was eye opening and was his first major project in the sector. It had been the first few steps in building a community which formed from the ashes of the tragedy that kept the sector blinded for so long.

As they entered the tunnel, Grey's eyes were drawn to the graffiti on the inside of the tube. He chuckled as he eyed each piece carefully.

Still impressive, even after seeing them for the hundredth time . . .

Once the hospital had been cleared of the previous tenants, Grey and his team had gotten to work on reconstructing it. He'd organised the finance behind the operation and helped with the construction when he wasn't stuck doing paperwork.

We've come so far in such a short time.

Grey exhaled, releasing the tension built up in his chest.

Maybe it's time I put an end to these little nights out; I've got far too much to lose now.

⌘

5: REGRET

⌘

Janus sat upright in her hospital bed, scanning the room nervously as a perfect silence engulfed her. She couldn't hear the hustle and bustle of the staff, nor the beeps and whistles of the life support machines around her as she would have expected.

Something's not right . . .

Her eyes became fixated on the window to her left. It was a large pane of glass through which she was able to see out and over the large tarmac of the airport. The items in the room were sparse, adding to her anxiety.

I've never seen such a barebones hospital room.

Janus felt claustrophobic as she pushed herself against the mattress, which had no sheets or pillows.

There's not even a door to leave this place . . .

The bed had been pushed right against the glass, adding to the pit forming in her stomach.

A frightening pang of dread pulled her eyes to the tarmac of the airport, manically scanning it for signs of life. In the midday sun, there was nothing, observing only the signalling lights scattered across the barren, manmade plain.

Janus was alone in the world.

"Everything's going to be okay," said Nathan from the other corner of the room.

Janus shook her head, ignoring him.

You've said that a lot . . .

She could not speak; she'd been left with only her thoughts.

"Don't worry, Janus."

She turned to grimace at him. He was leaning on the glass opposite her, staring at Janus with a knowing smile.

An explosion resonated through the halls of the hospital as if a train were coming through the corridors outside. The blaring echo rattled the foundations of the building before being engulfed in perfect silence yet again.

Janus exhaled before another bone-rattling explosion rang out in her room as the wall blew open, sending plaster across the polished, white floor. The anxiety-inducing blast sent a nova of sparks dancing across her prickled flesh, leaving her insides feeling heated and lethargic.

She closed her eyes as tight as she could, feeling terror reaching up to her from the pit of her stomach. Something demanded her attention outside; it was coming at her from the sky. The dissonance of the two threats caused her head to throb in a rhythm like a drum beat, unable to decide on whether to run through the hole in the wall or stay in the relative safety of the room.

Trembling, breathing erratically, and utterly terrified, Janus slowly turned around to the windows to inspect the sky, opening her eyes slowly.

"Everything's going to be fine . . ."

Why are you saying that!? Things are not fine! We are going to die!

The skies were clear. The sun was beaming brightly, and she could've sworn she heard some birds in the distance singing peacefully.

Glancing to the dark hole in the wall, she was unable to make anything out in the shadows that blocked her sight.

No way am I going through there . . .

Turning her head back to the window, Janus clenched her eyelids in an attempt to lessen the dry stinging sensation that afflicted her. A massive aeroplane appeared as she opened her eyes. The low hum of the engines could be heard through the window, growing louder and louder as the craft slammed into the ground floor of the building. The hospital bed rattled underneath her as the foundations of the building crumbled, a low roar echoing through the halls, this time even louder than before.

Janus couldn't move.

She was forced to watch the building slowly topple over; her room facing down to the pavement below, picking up speed as it came down to burn with the rest of the building.

Janus watched the ground come up to meet her as she found herself unable to catch her breath.

"Are you nervous?" asked Nathan.

There was no sound; there was no hope.

Only death.

⌘

Janus leapt out of bed carrying cords and tubes that were implanted in her skin, bringing them with her to the clean, polished floor as she fell on her backside. Sliding into the wall with her hands, scurrying like a wild animal, Janus's eyes manically scanned the window for signs of the plane as she screamed a terrible scream, consumed with the lingering panic from the nightmare.

Her father was dead, and her brother was lost.

Janus stopped screaming, her jaw hanging loosely as her eyes immediately watered.

"No . . ." she sobbed.

A nurse raced into the room.

The colour of the world became dull.

She became numb.

The nurse grabbed her by the shoulders. Janus watched his lips move, but she didn't hear him at all.

Tears streamed from her eyes.

Nathan was dead.

She began to sob uncontrollably as she fell sideways to the floor, curling her body into the foetal position.

Janus had gotten her father killed with her actions.

It was all her fault.

The nurse was still trying to appeal to her, lifting her as she became limp.

"Miss, please. You need to—"

Janus groggily pushed him aside as she stood up. It felt like she was underwater, her muscles sluggish and cramping despite the little amount of energy she'd spent so far. She pushed the door of her room open as her chest began to ache and burn, and with that, she couldn't catch her breath.

She fell to her knees, holding her chest with her hands as she tried desperately to take a breath. She gasped like a fish out of water, her eyes wide with disbelief.

A few more nurses scurried into the room, crowding her as they snatched her up with haste and escorted her back to the bed.

One of them brandished a needle, but she was too terrified to react to it as the feeling in her extremities became numb tingles. Janus did not feel the pin prick in her neck as she fell back into a nightmare.

An endless, horrible nightmare.

⌘

6: ADMITTED

⌘

Grey woke to the sound of falling rain.

Slowly opening his eyes, he took in the details of the room as he began to stretch his limbs across the hospital bed. He'd been asleep in the quarters closest to the door among four other compartments with patients sleeping soundly, hiding behind thin blue curtains.

As Grey hefted himself out of bed, he sat on the side as he rubbed the sleep from his eyes.

I feel terrible . . .

Touching the spots on his body where he'd suffered wounds, Grey found the skin completely sealed as if he'd never been hurt in the first place. He nodded with satisfaction.

Rising to his feet, he moved towards the door, observing the quiet pattering of the precipitation against the glass towards the right. A flash of lightning lanced the sky outside, illuminating the room for a brief moment as the thunder rumbled around the halls.

Grey turned to face the door, opening it by the rusted copper handle as he slipped out through the gap as quietly as he could.

The investments into Ciril Station are paying back in dividends!

As he entered the dimly lit hallway, Grey gently sealed the door before briskly walking to the nurse's station. The young man who sat alone behind the desk was reading a book but promptly slid a bookmark between the pages, looking up to Grey with a warm smile.

"Good morning, sir," he said as he placed the book on the white desk.

"Morning," said Grey, taking a look at the clock on the wall behind the nurse.

4:36 a.m.

"What day is it?" he asked, scratching his scalp.

"It's Thursday, sir," replied the nurse. "How are you feeling?"

I've been under for twenty-six hours . . . I should consider myself lucky I suppose . . .

Grey pressed against his ribs where his wounds had been. He nodded with a smirk. "I feel great. The surgery went well I suppose?"

I wonder if Duke's around here somewhere . . .

"Yes indeed," replied the nurse, "It's miraculous how quickly you've recovered, Greyson. One of these days you'll have to explain how you do that."

Grey tapped his hand on the table, turning away from the desk as he pondered what to do with himself.

"You want some coffee?" asked Grey as he glanced over his shoulder.

The nurse smiled. "Yes, absolutely . . . !"

"I'll duck down to the cafeteria," said Grey, tilting his head. "How do you have it?"

"Black with two sugars," he replied. "Thank you, sir."

Grey chuckled. "No need for that 'sir' stuff, kid. Just call me Grey."

His bare feet slapped against the polished checkerboard floor as he stepped over to the shoe rack near his room. Quickly removing his boots from the shelf, Grey slipped them over his feet before moving down the hall. He glanced around at the signage on the walls, squinting to read the text.

Third floor, Recovery Centre. Reckon these other patients will be here for a lot longer than I was . . . Should consider myself lucky I was only under for a day.

Dredge's recovered substantially quicker from wounds compared to normal human beings, but with the enhanced surgery techniques the hospital employed - thanks to the ongoing research at Ciril Station — that natural healing ability was multiplied considerably.

Hopefully we can apply the same tech on regular people one day.

The entire complex was eight floors high; however, they'd only managed to restore the first five so far. Resources had to be managed carefully due to the limited amount Grey had to work with, as the income coming through the sector was marginal compared to the other sectors in Menilax. The priority was the reconstruction of the Enforcement station at this point, and they were only a quarter of the way through construction after a year of hard work. Thirty percent of the resources set aside for the project had been invested in security. Due to the inherent risks of transporting materials and guarding the worksite, progress would be impossible without the substantial investment in protection; the route to the site went through Senper Square, after all.

Reaching the end of the hall, Grey made a right turn and opened the metal door to the stairwell. The rusted steel doors of the elevators were tempting, but power was limited here, and he knew it would be better to leave the limited use for patients.

I'd hate to come out down below only to see some poor doctor wheeling a patient's bed past me . . .

The damp, cold corridors of the hospital were uncomfortable, but the stairwells were even worse. Thankfully, Grey was used to the conditions of the sector, happy to stroll down in nothing but a thin hospital robe as rain peppered his head and shoulders from the holes in the roof. Peeling walls, large blotches of mould, and rusted metal guardrails were the only exhibits in the winding staircase, but he was in and out in a few minutes. Opening the metal door of the ground floor, the smell of rain and chlorine wafted into the stairwell as he quickly closed it behind him. To his right was the entrance guarded by two sliding doors that met in the middle, reinforced with bulletproof glass and steel frames.

Turning his head to the left, Grey observed that the reception desk was unstaffed. Grey walked behind the L-shaped desk and opened the bottom drawer tucked underneath. He'd kept his personal things in this drawer, and the staff knew not to rifle through it. Inside were three packets of cigarettes, a knife, a handgun, a set of keys, and Sithaleir's hilt.

Placing his hand on the metal and glass shaft that fit neatly in his hand, he rolled it around his palm anxiously. Considering how the fight with Sinew ended, Grey couldn't help but think how different it could've been if he'd have managed to summon the blade. Perhaps the fight would've gone his way, although he shuddered to think of the consequences if he was to succeed that way.

Maybe that's how this ends, with Sithaleir through his back. If anyone deserves such a terrible fate, it would be that monster.

Shaking his head, he placed the hilt back in the drawer and took a pack of the cigarettes and a lighter.

Stepping outside through the double doors, Grey took one out from the pack and lit the cigarette as he stood under the archway of the hospital, admiring the dark rain falling from the sky.

The courtyard had a large garden in the centre, maintained by staff daily. Among the flowers and rain-soaked soil stood a large, stone slab with a copper plate screwed into the stone. Grey knew the words that had been etched on the plate by heart.

In memory of Ciril Lorath. May we learn from the sins of our past and use them to motivate us to become the best versions of ourselves.

Smoking the cigarette, Grey rubbed his finger along his scar as he looked away from the garden. Scanning the massive walls that encircled the courtyard, Grey found six security staff on detail patrolling the catwalk accessible via the hospital roof. Thankfully, the security team only had to watch the Farley Tunnel for anyone coming or going.

Grey's office had been here when he was first finding his feet as a councillor. However, he'd quickly moved back to his house near the bar once he was satisfied that it was safe for it to run itself.

'My' house . . . Still doesn't sound right . . .

He waved to the men and women who were stationed along the walls surrounding the courtyard. Some waved back to him with their blue ponchos and rifles as a flash of lightning lit the sky on fire, if only briefly. Grey didn't recognise who they were, but he knew that at least half of them would be augurs. To effectively defend any zone in the Broken Sector, they had to have some men and women with abilities to match those who might attack to provide an adequate deterrent.

Deterrents . . . That's what we're aiming for. If anyone strong enough really wants to assault this place, it won't stand for long . . .

Thinking once again on Sinew and how effortlessly he'd dispatched the enforcers, he realised how frail his operation was. There was little room for error.

Let's hope we don't get anyone like Sinew coming here . . .

Visualising those enforcers dying and wailing in horror began to penetrate his mind. He could almost hear them crying out for mercy. Grey closed his eyes, taking a draw of the cigarette. He held his breath for a few moments before exhaling, feeling the nicotine flooding through his body. The rush of chemicals calmed his anxious mind as he stretched his neck around to relieve the tension of his taut muscles. Finishing his cigarette, Grey held his hand out from under the arch, allowing the rain to extinguish the burning tip.

"*I need some coffee,*" he said under his breath as he stepped inside.

⌘

"You're looking well."

Ducard stood in the doorway of the old doctor's office, which was still littered with models and old diagrams of the human body. Grey had meant to clear it out, but it'd started to grow on him. He looked up from his breakfast and smiled warmly at his old friend.

"Feeling well too. How was the ride over?"

Ducard shrugged, stepping inside Grey's office. "Didn't run into too many issues, which is always nice. How are you recovering?" he asked as he took a seat. "I can't even tell you almost died yesterday . . ."

Grey squinted at him, detecting frustration in his voice.

"Thanks for taking the enforcers back to the checkpoint," said Grey, changing the subject as he slid another spoonful of cereal into his mouth.

Ducard shook his head, leaning back into the chair.

"There's something we need to discuss," said Grey, dropping the spoon into the bowl. "Sinew's the one responsible for almost killing me last night . . ."

Ducard leaned forward, a shocked expression consuming his earlier face of irritability. "That explains a bit . . ." he said thoughtfully. "When was the last time you saw him?" he asked.

Grey shook his head. "I haven't seen him in over ten years. I wish I knew why he's back. It can't be a coincidence . . ."

Grey had a cup of coffee in his hands, his third since waking.

"Did anyone *see* you?" asked Ducard with concern.

Grey took a deep breath, holding eye contact with him. "No."

Ducard nodded, sighing with relief as he leant back into the chair. "What about Sinew?" he asked. "Did he recognise . . . *you?*"

Grey nodded. "Yeah, he seemed to . . ."

Ducard took a sip of his tea, mulling over Grey's words carefully.

"I'll check with the base," he said finally. "See if anyone's heard anything about him."

The two of them shared the silence, quietly mulling over each other's words as they sipped on their drinks.

"By the way," said Ducard, gesturing to Grey. "You know the girl you rescued six weeks ago? She woke up last night. Looks like she's gonna make it."

Grey grunted.

Janus. . . So the lung transplant held up after all . . .

"She's a lucky one . . ." mused Grey. "How's Adalia holding up?"

Ducard shrugged. "She sounded flustered, stressed. She's taken a leave of absence from her company, hasn't publicly announced why yet, although there are plenty of reporters speculating on her situation."

Grey nodded, finishing the coffee with one last gulp.

I'm surprised STARCOV managed to keep the lid on this one.

He scoffed.

A rogue operator hunting insurgents in a public place? Quite the shitstorm . . .

"Janus must have had some pull within STARCOV, considering the bullshit statement they released on how it all went down that night . . ." said Grey.

"Yeah," said Ducard, nodding in agreement. "They didn't even mention the dead augur you found there . . ." Ducard scratched his nose. "What was his name again?"

"Desiriah," he answered immediately, "I met him once when he came to the temple, never really liked him. But he was considered quite powerful for a shifter."

Wonder how Janus managed to take him down . . .

As far as Grey knew, Janus was not augmented. It'd be one of the questions he'd ask her, assuming she was capable of holding down a conversation.

She took a real beating from those people . . . Fingers crossed she pulls through . . .

Finishing his coffee, Grey stood up and raised his chin towards Ducard. "I might head over to see her, find what she remembers from that night."

"Do you need a ride?" asked Ducard.

"Couldn't hurt," replied Grey. "Might be good to take it easy for a while. Are you ready to go?"

Ducard shook his head, and closed his eyes for a brief moment. "There's something I need to say . . ."

Here we go . . .

"Leave it alone, Duke . . ."

Ducard squinted at him as if the words forming in his throat were causing him discomfort. "If you want my help . . ." said Ducard, "then you'll hear me out. I think I've earned it."

Grey stood up from the chair and began to move towards the door. "I think I'll walk."

As he walked outside the office, he saw Artemis closing the door to the stairwell at the end of the hall.

"Arty . . ." said Grey, shaking his head. "What are you doing here?"

Grey's oldest friend walked towards him with a defeated gait. Artemis had been known to tie his hair back into a ponytail, but at the moment, his long black hair ran over his shoulders, and down his back. He'd recently shaved, making him appear more academic with his dark brown skin and confident, determined features.

"You were in the hospital overnight as a patient. Did you not think I would come?"

Grey nodded solemnly. "I suppose . . . But I'm on my way out, so . . ."

Artemis held his palm to stop Grey as he stood before him.

Grey crossed his arms. "So you're going to give me a lecture too, eh?"

"You almost *died*," said Ducard from behind him.

Grey shrugged. "*Almost* dying and *actually* dying are two very different things."

Artemis shook his head, disappointed. "You're going to have to do better than that this time."

Grey moved back inside the room and sat on the desk next to Ducard. "Speak your piece then so I can get on with it . . ." said Grey

Artemis joined him at the table.

"I understand why you went after Jone, I really do," said Ducard. "But putting yourself at risk when you go out of your way to fight these augurs—"

Grey clenched his jaw.

"It was *Sinew* that did me in, not some *fat* corporate slug. How was I supposed to know he was going to be there?" proposed Grey, gesturing wildly.

"Life is unpredictable," commented Artemis. "You are correct in the assertion that you would not have been able to anticipate his presence that night. But *your* presence may have attracted Sinew to that place, at that specific time. Have you considered this?" Artemis shrugged. "Perhaps, it was your participation that got those enforcers killed."

"Before you react—" continued Artemis, raising a palm to Grey's angry expression. "I am not assigning blame. I am merely reminding you that any person's presence in a situation can change the outcome dramatically despite the intentions of said person."

Grey laughed mockingly. "So I should just lock myself up at the bar then? Let that piece of shit have his way with those children?" Grey gestured dismissively.

Ducard placed his hand on Grey's shoulder. "Remind me again why you decided to do all of this?"

"Do *what?*"

Ducard gestured to Grey assertively. "You, becoming *this*. You told me you wanted to be a councillor, to help rebuild the Broken Sector." Ducard shook his head before continuing. "You wanted to live a legitimate life of public service, to repay your debt . . ."

Grey sighed.

"If Sinew had killed you that night, who would replace you?" asked Ducard. "You've got so much to live for. It boggles my mind how you can be so careless with so much on the line here . . ."

The three of them sat in silence for a few quiet moments.

"Are we done?" asked Grey sternly, glaring at Ducard with his jaw set.

"That depends on you," said Artemis. "Are you willing to throw away your friendships because you are too stubborn to listen to reason? What about the treatment you promised you'd get? Ciril Station is only a few hours away, and if you would only—"

Grey stood up and smashed the table with two empowered fists, causing Ducard to jump as the metal table bent in half. Artemis remained neutral, not reacting in any significant way.

"Don't you sit here and talk to me about throwing friendships away! Do I need to remind you who *you* work for!?" Barked Grey, jabbing a meaty finger in Artemis' face.

Ducard took a deep breath.

"We're talking about *you*, not Artemis," said Ducard.

Grey threw his hands up.

"I'm rebuilding this sector with my bare hands. I spend every waking moment trying to fix something, or sift through page after page of bureaucratic bullshit, and all I ever hear from you two are criticisms."

Artemis gently raised his palm. "You need to take a step back and see what you are really doing," said Artemis, tilting his head as he sighed. "You are not well . . ."

Grey felt like he wanted to punch his way out of the situation.

Artemis crossed his arms as Ducard took his turn to speak.

"We have allowed you a great deal of slack. Both of us know the things you've done to get here, but you promised me that once things settled down, you'd spend some time on bettering yourself . . ."

Grey took a deep breath through his nostrils. "Once the sector's back in good health, then I'll focus on me."

He took one last look at the two of them before promptly walking out into the hall.

⌘

95

⌘

7: INVIGORATION

⌘

Ever since the nightmare of the plane crashing into the hospital, she hadn't slept well.

Her nightmares were so disturbing and vivid that she'd done everything to avoid sleeping. Janus's doctor had told her that she needed to sleep naturally, advising her that they wouldn't prescribe medication unless they absolutely had to. She shuddered to think how terrible the nightmares could become when fueled by narcotics. The last time she took something to help her sleep—during the early days of Oscar's disappearance—her dreams had become so terror-inducing that they'd traumatised her; the scars rivaling those she'd gotten in the real world.

Without sleep, however, she felt her weakened grip on her sanity slip even further into the abyss she'd fallen into. Despite her pleas to be released from the hospital, the staff told her that the recovery stage of her admission couldn't be expedited, especially considering she'd almost died the last time she got out of bed.

Assuming she were still an active member of STARCOV, it would've been a lot easier to have the surgery, with the better surgeons and doctors on reserve for operators in need. Not only did she have to shoulder the reality of losing her loved ones, but now she was unemployed.

I can't deal with all of this . . .

The reality of what was lost from her overzealous operation hounded Janus through every waking moment. No matter which way she justified it, her conscience refused to let her spin it into anything but a disaster.

My brother, my father, my career . . . I've lost everything . . .

She felt so empty, so lifeless. Everyone she'd ever trusted was gone. Adalia was around, of course, but she'd been as distant as ever.

Every time I see her, she makes me feel like crap . . .

Adalia had slapped her when she'd first saw Janus awake, shocking the both of them. Her mother had left the hospital afterwards, leaving Janus alone for another twenty-four hours before returning, not saying a word about it. Pretty standard fare for what she expected from the woman.

Janus had made a promise to stay out of trouble to her face, but deep down, she knew that she couldn't leave it be. If fate had deemed her worthy of having one more chance to strike back at those responsible for destroying her family, then she would take it with both hands. Letting go would mean distancing herself from the situation, and she knew that would never happen, not when the words of Keynan were branded in her mind.

. . . you do not possess the gift that your sibling does . . .

Still have no idea what "gift" he was talking about . . .

Although the duty was a disaster, Janus had at least learned who she was dealing with now. They would believe her dead after the state they left her in, and with enough preparation Janus would be ready next time.

I need to find some augurs and convince them to help me bring those bastards a taste of their own medicine, especially that Pioneer basard . . .

Pioneers were thought to be exterminated after the war, but apparently, there was at least one still walking around Vale. They could be destroyed, the invasion was proof of that. Years of training and experience had brought her here, and it seemed as if everything she'd gone through was a precursor to taking them down.

Dad's rounds took down that bastard in the purple robe, before he rose again at least. Catching them off guard is the key, but how to make sure they stay down, that's the tricky part . . .

She had to stay determined and not focus on her loss.

Janus would make it right, one way or another.

Rubbing her tired eyes had allowed a nurse to come into her room without her noticing. When Janus opened her eyes, he was standing next to her bed greeting her warmly.

"Good morning."

It was the same nurse she saw when she first woke up, but rather than bring it up, the nurse monitored the machines next to her bed as he began to jot a few things down.

"Good to see you up," said the young nurse. "How are you feeling?"

Janus groaned as she propped herself up against the pillows. "What time is it?" she said, stretching her arms and legs out on the bed.

"It's about 4:30 p.m.," he said. "Your brother's been waiting for you to wake up for a few hours now. Would you like me to send for him?"

My brother . . . ?

Janus shook her head, confused. "My brother's . . ." She sighed, nodding to herself.

It's Morgan.

"Hmm?" he said, stopping midsentence to gauge Janus curiously.

Janus rubbed her face with her hands, not noticing until now how clammy her skin was.

I desperately need a shower.

"Sorry," said Janus. "Send him in, please."

The nurse nodded politely to Janus, quickly writing a few more notes discerned from the devices before stepping outside. Janus inched her back further against the bed, sliding a pillow under the small of her back to keep herself upright.

Morgan Bartin was Nathan's son, but from a previous relationship. Not only had Adalia refused to take Nathan's name when they married, but she refused to let Morgan in her house as if denying his past. Nathan had privately kept the relationship going and had encouraged Janus to stay in touch with Morgan despite their different mothers. Her father had told her than Morgan was similar to him in his youth, sparking interest in Janus, giving her the opportunity to get to know a younger version of Nathan.

He stepped into the room, hands in his pockets with his hoodie over his head, bringing with him the smell of tobacco and beer as he leered at her. Morgan was in his late twenties and had started growing out his beard in recent months, giving him a menacing, borderline homeless look. She hadn't spoken with him since being accepted into STARCOV, but considering Nathan had been the one to organise outings, she doubted that they would stay in touch often. Janus mostly came along to humour her father in the later years, not really having much in common with Morgan since joining the unit. She wasn't looking forward to the conversation with him now, after everything that happened at the national park.

"Hey . . ." said Janus. "Is Adalia out there?"

"Why would I know where she is?" he said, shaking his head.

Morgan had always been this way. Introverted and passive-aggressive.

"What have you been up to?" she asked, trying to hide her disapproving tone as she quickly moved on from the comment.

He clenched his jaw. "What the hell were you thinking!?"

"Excuse me?" she replied.

Morgan moved aggressively, pushing the bed in as he stood over her, gesturing wildly.

"What happened to Nathan?" he growled.

She swallowed the bile building up at the back of her throat, looking away from him in shame.

"I'm sorry . . ."

"Don't be *sorry*," said Morgan, gesturing accusingly. "Be truthful. Tell me what happened."

Janus took a deep breath. "I can't . . . tell you . . ."

Morgan stared at her accusingly. "You're seriously not going to tell me?"

Janus sighed, feeling a wave of nausea rising from her chest. She had so many things she wanted to say, but the words became lost in a storm of anxiety and panic. Janus had agreed to keep what really happened to herself as part of her agreement with Captain Davis.

"Believe what you want."

She scrunched her brow as she rubbed her forehead, reacting to the pulsating headache forming across her head. Morgan was on the verge of losing it; she looked over his attire curiously as she tried to get a handle on the conversation. He wore a pair of ripped navy jeans, running shoes, and an unbranded grey hoodie. She saw a few bulges in his pockets, and she immediately recognised the shapes.

He brought drugs into the hospital. Of course . . .

Her stepbrother had an addictive personality and always stood by the notion that he was just a dealer, consuming his own product to "be sure of the quality" before selling them. The dry lips, bloodshot eyes, and twitchy neck told her all she needed to know about his current state of mind. He had the potential to be dangerous, especially if he was coming down from whatever it was he was on.

"You got him killed, didn't you?" Morgan threw his arms in the air. "How can you just sit there? I don't even know how he died, for Pioneer's sake . . ."

She took a few moments to catch her breath as a rising tide of anger and humiliation bubbled under the surface of her assertions. "Why are you here?" snarled Janus, "apart from making me feel like shit?"

Morgan scanned her face for a long moment before answering. "Aside from finding out how my father got his head caved in?" He sighed, straightening his back.

Janus scoffed. "You know I can't talk about it . . ."

Despite his apparent "need for closure," he had come for a completely different reason, she was sure of it. Morgan hated Nathan more than anyone, declaring to her privately that he'd refused to allow him into STARCOV alongside Janus, claiming that there was only one space available at the time. He blamed the state of his life on Nathan and consistently refused to discuss any alternative reasons as to why his life had ended up the way it had.

Morgan cleared his throat and looked at her sternly. "I've been offered a position in the military . . ."

Is he serious?

"I'm going to be flown out to a training facility for a year, so you probably won't see me again for a while," he said. "And considering what *you* did to my father, I've got nothing else here, so I—"

"Don't be stupid!" yelled Janus.

The sudden outburst shocked him.

"You're not even *close* to being in the right frame of mind for military service, and you're going to *use* Dad's death to justify that? How dare you!"

"Like *you're* in a position to say anything about how I live my life! You took away my—"

"I can't believe this!" she yelled, throwing her arms in the air. Her arms began to tremble, so she crossed them in an attempt to hide it. The sudden adrenaline pumping through her body made her anxiety feel as though it was going to explode through her pores like a volcano.

Take it down a notch, or you're going to push him away . . .

"You have to trust me here," said Janus softly, trying to calm herself down as she took a few deep breaths.

That's it, calm down. You don't need to put any more stress on Morgan, or yourself.

"I could talk to you for hours about how this is the wrong move for you . . . ." She sighed, not breaking eye contact. "This is a mistake, Morgan, and I think you know that too. Why else would you come here and try to justify it?"

Janus knew she couldn't convince her brother not to go. She looked into his eyes and remembered the things that they had done together. They'd been very close once. As she took a moment to read his angry and distasteful expression, she knew all too well that he'd already made up his mind.

He bit the inside of his lip—like he did when he was wrong—and rubbed his face with a four-fingered hand.

"Why is it right for you and wrong for me?" he proposed.

"It's not *right,*" she said quizzically. "If I could go back in time, I wouldn't choose this life. I had no idea what this life brings down on you, you're never the same after service, no one is." Janus took a jittery breath. "I know we don't see eye to eye on most things, but trust me, it's nothing like the streets."

"You're right," he said with his jaw clenched tightly. "You've always been so *focused* on everything to the point where you have tunnel vision." Morgan shook his head. "My life is in a mess right now. I need some stability, some honest work, and you can't get past your own garbage to see what I need."

Morgan looked sincere for a moment before he snarled and gestured at her dismissively. "This is how it is! So get over yourself for one damn second, and tell me what happened to my father!"

Janus sighed. "If you make this decision, you'll regret it."

Morgan stood up defiantly, his jaw set.

"You don't know me as well as you think. You've done your military thing, and I've . . ." He sighed, tapping his chest. "Well . . . I've done *my* thing. We're two different people now."

Janus looked up at her stepbrother, rubbing her wet eyes.

"*You* might not agree with the military way of life," said Morgan sternly, "but I will; this is where I'm supposed to be. Your words disgrace the brave men and women serving our city, and you disgrace yourself by not owning your decisions. So if you won't tell me what happened, then to hell with you!"

And just like that, he was gone.

Feeling distraught, guilty, and alone, Janus smashed the mattress with her fists over and over again in a fit of angry tears, grunting and groaning.

After a few minutes of belting her frustrations into the bed, Janus cried more than she ever had in her life. She cried for her father and her brothers. She wept quietly and profoundly for what seemed like an eternity. The nurse that had come in earlier saw her crying and stepped out of the room as quickly as he'd arrived. Eventually, she fell into a fitful, restless sleep, murmuring curses and promises of vengeance under her breath as she fell into the pit of nightmares that were waiting for her.

⌘

"Hey, darlin'," said a man's voice. "How are you holdin' up?"

Janus didn't turn to face him immediately; she'd been lost in her own mind for at least an hour as she watched the aircraft landing and rolling around the airport across from the hospital. As the afternoon sun began to vanish over the horizon, she thought about how warm it would've made the tarred runways. The repetitive dream of the plane crash and the subsequent building toppling over with her inside made her obsessed with the airport. She kept watching the skies, waiting for the vision to become reality at any moment.

Janus turned to look at the man for a few moments, her face sticky with the tears she'd shed earlier from her encounter with Morgan.

"I'm okay, thanks," she said, regarding him curiously, "Who are you?"

He slid a chair over to sit next to her bed as he began rubbing his hands together.

"My name's Grey," he said. "I was the one who brought you here six weeks ago."

So that's how I got back . . .

He had a scar running over his left eye, but apart from that, he was quite handsome for a man his age. He looked older than he probably was, with worry wrinkles on his forehead and spots of white hair across his brown hair and beard. He looked like he'd just woken up, with dark circles around his glassy, tired eyes.

"I'm sorry I couldn't get there in time," he said with a heavy sigh. "I knew your father; he was a good man, and—"

"I recognise you from somewhere . . ." she said, changing the subject immediately.

He cleared his throat. "I'm a councillor. I represent Sector Eight."

This is the councillor for the Broken Sector? He looks the part. Must be a tough job to oversee such a hostile place.

Grey had earned some easy respect in her eyes in that moment thanks to his position, although she remained sceptical.

"And what's a councillor doing in my hospital room so late?" She asked, squinting at him.

Grey looked into her eyes. She saw a glimmer of something genuine in those blue eyes at that moment, as if he really was concerned about her wellbeing. There was something familiar about them, although she couldn't put her finger on what.

"I wanted to ask you some questions about what happened, if you wouldn't mind?" He asked.

She crossed her arms. "I suppose it would be rude of me to deny you, considering you saved me. Although, how about we get a few facts right about your involvement first. What brought you to the National Park that night?"

Grey smirked. "I suppose you could say I owe your mother a favour or two. She'd suspected you two were planning something, so she reached out to the only augur she knew to follow you."

Mother has quite the collection of "friends" . . .

"You . . . you're like them?"

Grey squinted at her, tilting his head. "Like who? The men you fought?"

She nodded, still reeling that Adalia knew a man like Grey.

What else are you hiding, Mother . . . ?

"Well, one of the boys you took down—"

"Desiriah . . ." she said.

"Yeah, that's him. He's from *my* part o' town. Been trying to track him down for quite some time." Grey leant back into the chair, impressed. "Gotta say, that's some mighty fine work you did. He was *no* pushover; in fact, he was considered to be one of the stronger augurs in—" Grey scratched at his scar.

"Sorry, I'm getting off track . . . Anyways," he said, changing the subject. "I'm here to talk to you about what happened. Adalia's asked me for help trying to track down your brother, so any info you can pass on will be put to good use."

Janus perked up at that. "Thank you for helping, but . . . I'm a bit lost with the context . . ."

Grey raised a hand. "Of course, let me fill in the blanks for you. Where to start . . ."

Janus scratched her head. "How do you know my mother?"

Grey nodded respectfully. "Your mother's been awfully generous to our little sector; some of my citizens work for her company, and she's been instrumental in providing weaponry to the security team protecting our borders. With all that in mind, it would've been pretty rude not to help her out when she called me," said Grey, pulling his chair closer to the bed.

Janus nodded.

"Now," said Grey, "if you could tell me what happened from the beginning."

Janus hesitated, reminded of the gag order she'd received from STARCOV.

"You have my word that it won't leave this room, darlin'."

If he's an augur, he's the best person to actually get this done. If Mother trusts him, with her business smarts, and natural paranoia, then I suppose he must be trustworthy . . .

Janus sighed. It still didn't feel enough to trust him completely.

"Listen, this information could get my family into more trouble than we're already in," said Janus. "Why should I believe you?"

Grey nodded to himself, rubbing his chin for a moment before responding.

"I've been searching for one the scumbags you ran into for longer than I can remember."

He leant back into his chair as he continued. "If it *is* the same feller, well he comes and goes, kidnapping folk and killin' anyone who gets in his way. Your info might help me track him down and deal with him once and for all."

"And my brother?" interjected Janus sharply, "If he's still out there, do you think that . . . ?"

Grey reached a hand out to pat her on the leg, "I promise you darlin', if your baby brother's still out there, I'll bring him home."

The phrasing made her heart skip a beat, and it was at that moment that she knew any help at all was welcome, especially if there was a chance that Grey's involvement brought Oscar home. Janus went over her story in detail, explaining her father's position, her infiltration plan, the fight with Desiriah, and the confrontation with Sinew and Keynan in the attic.

"You're sure he called him 'Sinew?'" asked Grey.

She nodded. "I remember every word; that's definitely how Keynan introduced him,"

Grey scratched at his scar again before rubbing his face in his hands.

"Who is he?" she asked.

He looked uncomfortable at the question. Grey rubbed his stubbled chin, remaining silent for the better part of ten seconds.

"As I mentioned before, he's bad news," he finally said. "He's old, dangerous, and unpredictable, that much I *can* say. But unfortunately, we don't know much more than that.

"But as for that colleague o' his," said Grey. "The Pioneer? Well, I have a few contacts I can get in touch with, to see if we can track him down. Pioneers tend to stand out against regular folks after all." Grey crossed his arms. "If we can track down the Pioneer, we might find Sinew."

Janus nodded as she yawned.

"Well, that should get us started at least," said Grey as he stood up, taking her yawn as a hint. "I'll come by some other time and check up on ya', and I'll let you know as soon as we have any leads on these guys."

"Before you go," she said, drawing his attention back to her. "There was a symbol on his chest plate, the Pioneer," said Janus looking around for her notepad. She rifled through it, turning the pages quickly until she came across her sketch of the symbol. She showed Grey, who received the notebook from her. Grey traced the scar on his face as he inspected the logo, shaking his head after a time.

"Don't recognise it," he said, "but it could help us identify him . . ."

Janus ripped the page off, handing it to Grey. He folded it four times before he slipped it into his pocket.

"If I need to reach you . . ." she started.

Grey held his hand out, glancing to the notebook. She handed it to him along with a pen. Within a moment, he returned both of them to her, gesturing to the number confidently.

"You give me a call if you remember anything else of note."

⌘

8: POLITICS

⌘

"I do take a lot of walks through Sector Five, so I know the area pretty well," said Grey.

The enforcement detective was busy writing down notes, while the Inquisitor watched Grey intently. They'd caught him before the board meeting, seating him in a small room to question him about the night he encountered Sinew.

"I could see a bunch of Enforcement vehicles parked outside one o' the buildings—"

"Lornan Futuristics . . . ?" asked the detective.

"Yeah, could've been. I saw an older gentleman—wearing a purple robe—hassling a group of enforcers who'd surrounded him. As I approached, he seemed to . . . do things to them . . ."

"What sort of things?" asked the Inquisitor.

Grey took a deep breath. "He broke their bones, their necks . . . Did it all without laying a finger on 'em." The interrogator sighed, taking a moment to compose himself as Grey spoke of his experience. "By the time I realised what was going on . . . it was too late . . ."

The Inquisitor and the detective shared a look of concern.

"Have you seen this man before?" asked the detective after a moment of writing in her notebook.

"No. Definitely not . . ." Grey chortled mockingly. "This ain't the sort of person you forget . . ."

The Inquisitor probed Grey with a new line of questioning. "This 'ability' that the man demonstrated, have you ever seen this before?"

"No. Nothing like this."

"Did you confront him?"

"Yeah. As soon I saw the enforcers go down, I tackled him . . . I got a few good hits in, but he, well, he beat the hell out me . . . Left me for dead when he was done with me."

Grey scratched his scar, sighing heavily.

"The next thing I remember? I woke up bleeding, hurt probably more than I'd ever been hurt before . . ." Grey shook his head, rubbing his tired eyes. "I walked along the road back towards the checkpoint to find some help."

The Inquisitor took some notes; Grey could tell from the slight trembling in his arm that he was rattled by the account. He didn't envy their work.

The detective, however, seemed to be more settled. She took her notes a lot quicker compared to the Inquisitor, and seemed to have been around the block more than once when it came to augurs. The Inquisitor was Caucasian, wore small, square-set glasses, and had his head shaved. The detective was older; she was tall, had almond-shaped eyes, olive skin, and a serious, determined look in her eyes.

"I hope you guys find the scumbag," said Grey. "I wish there were something more I could've done for your friends; I barely got out of there with my life . . . !"

"Thank you, Councillor," said the detective, closing her notebook. "We'll be in touch if we need anything more from you."

They all slid out from under the table, exchanged handshakes, and left the small office. Grey followed them out into the hallway, moving quickly across the brown carpet. Hanging along the walls were framed pictures depicting the construction of Menilax, along with the invasion and subsequent war. It was the youngest city on Vale, created to serve as a beacon of research and development for improving the lives of those across the planet. After the invasion, it had become the primary source of weapons and defence development, supplying the globe with tools of destruction in case the Strin dared to return.

Sad way to spend resources . . .

Shaking his head, he only wished that more photos and awards were celebrating the citizens and public servants of Menilax rather than memorialise the event that sent the city into chaos.

Grey sighed, glancing out the window to find the weather had held up pleasantly enough. His walk to Sector Two was thankfully rather quiet, time that was sorely needed for him to process what had happened recently.

These weekly council meetings were held in a few different areas around the sector; tonight's took place in the community outreach centre, where various members planned activities, ceremonies, and events throughout the city. The offices on the second floor were quite standard, which made Grey feel a bit more at home. He felt ill at ease when the board rooms were overly fancy or sported expensive decorative paintings and sculptures. The simple brick building painted white on the inside was homely and simple, just the way he liked it.

The male Inquisitor pressed the call button on the elevator as the two of them quietly chatted between themselves while they waited.

"Have a good night," said Grey.

It made sense that he should be interviewed here of all places. Grey couldn't imagine them coming into the Broken Sector to find him, not without his own team coming to escort them. The weekly board meeting was the only thing he had scheduled outside of the sector, so most official things were done in and around these meetings. They were waiting for him as he entered the building but were polite enough to ask if it was a sensible time to conduct the interview. The guilt he'd felt as he lied about what had happened weighed heavily on his mind, but he had no other choice. Telling them the truth would jeopardise what he'd spent so much time working towards. He knew that he was the only man who could rebuild Sector Eight, at least until someone else stepped up.

The moment someone steps forward, I'll step down.

He smiled.

Maybe then I'll fulfil my promise to Ducard and go back to Ciril Station . . .

Grey greeted the two security guards in front of the boardroom with a handshake.

"Good evening, Grey," said the taller man.

"Evenin'" he replied. "Is everyone here?"

He nodded. "Certainly are, and they're about to get started."

The man opened the door for Grey. "Please go ahead, sir."

⌘

Grey stood before the other councillors confidently.

"I've been thinkin' a lot about what the Broken Sector needs next. I know you all have your own opinions, but I strongly feel as though we need to incorporate some law and order into the place. This is why I'm suggesting we start pushing for Enforcement to head back onto the streets of the sector, patrolling, helping out the community . . ."

He cleared his throat, looking around the room at the other board members.

"It's a big ask for any person to walk the beat. But if we can get somethin' goin', it'll make other things a lot easier. I've been spending most of my time and money on rebuilding the old Enforcement Station on Cardinal Point. Once we're back up and running, we should be able to defend the site rather easily. We've been able to keep the hospital upright and defended for two years now without incident, and that's with a minimal amount of staff. I think we're in good shape to hold other positions, assuming we got some help from the rest of the city in terms of manpower."

Grey looked around the room again. They all seemed to consider his words carefully.

The chairwoman raised her hand. Leanna Poltier had held the position for many years now, and she was very good at keeping everyone in check. She had long black hair, black skin, and faded jade eyes. She was tall, lean, and held a confident posture at the end of the table. Her tenure as a councillor had put her miles ahead of everyone else, and she'd led the board for over twenty years now. She was wise, middle-aged, and didn't have any patience for people wasting her time. It was precisely what Menilax needed to thrive.

"I agree with your solution, Councillor," she said. "But I don't see how an average person will stand up to an augmented individual, especially considering what they're capable of."

Grey thought on her words for a few moments before answering.

"I have a few volunteers that would be willing to put on the uniform," he suggested. "They're augmented, seasoned, and trustworthy. Could be a good way to get started, but we'd have to have someone show 'em the ropes on how to be an enforcer."

"You want to have people from the Broken Sector put on the uniform?" asked Tobias.

"Grey, I understand your wish," he continued. "In fact, I think it would be the best thing *for* the sector. But picking up random citizens and slapping uniforms on them? Doesn't sit right with me."

"They're not random," said Grey, gesturing firmly. "Some of these folks have been working with me for years now."

Grey extended his hand to Tobias, the Head of Enforcement, who rubbed his neatly trimmed beard as he listened to Grey. He wore his Enforcement dress uniform proudly, pinned with the medals of his career in the service.

"You can do the usual training and vetting you'd go through with any other recruits. All I would do is send them to you. You'd take care of the rest."

Grey raised his hand gently before continuing. "All I ask is that you treat 'em fairly."

"I assume that it's not just going to be augurs wearing a badge?" asked Tobias. "You're planning to have regular personnel as well, correct?"

His aged features, light brown complexion, and thick eyebrows gave him an esteemed look. The man was dedicated to the cause and had been the first to discuss getting boots on the ground in the Broken Sector all those years ago.

Grey nodded. "Of course. There aren't as many of us still around as you might think."

"I think the numbers of active augurs would surprise even you, Greyson. Tell me, with these enhanced people running the streets unchecked, how can you expect a regular enforcer to stand up to such threats?" asked Magdeline, the head of science and research. "No one in their right mind would accept such dangers. Look at what happened to the enforcers on Lornan Street for Pioneer's sake. And that was only one of them!"

Magdeline wore her long black hair tied behind her in a ponytail. Her caked on makeup, wide-brimmed glasses, brown eyes, and a tall, thin stature gave her the appearance of a stern business person. Her expensive suit was the real indicator of what she valued above all else.

The room looked toward Grey for a response.

Most of the time, he felt like he was pretending to be the person they expected. Politicking turned out to be a very different skill when compared to espionage, something he didn't consider would be challenging compared to the latter.

Grey's articulate conversational skill was still developing, but speaking honestly seemed to work for him most of the time. It had come back to bite him with Magdeline in particular, on occasion, but he was more worried about saying something disingenuous or false rather than being caught out. The more he did it, the less anxious he felt about the whole process. An irrefutable rule of life that he'd discovered after some time in the role.

Grey stood before them for a few quiet moments, gathering his thoughts. He'd made a list on his priorities once the hospital had come together; he took a few quiet moments to run through it in his mind.

First Priority: Get a working Enforcement battalion together.

Second Priority: Rebuild the sector's infrastructure: new homes, streets, jobs, and businesses.

Third Priority: Ger citizens documented and on the grid: We need IDs, birth and death certificates . . .

Grey cleared his throat.

"We all agree that we need order in the sector. Identification systems, monitoring, security . . . We can't have those unless we have Enforcement, so we need to work on that first. We've been installing some security systems around some marketplaces, shopfronts, and the like, which has helped us catch some criminals in the act."

Thinking of you, Jone . . .

"But it's not enough. I think if we had maybe one augmented enforcer for every regular enforcer, it might help keep things sustainable. To address Magdeline's point, it would be a struggle, ain't no one denying that. But what's the alternative here? Leave the sector lawless?"

He shook his head. "My security team is keeping the peace, even with the small numbers we have at the moment."

Jonathon, the Councillor representing the Industrial Sector, piped up. "We have something in mind that could help Councilman Grey with his suggestion . . ."

The overweight Councillor stood up quickly, forgetting himself as he cleared his throat.

"I do like the idea of having augmented people wearing a badge," he added. "That's something that the entire city could probably have more of. As for your regular Joe, I *do* have a solution to bring them forward as a threat to those who challenge Enforcement. We may still be a month or two away from deployment, however."

Deployment . . . ?

Grey noticed Magdeline's face flare up with anger for a brief moment as she stared Jonathon down. He seemed to ignore her reaction, although he was sweating more than usual.

What's that all about . . . ?

"You're gonna need to elaborate on this, Jon; what kind of deployment are we talkin' about here?" Asked Grey.

The chairwoman addressed Grey directly. "Jonathon is working on a . . . What did you call it again?"

She looked over to Jonathon quizzically.

"Uh, it's called an 'Exo-Skeleton,' madam chairman."

She smiled. "Yes, of course. Think of it as an armoured suit for a person to operate. It is designed to contend with the abilities of these augurs."

It's not a massive surprise that they've been preparing something . . . would've been nice to know about it though . . .

Grey thought about how much money would've gone into a project like this and who was funding it. He put stock in Magdeline having something to do with that.

"I'm interested in the specifics; what kind of suit are we talking about here?"

The board was well aware that Grey was an augur, which was one of the reasons why his application was approved. Who better to deal with augurs than one of their own, after all?

There was still some heavy stigma associated with his abilities, which was why some of the board members were still hesitant to trust him. Grey hoped that he could ease their fears with enough time.

"That is none of your business," said Magdeline flatly.

Grey raised an eyebrow to her.

"If you're going to deploy these units in *my* sector, then you'll be filling me in on the details."

She blinked at Grey slowly. "The suits are not ready to be used yet. Jonathon has overstepped the boundary of our contract by sharing the details with you all, which we *will* be discussing in private . . ."

"Well, it's a little late for that," said Grey under his breath.

"Pardon me . . . ?"

"It's out in the open now," said Grey, gesturing with a shrug. "So what's the harm?"

"Good point, Grey," said Jonathon, "while we're on the topic, we'll be putting together a unit similar to some of our other branches of military—like STARCOV. We originally thought of making a separate arm to Enforcement, however, we can combine the two if you'd all prefer it." Jonathon began to sweat bullets. Magdeline glared at him incredulously, shaking her head as she clenched her jaw tightly.

"I see," said Grey, "and how are you recruitin' for this little unit of yours?"

Magdeline scoffed. "Did you not hear me before? *This* is a private matter and is no where near ready for this board to discuss. Jonathon," she said. "Not. Another. Word."

She was in charge of the weaponry and design arm of the city. She was dangerous, cold, and ruthless. And yet she loved dogs, had a family, and loved to paint, shocking him that she had a life outside of her business dealings. Grey struggled to communicate with her at the best of times. They'd both had troubled upbringings and weren't the best at expressing themselves.

Grey clenched his jaw. "Let me make something clear, Mag—"

"Magdeline," she tried to correct him, which he promptly ignored.

"I don't want some disgruntled ex-enforcer beating on my citizens because of an overindulged drug habit on the side. We all need to be clear on this."

She squinted at him. "As I said before, the specifics are not your concern. Besides, we're months away from deployment. You will be consulted when, and *if*, we decide to use these suits as Enforcement assets."

Jonathon raised his hand between the two of them as they glared at each other. "Perhaps Councilman Grey and I could discuss this in private after the meeting. As you all understand, this is a . . . sensitive subject," said Jonathon, clearly becoming uncomfortable.

Grey sighed. "I ain't interested in bickering with you Mag, and it ain't anything personal. I'm just trying to look out for my people; that's all."

"I would be interested in learning more about this as well," proposed Leanna.

"Magdeline, Jonathon, we'd all appreciate some transparency on this project. Next week, we'll expect some proper documentation around this issue so we can assess how best to utilise these . . . skeletons . . . ?"

Jonathon cleared his throat. "Exo-Skeletons, madam . . ."

Leanna scoffed. "As you say."

"As I said earlier, Madam Chairwoman," Magdeline spoke more cautiously when addressing Leanna, "I would prefer it if we didn't go into specifics yet. I understand the need for information. That can be arranged and delivered to you when the project is near completion. But I feel it's highly inappropriate to share overly detailed information on the project with . . . other members before we're ready to share it."

Leanna looked at her incredulously. "You approved the construction of these 'Exo-Skeletons' without supplying the details to me. I propose that they are *indeed* used in Sector Eight, which means that Grey needs to be involved now; it's that simple. To suggest otherwise is illogical, and frankly, if you're so close to being ready, then it won't hurt to share some details on what these things can do."

Grey resisted the urge to grin.

I'm a big fan of your work, ma'am.

"As suggested earlier, get us some more detailed information on this project so we can begin plans on how best to tackle the recruitment and deployment. Jonathon—" said Leanna, "get back to me after your private discussion with Councilman Grey. It would be good to know what roadblocks we'll be tackling for this project."

⌘

9: CROOKED

⌘

Janus gasped as she sat up in the bed, panting and sweating from another vicious nightmare.

"Hey," said a croaky voice from the corner.

It was her mother, sitting up straight with an open book in her lap.

Swallowing dryly, Janus lay back down on the bed, blinking and rubbing the sleep from her eyes with slow, tired movements.

"Can I have some water?" asked Janus croakily.

Her mother nodded, placing her book on the table next to the hospital bed before leaving the room. Rubbing her face, Janus tried to recall the nightmare, but it was already slipping away.

Something about Darius, and Grey . . .

After her meeting with Grey, she remembered the many news reports about him becoming a councillor. She hadn't paid them any mind at the time; after all, domestic problems were Enforcement's problem, not STARCOV's.

Why can't I stop thinking about that man?

Janus leant back into bed, taking a deep breath as she gestated on the questions that had been forming around Grey.

How was he able to get me back to Menilax so quickly after picking me up at the national park? I doubt I would've been able to last more than an hour in the state Keynan left me in . . .

Once she was back on her feet, she'd seek him out.

Maybe I could help him with the search for Sinew, and Oscar.

She needed to keep her mind busy, so she'd spent a lot of time planning what she'd do after leaving the hospital. All of this lying around had been more hurtful than helpful to her mental health.

If you don't deal with your loss now, it's going to—

Janus cleared her throat and held back the knot that was forming in her throat. Looking around the room anxiously, she felt as though she needed a distraction.

Mother's book . . .

Janus picked up the book—which still had the price tag on it—and looked at the front cover.

Interesting design choice . . .

It was an incredibly detailed drawing of two hands gripping one another in a firm handshake. One of the hands had a long black shirt with black leather gloves; the other looked to have a black suit and a white business shirt underneath with an elaborate gold watch and a gold wedding ring. Crimson blood spots could be seen on both hands, a stark contrast to the otherwise colourless portrait.

Crooked, by Greyson Lorath.

"Grey," she said under her breath.

Janus remembered the book's release, although she'd never actually seen the author's face before, which is why she hadn't made the connection earlier. As she was about to put the book back, she saw the blurb on the back and decided to take a look.

"The kindred are considered by some as the greatest assassins in the history of Vale. Rivalling the skill of our ancient protectors, The Pioneers, these assassins kept the world in check by striking from the shadows at those who would seek to ruin the balance of the world—good or bad—and were relentless in their quest for personal gain and influence.

"This account is from a member of the kindred; a self-imposed exile who poured his heart out to me one week before his disappearance. Darius Malaroth was—"

She dropped the book to the floor.

Darius . . . I can't believe this . . . Grey dealt with him . . . ?

Her jaw hung loose.

Darius was the boy who was with me on my first operation with Captain Logan all those years ago. And he disappeared?

Adalia walked in with a jug of water as Janus cleared her throat, finding herself amidst the confusion and shock that had filled her body. She gestured to the book dismissively.

"How can you read this crap?" she said with a forced laugh and a trembling smile.

She shrugged, scooping it up from the floor. "Grey's told me that it's a transcript of the man he spoke to; he's just trying to raise a little money for his sector, that's all. It's a good read; you should give it a go!"

Adalia poured some water into the plastic tumbler for her daughter as she smiled at her warmly.

"Thanks," said Janus as she downed the contents in a single gulp. "I bet you bought the book *thinking* it was real, didn't you?"

Her mother looked at her incredulously. "If a secret organisation of killers is hiding around the corner, I feel I should know about it!" She shrugged. "What kind of mother would I be if I let my children walk the streets with such riff-raff wandering around?"

Her mother chuckled as she returned to her seat, glaring at Janus with a knowing grin. "Besides, this *'Darius Malaroth'* character is a *real* person. Apparently, Enforcement struggled to hunt him down for years. Fiction begins with truth, as you know."

Adalia spun the tumbler around as she gestured. She was always very animated.

She's only animated when she's drunk though . . .

Janus' shook her head. The signs were all there.

Adalia tilted her head as she spoke, "yes. Darius Malaroth. Vicious little fellow . . ."

She wanted to curse her mother for getting drunk in a hospital, but she knew better than to confront her on this. Her mind took her back to Darius as the lesser of two evils.

I never thought I would hear about him again . . .

She shook her head.

I need to speak with Grey. We never found any records of Darius after that night. If he wrote a book about him, then he must know a few things . . .

Janus rubbed her eyes again; they were dehydrated.

Or perhaps I could just read the book . . . ?

"Can't say I know him," she lied.

"He's one of the most infamous people in modern history! And apparently, he was a contract killer for a secret group of assassins called 'the kindred.' They used to contract out these young kids and send them around the world, killing for money, and it's all in here!" she said, slapping the binding.

Scoffing, her mother continued. "After what happened the other night, I would've thought you could suspend your disbelief on secret orders and such. What you witnessed was definitely not easily explainable, after all."

Janus tilted her head; her mother had a point.

This whole situation . . . it's only going to encourage her now . . .

"Actually, it was," said Janus. "We didn't understand what these particular augurs were capable of . . . and it cost us—"

"My *husband?*" said Adalia, incredulous. "Indeed. A heavy price to pay for your *stupidity!*"

Wait a second . . . how did we get here?

"Are you really going to do this now?" Asked Janus.

"Don't you dare try to assert that *I* am doing anything out of order. After what you did to this family, you have a lot of nerve to dismiss *my* feelings. You tore this family apart, Janus, and to say otherwise is a complete lie."

Adalia's eyes became distant as she paused for a few moments before sipping her drink.

Janus's eyes began to water as she rolled over to the other side of the bed.

"Are you all right, my dear?" asked the nurse standing in the doorway.

She nodded slowly, wiping the tears from her eyes. "Yes . . . I'm okay . . ."

He nodded, squinting at Adalia accusingly before leaving.

⌘

10: BONES

⌘

The bar this time of night was alive and rampant, filled with people from all walks of life.

Grey lived for nights like these, where he could drink among citizens in the pub on equal terms. He rarely spoke with anyone. Instead, he quietly enjoyed the noise of others enjoying themselves. It was his refuge from the world. To be around so much happiness was a blessing, one that he was overjoyed to facilitate.

Seeing people dusty and clammy from a hard day's work, drinking and laughing with colleagues, strangers, and friends, instilled a sense of community in his jaded spirit. He'd never known how infectious a pleasant environment could be until putting the pub together, and he'd always made sure it was open until late, even if he had to serve people himself. With a small amount of funding for the entire sector, Grey made sure the establishment had enough coming through it to provide the patrons with cheap drinks and meals to encourage them to come back, strengthening relationships between everyone who came inside.

Looking out the window of the bar, Grey exhaled.

And here I thought it was going to be a quiet night . . .

Three armoured soldiers stood outside.

All he could make out from the barstool was their thick black armour and crimson red eyes beaming at him through the dirt-smeared windows. Glancing around the room, he was satisfied that no one else had spotted them yet. Finishing off his drink, he slapped the empty glass on the wooden table before stepping away from the bar.

"Grey?" said Peter, his long brown hair draping over the apron strapped over his shoulders. "You heading out for the night?"

Grey forced a smile and shook his head. "Nah, I'm not done yet." He gestured towards the glass door behind him. "Just getting some air."

Peter nodded as he turned to take an order beside Grey.

Opening the glass door, Grey was disappointed to find the night colder than usual. Turning to his right, he now faced the armoured soldiers. Threat analysis was critical for his survival during his earlier career; Grey's attention to detail coming into play immediately as his mind to began processing the trio before him. Slipping a cigarette from his pocket before lighting the tip, his eyes took in as much as they could as he walked towards them. The armour plating was incredibly thick, the corners accentuated with sharp, razor-cut edges, most evident on the shoulders.

These things are walking tanks. Not sure if Sithaleir could even cut through.

Grey kept his face neutral as he exhaled smoke, walking casually over to the three of them.

Hopefully, it doesn't come to blows here.

As he got closer, he couldn't help but pick up the scent of fresh paint and new machinery. It seemed that these plates covering their bodies were new, and as he scanned the armour up close, he noticed the areas around the joints, such as the neck and the knees, looked to be made of a light-weight mesh weave instead of the plate.

Could be a weakness.

The plate and the weave beneath the gaps were both the colour of a deep onyx. The only thing that wasn't as dark as night were the red eyes, which followed him curiously as he wandered over.

"Evenin'," said Grey, making a thin smile as he smoked away.

They held their crimson gaze on him, not giving anything away as of yet. They didn't seem to carry any weapons as far as he could see, but the thick plating likely hid a few surprises.

Be careful here. Can't risk these goons hurting anyone.

"Councilman Greyson," spoke a woman's voice, slightly distorted with a vocal disruptor to shield her identity. She held up armoured hands submissively. "We're not looking for trouble; we're just here to talk."

The armoured woman gestured softly. "We have a few questions we'd like you to answer."

"Where is Darius Malaroth?" One of the others stepped towards him, cutting the woman off; this one had the voice of a young man.

"We'll get to that . . . " she said, turning to the man who'd spoken, dismissing him with a flick of her wrist.

"Pretty forward line of questioning," said Grey confidently. "I imagine you've read my official statement on the boy? Not to mention the fact that I published a pretty damn good book about it, you know?"

Grey crossed his arms, liberally taking a few steps to close the gap between them, staring into the young man's helmet.

He wasn't sure how tall the people were inside the suits, but the hardware made them seem at least seven feet tall. They were behemoths, and the operators looked to be ready for a confrontation. Although he wasn't sure why.

Do they know? Or are they just not a fan of my political tact . . . ?

"We've heard that you're going to take over the program," said the woman.

News travels fast . . .

Grey smiled faintly, not taking his eyes off the boy.

I hadn't expected these things to move so quickly. Jonathon really was holding back on how far along the project was.

"We love your work, sir," she said. "And we know about your facilities, your hospital, and your schools. You're a hero to this sector." She shook her head, "but that man . . . " She jabbed an armoured hand at the hospital.

She's gesturing towards . . . the hospital . . . ?

"—He's a monster!"

Shit . . . they must've tracked Darius's blood samples through the new computer network. Guess I overdid it when I told the staff to put everything through the system . . .

"Listen," said Grey, "Darius is dead, don't know how many times I need to say it . . . "

"Then why was his DNA registered at your hospital recently?" asked the man in the back.

Grey tilted his neck around the young man's armoured suit to stare at the third one who was much larger than the others, querying him with a commanding voice.

"Are you accusing me of somethin' here, son?" Asked Grey.

"Son?" he replied. "I'm your senior, so you should show me a little more respect."

Grey stepped around the young man, continuing to smoke as he stared through the red eye holes at the other man.

"Hard to tell through your little toys here, you sound like your balls are a bit too tightly packed inside your little diaper there."

The large man in the suit craned his neck down, tilting his head slightly.

"It's a good point, councillor," asked the shorter man. "If Darius really is dead, then how did the system pick up his blood signatures?"

They're very well informed . . .

Grey turned around and looked at the young man. "Do I look like a fuckin' doctor to you, boy?"

They stared at each other for six seconds as Grey blew smoke into his face.

"Grey, please," said the woman in a gentler tone than before. "We're ready to serve you in cleaning up this sector. In fact, we're willing to work as aggressively as you, but we need to put this to rest."

"This country has suffered enough!" screamed the angry man behind Grey. "That monster needs to die!"

"Please help us, Grey," said the woman.

"That man *killed* my little girl . . ." said the large man. "You have no idea what he's done to this city . . ."

I think you'll find . . . that I do know . . .

"Let me think about it."

Those words meant he was admitting guilt for something, but these soldiers didn't dare fight him on their own. They'd be foolish to pick a fight with him here in the middle of nowhere. He doubted their excursion here was an official order; it was likely that they'd decided to act on whatever intel they'd gleaned accidentally, and considering how angry the larger one was, it seemed personal.

He turned to walk away, but as he did, a metal hand clamped down over his shoulder.

Grey ascertained much at that moment.

The metal is weighty, yet they can move frighteningly quickly.

He could feel tiny vibrations through the metal hand on his shoulder, which meant there were servos powering the suit. This would likely have assisted the wielder of the suit to control the bulk in a pinch. The metal was made of titan—typically reserved for aircraft—which could absorb a considerable amount of force before fracturing or bending. He'd spent enough time on interplanetary ships to know the metal well.

I wonder if Sithaleir's going to be enough to cut through this . . .

"At least give us the hospital records, mate," said the younger man.

Grey clenched his jaw. "You don't seem to understand the situation, kid." He stepped away from the three of them, moving back towards the bar.

They're clutching at straws now; this conversation is over.

He continued. "I'm not going to get involved in your little black duty here. I know you're not here on official business . . ."

Grey ashed his cigarette on the windowsill. "What'd the boy do to you three? Hmm? Is it worth threatening a Menilax official? Risking some jail time?"

"Sir, please—"

"Go back to your command and tell them to go through the proper channels." Grey crossed his arms. "If I see you here in my sector again, I'll gut all three o' ya. Understood?"

The soldiers didn't even flinch. Standing still, they kept their crimson gaze on Grey.

"We're going to have to insist," said the large man. "We wouldn't want anyone to get hurt now, would we?"

"Sean—"

"No more stalling! I've been waiting eight years to kill this punk . . . !"

Grey's brow deepened, and he clenched jaw tight as he stared back. "It ain't happenin'. Last chance, get the hell out of here or it gets violent." Grey grimaced, priming his muscles to move in a pinch in case they came at him.

The large man extended his right arm. A cylindrical contraption popped out from his wrist, encircling his arm as it began to spin clockwise at a frighteningly quick pace.

"Tell us what you know about him!" The guard pointed the weapon at Grey.

"You're not too bright, are ya . . . ?" said Grey mockingly.

"We don't have time for due process, *'Councilman,'*" said the large man as he stomped over to Grey. "We need to know now!"

"Let's just relax here—" began the woman as the large man pushed his fist towards Grey.

Grey reached out, clutching his fist from the air as he began to crush it between his enhanced fingers. The metal popped and cracked as Grey kept closing his hand, grinning threateningly at the Onyx Soldier who was trying to pull his arm away.

"You're seriously trying to threaten me?" said Grey with a crooked smile. "Let me tell you somethin'." His iron fingers continued to burrow into the flesh of the large man's hand. "You have no idea what I am capable of."

The shorter man raised his arm as the same ring-like mechanism spun up around his wrist. Grey released the large man's hand and darted towards the young man. Before Grey reached him, he fired the weapon as it launched tiny, almost invisible needles. Grey pushed his body towards the wall, narrowly avoiding them as they peppered the bar window behind him.

Oh no.

Grey pushed out from the wall and wandered to the bar window, peering through hesitantly. He felt his heart stop.

Tiny needles had punctured several citizens inside the bar. Some of them weren't moving, others were limping towards the rear exit, observing Grey as if he were a predator. Grey sunk away inside himself for a brief moment as a frenzied rage began rising through his chest, pushing away his logic and reason, the look on their faces all too familiar.

"Wrong move . . . !" he said with a low growl.

Grey unclipped the sword hilt from his back and flexed the muscles in his sword arm until they hit their breaking point. Black miasma exploded from the handle, pluming from the core as it spilled out around him, engulfing the street in shadow within seconds.

The Onyx Soldiers were mystified by the glowing green aura in the centre of the darkness. A black blade had formed from the hilt, inscribed with glowing green runes. The runes were burrowed deep into the metal, making it seem as if the core was made of jade, glowing brightly like a tainted star.

The thickness of the smoke choked the lights from the street lamps as they blinked for a few moments before malfunctioning, leaving the only light source in the street solely in Grey's hands. His augmented grip holding Sithaleir with a trembling rage, burning viciously across his muscles. It whispered to him, sending a tingling chill along his spine as if a spider crept across his flesh.

Bring them . . . to me . . .

The guards stepped away from Grey, trying to find their bearings and get a handle on the situation as they shared a look of fear. Their loud, machined breathing sounded panicked and worried.

Grey dashed forward, slashing Sithaleir outward at the apex of his manoeuvre, removing the murderer's head with a deft slash. The helmet made a thick clunking noise as it toppled to the concrete, blood spilling out from the stump as the body remained stationary, the weight of the suit keeping it in place.

Grey stepped forward, kicking the husk into the woman, who looked to be unsheathing a large rifle from her back. He sprinted to the large man, slashing horizontally at his chest plate as the woman was knocked down by the human projectile Grey had kicked her way. Sithaleir became embedded in the large man's armour with a metal clunk as blood began to pool from the flesh underneath. Grey cursed; the armour was too thick for Sithaleir to penetrate it completely.

Before Grey could react, an onyx fist came down on his head, slamming his cranium and concussing him instantly. If Grey hadn't utilised his ability before the blow came down, the impact would've easily crushed his skull like a melon.

That hurt . . . !

Raising his strength level, he flexed his muscles until they felt solid enough to deal some damage. Grey reached forward to the large man's chest plate and reefed Sithaleir free as the man brought his arm back up, ready to swing it again. As his foe leveraged the armoured fist his way, Grey dashed backwards, slicing vertically at the soldier's wrist and severing the operator's hand from his arm. As the soldier reeled, Grey pulled the blade back and stood ready to thrust it into the operator's exposed neck.

Seeing the move coming, the behemoth summoned a shimmering, silver blade from its other wrist, bringing the short sword forward as it snapped into place with an audible click.

Grey changed direction mid-swing and thrust the sword down into his opponent's chest. Despite the attack change, the black behemoth reacted with a surprising amount of haste as he parried Sithaleir with incredible resistance. With all of this happening in a few seconds, the two of them hung there, holding each other's blades in place with snarls and grunts as the woman who'd been knocked down finally stood up and unclicked her own needle weapon from her wrist.

The onyx guard sheathed the blade as it slipped inside the wrist mechanism. The move caused Grey to fall forward as Sithaleir clanged against the black armour. The large man snapped his arm forward and grabbed Grey's throat, lifting him into the air.

"You got lucky with him." It lifted him effortlessly into the air as Grey gasped and choked from his mighty metal grip, allowing Sithaleir to fall to the floor as he struggled to breathe.

"You won't get lucky again."

Grey had to apply most of his potential into his neck and upper body to avoid being crushed. His mistake was underestimating his opponents, the realisation came too late as the female moved close. She laughed, putting the needle weapon back into her wrist plate, confident that she'd no longer be needing it.

"And I was trying to play nice . . ." she said. "Do you think you're better than us? You and your kind, killing the rest of us like we're nothing but insects . . ."

The woman brought her arms back. "If you won't give up Darius, then it's going to be you who pays for his sins."

She began pummelling into his back and sides with brutally powerful strikes. He grunted and gurgled as he clenched every muscle in his torso, tightening the muscles as much as possible. Focusing some of his potential to his hands, he began to pry at the armoured fingers around his throat, but each blow from the woman threatened to smother his focus. If he allowed the agony to overwhelm him, he'd be dead in seconds.

"What the hell?" said the woman, continuing to pummel his back. "The other dredges were dead by now . . ."

"He's much older than the others," said the large man. "Might be more experienced. No matter, let's see how long it takes to break him."

She scoffed. "Blood for blood . . ."

The woman grunted as she punched him in the kidney with a vicious right hook. Grey cried out in agony as he clenched his jaw. Roaring in desperation, he finally freed himself, falling to the ground as he gasped for air. Applying strength to his right hand, Grey reached down to his sword.

He heard the air part above his head as the large man lifted his foot over Grey's head. Rolling underneath the armoured behemoth, he slashed at the back of the soldier's kneecaps, causing him to fall to his hands as he groaned.

He stood up to slash at the woman, but she'd spun up her needle weapon in the time it took for him to escape the grasp of the male guard, stepping back to avoid his attack as she fired it into his chest point blank.

To Grey, most bullets felt like an insect biting him, his augmented body stopping the inertia of the rounds immediately assuming he applied his ability on that part of the body in time to resist the velocity. But these needles were so tiny and fired so quickly that they penetrated his flesh, overwhelming his nervous system with incredible pain. Clutching at his chest, he fell to one hand, his body trembling and bleeding as he closed his eyes, his hands feeling the hundreds of little needles stinging inside him.

It was then that he realised what these soldiers were built to accomplish.

They were made to kill augurs . . .

The spinning mechanism disappeared into her wrist as the space on her shoulder opened up. The trooper pulled a sizeable automatic rifle out of the opening.

"We'll find him; you'll see," she said. "You've died for nothing . . ."

The massive black rod unfolded and clicked into place with tiny mechanisms and metal plates moving and shifting, building the unremarkable shape into a deadly piece of weaponry.

"These armoured suits of yours are fantastic," said Grey as he rose to his feet. "Your benefactors," Grey spat blood on the pavement as the woman raised her rifle his way. "They've done a great job."

Grey grunted in pain as he scraped the needles from his flesh with his hand.

"But they have one fatal flaw . . ."

He launched himself into the air.

She fired the rifle, sending a scorching beam of white light into the area where Grey was a moment ago. As he sailed through the air above her, he landed on her helmet, stomping her face as his enhanced weight sent her crashing into the ground like a hammer pounding a nail. Grey pushed Sithaleir into her chest plate, the blade piercing through her body and into the bitumen as she screamed terribly.

He hopped off and stepped away from her, panting and sweating as he chuckled to himself.

"They're being driven by amateurs . . . "

The woman raised a trembling hand to Sithaleir attempting to remove it, but she was unable to grasp the weapon. As her fingers wrapped around the frame her armoured palm hissed, melting the armour as if the blade hilt were made of magma.

"It burns!" she screamed. "Get it out! Please!"

Grey heard the last soldier rise to his feet behind him.

Unsheathing his handgun, Grey spun around as he squeezed the trigger, firing rounds at the behemoth as quickly as his fingers allowed. The giant soldier stood there, staring at him with fiery red eyes, smoke rising from the bullet holes. Grey reloaded the weapon and continued to fire at his foe. The metal behemoth now walked toward him with two hands outstretched, reaching for Grey like a monster, using the plating on his arms to protect his helmet from the gunfire.

Grey started to fire at the legs, gut, and chest of the armour, jogging toward the soldier in haste as he continued to fire, reloading when necessary. The behemoth took on the barrage effortlessly, trying to swipe at him with wild, feral blows when he got closer. Grey moved around him easily; detecting his growing weakness from sustaining so many injuries. Suddenly, the arms of the titan became lifeless, falling asleep and hanging limply from their sockets. Despite suffering so many wounds, the large man did not make a single squeal expressing pain.

This guy doesn't seem to feel pain . . .

Not feeling pain was an incredible advantage in a fight; he quelled the thoughts that naturally started to sprout, possibilities at how this could be achieved. Now was not the time for such thoughts.

The soldier walked forward despite his continual suffering and loss of limb control.

"You don't seem to understand," said the soldier. "You can't win this fight."

It reacted just as he thought, bringing an iron head down on him again and again. Grey responded with his own head-butt, meeting each blow with his empowered skull, countering the attack perfectly. He suspected it would try to kick him, but such an attack never came.

Maybe there are no servos in the legs . . .

By the time the outer casing of the helmet began to fracture, Grey could see the face of the operator. Wrapping his blood-flecked hands around the cracked mask, Grey squeezed it with enhanced muscles. As he did so, Grey heard something powering up like an electrical charge, and as he released his grip and tried to step away, electricity sparked out and around the soldier. One moment earlier, and he would've been electrified by the defence mechanism.

Sneaky little defence system . . .

When the electricity stopped, Grey put all of his focus on his right hand, shouting as his muscles strengthened and expanded so intensely that his flesh could burst like balloons at any moment. Grey punched the soldiers face, embedding his fist in the soldier's skull with a godlike blow.

"You monster!" yelled the woman.

He turned around to face her, satisfied to see Sithaleir still resting in her chest.

As he began to yank his fist free from the dead body inside the armoured suit, she'd managed to stumble over to him. The same electricity that his latest victim had tried to use was tempered into her arms now, so when she swung her armoured fist at him, the lightning blasted through his entire body. Grey screamed as loud as his voice would carry as the lightning held him in place, scorching his nerve endings.

For a few moments, he couldn't think or move; his entire world was engulfed in white-hot pain as the electrical charge bounced between the corners of his body. Then, he was launched across the road, slamming into the brick wall of an adjacent building. Grey stood up despite his twitching muscles while the behemoth's movement towards him caused the ground to rumble. Snapping her hands back, the woman brought out two short metal blades from the wrists of the suit, ready to exact vengeance for her fallen comrades.

He took a deep breath and quickly analysed his condition.

I can't risk an extended engagement. I need to end this fight now.

Grey knew that he had to get Sithaleir back in his hands to stand a chance.

The electricity made every muscle in his body tender and sore, so he'd be unable to summon any additional strength in his weakened state.

"Tell me where Darius is!" yelled the woman in a distorted voice. "And why do you have his sword!?"

"Like I said in my book," said Grey panting heavily, "Darius is dead."

Grey saw the silver blade from the angry man's wrist on the ground, having broken off during their fight. With the last of his strength, he sprinted over and snatched the blade with his palm, spinning it around to lob it at the woman. The edge punched through her throat and emerged on the other side, sailing through the air before slamming into the awning of the pub, dripping with blood.

The hulking soldier clutched at her seeping neck wound as she started to stumble and gurgle.

Racing over to her, he unsheathed Sithaleir from her chest and used it to remove her head from her shoulders with a quick horizontal slash. The head rolled along the road, slipping into a pothole near the sidewalk as the body remained stationary.

Grey winced as he stumbled onto his backside.

I need a strong drink . . .

⌘

11: STATEMENT

⌘

Janus pushed the bar door open hesitantly, cautiously scanning the patrons to find the councillor of the Broken Sector.

Have the conversation with Grey, and go. You don't need to commit to anything yet.

One of Grey's associates had called her at the hospital yesterday, and after discussing her plans to finally be discharged from the ward, he'd practically begged for her to come down, mentioning that there was something they needed help with.

I hope this isn't a waste of my time.

"Good to see you're back on your feet," said Grey smiling warmly as he approached her.

Janus turned her head to face him, grasping his handshake firmly.

"Want a drink?" he was already waving over the bartender before she gave her answer, walking to the table he'd been sitting at before coming to greet her.

Janus smiled, showing good manners as she approached. "I'll have water, thanks."

The last thing I need right now is something alcoholic; I really don't want to cloud my senses in the Broken Sector.

When the young lady with one arm walked over, she took their orders before returning behind the bar. Despite her disability, she was adept at preparing multiple orders at once, sliding mugs of beer around the long wooden bar to the other patrons.

"How're you feeling?" he asked.

"Still a bit woozy from the painkillers," she said smiling faintly as she joined him at the table, sitting across from him on a rickety wooden stool.

Nodding, Grey leant back as the waitress placed their drinks on the table.

"And how's your breathin'?" he said.

She absentmindedly touched her ribs.

He knows about the prosthetic . . .

She shook her head.

If I weren't born into a wealthy family, I would've died . . .

She usually didn't consider such things, but after being escorted to the bar in an old Enforcement cruiser, observing the sector as if she were a child, she felt fortunate. Along the way, she'd seen at least twelve dead people, a shooting, and a handful of junkies wandering around aimlessly. None of them would've received a prosthetic organ if they were hurt.

"Better than ever," she lied.

Staring into his glass, Grey pursed his lips.

"Good to hear darlin'," he said. "Going to be straight with you. I spoke with Adalia about . . . well, about a few things . . ."

Grey looked into her eyes. "The company that saved your life, giving you a prosthetic organ, is failing. Turns out people are more interested in buying things that kill people rather than save them . . ." Grey sighed, leaning back into his chair.

"I'll speak with Adalia, see what we can do," Janus sighed. "After all, I owe them my life. Don't worry Grey, I'll make sure they get some help."

She took a deep breath, suddenly noticing Grey's wounded state.

"Sweet Pioneers, are you okay?"

Really need to stop saying that . . .

He had cuts on his face, a bruised cheek, and his throat looked purple and sore. Grey chuckled, his reaction puzzling her.

"Yeah, I'm fine, darlin'. All o' this—" he said, gesturing to his own face, "just part of the gig, that's all."

"How did this happen?" she asked, leaning forward to scrutinise him.

He went on to tell her about a fight in the bar that occurred last night, but he said it so nonchalantly, it threw her off guard.

"You talk about it like it's a schoolyard brawl . . ."

"Trust me, darlin', when you live around these parts, it's become a part of everyday life. We lost a couple of good people last night, which is what set me off . . . but, well . . ." He sighed as he took a swig of his beer. "It's another thing we all get used to here . . ."

Janus drank the water in one gulp; the journey over had made her incredibly thirsty.

"I wanted to ask you a few questions if you don't mind."

Grey nodded.

"I need to know who you are."

Grey didn't hide his offence well.

"Excuse me?"

"Let me rephrase. You're a public servant, an author, a fighter, and, well . . . an arms dealer . . . ?"

He raised an eyebrow.

"I checked your records . . ." Janus scratched the back of her neck as she smiled thinly. "I learned some things from your past."

Grey shifted in his seat, meeting her gaze after a few awkward moments.

She politely watched him, waiting for him to react.

"Okay," he said, folding his arms. "I'm not looking to lie to you, but I'm not about to tell you my life story here. We don't have that kind o' time."

Grey traced his index finger along his scar before taking a deep and thoughtful breath.

Janus clasped her hands together, puzzling out which question to ask first.

"Well, let's start at the beginning of your career," she said. "You were an arms dealer?"

Downing his drink, Grey ordered another before formulating his reply. "Yeah . . . that's one way to describe it I 'spose. I took over the business from my uncle." He chuckled. "During the invasion—once the Pioneers were destroyed—he supplied the resistance with his 'illegal' weapons. After the Strin were all destroyed, he was arrested for war crimes."

He shrugged. "No one lost any sleep over an arms dealer going to prison. It ain't right what they did to him . . ."

When a second round came over, he sipped it before placing it on the table.

"So, I stepped up. After all, those guns weren't gonna sell 'emselves . . ."

Janus squinted at him. "What weapons did you primarily deal with?"

Grey smirked. "SABRE weapons, imports mostly . . . It's my turn to ask *you* something," said Grey, sipping his drink liberally. "Why did you come here, what're you hoping to get outta this?"

Janus hadn't stopped to think; it seemed to be a natural next step to find someone who could help her find Oscar. But taking a moment to herself—however brief it was—helped her clarify what she'd been thinking about recently.

"I don't know . . ." she said.

Grey clenched his brow, clearly expecting a different answer.

"Some surface answers . . . would be for vengeance, to find Oscar . . ." Janus shrugged as she rolled her glass over the wooden table, marked and dented from years of use.

"I don't know if Oscar's still out there . . . And I do want to kill the bastards who took him . . ." Janus rubbed the back of her neck. "I feel as if I've been blind to what's really going on behind the scenes of this city. My concept of how the world worked was shattered when a Pioneer killed my father, dropping him like a rock after throwing him into the sky without even laying a finger on him . . ."

Janus sighed, putting her hands on the table with her fingers locked together. "I feel like before I can move on—" She grimaced, feeling the knot in her throat weigh her down. "I need to know what's really going on, even if that means finding out that Oscar's gone for good . . . I just need to know, before I can let go . . ."

Grey pursed his lips. "Good answer."

"Okay, my turn . . ." she said, raising her hand to the one-armed bartender.

Screw it . . .

After ordering a stiff drink, she removed her jacket and wrapped it around the chair, sliding into it with ease as she pulled herself closer to the table.

"What really happened to Darius Malaroth?"

After reading Grey's book, the question had been burning in her mind. After researching the book, Janus learned there was substantial evidence that the kindred was a real organisation. The members were contract killers that traded their talents for stupid sums of money. Traces of their presence went far back into Vale's history, adding to the notion that they were ancient and exceptionally well trained. Darius Malaroth was suspected to be one of those members, and Grey was the last man to speak with him.

"Darius, eh?" said Grey as he sipped his drink. As he spoke, his eyes seemed to drift away to another world. "I'd worked with him occasionally through his youth, helping out his benefactors, talking about things in his secret little family . . ." Grey chortled, shaking his head as his gaze focused on the empty space to his side. "Knowing I was neutral, he came to me looking for help. Apparently, he screwed up big time . . ."

Grey rubbed his scar. "I told him what he wanted to hear at the time. But as soon as he left . . . I, uh, spoke to an old contact of mine who confirmed the kid had a bounty. I left it there, and I didn't report him."

Grey shrugged, as he looked back into her eyes. "He was already gone by the time I made the call, and I didn't need the trouble. A few days later, my contact called me and said they found him near my house; they'd taken the initiative . . ."

Janus nodded.

The book says pretty much the same . . .

"Do you feel guilty about it?" asked Janus.

Grey shrugged. "I barely knew the kid, but I suppose I do. I knew I did the right thing when I refused the bounty, didn't feel right . . . I didn't realise at the time, but he had one of the highest kill counts in the world." He lit up a cigarette before continuing. "He spoke of this 'kindred' group and how they were set on takin' him down for betraying them. That sort of story tends to stick with you . . ."

Grey drew the smoke into his lungs. "So, I decided to write about it. Whether it was real or not is beyond me, but it's made a hefty sum, so I can't complain. I put the coin I made right back into the sector."

He stared at her for a few quiet moments. "I don't understand the world's fascination with him, to be honest. I suppose the story is interesting in its own way, but sometimes I regret getting it published. I didn't realise at the time how much my own life would be put under the spotlight as a result."

He looked her in the eyes with a mocking smirk. "I want to focus on rebuilding this place; anything else simply gets in the way."

Janus nodded, crossing her arms as she spoke. "Why do you think they care so much about a dead assassin?"

Grey tapped the cigarette over the empty glass, sending flakes of ash into the shallow pool of spirits in the bottom. "The kid had a lot more to him than that, believe me . . ."

Damn . . . I think I hit a sore spot. They must've been close at one stage . . .

Grey stared into the empty glass pensively, lost in thought as he sighed. "I suppose all those officials want someone to pay. There's been a lot of unexplained murders over the years; trust me, I've seen some of those open cases . . ."

He smoked the cigarette. "I seriously doubt it's all on this one kid, and I'm sure they know that too . . . But hell, seems as though they'll take what they can get."

"All right now, guess it's my turn?" said Grey as he sipped his drink, nodding to her. "I think you need to take it easy for a while, kid. Let me take care of this whole mess."

No . . .

"You nearly died, Janus . . . You should consider what you're going to do with your life outside of this."

Janus was taken aback, feeling a cocktail of embarrassment and rejection nauseate her from within as she leant back into her chair and crossed her arms.

"Leave your brother to me, all right? I promise I'll do whatever I can to make sure he comes home." Grey took a drag from his smoke and stood up from the chair, picking up the drink that didn't have the ash from his smoke inside it. "You can finish your drink. I'll let the team know to take you back to the checkpoint."

Her feelings turned to anger in a flash as he turned and began to walk away.

Who the hell do you think you are?

"Hey!" she yelled.

Grey turned around, finishing his drink in front of her before waiting for her to respond, standing neutrally. It wasn't loud enough to get everyone looking over, but a few people did.

She wanted to sprint across the room and punch his smug face, but all she felt was deflation and defeat. The last thing she had expected would come out of her visit here was to be turned away.

"I can help you . . ."

He sighed. "No—" Grey took one last puff of the cigarette before dropping it inside his drink. "You really can't. Thanks for the information, darlin', but it's about time you were on your way. Try and take it easy for a while, and take care o' that mother of yours."

He gestured with the drink before turning around and ordering another.

Janus let her shoulders slump as she stared at the table for a few quiet moments.

Maybe it's for the best . . . I do need to take it easy.

Grey leant on the bar as he placed the empty glass on the table. "I'll be back; can I get a fresh one?"

The bartender plucked the glass from the counter, taking it over to the sink to rinse it. "Stop putting your cigarettes in my glasses, you grub."

Grey chuckled as he dashed over to the bathroom, pushing the swinging doors in.

Janus took a deep breath and slid out from the table before walking towards the exit. As she stepped out, she realised she'd forgotten her jacket. Cursing under her breath, she turned around to go back in when she saw a man follow her out.

"Hey," he said, "you got a minute?"

She kept her gaze with him. "Actually, no."

Janus gestured towards the Enforcement cruiser. "I need to get home."

The driver appeared to be napping in the driver's seat, a half-finished bottle of beer resting on his chest.

"I wanted to talk to you about Grey," he said, extending a hand holding her jacket.

She rolled her eyes as she walked over and snatched the jacket from him before walking towards the cruiser.

"If you genuinely want to help," said the man, "I think I have a way you can convince Grey to trust you."

Janus turned to him, shrugging with her eyebrows raised. "He didn't say anything about trust . . ."

He shrugged too. "Both of you've had a similar past . . . but you're an operator, a government agent. It's difficult for him to trust someone like that, you know?"

Janus squinted at him, trying to figure out his angle.

What are you after, little man . . . ?

"Even if he didn't specifically say it, it's a trust thing. *That,* and he doesn't really know you. He only knows your mother. Having said that, I really do think you can help him, and he's *very* short on friends at the moment." he said flatly.

He explained how Grey had come to be at the National Park and how he found them.

She scoffed. "I know he came to the National Park; what I don't know is why my mother would ever associate with someone like him."

He raised an eyebrow, tilting his head at her. "Your mother's on the board of directors for a weapons development company; Grey used to sell weapons. The link there's pretty obvious."

Did Mother ask him to keep me out of the loop? Makes sense I guess . . .

"Your mother's *actually* a pretty big player in Menilax, despite what you might think." Janus allowed his words to simmer in her brain, nodding to herself quietly. "We need your help, Janus, and Grey will see that soon enough." He grinned. "You took down a Shifter, after all. That's reason enough to want you on our side."

The man raised his arms, grinning at her playfully, "and I think you're cute." His grin grew into a full smile. "So you know, there's that."

As he smiled, she realised how handsome he was. But he had more of a feminine appearance, like he could've been a model. He was an older man, possibly in his forties, although he'd aged incredibly well. His apparent innocence made her want to tussle his hair. He seemed so fresh and clean compared to some of the other faces in that bar.

You've got no scars, no bruises, not even a scratch on that pretty face of yours.

She chuckled. "*That* is a bad reason, but I'll take you up on the first one," said Janus with a hint of playfulness in her voice. "So, what do I need to do to earn the big guy's respect?"

As he opened his mouth, she said, "*And* if you say anything inappropriate, I'm going to hurt you." She smiled at him expectantly. "We clear?"

Nodding to her with his lips pursed, he laughed. "Fair enough."

Smiling broadly, he extended a palm out to her. "The name's Ducard, although my friends call me Duke."

Janus shook his hand fiercely. He had a firm handshake.

"Duke it is," she said with a grin.

⌘

After a few minutes of creeping through the Broken Sector alongside four members of Grey's security team, Janus decided to open the discussion a little more with her travel companion. "So what do you do for a living?"

Ducard looked up at her warmly. "I'm a pilot."

She'd never really spoken to any of the pilots in STARCOV. Talking about your role in the unit, or even your personal life was considered a faux pa. It compromised your conviction to the duty in the eventuality that an operator saw someone close to them get hurt, or killed.

"What made you want to be a pilot?" she asked.

"I studied aerodynamics as a teenager. Got lucky enough to secure a role in the armed forces soon after. I worked a lot during some of the refurbishment of the city around eight years ago, transporting cargo here and there."

Ducard shrugged. "It was a good living, but I grew out of it when they started having me transport armed soldiers and wounded people."

Janus asked him about it, warranting a shrug.

"I have a bit of a, uh, weak stomach . . ."

A bit strange, considering who your friend is . . .

"So . . . you and Grey . . ." she said with a telling smirk.

He smirked back. "Yeah, I figured you'd ask about him. I transported him . . ." He cleared his throat. "I transported weapons *for* him, rather. I would bring weapons on the side and take care of his interplanetary shipments. It became a monthly thing, then a weekly thing . . . Eventually, I was doing nightly trips for him."

She looked at him curiously. "Makes sense," she said. "A former gunrunner using a pilot who specialises in transporting guns."

They both turned onto another similar-looking road to the last; the difference was, however, that Janus was able to see the massive concrete wall separating Sector Eight and Sector Seven. Ducard and the security team followed the path along to the right as he continued to speak.

"Yeah, I suppose it does. Grey's not in that business anymore of course. He's trying to straighten his life out a bit, do some good in the world."

Janus looked at him incredulously. "Is becoming a politician really the right answer?"

"I think so." He nodded warmly, his dark blue eyes enhanced by the blue, moonlit sky. "The man's got a long list of things he believes could've been done better. I suppose you could say that's what drives him now, to repay the world for mistakes he made when he was younger. When it comes down to it, he's really the best person for the job. It takes someone special to take on a role like that, after all."

Janus scoffed. "Seems like you'd have to be crazy to step into those shoes . . ."

As the side street turned onto a long, six-lane road, Janus saw the checkpoint rising from the ruins of the old highway, towering over them on the left-hand side. Ducard flashed his pass in front of the security camera embedded in the wall. As the doors began to slide open, Ducard took a deep breath through his nose as he turned to face her.

"I don't know of any politician that isn't a little crazy. But when it's all laid out on the table, saying it's complicated would be an understatement." He sighed.

I can relate to that . . .

"I think you should consider Grey as someone who tries to do the right thing above all else, even at the cost of his own wellbeing . . ."

Ducard nodded to the security team. "Thanks, guys n' gals. We'll be all right from here."

The young, dark-skinned woman in fatigues nodded with a smile.

"Have a good night," said Janus with a curt smile.

"You too," replied the woman, winking to Janus.

Janus smirked as she looked at Ducard incredulously.

He chuckled to himself, seemingly tickled at the interaction. She was about to ask him what he told the security member, but her eyes became fixated on Sector Seven as they stepped through the door.

It's been over a year since I stepped foot inside this place . . .

Observing the differences between Sectors Seven and Eight, Janus realised, was a rather sobering experience. The Broken Sector was full of dilapidated buildings, ruined slums, and hopeless citizens, while Sector Seven boasted the largest military presence in the city. With armed soldiers patrolling and plenty of guard towers watching over the large sheds and buildings, an army of augurs would struggle to penetrate the heart of the Sector. As they began to walk beyond the gate, Janus noticed ample space between the checkpoint and the first row of storage sheds, likely to give those guarding the checkpoint enough time to assess any threats who came through.

"So," said Janus, "where are we going?"

"I'm going to my house; then I'll be heading out on my ship. An old buddy of mine needs some transport work done, so after I show you what I had in mind, I can drop you off anywhere you need to go."

"Thanks. I appreciate that," said Janus. "Who's this buddy of yours?"

"He works over in Silver City," said Ducard. "He's looking to rebuild one of the old Pioneer medical centres there, told him I'd give him a hand."

"Is he paying you?" asked Janus curiously.

"Well, he is, but it's mostly my expenses. I'm doing it more as a favour."

The two of them reached a line of military personnel who were watching them as Ducard took the lead, walking confidently between a gap in their formation. Each soldier sported grey and black fatigues, beanies, and held large automatic rifles, observing Janus with curiosity as she followed closely behind Ducard, hoping none of them recognised her.

With my operator status revoked, I can't imagine anyone who knows will be happy that I'm here.

Diverting her anxiety, Janus focused on the weapons the soldiers carried instead.

Looks like the SABRE Kantrino 664, pretty heavy duty . . . Although living next door to the Broken Sector, you'd need something powerful to keep the riffraff in check.

"Good evening everyone," said Ducard cheerfully.

"Evenin', Duke," replied one of the shorter men. "Who's your friend?"

"One of Grey's associates, giving her a ride out of here."

"Hey," she said politely.

As they walked between two of the large warehouses, Janus nodded to herself.

"Sounds like you've got a pretty cruisy life," she said.

"Well, it has its moments . . ." Ducard gestured as he drifted back to her, walking beside her as he smiled.

"I try to stay out of the politics when I can. My interest lies in . . . well, Grey's success of course, but I tend to get swept up with the Councillor and his problems probably more than I'd like."

Janus curled her lip as she nodded to herself. Ducard let the subject dissolve amidst the silence.

After ten minutes of walking along smooth concrete roads and weaving between warehouses, vehicles, and more patrols, they reached Ducard's hangar. It was dull looking on the outside, appearing like a medium-sized shed with two massive sliding doors on the front, painted a dull sky-grey.

"Would you like a drink?" said Ducard as he opened the thin metal door for her.

She nodded. "Something strong."

I've already had one tonight, may as well go for broke . . .

Janus took off her jacket as she walked inside, grinning as her eyes discovered the extraordinary interior of Ducard's home. The floor was smoothed out concrete, and around to the left was an L-shaped staircase, which led to a small hut on the edge of the warehouse. Directly in front of her, polished and tidy as if it had just come from the factory line, was Ducard's aircraft. It had the familiar shape of a SABRE Mark Twelve, although it was a tad flashier with some larger engines and a sleeker red canopy. Janus asked him about it as he closed the door.

"SABRE had me test the old girl when they were prototyping the Mark Ten. It was way ahead of its time when they eventually let me hold onto her."

The manufacturer was well known in Menilax, serving as the primary developer of defence technology before the invasion. Since then, there was a lot more competition, and every business wanted the contracts that SABRE still held onto.

I remember hearing about how close Lornan Futuristics was to securing the government contracts that SABRE held. I wonder if that's all out the window now that Jone Lornan's out of the picture.

The CEO of the company had been missing for two weeks straight, and it wasn't looking favourable for Lornan Futuristics lately without its leader.

I wonder what happened to him. He seemed like such a noble man.

Janus made a thin smile as the thought sobered her.

He gave to charity, had three children . . . They must miss him to bits . . .

"I see you know your aircraft," said Ducard with a genuine grin.

She shrugged. "Weapons were more my thing, although I know enough to get me by."

"Weapons, huh? Yeah I can see that."

Ducard gestured towards the stairwell. She saw a workshop sitting underneath the cabin as she moved, with various tools strewn across the wall, some of them caked with dust and others with grease. She saw a large motor sitting on the table, which caught her eye.

"What are you working on?" she said, gesturing to his workspace.

"Oh, that? It's an old generator motor. When I come across one, I typically try and get it up and running for Grey. They still don't have electricity in most areas in the broken sector, so these things are worth their weight in gold, you know?"

Makes sense. I wondered why the pub had lights and refrigeration . . .

As they ascended, the rickety stairwell sent echoes bouncing around the warehouse, wiggling a little too much for her liking. Entering the cabin, Janus observed the contents of the room but took note of the brown leather couch to her left. Leather furniture was quite uncommon in Menilax.

"You're not originally from here, are you?" asked Janus.

Ducard tilted his head with a smirk. "What gave it away?"

She scoffed. "Just a hunch."

He smiled. "Silver City."

Janus grinned. "Explaining how you and your friend know each other."

He smiled. "You'd make a good detective."

Ducard moved towards the far end, reaching on a shelf next to the fridge to nab a bottle of brown spirits, stepping around the dining table as he did so.

Janus slipped into the cold leather, crossing her legs as she leant into it.

"Is whiskey okay?"

"Whiskey's more than okay, thanks."

"Try this," said Ducard as he handed her the glass.

She smelled it excitedly.

I can smell the wood of the barrel it was kept in.

Taking a swig, she let it soak into her tongue for a moment before swallowing.

Smokey, and . . . sweet.

She smiled warmly as she sipped it a second time.

"That's not bad; what is it?"

"It's from Raschta, made from Tima berries," Ducard said as he sipped it liberally.

She nodded her head pleasantly.

"So how did you manage to get your hands on this place?" she asked. "I didn't realise they allowed private contractors to rent space in Sector Seven."

"Menilax keeps a few of us around, just in case of an emergency. They pay me a small retainer and let me stay here. It's a good arrangement, but I'd practically be conscripted if there's another war. So," said Ducard, "to business?"

She leant back in the chair and crossed her arms. "To business."

He took a large sip of his drink before placing it on the glass table in front of them. "Grey was attacked by a military team last night."

Janus nodded, her expression morphing into a serious one.

"These . . . soldiers . . . they had some *crazy* advanced tech, more so than anything I've ever seen before. They were being operated by mercenaries, it turns out, although the nature of how they were selected is still being looked into. We don't know a great deal about them yet, but I have been able to find out where the equipment's being manufactured."

He met her gaze. "I've seen your records, Janus. I know how good you are at infiltration."

She raised an eyebrow. "I only just got out of the hospital, you know . . ."

Ducard nodded as his eyes snapped back to his hands, which were held together tightly over the glass of whiskey. "Of course, I understand," he said in defeat.

It would be good to get my hands dirty again though . . . And it's not like I have anything else I could possibly lose. If I don't get Grey's help, I doubt I'm going to find those bastards that took Oscar.

"I'll drop you off, and we can call it a—"

"Tell me more about this facility," said Janus, making up her mind.

Ducard looked up at her, smiling with his teeth exposed.

"Well, we don't actually know a great deal about it, but we do know that it used to be an old airbase for Daenodil. They went into administration around ten years ago, after which *someone* bought up most of their assets, totally off the books of course."

"How did you find them?" she asked curiously, sipping the whiskey.

"Some of the armour pieces had frost burns, and I don't think their little skirmish to the Broken Sector came with transportation, meaning they would've had to make the journey on their own."

She nodded.

"The mercenaries were sloppy. They probably didn't even realise the signs they left behind. Although when you see what the suits were packing, I suppose I can't blame them for believing they were in any danger of failing. These things were built from the ground up to fight augurs, and they were out hunting one."

Could've used some of those suits six weeks ago . . .

"So," she said, leaning forward, "what do you need me to do?"

"We're hoping to find out who's funding them, and maybe get some schematics and data if we can manage it."

Ducard got up from the lounge and picked up a folder from the dining table, handing it to her with an outstretched arm. She flipped it open, revealing numerous photos, a list of objects recovered from the bar fight, and a few written accounts by those who were present. Scanning them quickly, she could see that some of these observations were written by Grey.

He writes well for someone rough around the edges.

"We don't have enough information to understand who's funding their operation, but we know that at least two councillors are involved. If you can get us something, anything that we don't currently have, it'll help us understand what these things are really built to do, as we're running mostly on assumption at this point."

"So *this* is why you called me down to the bar then?" she said, sifting through the documents.

"Yes. I assumed Grey would've been more than happy to have you on board, but, well . . ." He sighed. "The point is, we could really use your skillset, Janus. I know you're looking for your brother, and although Grey doubts you at the moment, once he sees you're willing to work with us on this, well . . ." Ducard gestured softly. "Trust me, he'll come around."

Janus was taken aback. "He's unsure of my ability?" she placed the folder on her lap, looking into Ducard's eyes as she crossed her arms.

"Don't take it the wrong way," he said defensively. "Like I said, he doesn't know you, but if you can show him what you can do?" He smiled. "He'd be foolish to disregard your help."

The corner of her lip curled sardonically. "How can you be so sure?"

"Because I know him. He's a guarded man, but I'm sure he's just trying to do the right thing by your family."

She nodded warmly, but her mind drifted away on a train of thought.

That sells it then; he is definitely dismissing me on Adalia's word.

Doing this thing doesn't guarantee that he'll agree to have me on board, but I suppose it's worth a shot. I don't know what else I'm going to do with my time, and maybe this will help me get in good graces with these guys.

Janus traced her left hand over her cheek.

Oscar's still out there; I can feel it in my bones . . .

"You really care about Grey, don't you?" asked Janus with a gentle tone.

He nodded without hesitation. "Yes," he said mirthlessly.

"I can tell you mean it," she said with a warm smile.

He clapped his hands on his knee, his emotions changing gears dramatically. "I can fly you there right now if you're ready?"

Janus almost dropped her drink, coughing as she swallowed her sip of whiskey awkwardly. "Well, that's a little quick . . . isn't it?"

He shrugged. "I don't know . . . Is it?"

Unable to suppress her laugh, she scolded him playfully about his naivety. "It takes *days* to plan an assault of any kind, let alone one where I need to move undetected through an *armed base.*"

Janus laughed genuinely, caught in a laughing fit.

He shook his head, rolling his eyes, her laugh amusing him despite the clear jab at him.

"Seriously now," she said sternly. "I need to know their security systems; how much staff they have, what weapons and equipment I'll need to get inside and out in one piece . . ." She took another sip of her drink, as the two of them tittered for a few moments. Janus groaned as she took a deep breath.

"Pioneers . . ." she said, "it's been a long time since I laughed like that."

Ducard bowed before her in a mocking gesture. "I'm glad to be of service."

She chuckled. "When do you get back from your trip?"

He scratched his scalp. "I should be back in a few days at the latest."

She smiled with confidence. "More than enough time to prepare."

⌘

12: LINGER

⌘

Silence. An overwhelming, crushing silence pushing everything else in the environment beyond the senses.

Depression. A drawn-out drumbeat that grew louder, incessantly punishing him with each passing day. Throbbing, pulsating, a numbing ache that refused to vacate, coming and going with varying intensity.

Alcohol. This liquid would grant Grey some reprieve from the relentless guilt that cursed his existence and plagued the dreams waiting for him at night. But now, after abusing it for so long, the effect came on tenfold.

These things combined to shut down Grey's overactive mind.

After an hour of drinking in silence with no thoughts running through his mind, he began to embrace the numbing as he quietly traced his fingertip across the rim of the glass. Vertigo made his head swim, drowning out the expected racing, intrusive thoughts that hounded his every thought and action. A small part of him wanted to get up from the bar, head back to his house, go visit friends. But he couldn't.

Despite having the inkling, it would never progress further than that, as it never had before. It was a self-imposed cage, and despite every effort to avoid it, Grey would always end up here. The best thing he could do was to succumb to it and ride out the pain.

Fighting only seemed to make it worse.

When he downed the last of his drink, a hand reached out and replaced it with a full glass.

He knew he should thank the person.

Grey felt a hand touch his shoulder. He ignored it.

He grabbed the perspiring glass and swallowed a mouthful, barely tasting it as he blinked slowly. The only thing he felt in his body was a tingling in his head and his eyes swimming and waving as he blinked slowly, trying to settle himself. A stray thought, an inkling spurned his subconscious, asking him to turn around and confront the person, to greet the owner of the hand on his shoulder.

But nothing came of it.

He heard a voice, distant and unclear as if he were underwater. The hand released from his shoulder as a person pulled up a stool beside him.

He took another sip, blinking his eyes lazily.

The man ordered a drink, sitting with him quietly.

Grey sat back in his chair, rubbing his face with both hands.

I need to get some help for whatever this is . . .

As quickly as the thought came, it vanished, sinking like quicksand into nothingness.

What was I . . . thinking about?

He shook his head.

Sighing to himself, he looked over to see Artemis drinking with him.

Artemis looked at him with his long nose and clean-shaven face, saying something to him with concern in his eyes. To Grey, it sounded like mumbling.

Grey nodded, returning to the drink. As he looked into the glass, he felt a wave of nausea flush through his body. As he closed his eyes, Grey felt the world spinning around him. He groaned as he rubbed his face and opened his eyes, causing the sensation to dissipate in a few moments.

Artemis touched his shoulder, snapping him from the train of thought that lead back to that place. "Do you remember contacting me?"

Staring at him, Grey blinked as his vision warped from left to right, encouraging his rising nauseated feeling.

He smiled sadly, shaking his head. "I'm sorry . . ."

Artemis nodded thoughtfully, staring at Grey with concern for a few moments.

Then he patted him on the shoulder and stood up.

"Let's get you home."

⌘

"I want to see her."

"Get out of here, kid."

"You won't stop me; you know that."

Darius was determined to get through Grey, no matter the cost. There was no other choice, and he could see it in his eyes. They both knew what was about to happen.

Grey raised his shotgun, grimacing at Darius with determination in his heart.

"She don't wanna see you, kid."

The sun outside of Grey's house became blanketed in shadow.

The two men gazed at each other, ready to do whatever it took to get what their heart demanded of them. As the darkness came inside, they both closed their eyes, allowing the shadows to envelop their faces, transforming their identities in an obsidian cloak of obscurity.

Darius unsheathed Sithaleir.

"You have no idea what you're doing, do ya?" barked Grey.

Darius moved toward Grey confidently, Sithaleir swinging around his hand and fingertips. He swung low as Grey stepped aside, grunting in hatred for what the boy was making him do.

"I'll shoot! Stay back!"

Darius reached out to him, slashing outward in an attempt to catch him off guard. Grey stepped under it and punched the boy's stomach, hard.

"You . . . You can't keep me from her . . . !" he said as he slowly rose to his feet.

"You don't deserve her," said Grey in a low growl. "I'll kill you if I have to."

Darius charged forward recklessly.

Grey slammed his boot toward Darius, and as he rolled around to evade the kick, Grey was there, holding the shotgun at his chest. Grey squeezed the trigger. The shot blew a hole into the young man's chest, sending him lifelessly across the floor in a pile of twitching dead meat.

Grey pumped the shotgun and blinked once. As he opened his eyes, Darius was there again without a single wound.

"You know how this ends," he said. "You can't change what happened."

Grey fired again, ruining Darius's head, blowing it apart as the body fell quietly to the floor. Pumping the shotgun, he kept his eyes on the body.

Don't . . . blink . . .

Grey's eyes were burning and twitching, demanding he blink to relieve his distress.

"Imagine how he felt. When you overpowered him . . ."

Closing his eyes, the boy was in front of him by the time he opened them, clutching Grey by the throat with one hand and holding Sithaleir over his heart with the other.

"I am not a monster!" he screamed in Grey's face.

Grey shed a tear. "Yes . . ." he shook his head, grimacing against the vice grip of Darius's hand. "You . . . are . . ."

As Darius thrust the blade at his chest, Grey clutched it with his hand, trying to push against the frenzied strength of the youth who wanted to impale Grey with the glowing artefact.

"Ciril . . ."

Darius rammed the blade inside his chest, causing Grey to scream out in agony.

⌘

Grey gasped as he opened his eyes, sitting up and panting heavily as he glanced around anxiously with his heart beating out of his chest.

"Are you okay!?" Artemis was in the doorway, his face consumed with fright.

Grey looked over to him, suddenly realising he was home, as he nodded to his concerned friend.

"You were having a nightmare . . ." said Artemis, lowering his arms.

"Water," he managed to croak out before he flopped back onto his pillows.

"What happened!?" said Artemis as he jogged into the kitchen.

Grey sighed. "Same dream . . .!"

Artemis returned and remained quiet as he passed him the water.

"You know how I feel about what you're doing," said Artemis. "Do you genuinely believe that drinking will make the nightmares go away?"

"Please, don't start."

Artemis nodded. "Tell me what's happened recently, at least? You've been coming apart at the seams lately."

"Lately?" Grey chortled. He coughed heavily before downing the water in one gulp. "Where to begin . . ."

Grey sighed.

"I saw Sinew, who almost beat me to death *and* wiped out an entire squad of enforcers while he was at it. I couldn't do *shit* about it, just had to sit there and watch him do it . . ." He gestured erratically.

"I killed three soldiers, who'd killed *eight* civilians by discharging their firearms into my bar. How the hell am I supposed to avoid taking lives when these people don't share the same values?" Grey wheezed as he tried to catch his breath, face dripping with sweat.

"I swore to myself that I was done with all of this, but trouble just seems to follow me . . . I do one thing right, and two things go wrong. Can't seem to get ahead of it all . . ." Grey groaned to himself as he rolled over to the side of the bed, placing the empty glass on the bedside table.

"Things have been hell lately, and I can't see it getting any better." Tilting his head, he looked to Artemis with a challenging grimace. "So I had some drinks, and it got out of hand. Don't you think I deserve a break?"

"Yes," said Artemis, grabbing the empty glass before refilling it in the kitchen. He returned a minute later, sitting on the bed as Grey downed another glass of water.

"But what you're doing isn't a break; it's a full-time habit, an addiction. It is time you slowed down, I think. Being a dredge does *not* make you invincible."

Grey wiped the sleep from his eyes.

"So last night. You called me . . ." said Artemis impatiently.

Looking up at his friend, Grey reminisced about the events of the last few weeks, looking for the reason why he'd have called Artemis to meet him at the bar.

What was that all about . . . ?

Grey traced his thoughts back to Janus Scitilliant and her duty in the National Park.

Of course, the Pioneer . . .

Grey slowly edged to the side of the bed before launching himself hesitantly to the chest of drawers. He slipped into his black pants and snatched a piece of paper from the top of the drawers.

"Janus—Adalia Scitilliant's daughter—ran into Sinew *and* a Pioneer on the same night."

This warranted a look of surprise on Artemis's face, a rare sight indeed.

"Apparently, they were working together," said Grey. "She said that the Pioneer was wearing a dark blue, metallic chest plate which had *this* symbol engraved on it—" Grey handed the drawing to Artemis. "Wondering if you'd recognise it?"

Artemis inspected the shape, showing the same curious expression that Grey had when he saw it, and yet, he saw a hint of recognition in Artemis's brown eyes.

It was an upside down sword hilt with a jagged circle surrounding it. The shapes were drawn as if they were made of serpents weaving in between each other.

Artemis had a mug of strong coffee, which he sipped liberally.

"Did you drink the last of my coffee?" asked Grey.

Artemis smiled at him. "If a Pioneer were displaying it proudly, then it would be some sort of designation or rank," he said, ignoring the question.

Grey walked past Artemis and entered the kitchen at the end of the room, refilling the glass with water.

"I'll need to look through the archives," said Artemis as he joined him in the next room. "With enough time, I will be able to find out which specific designation it was."

They both took a seat next to the circular, timber table in the middle of the room. The old, weather-worn house had a massive hole in it to the right, allowing him to glance out into the overgrown yard, which looked more like a small forest than a lawn.

Looks like it's pretty cloudy . . .

He chortled.

Matches my mood . . .

He hadn't been out in the yard for a very long time and had no intention of going any time soon. Grey's vision drifted over the ruined shed at the back of the yard, and as his eyes began to adjust to it, he snapped his vision away, refusing to look at the ruin.

Seems like it was yesterday that I was sitting out there, watching those I cared for die by my hand . . .

"I wanted to ask you about Sinew," said Artemis, breaking his attention away from delving any further into the painful memory. "Did he demonstrate any other abilities? Ones that you have not seen him utilise before?" he asked.

"Same old tricks, at least from him," replied Grey, setting the cup on the table as he squinted at Artemis. "Strange thing is, Janus told me that the Pioneer was able to control her and her father," Grey tapped his fingers on the table. "I thought Sinew was the only one who could do that. Seems he's been able to teach it to someone else, although the way she described the two, it was the Pioneer calling the shots."

Artemis nodded, "Every time we've come across Sinew, he seems to have developed new abilities without fail. If what you're saying is correct, then in the last ten years, his evolution has stagnated . . ."

"I would agree. In fact, if anything, he seems almost . . . slower . . ."

"Physically?"

"No," said Grey. "Mentally."

Artemis sipped his coffee. "Perhaps he is getting old. He is not a Pioneer, after all."

Grey tilted his head, considering the statement.

Pioneers are practically the same as augurs, excluding their immortality. Usually they'd have one power or another, to a varying degree. Seems that Sinew's power is an extension of being a drege, so maybe only dredges can learn it.

"So this woman, Janus, can she be trusted?" Asked Artemis.

Grey sighed.

Hard to say . . . I've never really trusted STARCOV after that duty I had. Then again, I'm sure Janus can relate . . .

He chortled.

Artemis raised an eyebrow, still waiting for an answer.

"Remembering the first duty I had with STARCOV . . ."

"Ah, yes, of course. That was quite the train wreck," said Artemis.

"Can't tell whether it's just me, you know? I mean, my experience with most people has been a negative one." Grey shrugged. "She seems genuine enough, I suppose. Although she's a lot colder compared to when we first met all those years ago."

Artemis didn't reply immediately, choosing his words carefully. "Do you think she suspects you?"

Grey shook his head, "No, I don't think so."

"I don't think she'd react well if she figured it out," said Artemis, gesturing softly, "either way, do you trust her account of the event?"

Grey nodded. "She's a reliable witness. I have no reason to doubt her."

Artemis crossed his arms, looking into the mug before finishing the contents. "If it was truly was a Pioneer working with Sinew, then that narrows it down for us considerably. The number of Pioneers left alive is very small."

Grey put his hands behind his head, lounging in the chair. "Know where any of them are off the top of your head?"

Artemis nodded with a smile. "I know where one of them is, at least."

His friend brushed his hair back from his forehead. "I wouldn't get your hopes up about finding all of them, however. Most have made a considerable effort to remain hidden from the public eye."

Grey patted his pockets down, searching for his cigarettes. Artemis chortled, scooping them out from under a pile of documents. Grey gestured for his friend to toss him one.

"I've only met one Pioneer," said Grey, tapping his hands on the table impatiently.

"Westermann, I think his name was. He was getting started over in Silver City when I ran into him. Seemed like a decent man."

Artemis slid the packet over to him.

"Wait a moment, did *you* meet him? Or was it—"

Grey smirked. "*I* met him. It was when I was training."

Artemis nodded.

"These Pioneers . . . I always put them on a pedestal as if they were better than the rest of us. But if they're capable of working with someone like Sinew . . . ?"

"We do not know the full context," said Artemis. "It can be easy to make assumptions, but I shall defer it for now."

Grey looked at him dubiously. "What possible explanation could justify working with such a monster?"

Artemis tilted his head slightly. "This world is not so black and white. You of all people should know this."

"You didn't answer the question, Artemis. What is a Pioneer doing with a *creature* like that? Hmm? You got an answer that doesn't prove they aren't as shitty as the rest of us?"

Artemis sighed, his eyes searching Grey's face for his real state of mind. "Nothing you do will change the past."

Grey rolled his eyes as he stood up. "This isn't about my god damn past!"

He watched the overgrown lawn dance against the wind, the soft howl of the unseen force settling his rising anger. Grey took a deep breath, taking in the morning air of the Broken Sector.

It's so much cleaner here compared to the rest of the city.

"This is about answers, Arty. Pioneers save—" He shook his head. "Damn it, I can't stop saying that stupid phrase!"

Artemis clicked his tongue. "Do not worry, we all say it . . ."

Grey exhaled, letting his frustrations flow out of his chest and into the wind.

"After all this time, I'm still searching for signs that good prevails, that there is some sense of justice in this world. Seems like that theory is disproven every day, and yet, the Pioneers were always there as an example to strive for. Like my dad, a man who believed that justice prevailed over everything, and no one could escape it."

Artemis remained silent.

"But even he failed to live up to those expectations, and the rest of his kind are the same . . ."

"Your father . . ." said Artemis, causing Grey to turn around. "He's still harassing you?"

Grey chortled. "Yeah, he wants to make up for lost time, get to know me as a person . . ."

Artemis made a thin smile. "You could learn a lot from that man if you'd be willing to talk to him."

Grey shrugged. "Got enough to worry about without pandering to his guilt."

The two of them stayed quiet for the longest time as Grey sat down and dangled his legs over the hole in the wall. His bare feet rested over the top of the grass, tickling his toes as he gestated on the conversation a little too much.

"You need a shave, my friend," said Artemis as he came to sit beside him.

"I've heard the beard suits me," replied Grey with a smirk.

"For someone living in the Broken Sector? Absolutely. For a councillor? Not so much." Artemis gestured sharply. "It would be a mistake to assume they are all of the same mind, I think. Especially after what some have turned into following the destruction of the Pioneer order. Just because they are immortal does not make them perfect."

Grey lit the cigarette he'd been fiddling with as Artemis continued. "Did you know that they had the equivalent of assassins in the Pioneer order?" quizzed Artemis. It is all rather fascinating. I could provide you with some of the old tomes if you wish. It might help for you to know who you are dealing with. After all, it doesn't sound like you have the right idea about what they *really* were."

Grey chortled. "Reading was never my strong suit, but I suppose you're right. Couldn't hurt to learn more about these guys."

"Well. It wouldn't be the original tomes, of course," said Artemis, "but copies."

Grey placed his hand on Artemis' shoulder. "How are you doing anyway?" asked Grey.

Artemis' jaw hung loose, an expression that threw him off guard. "I can't remember the last time you actually asked me that . . ."

Grey shrugged. "What can I say, I've had a lot on my mind lately."

Artemis scoffed. "The sheer amount of synapses firing off in that head of yours . . . I am surprised you're as stable as you are."

He laughed. "Who says I'm stable?"

Artemis pursed his lips, tilting his head in mock agreement. "I'm doing okay," said Artemis. "Chance and I have been spending a lot of time reorganising the archives as the old system is a bit archaic."

"Good," said Grey. "It's always nice to be busy. How are you two doing?"

"Better than ever. I managed to get him into the archives with me full time, which should keep him out of trouble. We live together now too, he keeps me sane when the Eminence is laying the stress on thick. Either way, we are both keen to be done with fieldwork, I think."

Grey nodded with contentment.

"Would you two ever consider leaving the kindred?" asked Grey. "There are plenty of other opportunities around for scholars, particularly ones that don't condone killing for money."

Artemis blinked slowly. "You know that is not why we stay."

"Your inaction says otherwise."

"Grey," said Artemis. "I respected your decision to 'leave it be' when you woke up, this morning and in your hospital." He stared daggers into Grey's eyes. "I expect you to give me the courtesy."

Looking down at his hands, inspecting the wrinkles and small scars across them, he sighed. "You're right. I'm in no position to judge . . ."

Rubbing his sore, tired eyes, Grey took a deep breath.

Need to get stuck into it, I guess.

He sighed.

There aren't enough hours in the day . . .

"Ducard wanted me to let you know that he's gone off-world for a few days," said Artemis as he sipped the coffee liberally.

Grey nodded, rubbing his finger around the rim of the glass. "Did he say where he was going?"

Artemis shook his head. "Unfortunately not. Although he did mention that it was of a personal nature."

Stretching his arms back, Grey yawned as he got up and walked towards the pile of documents demanding his attention. "I'm heading to Cardinal Point tonight," said Grey. "I'm hoping to get some more supplies and staff to the team I have out there."

"I see," said Artemis in between sips. "How is progress there?"

"It's going very well. Things are progressing a lot quicker than our other projects."

Artemis raised his hand, along with a challenging query. "How are your citizens handling the news about your plans?"

Good question.

After decades without any actual policing mechanism in the Broken Sector, Grey was close to rebuilding the infrastructure to bring it back. It included jails, staff, weaponry, and vehicles, which had initially caused a significant divide in the community. He thought about this as he sat down at the table, sifting through the documents to find where he'd left off from yesterday afternoon.

"We haven't had any raised in a while," said Grey as he rifled through. "I think people are starting to come to terms with the idea though."

"Law and order is an essential part of any civilisation. And your security team can't hold the fort forever. You need the rest of Menilax to help."

Grey stretched his neck, closing his eyes as the words thrummed in his skull.

Story of my life . . .

Dealing with criminals had been one of the first problems he'd been presented with. The council couldn't help him despite his initial pleas. They weren't willing to have augmented people in regular prisons, nor were they willing to lend resources to such a delicate part of Menilax. The only option was to have them banished from the sector.

Execution had been thrown around by some of the more calloused members of the security team, but Grey had dismissed the idea altogether. They were on the verge of completing the construction of the Enforcement building, including the prison, which opened up potential options for dealing with those who refused to obey the law of the sector.

"I should make a few calls," said Grey.

As he stood up, Grey stared at Artemis for a few quiet moments, nodding respectfully to his oldest friend. "Thanks for coming to pick me up, Arty . . ."

Artemis smiled genuinely. "You're always welcome."

⌘

13: RE-ENFORCEMENT

⌘

The trip to the building site was filled with hazards, and although any trek from one side of the Broken Sector to the other was treacherous, this particular route was avoided by every sane soul left alive.

Anyone wishing to make their way to Cardinal Point needed to pass through Senper Square, and considering there was no other way to the Point, Grey had insisted on leading the convoy personally. Being one of the rare few to come through this place on his own and live to tell the tale, he'd organised to make the journey during the early hours of the morning. The fanatics that claimed Senper Square were violent, zealous, and far beyond reason. Thankfully, the thick cloud cover would drastically reduce visibility as they navigated the road west of the square. Navigating through without any encounters would be preferable.

Grey sighed. He knew that he'd have to deal with the cultists one day, but there would be casualties, and he didn't feel comfortable committing to losing anyone on his team, nor the innocents who'd been swindled on the cultist side.

Grey craned his neck upwards as he passed under the archway welcoming them all to Senper Square. To the right was their road leading towards a series of underpasses, and in the distance, the Mortaroy Tunnel. To the left was another route, but this one would take them into the heart of the square, and in all likelihood, their deaths. With such a large convoy to transport, their choices for getting vehicles through the Broken Sector were minimal as most roads in this sector were destroyed.

As usual, his eyes were drawn to the massive mineral pool in the middle of each road. Spanning one kilometre in length and half that in width, the pool was once a place of quiet reflection for many citizens. Now, it was scorched, and the once majestic statue of Tobias Finlay, the Pioneer responsible for Menilax's infrastructure, was now a crumbling ruin caked with moss and ferns.

His eyes followed the path to the left, all the way to the edge of the square, where numerous buildings surrounded the road. Once occupied by humble shopkeepers and tradespeople, the area was now housed by the Ashen Faith. The cultists were convinced that the deities who watched over Vale before the invasion, the Pioneers, would rise from the grave and destroy those who'd wavered from their holy tenants. Aiden, the luminary of the faith, had taken residence inside the old Pioneer temple sitting at the apex of the road surrounded by the old businesses. Despite the dangers around the square, Aiden held the territory with the tenacity only a religious leader could muster. Such determination helped him construct the cult, employing his natural charisma to instil his followers with the unshakable belief in him and the tenants he enforced.

All his life Grey knew what the Pioneers were, but it seemed this logic hadn't been passed down to ordinary people. He'd learned quickly that the rest of the world thought highly of Vale's ancient protectors. In reality, the Pioneers weren't so different from augurs. They were still flesh and blood and were cursed with the follies that afflicted all of humanity, a fact that he'd only considered recently.

In a way, he'd adopted the Pioneer methodology when putting together the Broken Sector's security team. Each member of the group had been handpicked based on a few key traits, bringing the team to its elite, unwavering status. Rather than choose outright strength, academic intellect, or reflexes, Grey had placed great emphasis on a person's character. The team's composition had become one of his most significant accomplishments as a councillor, and as he glanced around to those that had come with him this morning, he smiled with satisfaction.

I suppose if you're looking to grant regular folk the gift of immortality, you want them to be decent people.

Despite looking pensive, he knew everyone on this duty would be incredibly alert and ready for anything. It was a shame that his people needed to focus on threats, as under different circumstances, one could learn a lot about the war by analysing the square. After all, this place had been one of the forward operating bases of the Strin invasion force when they landed.

During the uprising, the resistance struck these incursion sites with surgical precision, targeting the many fuel containers around the base. Little did they know, the fuel's composition made their demolition efforts disastrous for those who survived. Lambent radiation, a highly volatile and experimental substance, was the primary energy source for Strin transportation. While the origins of the material still remain a mystery, those who had survived the invasion had learned of its destructive potential when released from the sophisticated container that kept it docile.

When the containers were destroyed, the residue melted through Vale's crust, leaving behind radioactive fingers that stretched deep into the ground. Getting too close to these rifts would result in a slow and painful death, punishing the natural curiosity of those who ventured too close. The beautiful luminosity they radiated claimed the lives of many, with patients still checking in to the hospital with radiation sickness as a result of these sites. Those who'd chosen to stay here had serendipitously gained some visibility during the night, with each crater serving as a volatile torch revealing those who dared to trespass on their coveted land.

Keeping a brisk pace, Grey led the convoy along the road where they would eventually reach the Mortaroy Tunnel leading them up to Cardinal Point. Thirty of his own staff were housed at the Point, so with the additional eighteen souls they were escorting, the pace of construction would be ramped up considerably. While it was a lot of work keeping the construction site defended, leaving it unoccupied was entirely out of the question. Grey had enough staff to cover one project at a time as if the team were spread too thin, they wouldn't be able to defend the worksite effectively. Workers and security members had to be deployed carefully after all, and materials needed to be escorted by a formidable security team to prevent greedy hands from attempting to snatch away the resources.

It wouldn't be too long now until they reached the first underpass. The Faith would likely have people watching for threats, even at this time, so they'd have to proceed carefully. Grey signalled for the convoy to slow as they approached.

Grey realised early in his career that progress would be difficult and demanding; The Broken Sector didn't have experienced people, reliable resources, or proper training institutions, and without these things, opportunities for creating roles within the community were poor. The little number of jobs that were consistently around had been created by the individual, selling and trading food and other materials to others. This trade had become the primary source of income for most looking to survive; operating and maintaining stalls at Kensir Plaza allowed each person to generate enough currency to maintain the status quo. Grey exercised considerable effort in placing people into roles around the other sectors of Menilax, but they came far and few between.

Grey doubted he could fix everything in his lifetime, especially considering that any one of these days could be his last. Along with the many random threats he could stumble into within the sector, Grey had his share of political rivals, and a few veiled dangers leering at him from the shadows. The weight of the past was crushing him from the inside, gradually corroding away at his lingering sanity. Grey knew that he couldn't keep the past locked away from the world forever, but while he still drew breath, he would continue to work as much as he could to relieve his conscience.

Things will catch up with you soon, Grey . . .

Patting his hand on his chest, he found his pistol resting quietly in the holster. The brown leather strap brought his mind back from reliving the past, which yawed at his subconscious, begging him to delve inside and relive them once again. The nauseating sensation hit him in waves as he mentally blocked it, resisting the clamouring of his nightmares pulling him inside. Then, he reached around under the back of his shirt and felt the ice-cold hilt of Sithaleir, which was strapped over his back with a cotton band. His mind returned from the endless depths of anxiety and crippling neuroses after exploring the engraved runes with his fingertips, the intricate twisting metalwork, and the cold glass frame reviving him. Gripping the artefact, he felt a cold snap ripple along his flesh.

"I . . . am here . . ."

I know . . .

"You . . . do not . . . know . . ."

Grey rattled his head.

"Invoke me . . ."

Grey released his grip on Sithaleir.

Focus your mind. Concentrate. You don't need it right now.

He remembered the words of his teacher, Disciple.

"Your mind can be like a magnifying glass. If you leave it to its own devices, you will focus on trivialities, cluttering your mind with distractions. Take control of it, the same as you would any other tool, and fixate your attention on what is essential in the moment."

Exhaling forcefully, Grey's hand instinctively returned to his pistol. As he rubbed his index finger over the blue lightning bolt impression, he smiled, satisfied with his decision regarding the team's armaments for this duty.

"Are you all right?" asked Lionel, who'd placed his arm on Grey's shoulder.

Lionel, the young man from the tunnel, had decided to take him up on his offer to join the team when he'd left the hospital last week. Upon seeing his concerned face, his fear and anxiety melted away, snapping him out of his mental torment.

You inspired this kid to be better, to protect those who need protecting.

"Yeah . . . I'm good, kid," said Grey, slapping Lionel's arm as he passed him.

The young dredge showed incredible promise. It took a lot of guts to stand up and defend the innocent, as joining the security team was pitting yourself against the dangers of the sector. With Lionel's addition, they had six people on protection detail, each one of them responsible for protecting three trucks, two vans, and the newly acquired Enforcement cruiser still plugging along despite its age, not to mention the workers and drivers. So long as they moved through without alerting the cabal of the faith, they should be able to manage the duty with the members they had. In the event they encountered the cultists, Grey prepped the team's arsenal with non-lethal weapons, enabling them to neutralise the opposition without bloodshed. Scitilliant A.I.S. were the supplier, of course, but the acquisition was not as easy as acquiring their lethal counterparts. According to some of the engineers involved with the development of the tech, Grey had been the first client to show interest. Preserving lives, as opposed to taking them, did not rank as a priority for investors.

As they approached the Ulysses Overpass, Grey turned to gesture at Sornus, his lieutenant. The woman turned and began addressing the others, giving them the order to hold their positions as she paced between the formation. Underneath the giant, U-shaped gateway was a makeshift barricade, which hadn't been there the last time they made the route. The fact that it was empty was a concern, meaning an ambush was likely. Of course, they would have to clear it before they could proceed; only the cruiser would be able to roll over the rubble and refuse in one piece.

There are threats here. Only question is, where are they hiding . . . ?

Grey moved with haste to the right-hand side of the arch. Tiptoeing along the wall, he remembered from the last time they passed that the maintenance staircase was built into the side of the structure. Leading to the broken highway above, the stairs used to be one of the routes for service staff to get up to the PulseWay. Now, it could've been where the Ashen Faith were planning to ambush the convoy.

As he walked along the ramp, he placed each step with careful consideration. The area around the corner was covered by the ruined PulseWay above, but apart from that, it was exposed. As he approached the opening, he could hear murmurs and rustling.

Peering around the corner carefully, he found himself staring at the shadows, which danced across the floor erratically. They were projected by a crackling fire, which logically must've been on the other side of the ramp. He took a few quiet breaths, considering his options rigorously.

He turned to face the convoy and saw his security staff watching him nervously.

Grey waved his hand at them before holding up three fingers. Then, Grey swung his arm in a half circle before gesturing to the row of rusted cars adjacent to his position. With these gestures, he had given the order for three of them to take cover directly across from him, evident in the fact that the team obeyed, sprinting over as per his command. Sornus was there immediately, showing her proficiency as a dredge.

Channelling his augmentation, Grey prepared his body for balanced enhancement, divided evenly between strength and speed. Peering gradually around the corner, he gleaned eight Ashens, and it seemed as if they were preparing themselves for combat. Strapping on vests and loading automatic rifles, each of them appeared rushed, hastily getting ready to defend their land from Grey's crew. As he continued to lean, he saw a muscular woman leaning against the wall. She reached out to him with an open palm, growling at him as her fingers stretched out to his face. Grey brought his right arm around and pinned her arm to the wall by the wrist. She was stunned at his supernatural speed, allowing Grey to yank her towards him as he embedded his knee into her diaphragm. She yelped and she bent over his knee, coughing saliva onto the pavement. Releasing her wrist, Grey snapped his hand to her throat, lifting her into the air as if she were a toy, doing so in the blink of an eye as he squeezed her jugular.

As the other Ashen Ones turned to face him, Grey tossed her like a garbage bag, knocking three of them over as they grunted from the impact.

Eight threats, four momentarily incapacitated.

Grey optimised his muscles for speed. When the older man at the end of the row began to raise his weapon, Grey leapt towards him. By the time the Ashen man had shouldered the rifle, Grey was behind him, wrapping his lean arms around his neck. Using the momentum he'd gained from the dash, Grey swung his captor around, lifting and spinning him around. He used the man's boots to pummel a woman's head who had only just turned around to try to keep up with Grey's movements. The blow knocked her out cold, launching her into the railing to the left with a solid thump. As Grey released the man from his grip, the human projectile sailed through the air, plunging into the muscular woman he'd dealt with initially as she began to rise.

Another woman had managed to get behind him somehow, taking advantage of the gap in his awareness. She wrapped her arms under his and held him tightly with her palms secured around the back of his neck.

"I have him!" she yelled.

The strength she displayed was something only a dredge could've managed. He'd underestimated the situation, which now called for him to readjust his strategy. Time slowed to a crawl for Grey, as his mind raced with possibilities.

Six threats remain, including the dredge . . . She's formidable but untrained. Her strength is adequate, but she's committed to the grapple, gambled everything on its success. Overconfident with her approach, not expecting a counter attack.

Bringing his head forward then backward as hard as he could, Grey expected to feel her nose crumble under his skull, but she was ready. Using his momentum, she leant back, carrying him over with her in an attempt to slam his head into the pavement. As Grey fell backward, he strengthened his arms and fingers before reaching down to clutch her sides, jamming steely fingers into her kidneys. Using her momentum against her and tunnelling his augmentation into his upper body, Grey tucked his legs in and landed on his feet. Her gasp of pain was followed by a loss of strength, allowing him to lift her body above him as he snarled, growling at the exertion required for raising a dredge. Lifting her bulk above, Grey roared as he threw her over to the other Ashen Ones with a mighty toss, knocking them over like bowling pins as she continued to soar over the railing.

You're a dredge, so you can handle more punishment . . .

He kept his eyes on her for a brief moment as she sailed through the group of people and landed beyond the ramp, sliding across the dirt near the security team. She'd barely managed to stop tumbling over and over before six shock rounds riddled her body in quick succession.

You aren't getting up anytime soon . . .

The two Ashen Ones that were knocked down with the initial human projectile were almost up now, but the more pressing threat stood to the left. A short, brown-haired woman with a burn mark across her face had managed to raise her automatic machine gun, training it at him with a snarl.

Knowing he'd have to take a few rounds, Grey adjusted his muscle composition again. Flexing and preparing his muscles, he changed the balance of his ability by making his skin tissue durable rather than light. The weapon roared at him, spitting out scorching hot lead in rapid succession. Instead of penetrating his flesh, each shot caved in on itself as it met the unstoppable force of his enhanced muscle. Grey grabbed the rifle from her arms, crushing the chassis as if the weapon was made from wet paper. He took advantage of her disarmament to thrust his palm into her chest, knocking the wind from her and sending her reeling into the railing.

Unclipping the safety strap on his chest holster, Grey unsheathed the Surge pistol, turning around to face the remaining four threats. They'd managed to turn to meet him, but only one of the Ashen Ones had actually managed to ready his rifle. The other three were still in the process of loading the weapons.

Damn, these people are slow to prepare.

Grey shot two rounds at the man's neck.

With the remaining three threats, Grey didn't think it necessary to take them down as quickly as the others, so he fired a single shot at each of them. The man who'd taken two rounds was out cold in less than two seconds, while the others took twice that before collapsing.

Glancing at each of the people he'd neutralised, he was happy to see they were all breathing. With the immediate area clear, Grey slipped his pistol into the holster and moved to the opposite side from which he'd entered. From here, Grey could see the next obstacle, the Keltway Overpass, running in parallel to the Ulysses. Thankfully, he couldn't see any threats between here and there, but there was a lot of rubble, rusted cars, and old buildings on either side of the road, which could be responsible for hiding more Ashen threats.

Leaning beyond the railing, and peering above, Grey decided to check the top of the overpass before clearing the barricade and moving the convoy forward. Once he was up there, the elevated angle would allow greater visibility of the area.

Grey moved quickly to the door, placing his hand on the cold, rusted metal. The latch whined as it opened; the resulting echo resounding through the stairwell as he glared into the darkness expectantly.

Scanning the winding stairwell from his position, he felt satisfied that it was free from any souls. It was quiet enough inside that if there was someone hiding, he would've detected them by now, but as he could not hear movement, heartbeats, or breathing, he knew it was clear.

Grey thought carefully on his next move. Inside the stairwell, his mobility would be limited. With the structure being so old and flimsy, any serious manoeuvrability could bring the entire thing down. If there were threats deeper within the complex, bringing the whole overpass down would kill them. There could still be surprises waiting for him on the top of the bridge, or inside the offices below, and he couldn't check it all as quickly as he would've liked.

Need some backup, just to be safe.

Backing off from the doorway and approaching the edge of the concrete platform, Grey hailed the team with an outstretched arm. As their gazes locked onto him, he held up two fingers before waving them over. One of them remained, while the other two began the short sprint over to him as they dashed around their makeshift cover.

Grey returned to the door, listening for movement, but all he could hear was the stomping gait of his team, their boots pounding the dusty earth. Hopping up to the concrete platform, Grey turned to face them both. Considering his word choice carefully, he contemplated the best set of tactics for navigating the space ahead. Tienzin and Sam, two honest and hardworking members of the team, stood before him, panting slightly from the sprint over.

Tienzin was a middle-aged man, born with the sun-kissed skin of the Sashiryu. Along with the rest of his kind, his facial hair was sparse and small, while his eyelids—acute and perceptive—were thin. Despite his determined look, Tienzin had a good sense of humour, something that Grey sought out more and more when choosing team members.

"I'll take the roof," whispered Grey. "You two head downstairs, and don't get ahead o' yourselves." Grey glanced between the two of them, gauging their mental state. They seemed attentive but nervous. "If you stay together, you'll do fine. Just make sure you sing out if you find anyone."

They shouldered their rifles, confirming their readiness with sharp nods.

Grey unsheathed the stun pistol before stepping inside and snapping the weapon to eye level. Gesturing below with an extended hand sent Sam and Tienzin downstairs to the offices, keeping their footsteps quiet. Sam's dull red hair had been tied back into a ponytail as usual. Her pale skin, brown eyes and sharp features gave off a very professional vibe, although her worry lines made her look older than she was.

Reaching out to the metal safety rails around the edge, he shook one of the bars gently to confirm the durability. Strangely enough, he could feel the chill of the night air inside, causing him to crane his neck up to find the roof of the staircase destroyed, leaving the stairwell at the mercy of the elements. As Grey moved up the stairs, he felt the concrete and steel groan underneath his feet, shuffling and wobbling as he stepped carefully.

Ascending carefully, his eyes became fixated on the corners of the staircase. Grey concentrated on his breathing to keep his mind clear and ready to react in a heartbeat.

A loud wheeze echoed through the stairwell.

Snapping his pistol over the railing, Grey scanned the bottom of the shaft intently. Within a moment, Sam raised her hand out and waved to him, before poking her head up with her eyebrows raised, mouthing the word "sorry." Grey smirked, shaking his head as he resumed his ascent.

Within a few moments, he reached the apex.

As he hiked beyond the final step, he was greeted with the breach that allowed the night air in. Grey peered through the void, admiring the view of the road and the two remaining overpasses.

Keltway is next, then Perch, then the tunnel. I hope they don't have positions in each one, or this is going to take a while . . .

Perch Overpass ran parallel with Keltway Overpass, both of which he could see stretching out to the southwest. They used to connect to Sectors Five, Six, and Seven, but now they led to nowhere. The barriers that were constructed after the invasion blocked them off, although considering how ruined the PulseWay was, it was unnecessary.

One day I'll rebuild this old thing better than before . . .

Grey sighed as his eyes drifted back to the road and to the duty at hand.

The remaining parts of a ladder could be seen strewn about, noticeable by the broken metal tubes sticking out of the rubble. Peering above, Grey could see the PulseWay proper, within jumping distance for a dredge. Bending his knees, he exerted a small amount of power, channelling it into his lower body before launching himself up. Grey soared into the air, quickly clearing the debris and landing gracefully on the bitumen of the PulseWay.

Grey scanned the road stretching behind him, satisfied that there were no signs of life. Turning around and facing the way that led towards the cabal of the Ashen Faith, he could see a man clumsily shuffling along. The gaping holes in the PulseWay did not seem to slow him down as he leapt across them without much strain, although the man was not graceful in his movements. Instead of landing on his feet, he seemed to fall on his hands and knees as if he wasn't sure what he was doing.

He can't be augmented . . .

Squeezing the grip of his handgun, he thought about taking a few shots at the clumsy leaper, but considering the short range of the Surge rounds, Grey decided against it.

I have to chase him down on foot, can't let him warn the cabal . . .

Grey funnelled all of his strength into his legs, crouching so he could push off and get a good start. The man was at least four kilometres away from him, so he'd have to push his body hard to get to him in time. Gritting his teeth, Grey took off with incredible momentum, launching at a speed that would've crippled an average human. Racing across the remnants of the PulseWay, Grey sailed over the gaps with slight hops, and within a few seconds, he was in front of the man, stopping himself by lowering his profile and digging his feet into the bitumen.

Small chunks of road pelted the man's back, causing him to turn around. His eyes were wide with shock as he stared at Grey, who grimaced at his nervous display. He was trying to say something, but fear had taken hold of his senses, preventing him from reacting as he stammered and backed away with his arms raised.

"Well now," said Grey, "where do you think you're goin'?"

The man was bald, pale, clean-shaven, and slightly overweight. He wore a long sleeve jumper, black pants, and some odd mechanical shoes that he didn't recognise. He reeked of alcohol with his jumper having various dark stains littered across it.

"Think you an' I need to have a little chat," said Grey as he stepped over to him confidently.

The man gasped and turned away from him, dashing inside the nearby staircase before slamming the door behind him. Grey adjusted his augmentation for upper body strength, slamming into the door with a tackle and knocking it off its hinges. Grey stood directly in front of the man as the door flung past him and over the railing, clanging around the steel and concrete infrastructure as it bounced down the stairs.

The man's face was overwhelmed with shock. As his jaw began to tremble, he stepped away from Grey, losing his balance as he teetered over the edge. He yelped as Grey clutched him by the scruff of his shirt, snatching him away from the stairs and lifting him up with a snarl.

"Where are your friends?" he barked.

"Right here!" said a woman's voice behind him.

Grey growled as he reached behind and clutched the woman's throat with a grimace, bringing her next to the bald man and glaring at them impatiently. He held them up like pests, shaking his head, wanting to simply get on with things rather than deal with them.

"Is there anyone else here with you?" he asked the woman.

"I would rather die—" she wheezed as he gripped her neck tightly, "—than tell you where my brothers and sisters are . . ."

Grey sighed.

Need to calm down . . . The adrenaline's getting to me . . .

He took a deep breath.

"If I release you," he stated calmly, "will you talk?"

She snarled at him. "You can say whatever you want, snake!" She spat in Grey's face. "When the Pioneers return, you will know their wrath!"

Grey grumbled, failing to quell the white-hot anger swelling inside his chest as her saliva rolled over his scarred cheek.

"And you!?" said Grey, yelling in the man's face as he shook him.

The man was trying to say something, but he kept glancing at the woman nervously. She had a scar running across her nose, which had deformed the flesh around it drastically. She had long black hair, which messily draped over her face and pale skin. The muscles around her nose and upper lip quivered with rage as she glared at the man. If he let her go, she would not be cooperative. He sighed as he glanced at the bald man.

He's not going to talk with her awake.

Grey let go of the man as he unsheathed his pistol, firing a single slug into her neck before returning it to the holster. She writhed in his hand for a few moments as the Surge round pumped electricity through her system, sapping her muscles of energy and stressing her internal organs severely. The man watched the woman spasm as Grey placed the now unconscious woman to the floor as gently as he could.

"I just wanna talk," said Grey, tapping the holster on his chest where he returned the pistol.

"It looks bad, I'll give you that. But I'm using nonlethal rounds. Understand?"

The man nodded, swallowing dryly as he looked over at the woman, no doubt noticing her rising chest. Grey gestured to the direction where his convoy was as he spoke.

"We're transportin' supplies to Cardinal Point," he said. "If I *let* you get back to the church, there would be bloodshed. And that *is not* our goal here."

"Y . . . Yes . . . I understand . . . But—"

"Now listen up," said Grey, pointing his finger at the man's face. "I haven't killed any of your friends; they're okay, same as this one," said Grey, gesturing to the woman resting on the ground. "Now I really wanna trust you here, but I can't let you go if you're gonna go straight over to your friends, so—"

"Just . . . Before you continue . . ." said the man, raising a trembling hand. "They aren't my friends, Councillor."

Grey relaxed his shoulders a little, nodding politely as he crossed his arms. "Okay, so why were you running inside here to have *this one* help you?"

"I didn't know she was here!" he stammered defensively. "I saw you and your convoy coming, so I hop-tailed it out o' sight. I was just looking for somewhere to hide, that's all."

Grey rubbed his chin for a few moments, weighing the man's story carefully.

"You called me councillor . . ." he said expectantly. "You know who I am?"

The man smiled broadly before nodding nervously.

"Yes, I know who you are, sir. I didn't think you'd be this friendly. Your reputation around these parts is pretty unforgiving, especially among the faithful . . ."

Grey chortled.

Ironic . . .

"What's your name?"

"Excuse my manners, sir. My name's William," he said, extending his hand to Grey.

Grey nodded, uncrossing his arms to shake the man's hand. His eyes drifted down to the strange shoes Will wore, gesturing to them curiously.

"Interesting tech you got there . . ." said Grey suggestively.

The boots were gargantuan, more so than any other footwear he'd ever seen. The mechanism looked to clasp halfway up his ankles, and the bottom seemed to branch out, looking more like an animal's hoof than a boot.

"Oh, these?" He smiled. "Thanks. It's a, uh, work in progress, you could say . . ."

Will explained that the soles contained thrusters, propelling the wearer into the air with a quick burst of kinetic energy. Generated by movement, the power was stored inside the capacitors, ready to be utilised once enough energy was stored, explaining how he was able to get across the gaps in the PulseWay. He advised that there was a short window for using the boots in its current build before the energy dissipated, so he still had more work ahead of him before they were ready for mass production.

"The amount of running required to gain a sufficient amount of kinetic energy is not as efficient as it could be," he said. "That's actually why I was up here. I usually come up at night to give them a bit of a test run; I've found the PulseWay to be a fantastic place to give them a good whirl."

Grey smiled warmly. "I've never seen anything like it. You could make some serious bank if you perfected that thing."

William tittered anxiously. "These boots are a *long* way away from anything like that, although it would be incredible to see them manufactured on that scale. If I can finish, I'm hoping I can use the money to get us out of this place . . . Assuming I can convince Aiden to let us leave . . ."

Grey crossed his arms.

"Tell you what. When it's ready, come and find us." Gesturing to his own chest, Grey continued. "I've got a good relationship with the CEO of Scitilliant A.I.S., and I know for a fact that they would love to get their hands on those boots o' yours."

The engineer scratched the back of his head. "Yeah okay, sure."

Grey slapped the jittery man on the shoulder, holding it firmly for a few moments. "You mentioned an 'us' . . . Got a family?" he asked gently. "They with the Ashen Faith?"

He nodded, his face shrinking back to a more serious reflection of his inner workings. "It's complicated . . ."

Grey tilted his head. "These things always are. Will, you seem like a good man. You make sure to come and find me at my bar when you're ready. Do you know Jenior Pass?"

Will nodded.

"The bar's north of the pass. If you're feeling up to it, come and see me. We can work somethin' out, and I'm sure we can get you all to safety one way or another." Grey tilted his head. "You take care of yourself, Will."

With that, Grey stepped back onto the PulseWay and into the fresh night air.

Will followed him out, calling after Grey with a dubious tone. "So . . . you're just going to let me go?"

Grey pulled out his pack of cigarettes from his belt, slipping one into his mouth before lighting.

"You don't strike me as the sort o' man to stir up trouble." Grey casually turned around, raising his head towards him. "That is unless I'm wrong about you . . . ?"

Will nodded. "I won't say anything. You have my word."

Nodding slightly, Grey waved his hand once.

"Take care o' that family of yours," said Grey.

He moved toward the edge of the PulseWay as he lit the cigarette, breathing the smoke into his lungs and holding it there for a few moments. Leaning over the guardrails and inspecting the area around him, he exhaled, glad to see that there were no signs of life in Senper Square.

I'm so close now. I wonder how long it would take me to leap down and take care of that worm . . .

If he chose to, he could go looking for Aiden and rid the world of him once and for all, guaranteeing that no more minds would be corrupted by his false doctrines.

Grey pushed the feeling away.

It was getting easier to dismiss the impulse to solve his problems with violence. The more he resisted, the quicker he could set the mood aside. Knowing that it would only bring misery to himself and those around him was helpful in adjusting the intense conditioning he'd been subjected to as a child. No matter how hard he tried, the urge continued to rear its malevolent head, and after a lifetime of training towards aggression and tactical planning, it came as no surprise that it would be a problematic impulse to neutralise entirely.

He suspected he would never be free of such urges, making vigilance his only defence against the incessant noise of his anxious, violent mind.

You can't trust your feelings. Put your faith in the man you want to be tomorrow.

As he walked along the bitumen, his heel fell through a small hole in the road, aggravating his wounds from the fight at the bar recently. Pins and needles danced over his body as the sensation left him breathless for a moment.

Paranoia had set in immediately after the bar confrontation; the onyx soldiers seemed to know a whole lot about Grey, and Darius for that matter. He'd been waiting to see if more of the soldiers came looking for their fallen comrades, so as a precaution, he'd had the suits and bodies relocated to a secure location. With Ducard's help, he'd removed the tracking units built into the suits before loading them into his aircraft. Once the remains had been relocated, Ducard had promised to get him some more information on where they'd come from, which he was immensely grateful for. After all, Grey had enough to worry about as it was.

Still can't believe they were hunting Darius . . .

Grey sighed heavily, closing his eyes for a moment.

I would've thought they'd have stopped looking by now.

He rubbed his face with both hands.

How long am I going to have to deal with the demons of the past?

Grey knew the president of the board would shut down the program after he told her what had transpired, but it would be a waste to discard all of that work, especially considering what the suits could do in the right hands. Inspecting the material of the suits personally, Ducard had confirmed that the plating was typically used for reinforcing the chassis for interplanetary craft. It was incredibly dense, and yet they'd carved thin enough pieces to prevent the operator from being weighed down too much. The little servos and motors around the joints and limbs helped propel movement to compensate for the weight, confirming Grey's assertions gathered during the fight.

A fledgling augur would've been torn to pieces by one of those things.

Grey sighed.

One problem at a time . . .

Tossing the spent cigarette, he began enhancing his legs. After a moment of concentration, Grey began the short sprint back to the convoy. As his energy was finite, he'd need to conserve it whenever possible. The night was not over yet, after all.

William, I hope you don't go back on your word . . .

Grey took a deep breath, hoping his mercy wouldn't come back to bite him. When he approached the halfway mark, he saw Sam leaping across one of the first few gaps.

"Damn," she said as he leapt over to her platform. "I'd forgotten how fast you are . . ." She chuckled. "Everything all right?"

Grey nodded to her as he glanced down to the convoy below. It appeared as though they'd cleared the barricade already, much to Grey's satisfaction.

She glanced at his shirt with a furrowed brow. "Are you sure you're okay?"

Looking down at his black, thin shirt, he could see flecks of rusted metal and dust, as well as a small streak of blood. The wounds he'd suffered from the fight at the bar had opened up, causing them to weep. He'd pushed his body considerably tonight, against his doctor's orders.

He nodded, blinking slowly. "Yeah, darlin', don't you worry about me."

After a quiet moment, Sam let it go. He could tell she wanted to inquire further but wisely decided against it. They both looked down at the convoy; the rest of the team were waiting for them, except Tienzin, who Grey asked about.

She swallowed, gesturing below nervously.

"He's down below. We found a few offices on the bottom floor, along with some stragglers." She blinked, staring at him expectantly. "Thought we'd wait for you . . . to make a decision."

"Well, all right," he replied. "Let's go."

Grey gestured to the convoy below. "Can you make it down on your own?"

She grinned. "You serious?"

Grey's mouth curved into a smile, bowing mockingly as he gestured toward the convoy.

"Well then, Ladies first."

She shook her head. Hovering her foot over, she winked at him before falling off the edge. Grey strode over unceremoniously, leaping off with a booming laugh and falling like a rock to the road below. The pit that formed in his stomach was thrilling, reminding him of his reckless childhood, where he'd spent many a night testing his limits.

The ground crumbled beneath his augmented weight, spraying rubble around the road. Looking up to Sam, he watched her delicately glide down to meet him, flecks of blue energy sparking around her feet. She had a playful grin etched on her face.

"If we were racin'," said Grey, gesturing brashly, "this'd make you the runner up, darlin'."

She chuckled at him as she glided the rest of the way, smiling broadly as she landed.

"Don't ever change, Grey."

Interesting choice of words . . .

Grey rubbed at his scar as he moved through the darkened underpass.

"Let's go check on Tienzin," he said. "Then we can get back on the road."

Unsheathing his handgun, Grey stepped around the broken boom gate, taking in his surroundings with cautioned curiosity. To the right, he saw a small row of parking spaces, two of which were occupied with rusted cars. In front of the cars were a series of broken windows, but it was far too dark to make out any detail beyond them from where Grey stood. As he moved closer to the windows, Grey peered through to get a clear view of the darkened office. Sam walked beside Grey, holding her rifle as she scanned the windows acutely.

"Tienzin?" His voice echoed through the pitch-black office.

"I am here!" he replied. "Awaiting your presence, fearless leader!"

Grey moved briskly to the caved-in door on the right, stepping into the darkened office space without hesitation. Twisting the dial on his chest lamp activated it, sending a bright beam of light before him, revealing the secrets of the darkness. Cubicles and desks lined the area, although they were scattered and broken, like everything else in Sector Eight. The once humble workspace had been ransacked, likely during the early days after the war. There were many offices like this along the PulseWay, housing the government staff responsible for maintenance, finance, and administration. The overpowering stench of mould hit him immediately, but after years of living in the sector these strong odours didn't have much of an effect anymore.

Grey could hear heartbeats towards the rear of the office, thanks to the relative silence of the area. Sam followed closely behind him, the mushy splash of their footsteps the only audible noise.

Grey stopped for a moment, looking over to the left, illuminating the hallway that stretched before him. It appeared to lead to some old restrooms, private offices, and a lunch area at the end.

No signs of life this way . . .

Grey turned back to the right and moved immediately through to the rear office, which would be close to the stairwell Grey ascended earlier. As he stepped through, he saw four people with their hands behind their heads, lying face down on the ground. Tienzin was sitting on the stairwell, puffing leisurely on a cigarette. The faint glow of the burning herbs lit his features, showing his bored face.

"These ones, I leave to your discretion Grey Son."

Grey chuckled.

Still can't get used to him calling me that . . .

"Now listen here, folks," said Grey, sheathing his pistol. "We're only looking to pass through. We haven't killed your people; in fact, we're using nonlethal ammunition."

"You cannot fool us!" screamed a man as held up his head. "The one who offers his hand in peace after showing nothing but violence cannot be trusted!"

Taking a deep breath, Grey continued. "No Ashen blood has been spilled tonight, I can promise you that. All I'm asking is that you let us pass in peace, and we'll let you go."

"If you cared about us *so much*, then why are we face first on this filthy, scum-soaked carpet?" a young woman snarled.

Grey nodded, pursing his lips. "Fair enough. Everyone stand up, let's head outside."

They all stood up, albeit hesitantly at first.

"No funny business now . . ." said Grey as he gestured back through the offices.

The cultists shared suspicious glances, eyeing each corner carefully before committing to the walk ahead. As they all marched out into the faint moonlight from beyond the overpass, they all turned to face Grey and his team.

"See?" said Grey. "Ain't no one here tryin' to trample on your sacred land." Grey gestured to the convoy. "We're only lookin' to move supplies to another part o' the sector. Unfortunately, this here's the only way we can get all o' these vehicles through." Grey gestured around him. "The only other way was the PulseWay, and, well . . ." Grey chuckled. "Don't need to tell ya'll about *that*, now do I?"

The woman raised an eyebrow at Grey. "How do *we* know that you ain't hustlin' weapons?" she asked sceptically. "We know who you are, Councillor. You might think you're different now that you're a big shot politician, but we all know where you came from."

Grey shook his head with his eyes closed. "Ain't doin' that no more, darlin'. Gave up the arms trade a long time ago. Nowadays, I'm tryin' to make things better for the rest of us."

Using his chin to gesture to the convoy, Grey continued. "Why don't ya'll come and take a look at what we're sportin'?"

Grey moved past them, turning his back and moving briskly outside.

"It's a trick!" said the old man. "They're going to take us away! Transform us into his faithless slaves!"

Tienzin gestured for the old man to move up.

"Get your hands off me! You faithless demon!"

"Move onwards, Ashen One, and I will have no need to violate your space again."

Grey threw up his arm. "Hell, you're more than welcome to come with us if you want, but no one's going to take you away against your will. But if you wanna tag along, you gotta earn your keep," he said. "Each o' my crew here pulls their own weight. As long as you contribute in some way, I'd be happy to have you join us."

"We'd never join the likes of you!" yelled the older man as the other three ignored him and followed behind Grey. "I see through your lies! You'll all be taken by the Grey! You will see!"

The Grey . . . ? That's new . . .

Grey sighed, approaching the convoy casually.

"Sir?" quizzed Sornus, her brownish-grey hair draped casually over her shoulders, concern plastered across her grizzled face. He raised his hand before lowering it slowly, letting her know he had the situation under control, although she certainly didn't seem to think so.

"Come on now," said Grey, turning to gesture to the others. "Don't be shy; we won't bite."

Stepping around the rear of the van, he knocked on the doors with the back of his knuckles.

"It's Grey!" he yelled.

The two women and the young man came around to the rear of the van, while the older man stood a few meters away, snarling at them with his arms crossed and muttering inaudibly to himself.

"Grey?" Sornus rounded the corner of the van. "Are you sure this is a good idea?"

The double doors opened up, breaking the moment before he needed to answer her.

"Sorry Grey!" said Luna from inside the truck. "The keypad broke again, had to use the lever to open her up."

Grey chuckled as he hopped up inside the cabin. "Good to hear the lever works at least. I'd hate to see ya'll live in that truck for the rest o' your lives."

Luna's broad smiled faded as soon as she saw the muttering old man 'round the corner.

"Don't mind these folk," said Grey. "They may look intimidating, but they're just like us, only lookin' to survive."

Grey looked to each of the Ashen Ones, gesturing around him. "Go on now, take a look."

They approached the truck, looking at the supplies curiously.

Inside were five people sitting on makeshift stools welded to the sides of the cabin. Throughout the cabin were many supplies. There were bags of concrete, steel pillars, safety equipment, food, and water, all packed as tightly as possible to fill every inch of space with the stuff.

"As you can see, we're on a duty to rebuild, not to injure. We're only looking to pass through so we can get to where we're goin'."

They all shared a shocked, perplexed look.

They really were expecting trouble . . .

"You won't take them from me!" screamed the man as he charged over to them brandishing a knife. They all turned to face him flailing the serrated steel manically.

Everyone around Grey panicked. His security team raised their weapons, and the Ashen Ones stood defensively. Preparing his body for speed, Grey readied himself to dash over and incapacitate the man. As he was about to step off the cabin, six slugs pelted him, fired from Grey's team.

"No!" yelled the Ashen woman.

The three of them went to move inside the truck as the woman snatched Luna's wrist, attempting to pull her from the cabin. The workers inside the cabin fired their own Surge rounds into the insurgents as they fell to the floor, twitching from the electrical charges circulating their nervous system.

Grey leapt down to the road, cursing aloud. The exchange hadn't gone as he'd hoped.

"I'm sorry, Grey," said Sornus, lowering her rifle. "We couldn't risk them hurting the workers."

Grey looked up at those in the rear of the truck; they were holding their pistols with trembling hands, looking down in horror at the Ashen Ones on the floor, their bodies writhing and twitching on the ground.

He'd placed the entire duty in jeopardy, not to mention the lives of the crew, all to show some good faith to strangers.

"It's all right," said Grey, scratching his scar roughly. "You did what you had to do . . ."

Inhaling restlessly, Grey hoped to vent some of the anxiety and guilt from his body.

No one got hurt at least, but still, I put their lives at risk unnecessarily. Their willingness to help rebuild the sector is the only thing that's going to carry us forward. I need to prioritise the lives of my own against the lives of strangers . . .

He sighed.

Need to drill it into my skull. I can't rescue everyone . . .

His fingernail cut into his scar as he scratched it, causing a small flash of pain to spark across his face. Drawing his hand away, Grey stared at the smear of blood on his fingertip.

After a lifetime of ruining lives, destroying families, and crippling governments, I should've learned the damned lesson by now . . .

A stinging nostalgia pinched at his brain, washing away his reason and narrowing his perspective. The stress pushing against the walls of his skull, as the sting became a throbbing ache. The icy, unrelenting hammering of guilt and regret resurfaced, returning to punish him for the slightest error. Grey needed a drink, it was the only thing that helped when he felt this shitty.

"Let's get these people under cover," he finally said, gasping for breath. "Don't want them out in the rain when it starts pouring, you know?"

Grey looked at each of those around him, taking a deep, exhausted breath.

They were all still stunned. Except for Sornus, who shook her head at him before walking away.

"I'm sorry . . ."

⌘

14: PROVISIONS

⌘

Adalia would've lost her mind if she knew what her daughter was up to.

Scanning the streets from the backseat, Janus observed the many commuters with curiosity as workers, shoppers, and business people walked hurriedly along the sidewalk. Each of them came rugged up to counter the cold winds, billowing between the mighty skyscrapers of Sector Five. The warm cabin was filled with the subtle hint of coffee beans as the driver sipped his large paper cup liberally, making the slow turn onto Cypris Street.

"We're five minutes out, ma'am," said the driver.

Janus leaned towards the centre of the cabin as he nodded to her through the rear-view mirror, her eyes wincing against the sunlight, peering through the windscreen.

She'd read that the clouds would clear completely by tomorrow, but today, Menilax would be covered with intermittent showers. The commuters didn't seem phased by the spattering rain; in fact, everyone looked as if they were on autopilot, their eyes locked ahead with blank expressions.

The facial aspects of the commuters reminded her of Adalia following their conversation earlier. After sharing an awkwardly quiet breakfast with her hungover mother, Janus had chosen not to disclose her intentions to her yet. Instead of confronting her, Janus had snuck into the master bedroom and swiped the electronic access pass to Scitilliant A.I.S. Being the founder and CEO of the company, Adalia certainly had a lot of influence over the many functions of the business, which would allow Janus to navigate Scitilliant A.I.S. as she saw fit. With enough guile and social engineering, she was confident in her ability to access the showroom and take what she needed for Ducard's duty.

The showroom. Where dreams are born . . .

Janus chuckled to herself.

Well . . . where my dreams are born . . .

Rubbing the ID card between her fingers, she thought on the current state of her mother. Adalia would never forgive her for what happened to Nathan. Perhaps there was some hope despite the dwindling numbers of the family unit.

It's either Oscar or bust now. No more excuses.

The only way to find him was through Grey, who seemed to know a lot more than he was letting on.

"We've arrived," said the driver.

Janus pulled her leather wallet from her backpack, slipping out a plastic payment card and placing it in his palm. He swiped it through a card reader built into the dash before handing it back to her.

Strapping the bag around her back, Janus grasped the door handle, pulling on it quickly to open the door. As she did so, the cold wind carrying small raindrops assaulted her senses, causing her to gasp as she stood outside, shocked by the sudden change in temperature.

Thank the Pioneers I rugged up too . . .

The Scitilliant Plaza had taken a considerable amount of time to develop. Paved with large stone blocks and covered with glass panels, it was impressive to say the least. Each side of the ample space was lined with small businesses and Scitilliant branded outlets, making it a great place to visit for anyone looking to glimpse a slice of the future.

I could be a salesman for ST branded weapons.

She tittered at the thought.

Janus had the product knowledge, although she wasn't sure how corporate life would suit her; commuting to Sector Five every morning in peak hour would be tough, especially in adverse weather. She was wearing a thick grey jacket with a matching scarf and beanie, although she could still feel the cold piercing through the layers. Reaching over to the other side of the cabin, she grabbed her large duffel bag before closing the door. The numerous hums of car engines reverberated through the pavement under her feet as her ride took off down the busy street. While the wind and bustling footsteps of the people around her made her feel relaxed, it had been a while since she'd been to this sector, giving Janus a small amount of anxiety.

Janus smiled broadly despite her feelings.

Let's go look at some new toys!

She smiled and rubbed her hands together, as she hopped into the crowd to join them.

The reception's only a few minutes' walk from here, thankfully.

The plaza was reasonably protected from the weather, but the cold still found its way inside.

Scitilliant Advanced Intelligence Systems: Still feels good to see it after all this time.

Scitilliant A.I.S. had been a significant competitor with Lornan Futuristics ever since the war. The two companies considered the largest manufacturers of weapons in Menilax, although Janus had a feeling that Lornan would be tanking unless they could get a handle over the CEO's recent debacle.

Sick pig . . . Can't believe Enforcement tried to keep it under wraps . . .

Although the story had been in the paper a few nights ago, she'd only read about it this morning. Someone had leaked various forms of content implicating the CEO; surveillance footage made up a large portion of it, which showed the man kidnapping small children. Among the leaks were photographs of those same children's rotting bodies dug up weeks later, although who had been the one to take the photos was unclear. Apparently, a few Enforcement officials were trying to keep a lid on it and were implicated along with the leaks of Jone's activity.

Perhaps he knew what was coming and left before the news broke. A man like that would have enough money to disappear forever.

She sighed.

I hope he gets what's coming to him. I can't imagine what sort of creature would want to do that to anyone, especially to children . . .

Janus shook her head at the thought. She didn't think him capable of such monstrous behaviour before reading about it.

Passing under the archway, Janus didn't break her gait as the glass doors slid open. Directly ahead of her was the reception area; the desk and floor were both made from marble, spotted with black over the primary crème colour.

The receptionist was a cute young man who greeted her with a warm smile. His short black hair and clean-shaven grin were adequate for such a role, considering he'd be the first face someone would see when entering the building. He observed her approach with his arms folded over the counter.

"Good morning," he said with a deep voice. "How can I help?"

He must be new.

"Just here to check on a few of the new weapons." Said Janus, slipping her Scitilliant Identification pass out from her back pocket.

The man received the pass and checked both sides before responding, "Miss Scitilliant, wow, you're related to the CEO?"

Janus nodded curtly. "I'm her daughter."

He nodded, passing her ID back to her. "What's Adalia like?"

She gave him a fake smile. "She's smart, hardworking, intense . . ."

The man smirked, nodding as if he knew something she didn't. "She's a genius, so none of that surprises me. Have you seen the prototypes for the new ST-34?"

Janus nodded. "I have indeed; in fact, I've even tested them myself."

"That's incredible . . . How was the recoil? Was it—"

"Listen, I've got so much paperwork I need to catch up on, so if you wouldn't mind . . . ?"

He scrunched his eyebrows, taken off guard by her interruption.

She smiled faintly at him, waiting impatiently for his reaction.

"Uh, yes, of course . . ."

Pressing a series of keystrokes on his computer unlocked the elevators behind him. Janus nodded as she moved briskly around the desk and stepped inside. He watched her as the doors closed, embarrassment occupying his face.

Don't have time to be kind today.

She pressed the button for the showroom, launching the elevator down. Within a few seconds, the elevator slowed to a halt as a pleasant musical tone echoed through the cabin. The doors drifted open, revealing the elaborately designed showroom.

Now we're talking!

Janus rubbed her hands together in anticipation as she left the elevator. If she sprinted from one side of the floor to the other, it would take at least five minutes. The walls, ceiling, and floors were all polished white, and the pathways splintered off from the elevators like a spider web, paved with brown wood panels to indicate the suggested routes. Looking at all the prototypes with their polished metal and block-shaped designs gave Janus an easy smile. She knew Nathan would've hated these weapons.

You were always so set in your ways, that old Lance rifle of yours was a relic!

Janus stopped moving, stunned by a sudden realisation. She'd completely forgotten about her father's rifle.

It must still be at the National Park!

Swallowing dryly, she felt a wave of guilt wash over her. Far too much focus was paid towards her search for support, with Nathan's memory locked away behind the pain of that night. The Enforcement report hadn't mentioned the gun as a recovered object, meaning it might still be around the site.

It's not going to be easy going back there . . . but I'll find his rifle if it kills me . . .

Every time she thought about her father or her brother, a pang of anxiety jolted her body, making her feel flushed and breathless as her mind seemed to take her back to those moments of pain. It was like reliving them all over again.

Pushing the feelings away made her feel better temporarily, but she could only quell it for so long. Each resurgence was worse than the last, making her want to curl into a ball and cry, scream aloud, or knock out a stranger.

Please . . .

Janus closed her eyes, praying silently to herself.

Let me get the bottom of this. I'll go back to the Inquisitor's Office; I'll get help. Just please let me find Oscar first.

Jittery muscles made her rapid breathing rattle in her throat, as a panic attack began to consume her thoughts. Putting her hands on her diaphragm, she inhaled deeply and slowly for a few moments to regain her composure, remembering the Inquisitor's words from her sessions as a teenager.

"You're not in danger right now. There's no need to worry. Your mind is reacting to a past event; you do not need to fuel the experience with further thinking."

She opened her eyes, visualising her stress melting away like candle wax as she exhaled to regain her composure.

As she began moving forward, Janus focused on the duty she came here to prepare for. She would have to make some challenging decisions about her loadout; Janus didn't want to be weighed down with too much equipment, so selecting lighter variants would be necessary. There was a lot to lose if she made a mistake up there, and she'd always felt more confident in her natural mobility compared to her accuracy and tactics. Despite her own personal health, she would be putting her mother's company at considerable risk if she was discovered or killed. Adalia Scitilliant's daughter caught as a terrorist would be one thing, but if the world found out that her equipment was supplied by the company, things wouldn't end well for either of them.

She'd had one of her old STARCOV contacts get in touch with the contractors who worked on the renovations of the building site. For a considerable fee, they were willing to dispense information that'd make the duty manageable, thankfully money wasn't a problem for Janus. A soundproof energy shield had been installed to keep out the harsh weather of the Blue King Mountains, masking the hangar from the outside world with a camouflaged exterior. Janus would have to take it down before she could enter; if the barrier came down, the noise of the blizzard would help mask her presence. Looking at the weather reports for the day of the operation, the blizzard would be raging, suiting her nefarious needs perfectly.

Janus had no clue who these Onyx Soldiers were affiliated with, but she assumed it was a private company. The only person who could fund such an operation—at least in this city—was a councillor. The implications were dire, which would've no doubt been plaguing Grey's already burdened mind.

No wonder Ducard called me into this. I couldn't think of anyone else who'd be willing to help them.

Stepping around the racks of equipment, Janus felt like she was walking through a furniture store. There were thousands of pieces displayed on stands and glass cabinets. The distinct aroma of polish and oil seemed stronger in some parts of the showroom, the scent reminding her of the gunsmith lockup at STARCOV headquarters.

I do miss that smell. I spent days at a time inside that lockup working on my weapons . . .

As she reminisced, she stumbled into the apparel and protection section of the showroom. The coordinates that Ducard had provided pointed to one of the more towering mountains in the region, so a thermal suit would be mandatory to keep her alive.

Standing before a display of suits arranged in the shape of an arrowhead, she inspected them carefully. At the apex of the exhibition was a bland looking bodysuit, but on either side were coloured, environment-specific variants. There were five models available: standard, snow, shadow, forest, and ocean. She read the description of each one carefully, feeling butterflies in her stomach as her spine began to tingle with excitement.

Stealth, Assault & Breaching series.

The weave is bound together using the patented Rutinov micro-plating. This advanced armoured system allows the wearer to manoeuvre quickly while still providing robust protection against most man-made threats. Ideal for the adventurer or special duty operations, the S.A.B. suit is highly versatile, suitable for a wide range of environments. Using state of the art sensors, the suit can adjust the gradient of the fabric to better conform to the environment, and can even warm or cool the user depending on the weather conditions.

Janus grinned like a fool until she read the addendum at the bottom.

Just as you'd expect, however, the ever-present flaws in Rutinov plating are more abundant here. The material is incredibly rare and ludicrously expensive and is very susceptible to sustained exposure to fire. The heat generated from environmental factors are manageable, but this suit will not handle manmade heat or explosive weaponry.

She sighed, nodding her head as she finally understood why the suit was sitting here in the showroom. A universal suit that could adjust to any spectrum would be far too expensive, and you'd be ruling out a large portion of operations due to its flaws.

For what she needed it for, however, the suit would be perfect.

Don't get set on fire or blown up. Sounds easy enough . . .

She clutched the snow variant and stuffed it inside her duffel bag.

When it came to guns, Janus had only one preference, the ST-31s. It was one of the older Scitilliant models, but she preferred the reloading mechanisms and the fast chambering of the rounds compared to the larger calibre models. The newer models tried to fix something that was already perfected in her opinion.

She still needed to repair her own ST-31s, thanks in no small part to the augur who jammed his oversized blade into it. So on the way over to the firearms, she nabbed two models similar to her own, and a handful of bullets and magazines from the displays.

Better to have spare ammo, just in case.

Mentally going over her list, Janus nodded to herself as she moved to the next section.

Before she'd breach the facility, Janus would need an electronics jammer to black out the site when she entered, and a rifle to take down targets from range. When it came to the people who were inside the facility and the equipment they were carrying, she was completely blind. There could be one person, or fifty; no one knew who or what was going on inside that place.

Either way, you're going to have to get your hands dirty . . .

Once the electronics were destroyed, she could move around the facility without worrying about surveillance systems interfering. Thankfully, the S.A.B. suit covered all but her eyes, providing some anonymity when she wore it.

Wandering down the path, Janus spotted the vests and ballistic protection area of the exhibit. She considered taking something to slip over the top of the suit, but it would only slow her down. The suit would protect her from small arms fire, knives, and blunt objects, so Janus only had to worry about high powered weaponry. Looking around the show floor exhibits, she failed to find any climbing gear.

If there's none here, I'll have to pick some up on the way home.

She saw many technologies presented elegantly during her wandering. Energy shields, mechanical limbs, vehicles, there was far too much to see in one day alone. As incredible as it was spending time here, Janus knew she had to leave soon, although she couldn't finish up until she found one last thing.

Where are you . . . ? I hope they still have it . . . !

The rifle she was looking for was never put into mass production; in fact, it had been considered inhumane by the council. The only one they'd ever managed to produce outside of this place was the non-lethal variant, although she couldn't imagine who would want to purchase a weapon that didn't kill.

If your goal isn't to kill your target, then stay away from firearms.

She chortled.

Can't imagine who would want a non-lethal gun . . .

Assuming that one could move past the moral implications of using the rifle, it was incredibly beneficial for stealth operations. It fired slugs filled with a specialised pathogen that drained the body of specific organic chemicals, which were responsible for muscle and nerve control. The end result sent the human body into a rigor mortis like effect within a few seconds of the chemical cocktail entering the bloodstream. It was a horrible way to die, but it was also a quiet way to eliminate a threat, making it useful for insurgents to remain undetected.

Janus was horrified at what the rounds did to people when she'd initially heard about it, but it had stuck in her mind ever since. Such practicality could not be ignored, and considering this would be a one-person duty, every little advantage could be the difference between failure and success.

On the way to the rifle section, she found the "Disruption and Detection" area.

Among the first exhibits she came across, Janus found a rifle with a contraption that bolted around the user's shoulder. It was long, white, and had a large barrel that protruded from the core. Next to the weapon on a slab of white foam were many different kinds of projectiles. The EMP rounds were reasonably small compared to the other ones, with the dull red fluid swishing around inside as she handled it curiously.

This'll do the trick!

Slipping between the exhibit, Janus opened one of the white containers and took one of the rifles from the crate, along with a handful of the EMP rounds. The EMP rounds would overload mechanical and computer systems by shorting out the circuitry of anything connected to the target. Judging by the brace that clamped over the shoulder, launching the rounds would give her one hell of a jolt. As she loaded the equipment into her backpack, she lifted it up and down for a few moments, considering the weight of each item.

The bad is already quite heavy . . .

I might need to dump the EMP launcher before I leave the transport . . .

It would be risky not to take it inside the hangar, but if she were going to be doing any sort of climbing, it would be advantageous to leave it behind once she used it. She rubbed her hands together as she moved along the wooden path, stopping in her tracks before the Surge Rifle.

So this is it . . .

It was an awe-inspiring piece of design. She picked it up and held the platform in her hands, inspecting it with grave respect.

This is lighter than the one I remember . . .

Janus shouldered the rifle and looked down the sight. The battery seemed to be dead, so she couldn't see the intended magnification and crosshair inside of the scope. They'd added a soft foam layer to the operator's end of the rangefinder, allowing the wielder to keep their eye on it without feeling the cold metal against their face. The bolt was on the right-hand side, just as she'd remembered. Janus pulled it back and loaded one of the slugs into the weapon before pushing it back into position. As expected, the mechanisms were new, so they struggled to load the round smoothly.

Need to oil this up before I use it.

She picked up the shoulder strap that was in a little container next to it before quickly dismantling the rifle, slipping the individual components into her bag.

It's an almost inhumane weapon to use. But I have no choice.

Janus began walking back through the exhibits, content with her choice of equipment.

Here's hoping there aren't any more surprises waiting for me in the mountains . . .

Judging on her luck, she doubted that very much.

⌘

15: CARDINAL POINT

⌘

Their destination was close now.

Grey could see the light shining through the mouth of the Mortaroy Tunnel exit, growing brighter and brighter as they approached, forcing him to detach the plastic sun blocker from the roof and position it to shield his tired eyes.

Enduring the slow journey through the tunnel had pushed him beyond fatigue. However, he hadn't checked on the rest of the team in a while due to being lost in his own thoughts. As he turned around to face the three in the back of the cruiser, he observed them all resting quietly, exhausted from a long night. Their bodies bumped up and down without resistance as the vehicle rolled over the uneven road. The sensation of pins and needles dancing across his shoulder didn't go away completely, but overall, he felt better compared with the start of the night. The quiet drive through the tunnel had given his body time the time it needed to heal, it seemed.

Grey felt satisfied that no one had been injured during the journey as it would've required the team to separate. Lucky as they were, they all made it through Senper Square in one piece.

One day we won't be so lucky . . .

After the run-in with the Ashen Faith at the Ulysses Overpass, the rest of the journey was whisper-quiet, which they'd all been thankful for. His body pained him, his eyes were burning, and he felt lethargic, but he was still kicking.

Although he'd dismissed the idea of seeking out Aiden earlier, he had revisited the approach in his mind. It'd been a while since his duty dealing with Jone, and he had been itching for another midnight operation to deal with another scumbag who thought himself above the law. Perhaps Aiden would be next.

Aiden isn't augmented, so unless I'm the unluckiest person in the world, I doubt I'll run into any serious complications if I do it right.

The only downside would be the fallout of the Ashen Faith. Aiden had already done considerable harm to the community, and without him, his underlings could prove dangerous.

Revisit this later, no need to stress on it now.

Despite his overwhelming exhaustion, he'd refused to allow himself to drift off. He used the handle to wind down the window, allowing the chilling morning breeze to keep him uncomfortable yet awake. His nightmares were too intense to handle lately, and the feelings and images experienced during his restless sleep became burned into his psyche during the waking hours. It was as if his dreams could traumatise him, a strange affliction that he wasn't sure how to deal with.

Grey did whatever he could to keep from sleeping most nights, relegating his rest to only an hour here and there. It had become normality for his patterns of rest to be scattered.

A broken sleep schedule for a broken mind.

As the enforcement cruiser passed the tunnel exit, the road separated into three different paths. Directly ahead was a massive, twenty-story building where the route passed underneath an archway built into the ground level. During brighter times, the building served as the head office of the sector's administrative staff. The design was a rarity in Menilax, and as far as Grey could see, it hadn't been used anywhere else.

"Wow, would you look at that," said Lionel enthusiastically. "This place looks untouched!"

It was a sensible sentiment, a thought that crossed most minds when they witnessed Cardinal Point. The fact that it was so far from the rest of the sector made it difficult for people without a vehicle to make the journey, so most citizens had opted to stay away from the Point. Not to mention that the only route to this place was through Senper Square, which was enough of a reason to stay away.

Grey had big plans for the area, but he didn't want to get too far ahead of himself yet.

The Point, among other things, was a place where Enforcement could literally watch over Menilax. High walls around the point kept outsiders away, while the cliffs holding up the infrastructure made it dangerous for those willing to risk the climb. There were airports, Enforcement barracks, garages, and military warehouses around the area, all of them in decent shape. All that he needed was the resources and staff to get it back into working form.

Sornus turned the wheel gently to the left, making the turn as the rest of the convoy followed her route; leading them to Cardinal Point Jail.

As they drove quietly along the unbroken road, he scanned the graffiti painted across the fractured concrete walls. Many words had been painted across them, like "Ballistan," "Kristof," and "Thatch." The titles belonged to the gangsters that had claimed Cardinal Point after the war. There were also more vibrant words like "war," "vengeance," and "kill," along with plenty of other instances of hateful language.

Just another thing on the list for repair . . .

Once the war had come to its bloody end, the Ballistan crime family had dispatched a small group of loyalists to move in and claim the area for their own needs. Halfway across the world was their home city, Dragnus, where they were one of three significant families ruling among hundreds of smaller ones. They were quick to use the area for human trafficking, narcotics production, and prostitution, among other things.

The Ballistan presence in the sector had been snuffed out by Darius, who had prioritised clearing Cardinal Point above other strike zones. It was all a part of his merciless crusade through the sector, and afterwards, Grey had left a few stalkers in the area to keep an eye on proceedings.

He'd felt guilty about how brutal Darius had executed them all; another thing in a long list of deeds that plagued his mind, but thankfully in this instance, it was now mostly quiet around the Point, with the rare exception of a few stragglers visiting the area. Grey and his team had been quick on the scene to recover anything useful after Darius's handiwork, pooling the collected goods and spreading them out across the sector.

"We're here," stated Sornus.

As the convoy stopped in front of the construction site, Grey turned around to check on the rest of the team. Each of them began stretching and yawning, trying to shake off their fatigue. Grey quickly stepped out of the vehicle and moved towards the construction site.

Considering the sun had only started to rise, Grey assumed that most of the team stationed here would still be asleep. The foreman and the head of security here were up at least, both of them turning to greet him as he approached. Karen, sporting a red safety hat and high visibility overalls, looked to be in good spirits. While Quen had his arms casually draped over his rifle, smiling at Grey as he approached.

"Thought you were coming a few days ago?" he said with his lip curled into a grin.

Grey shook his hand firmly. "Ah hell, you know how it is. The political game ain't gonna play itself."

Quen's firm features cracked into a full smile as he playfully slapped Grey on the shoulder.

"You look like *ass!*" he said, "You takin' care o' yourself, old man?"

Grey shrugged. "Ain't got time to take a piss, let alone 'take care o' myself.'"

Quen shook his head, chuckling to himself before moving to greet the rest of the team.

"How are things goin' around here?" Grey asked, nodding to the construction site as he stepped over to Karen.

She raised an eyebrow at Grey before looking him up and down. She wore her wisdom and experience on her face; her fierce gaze looked strong enough to shatter anyone willing to have a staring contest with her. Her wispy white hair, short stature, and lean yet muscled physique gave her an elegant, knowledgeable vibe. Thanks to these reasons and more, Grey had chosen her to lead the construction projects he'd been organising throughout the sector.

He blinked slowly, growing impatient with her staring. "I am fine, darlin'," he said with a false smirk.

She clicked her tongue. "Keep tellin' yourself that Grey."

He chortled. "Don't you worry, I will. Who knows, maybe one day it'll actually be true."

They hugged each other warmly.

"Now, how are we lookin' here?" he asked.

She looked into his eyes for a few quiet moments, holding an amused look in her eyes as she said nothing for what seemed like an eternity. Any time a gaze lingered too long or a look began to turn into a stare, he couldn't help but feel as if they were looking right through him, seeing the scared and fractured man he really was hiding underneath the hardened exterior. During these moments, he had to put on a brave face and weather the storm of nerves.

She doesn't know . . . Just relax . . .

"We're okay," she finally said, allowing Grey to exhale slowly. "Although that sniper of yours is causing a bit of trouble with the rest of the team."

Holding her hands on her hips, she tilted her head to the roof of the construction site. Grey squinted as he followed her gaze, spotting the familiar silhouette of an old friend. Grey waved to her as a faint wisp of smoke wafted out from under her darkened hood.

She gestured to Grey obscenely. "Can't imagine why," he said with a chuckle. "She's great with people."

He grinned foolishly, and Karen rolled her eyes at him. "She handles that rifle pretty well, but she *ain't* good with people. Can't you—"

Grey raised a palm, nodding to her gently. "She's an old friend o' mine; you can trust her." He raised his voice so Bosh-wa could hear him from her perch. "Even though she can be a *pain in the ass* at the best o' times!"

He smiled widely as he stared up at her.

"Beyond all o' that," he said sternly, "she's the best sharpshooter I know. She'll keep you safe, even if you don't get along with her."

Karen sighed, staring at Grey for a few moments before shrugging. "It's your show."

Grey nodded.

Agreeing to disagree is better than an outright disagreement . . .

"I'm glad you decided to show that handsome mug of yours, at any rate," said Karen.

"Gotta make an appearance every now and then, keep you on your toes." He smiled. "So tell me, how are things here?"

"We've been pretty desperate for food, but overall, we're managing. Can't say the progress is as smooth as I'd like it to be, but I know there's not much to be done about that.

"So," she said, "What did you bring for us this time?"

Grey turned around and watched the team members mingling and discussing the trip.

Always warms my heart to see the team getting along . . .

He smiled. At that moment, all of his stresses and anxieties melted away. Watching life in its purest form, where people could be themselves and express their natural thoughts and feelings, made him feel privileged that he could be a part of it all. Being the facilitator was enough of a reward for him to sustain himself.

Grey discussed the new staff with Karen, pointing to each of them and sharing their names with her.

"Apart from the staff," he said, "I brought some old iron bars we found in some old precincts throughout the sector, along with some concrete to make sure they won't break on us. I'm hoping it'll be enough to fix up the cells."

"I like the way you think, Councillor. Now all we need is something to keep the augurs in check, and we can start policing this sector again."

"Speaking of augurs," said Grey, "how are the Seekers going up here?"

Karen smiled warmly.

"You know what, those people are some of the kindest people I've ever had the pleasure of talking to. Admittedly, they can be quite scary at first, but beyond that, they're a real asset to the team here."

Grey smiled broadly. "That's great news, darlin'."

And here I was worried they wouldn't play nice.

⌘

16: SERENN

⌘

Darius walked along the quiet morning streets of the Broken Sector.

Can't stay around here like this for too long . . .

He'd found mornings to be the safest time to wander about. Although he was more than capable of taking care of himself, he had to stay out of sight. His face was rather infamous, after all, especially within the boundaries of Menilax.

Most people were well out of sight by now. The first sun rays of the day beaming over the broken cityscape never revealed danger; during this time the undesirables retreated to their own little respites. Grey had been keeping the roads relatively clear of violence, with the help of the security team, of course. But it was always happening somewhere in the sector, and wouldn't be going away any time soon.

One day, things here will be the same as they used to be . . .

Darius turned onto Livingstone Street and found a person lying on the sidewalk.

Damn it . . . not another one . . .

Racing toward the body lying quietly on its side, Darius gently rolled the person over. It was a teenage girl.

She looks young. I'd say no older than fourteen . . .

Her youth was tainted by a freshly bruised eye, various cuts and scabs, and dirt smears over her face. She also smelled of rotten flesh, the stench growing strong as her mouth fell open.

Sighing to himself, Darius pressed two fingers over her freezing cold neck, and felt a heartbeat, although it was far too weak for a girl her age.

"I can't just leave you here . . ." he muttered.

Lifting her by the arms, Darius began to gently shake her. Her clothes rustled as he moved her body, causing a small, orange needle to slip out from her clothes. The inside of the needle was stained and from the plastic leaked the strong scent of chemicals and aniseed.

She's taken Mersi . . .

Searching either side of the road, Darius looked for a secure house or a halfway habitable space to leave her. Hefting the light young woman over his shoulder, he walked along the sidewalk scanning the dilapidated buildings. After a few minutes, Darius discovered a house that looked safe enough, although it appeared as though the second floor had been completely decimated. Stepping inside the open doorway without hesitation, Darius began listening for any signs of life within the walls.

In front of him rose the shattered stairwell, leading to what used to be the second floor. He could see a hallway ahead, which seemed relatively intact, apart from the slivers of morning sun passing through the gaps in the ceiling. To the left was the lounge room, but it was visible from the street, presenting a possible danger if someone noticed her lying alone.

I feel bad enough leaving her here unconscious, gotta make sure she's as safe as possible . . .

Walking down the hallway carefully, Darius stumbled into what used to be a kitchen, surprised to see it completely filled to the brim with people, all of whom were sleeping soundly. The aniseed smell was thick here, and upon scanning the room he found packets of Mersi littered across the kitchen bench, along with some crusty food packaging, cigarette butts, and empty bottles.

Seems like this part of the sector is filled with scenes like this . . .

Darius turned away and walked back onto the street.

Can't leave her here . . .

Walking up the quiet road with the young woman still over his shoulder, Darius eventually managed to find an old barber shop a few doors up. Thankfully, it was empty, so he left her in the storeroom, wrapping her in a dirty old towel to shield her from the cold.

Hope you get yourself sorted out one day soon . . .

Before he left the storeroom, he found a stained piece of paper in one of the boxes. Finding a pen amidst the refuse, Darius began writing a message for the young woman.

If you're looking for treatment, head on over to the hospital in the south-eastern corner of the sector. The team will take good care of you.

Placing his initials on the slip of paper, Darius slipped it under the key to the storeroom as he stood over her, observing her quietly.

Maybe I should take her to the hospital myself. It's far too dangerous to—

Darius sighed, shaking his head.

You did your share of helping the community yesterday, and this morning even. It's time to take care of your own needs now. You can't save everyone, remember?

He watched her resting quietly for a few more moments, sickened at how vulnerable she was. Then, Darius left the old shop, closing the door behind him and praying that she'd be safe inside.

It seemed strange to him that he should be walking alone, at risk of being seen at any given moment. But he had to get out into the world, even if for a few hours when the occasion called for it. Darius grew stir crazy sitting on the sidelines for too long.

Eventually, after another few minutes walking along the quiet road, he made it to Serenn's home. Standing before the blackened, crusty lawn, his eyes traced the faded picket fence that girded the property. As it had many times before, his overactive mind rebuilt the home to what it must have looked like before the invasion.

The dark brown bricks that held the house up showed how old the house was, but it was still sturdy. Anything that still held up against the many years of desolation and war was a testament to those who built homes like these.

Stepping through the broken gate, his eyes regarded the familiar home as if it was his own.

Hell, I've been here enough in the last few years. Might as well be . . .

How Serenn managed to keep it maintained wasn't the question; it was how she kept those wishing to destroy it out of her property. It was a mystery he'd probably never get to the bottom of. Or perhaps, more likely, a problem he pushed to the back of his mind. Serenn hadn't spoken much of her past, but then again, neither did Darius.

Both of them preferred it that way.

As he walked along the cracked concrete path, he ducked his head under the overgrown tree trunk before ascending the old set of stairs and entering Serenn's home.

Moving under the handpainted white doorless arch, he saw that the floorboards had been polished recently, and in the middle of the ample, open space was a rusted metal step ladder extending up to the third floor.

Guess I don't need to jump up anymore.

His brown dress shoes clapped against the floor as he walked towards the ladder. Within a moment he was ascending, ignoring the creaking and scraping of the ladder as he gripped the handles cautiously. Darius felt his backpack slipping from his shoulder, so he paused his climb for a moment to fix it before resuming. Passing the second floor, which contained a dining area, a few bedrooms, and an entertainment area, he could see that Serenn had barely started renovating this floor. Pulling himself up over the top of the ladder and onto the third floor, he looked over to the right, finding a new, slightly faded rug sitting before a freshly polished wooden desk. The smell of lacquer filled the space up here. It was a lovely scent to pick up on, especially after witnessing the horrid stench of the Mersi-filled homes he'd stumbled upon earlier.

"Over here!" yelled Serenn from outside.

Darius smiled as he craned his neck to the right. She was standing on the balcony, dressed to kill and smiling from ear to ear, showing her perfect white teeth as she waved him over.

He absentmindedly rolled his tongue across his teeth, feeling them to be coated in plaque from going days without brushing.

Smooth . . .

"Hey there," he said as he strolled over, pulling his backpack around from his back.

"Hey, yourself," she said, raising an eyebrow. "Thought you'd left this city for good."

Darius tilted his head playfully. "Thought you could get rid of me that easily?"

She scoffed. "I'd hoped so!"

They both laughed heartily.

Slipping out a bottle of aged wine from Sashiryu City, he handed it to her with both hands.

Serenn's eyes flicked down to the bottle.

"My favourite," she said hungrily, receiving the bottle gracefully. "How'd you get your dirty little hands on this bad boy?"

Darius smiled. "I have my ways."

"Do you want one?" Serenn uncorked the bottle and began pouring it into a soot-stained glass.

He raised a hand, but as he began his protest, she poured one for him.

"Please," she said, "don't make me drink alone now."

He scoffed and lowered his hand. "I'd love one . . ."

"That's more like it!"

She turned around to sit on one of two plastic lawn chairs, both of which they'd hoisted to the third floor quite some time ago. Darius couldn't help but notice her attire, making his heart skip a beat as he slid onto the chair next to her.

Her long, pale legs poked out from a short, ocean-blue dress embroidered with a handful of gold butterflies and red flowers. There were no sleeves, allowing her slim, lean arms to glisten against the morning sun. Her shoulder-length black hair draped behind her ears, framing her beautiful, flawless features and blue eyes like a photograph. She looked into Darius' eyes as she sat down, although some of her features were now covered up, thanks to the unusually large collar of the dress. She'd worn similar outfits in the past, although he still couldn't put his finger on where he'd seen it before.

That smile . . .

Darius sighed wistfully.

It would've levelled me ten years ago . . . but now . . .

He thought about Ciril for a brief moment as his eyes sunk to the floor. He pictured her beautiful brown eyes, milk chocolate skin, and ruby red lips smiling at him.

Damn it.

He felt his hand begin to tremble as he rubbed at the scar across his face.

Ciril . . . I miss you so much . . .

"Are you all right?"

Darius was staring at the ground, and as she caught onto what he was doing, he snapped his gaze to meet hers, noticing the concern in her thin eyes.

"Yes. Sorry," said Darius, stretching out against the lawn chair. "Just have a lot on my mind is all . . ."

She scoffed. "You and me both . . ."

They didn't say much for the next few minutes as they quietly sipped the alcohol Serenn had served them. It was not an awkward silence as they'd spent a lot of time together over the years in the same conditions. Admittedly, Darius had not seen her since Grey had taken the spotlight, but he earnestly wanted to rekindle something with her.

Serenn rubbed her index finger along the scar on his face, causing him to flinch.

It's so obvious. I need to try to get rid of it one day . . .

He looked at her regretfully as she traced the red scar tissue, irritating it. He scratched at it after she pulled her hand away.

"What happened here?" she asked.

He made a thin smile.

"Happened a few years ago . . ."

She nodded, pursing her lips as her eyes searched his face for an answer.

"I thought you could heal your wounds . . ." she said matter-of-factly.

He nodded with a fake smirk.

"Then, why hasn't it healed?" Her hand reached out to touch it again, causing Darius to gently grasp her dainty fingers and delicately push them away.

"I'm sorry . . ." he said, "It's a sensitive subject . . ."

"Say no more," she said, placing her hand on her leg as she nodded.

Serenn leant back in her chair, reaching down below to pick up a packet of cigarettes. "You don't smoke, do you?"

He shrugged. "I have been lately . . ."

Serenn sipped her wine earnestly before taking two cigarettes from the packet, handing Darius one before lighting them both. Darius leant back in his chair, smoking like he'd been doing it all his life.

She clicked her tongue at him, causing him to look at her with a slight grin on his lips.

"What . . . ?" he asked with a smirk.

Serenn hid a knowing smile. "Judging on the way you're sucking down that herb, I think it's beyond smoking 'lately' . . ."

He chuckled. "Observant, as ever."

"You can be honest with me, Darius. Are you sure you're all right?" she asked with compassion lining her tone.

Darius sighed, looking to her quietly for a few moments. "No," he said finally. "But what else is new."

Serenn chose not to reply straight away, allowing his mind to gestate on his problems for a minute or so as he began to form something, anything to give her confirmation that wouldn't give away too much.

"I feel as though this world doesn't need me anymore . . ."

Sitting up and putting her glass down on the chipped pavement of the balcony, she stared at him sternly. "Don't say things that like."

He closed his eyes and shook his head. "Don't get me wrong, I'm not saying that I . . . want to die, or anything." Darius looked into her concerned eyes. "But I feel as though my time is running out, you know? Grey's proven that I'm not needed."

Darius had been forthcoming about his situation, explaining everything to her in detail during their previous visits, which made Serenn one of a handful of people who knew what was going on behind the scenes.

"Have you thought about taking a break?" she asked. "Maybe you've been spending too much time—"

"No," said Darius dismissively. "It's not that . . ."

The ash of the cigarette began to grow long.

"I feel as though I'm losing myself here, you know? If I keep walking around like this, one day, it's going to come back and bite me, but I can't keep hiding away not showing myself at all. The last thing I want is to jeopardise the role too. Seems I can't win either way."

Serenn nodded, processing his words carefully. "Sounds like you need a break, but, well . . ."

Darius felt a bolt of pain pass through his neck. Moving his head back, he rolled his neck around hoping to release the knot building up in his tense and stressed muscles.

"When was the last time you got laid?" she asked as she sipped her drink with a smirk.

The tension in his body released as he laughed genuinely and wholeheartedly.

"What!?" He was incredulous, shaking his head.

"Serious question," she said with a cheeky smile. "Last time you got your rocks off, hit me."

He laughed, blushing nervously. "Since Ciril, you know . . . I haven't exactly . . ."

"How long has that been now?" she asked, pouring herself another drink.

Darius went to smoke his cigarette, only to notice that it'd gone out. He gestured to her lighter, which she picked up in her hand. It was chrome and had an indentation of a butterfly on it. She flipped the lid off and sparked it.

"Not long enough where I'm thinking about . . . well, *that* . . ."

She nodded. "I understand."

"How about you?" asked Darius, sipping his wine.

She eyed him curiously. "Do you really want to know?"

He shrugged. "Don't see why not, I don't have any hard feelings."

"I've been seeing someone," she said with a smile. "Nothing too serious, but it meets my needs. Daltan's out on his own now," said Serenn, "so I have a bit more time to myself."

Darius looked over to Serenn, observing her quietly.

I wonder how different my life would be if we stayed together. I wasn't ready to be a father, a partner to you, let alone walking away from the Kindred. Never thought that fling of ours would lead to a child either; Pioneers I was naïve back then . . .

"Speaking of Daltan," said Darius, "how is he?"

She eyed him from the corner of her eye. "He's good. I got him working with me now, although he's got a sliver of craziness that's hard to reign in sometimes. I think he gets that from your side . . ."

Darius nodded with a hint of concern in the corner of his smile. "Seems a little young for that line of work . . ."

She tilted her head mockingly. "I think we both started out younger than him."

Darius smoked his cigarette, enjoying the familiar, tingling sensation that buzzed around his skin as he exhaled the smoke.

Hard to argue with that . . .

"Does he ask about me?" probed Darius gently.

"No. But then again, as far as he's concerned, you're dead." She replied, sipping her wine liberally.

Oh.

⌘

17: MARKETING

⌘

Grey despised paperwork.

Despite copious amounts of time going through pages, documents, and binders, he still struggled to flip through them consistently. His mind nagged at him incessantly, convincing him that he wasn't skilled enough for this line of work. He could only force himself to sit and endure a certain amount before he needed some time to breathe, so he suffered through as much as he could before venturing out into the sector. There would always be work to do, but this wasn't a sprint.

It's a marathon. A boring, pen and paper marathon . . .

After waking up from another surgery in the early morning, Grey had felt like a new man, and as he walked through the sector with the warm afternoon sun on his face, he felt content. The enhanced healing procedure ensured he was in and out quickly, which was good for him and the staff. The hospital had come such a long way from the sad state it had once been, and for once in his life, he finally felt as though things were really coming together for him.

Seeing the team work together yesterday on the construction made it all worthwhile . . .

The hustle and bustle of the Kensir Square markets became more prominent the closer he got, the noise pushing the last remnants of loneliness aside as he focused on what he needed to purchase.

Now was generally the quietest time to visit, but in terms of product, it was the worst time. Most of the stalls would've sold out by now.

The freezing wind and the warmth of the sun seemed to cancel each other out, making the day practically perfect for wandering outside. With plenty of streets and buildings surrounding Kensir Square, the landmark certainly had a specific personality to it. It was by far the largest open space in the sector, so it made sense that the marketplace made its roots here.

Being over five hundred meters long and seven hundred meters wide, the square was easily the busiest place in the sector. Surrounded by the square were dilapidated buildings where shops and business used to be. The buildings that remained were still relatively intact, making them useful for the folks that ran the marketplace, who used such spaces to store their goods and sleep close to the stalls that kept them alive.

As he reached the end of Ard Street, he came between two mighty buildings. Once the headquarters of Illian Financial, the bank had been unable to sustain itself once the riots had forced the staff to leave. The Broken Sector missed the presence of a bank, along with many other services, but they'd managed without so far. Every sector within Menilax used the Minial as their currency, but the trading value in the Broken Sector was a lot lower. Most citizens used coins, with the smaller denominations of notes being rare, and the higher value notes practically unused and unseen.

As he moved briskly between the buildings, rows of individual stalls stretched out before him, each one different from the last. Some were made of bricks and tin, others from tarps and steel, while some shopkeepers had simply set up a tent to house their wares. Security personnel patrolled the rows vigilantly while citizens wearily wandered around haggling, discussing, and commuting with their goods.

All right then, what do I need to get . . .

Grey had left everything to the last minute, as usual. He had to get food, soap, coffee, writing materials, and some meat for the wolf – a senior animal that would stop by on occasion for food and water.

It's been a while since she's been around. Hope you're okay girl . . .

He had never entertained the idea of a pet before, but the wolf had been following him around for many years now and he didn't have the heart to send it away.

All things considered, It would be a heavy load to bring back to the house, but his augmentation would help him get it all home. He could've used one of the vehicles or asked the team to help him carry it all back, but he enjoyed the time spent here so much that he preferred to go alone. It was a pure joy to be within the community, and he didn't want to spend the time discussing politics, giving orders, or detailing his future plans.

Can't thank these people enough for believing in me. The courage it takes to set up a stall . . . to tend to it every day . . . They're risking their lives every day by coming here. I hope that one day they'll be completely free from risk for the little things.

Grey had placed considerable resources here to ensure people had a sense of normality. Perhaps one day, the sector's economy would return to what it was before the war; Grey knew that the marketplace was the most crucial part of the economy, so it was tremendously important that it remained stable and secure.

"Councillor!" said an older man's voice behind Grey.

As he turned around, he smiled at the presence of Cameran Senpo. The senior man was once a general in the Pioneer's Tactical Response Unit and had earned himself leagues of credibility during his time in the service. Now, Cam spent his golden years running a stall selling building tools, convinced that construction was the way forward for the sector.

"Cameran," said Grey, extending his hand. "Always a pleasure."

The two men gripped each other's hands firmly.

Firm handshake.

"Got some new equipment this morning," said the old man. "Reckon you should swing by as you make your rounds?" Cameran winked at Grey. "You should see the new hammers I got. They have rubber grips on the handle, reinforced steel in the head, and they're lighter than ever. You should take a few; your construction crew'll love you!"

Grey smiled. "So business is good then?" he asked. "Have you had any more problems with Enforcement trying to get all o' this through the checkpoint?"

Cameran's reputation had only taken him so far when it came to the border security; however, with enough politicking, Grey had been able to secure some licenses for those wishing to import goods into the sector. Cameran had run into some trouble once he started importing knives and some more cumbersome tools, but thankfully, Grey had managed to get him clearance. The compromise involved imprinting goods with serial numbers in various places across the packaging and the item itself, and to ensure that proper records were kept. He'd understood the need for logging each purchase, so he'd happily obliged, working closely with auditors to ensure the products met the standards required.

"Not one!" he said cheerfully. "It's been great!"

Cameran chortled. "Well, we do have the occasional thug try and swindle me when I'm transporting goods to and fro, but my wits haven't left me yet!"

"Well, that's good to hear," said Grey. "I'll make sure I stop by in a little while; I'm sure we could use a few more hammers."

Grey patted the old man on the shoulder as he walked by.

"Pioneers, bless you, Greyson."

The afternoon sun lit up the stained pavement below. The scent of cooked meats, herbs, and cleaning products wafted around the square, although some parts unfortunately smelled of human waste. Most had come to terms with such unpleasant odours in the sector, especially when it came to the markets.

Pulling out a clump of plastic bags from his back pocket, Grey slipped one out from the bunch, stopping at a vegetable stall as he greeted the merchant warmly.

"Greetings, Councillor!" said the young woman. "These were all picked this morning, and you're just in time for our afternoon special; buy five items, get the sixth one free."

She gestured around to all of the baskets. However, at least half of them were empty.

"Good to know, might take you up on that," said Grey. "How's business?"

He sifted through a couple of the baskets, eyeing the products as he scanned the items that were left.

She smiled faintly. "Business is okay. What would you like?"

Grey took note of the half-hearted answer, collecting an assortment of vegetables as he placed them gently in his bag, handing her a few old coins in exchange for the goods.

"Thanks, darlin'," said Grey. "I haven't seen you around here before. What's your name?"

She smiled with her teeth showing a few gaps, sad to see at such a young age.

"My name's Jesika," she replied. "My dad usually runs things here. But he's being treated at the hospital, so I'm minding the store for him."

Her half-sincere smile faded entirely as the words spilled out.

"Is that right?" said Grey, rubbing his scar. "Is everything okay?"

She began to nod but adjusted it to a worried shrug.

"He was mugged leaving the square a few nights ago . . . He was pretty banged up, but he's okay now. Thank you so much for keeping the hospital running, Grey. I don't know what I would've done if he didn't make it . . ."

"Well," said Grey, "I'm glad it's nothing too serious. I'll make sure I check in on him next time I'm there. What's your old man's name?"

"Brice," She replied.

"Don't you worry, darlin'," said Grey. "We'll take good care of him."

Grey flagged Kara, one of the security team who just so happened to be wandering down the aisle. "I'm going to have Kara here give you an escort home over the next week or so, at least until your old man makes it back."

The young lady nodded happily, scrunching her face as she tried not to cry. "Thank you . . . so much," she said, smiling.

He nodded politely before patting Kara on the shoulder. "Any problems today?" he asked quickly as they walked away from the stall.

"Not at all," she said with a smile. "Pretty quiet one."

Kara was in her mid-thirties and had yellowish skin, blue eyes, and a welcoming smile. She didn't seem to let the reality of the sector into her heart, always staying relaxed and friendly.

That's why you're here, Kara. You have a warmth that people crowd around, need people uplifted when they come to the markets.

"Feel free to get a few of the team together if you're looking for some extra backup to escort Jesika, doesn't hurt to be careful," said Grey as he continued along the aisle. "Thanks, Kara."

"Anytime, Grey."

The aisle he'd chosen seemed to be mostly foodstuffs, so he'd have to check out a few more aisles to purchase the other products on his list. As a general rule, he always made an effort to visit the newer stalls in the market. People seemed to appreciate his presence there, at least most people did.

He came across such a stall which had a weary-looking man in his mid-thirties sitting behind a desk trying not to drift off. The esky containing the meat had half-melted ice, which was protected by the tent he'd set up to keep it out of the sun. There were only a few sausages left at this stage, which would be excellent for his dinner that night.

"Hey, there," said Grey, extending his hand to the man.

He jolted awake, standing abruptly as he held up both hands. "Please excuse me, sir, but my hands are not sanitary," he said. "I've been handling raw meat all day, you see, so grasping your rather masculine hand would not be very pleasant for you." The man chuckled as he wiped his greasy hands over his apron. "What can I get for you, on this fine, Sector Eight afternoon?"

Grey smiled at the question. There wasn't much in the way of choice. *Sausages . . . Or Sausages . . .*

"I'll take the rest o' those snags," he said. "You think they'll keep for a few more hours?"

He raised his hand before grabbing a green bag from under the table he'd been sitting behind. "They will with one of these; that is certain!"

The man scooped some ice into the bag before slipping the meat inside.

"Don't suppose you've got any leftovers for pets?" asked Grey with his eyebrow raised.

The man nodded promptly. "Absolutely, sir, for what kind of animal?"

"A wolf, a big one."

He pursed his lips, nodding to him with respect, "a wolf is a difficult creature to tame, you must have a commanding constitution to have it stick around, good sir."

Yanking a large brown sack out from the counter, which appeared to be filled with offcuts and other meat products, the merchant grasped it firmly by the top.

"The name's Grey, by the way," he said as the man handed him the bag.

"It's a pleasure to make your acquaintance, sir; my name is Christopher. My sincere apologies about the current selection; typically, we sell out of our best products early in the morning."

He smirked, whispering in Grey's ear mockingly. "Might I suggest you stop by a little earlier next time?"

Shrugging casually, Grey replied "My schedule's a little all over the place, but I'll try."

"Please do so," Said Christopher. "Our steaks, although quite thin, will blow your mind, sir. And let me tell you, a mind-blowing steak in our sector is quite a rarity."

Grey held back a laugh. The man was a natural born salesman.

Damn, I want one of those steaks now.

"That'll be thirty-seven Minials, Grey."

Grey handed him a handful of coins.

"You take care of yourself, Christopher," said Grey.

"May the Pioneers watch over you, Grey. Until next time!"

Hefting the wolf food over his shoulder, Grey continued down the aisle.

With his other hand, he jiggled the two bags with a smirk.

Hopefully, someone's at the pub to cook these . . .

During the early stages of his career, he felt incredibly anxious about living in the Broken Sector. After the chaos that Darius wrought, he'd tried to stay at the house on his own, but he couldn't stay inside for too long without losing his mind. It felt cursed, although he wasn't sure if it was the loneliness, or the house itself that made his anxiety flare beyond control.

Too much has happened there . . . I really should find somewhere else to live . . .

Grey continued to weave among the stalls, waving to a few friendly faces along the way, casually strolling through the square and taking in every detail with a smile of contentment. After a few minutes he came across an empty fruit stall which belonged to Preston Lars.

Must've gone to the toilet . . .

Plucking out a stained bronze coin, Grey placed it behind the counter before snatching a handful of berries from the stall, which were slightly wrinkled from being in the sun all day. Quickly moving on, he found that he'd finally reached the end of the aisle.

As he turned down the next row of stalls, he came across Tracey Demlen's store. A senior woman in a wheelchair, Tracey ran a smoking store in the marketplace. Unfortunately for her competitors, she was the only one who sold his favourite brand, making her the sole recipient of his coin. Grey's eyes scanned across the product line behind the wooden stall, spotting at least twenty other brands, all attached by a string from a steel pole running along the roof. He glanced at the bronze and blue packet hanging by a rope as he approached.

That's Grey's brand, all right . . .

"Grey!" she said with a cheer, rolling around from behind the stall. She hailed him over with both arms demanding a hug, giggling to herself with a croaky, tired laugh.

Grey chuckled as he walked behind her desk, leaning down to return the cuddle. She squeezed him weakly as her body trembled, which wasn't out of the ordinary considering her age.

"How you doin', Trace?" he asked as he stood back up, leaning on the stall casually.

"Same shit, different day," she said laughing.

Grey pursed his lips. "Ain't nothin' wrong with a good routine, darlin'." He flicked his head up towards the young boy who walked out from the back, his eyes fixated on a book with black binding.

"Mikey, how are ya?" he asked.

Without looking up from the page, Michael grunted as he took a seat in the corner.

If looks could kill, Tracey would've burned a hole right through the young bookworm's skull. As she raised a newspaper, about to whack him over the head, Grey raised his palm to her.

"Ain't no need for that," he said politely. "Leave the boy to his readin'."

She mockingly whiffed the air around her with the newspaper. "Bah!" she moaned. "Kids these days!"

Tracey leant under the desk, groaning and muttering curses as she pulled herself in with the wheelchair, which creaked under the change in weight.

"Got your goods right here," she said, bringing a box up on the desk. "And I got a couple more o' those metal lighters you're so fond of."

Grey opened the box, happy to find twenty packets of cigarettes inside. He held the package up to his nose, smelling it wistfully. With his eyes wide from excitement, Grey unwrapped one of them, slipping a fresh cigarette out and popping it in his mouth. The fresh scent of tobacco brought back a lot of memories, some good, and some not so good.

Wonder what you'd think about me smoking your brand . . .

Sealing his lips around the filter, he slapped his pockets as he searched for a lighter.

"Do you mind?" he said after a few moments, nodding to the cheap plastic lighters in the plastic contained behind the stall.

She squinted at him incredulously. "You've got three brand new lighters in that box!"

"Yeah, that's true," he said, pursing his lips. "But *those* are collector's items."

She chortled. "Give me one of your blues, would ya?" she asked. "These ones have been sittin' here for a few days now. I want me a fresh one!"

Grey nodded, slipping another out before handing it to her.

She reached over with a plastic lighter, sparking it with a wrinkled thumb as he held the front of the cigarette over the open flame, breathing in deeply as the smoke poured into his lungs. Holding his breath for a few moments, he closed his eyes, savouring the sensation of his first cigarette for the day. The cravings hadn't been so bad today, mostly because he'd kept busy.

Nothing quite like a copperhead . . .

"So when are we going to have electricity in this damn place? Do you know how much I miss my television?"

"It's on the agenda," said Grey, smoking leisurely. "But don't you worry, darlin'; we'll be back on the grid before you know it."

"Ha!" she said. "Typical answer from a politician!" she said with a dismissive gesture.

Grey reached out, touching the old woman on the shoulder. "You take care now."

She reached out and pinched his cheek. "You too, dear. I don't want to see any more cuts on that handsome face of yours, okay?"

Tracey gently slapped his cheek before smiling warmly at him.

Grey continued to smoke as he turned away from Tracey's stall, picking up the box and tucking it under his arm as he left. As he juggled the bags between his fingers, Grey realised that he had one more thing to collect before he could head to the pub.

Something to drink.

⌘

As the sun went down, Grey began pouring his first glass of Jake Walter's, a cheap yet high-proof bourbon that he'd quickly become accustomed to. Purchasing a couple of bottles from the market, Grey opted to keep them stashed at the bar. Storing them at the bar would remove the temptation to drink at home, which forced him to be sober during the times when he needed to focus on work.

He was planning to pour a bourbon for Artemis, but he'd insisted on drinking wine. Luckily, Grey kept a few bottles of his friend's favourite drinks at the bar, ready for them to be consumed at any time. Ducard and Artemis were the only friends who knew him before he'd chosen to change his life, so keeping a few bottles of their choice was the least he could do. He'd always felt incredibly welcome there, although he'd owed that to Kevin, the owner of Wolf's Blood Pub, more than anyone.

'We're always open to you and your friends, Grey.'

He'd handed the vegetables and sausages he'd bought to Kevin, who gave them to his son Liam. The boy quickly absconded to the kitchen to start cooking for Grey and Artemis, the savoury scents filling the room making his mouth water and his stomach grumble.

"Quiet night tonight?" said Artemis as he came out of the bathroom. "Seems quite, unseasonable . . ."

Grey turned around in his seat to inspect the room; there were only two patrons at the moment apart from them. He shrugged, turning to Artemis as he took a seat. "Can't really blame them for not feeling safe here anymore."

Artemis nodded as he joined Grey at the table and sipped his wine, swishing it around his mouth before asking about the Onyx Soldiers.

"What is the latest development on those soldiers, if I may ask?" asked Artemis.

Leaning over the table, he extended his palm helplessly. "Ducard told me he's looking into it."

"I suppose he does have the contacts to reach out to," Said Artemis. "He is off-world though, is he not?"

"Yeah," said Grey. "He told me that he had it in hand, so who knows . . ." He shrugged before continuing. "Anyway, what matters is what I tell the council. I've prepared a detailed report. If I can help it, I'd rather not shut down the program completely. In the right hands, those suits could help us enforce the law, get some regular people driving them, you know?"

Artemis agreed.

Taking a sip of his wine, Artemis took out a stack of folded paper from his pocket before placing it neatly on the worn table.

"I have a lead on one of our 'friends,'" said Artemis, smiling with satisfaction. "He is located in Menilax, hiding in a rather precarious part of Sector Four . . ."

Sliding over the stapled report, Artemis continued. "Through a substantial amount of research, I have found a great deal of information on this particular Pioneer. I have taken the liberty of summarising the important parts for you on page one."

Grey leaned in as he picked up the stack of paper.

"Perhaps with some deliberation, we'll be able to—"

"Do you want to go tonight?" interrupted Grey with a smirk.

Artemis shook his head in surprise, gesturing to the report with a frustrated smile. "Do you . . . not want to read it first?"

⌘

18: GLACIER

⌘

Flecks of snow permeated the violent winds, whipping against the aircraft as they ascended through the peaks and valleys of the Blue King mountains. Observing the blinding snow from the cabin of the aircraft, Janus felt confident, now more than ever.

She was in her element. Her plan was going to work.

Such extreme weather was nothing out of the ordinary for this part of the world. It had plagued the mountains so frequently, most people avoided them entirely as a result. With a lack of tourism and a small population focused around the base of the mountains, the peaks were left mostly to those brave enough to weather it all.

Such desolation attracted two parties: businesses looking for privacy and folk looking for extreme experiences. And with so many corporations seeking solitude in the modern era, it wasn't a surprise that opulent corporations fought for control over the space. This particular facility had changed hands a few times, meaning the blueprints she'd managed to get her hands on would've been out of date by now, especially with yearly renovations being all the rage in the corporate space. Specific locations hadn't been included in the documentation, so she'd be flying blinder than she would've preferred once she made it inside.

"Stop here," said Janus through her headset.

"I gotcha," replied Ducard.

The aircraft slowed, hovering in mid-air across from the hangar entrance.

Janus lifted the shallow, soft plastic goggles over her eyes as she handled the cold, steel handle of the cabin door. With a tight grip, she depressed the switch on the handle before using it to slide the door open. The low roar of the aircraft became consumed by the storm as the tempest swept through the cabin in a rush. Janus stood vigilantly as the storm swam around her, eyes staring boldly into the hazardous white before her. After meditating silently for a few quiet moments, she turned and moved to the rear of the aircraft, clutching the white rifle.

Using her right hand, she pushed the stock against her shoulder. The sensors on the brace activated, causing the memory foam to clamp over her arm, locking the rifle onto her body with a crisp snap. The warm padding was pleasant in contrast to the cold snap of the storm, possibly the last comfort she'd be privy to for some time as she returned to the precipice and took a knee.

With her mask already over her face, she pressed her goggles against the cold metal of the scope, squinting to find a suitable review angle. She centred the crosshair above the hangar entrance where the barrier was presently active. Janus held the weapon steady, and with her index finger, she gently squeezed the trigger, feeling the subtle spring giving way under her considerate movement. The slug fired with a whisper as it pearled out into the storm.

She lowered the weapon immediately, focusing on the hangar despite the low visibility. Within moments, the shimmering wall of energy dissipated, leaving her insurgency free and clear.

Janus sighed with relief before folding the weapon into its smaller form, slipping it into her backpack as she stood and barked into her radio. "The wall is down. Can you get me a little closer?"

"I'll try," said Ducard. "Although I can't get that much closer without anyone seeing us."

As she gripped the handle above her, the suit adjusted for the sudden change of temperature, warming her hand against the biting cold of the cabin handle.

"How's this?" said Ducard via her earpiece after a few moments of movement.

This is going to work . . . It has to . . .

"I can go lower if you want?" said Ducard.

Janus nodded to herself. "This is good, hold it here!"

Wasting no time, Janus turned away from the door and moved to the other side of the cabin, gently removing the spear gun from the brackets on the wall. She studied it for a brief moment before taking the safety bolt out from the gun, substituting it with a grapnel bolt kept in a metal bucket under the seat. Janus slid the bolt into the loading mechanism and unhooked the rope drum at the base before carrying it the edge of the cabin. Reaching down with the drum, Janus hooked it firmly to the pulley between the landing skids.

Don't look down.

Taking some quick breaths, Janus stood up and held the spear gun against her shoulder. The cold metal stock cooled her skin for a brief moment before the thermal systems kicked in. She waited patiently for the trembling in her hand to dissipate before placing the metal sights over her eye.

The bolt soared through the storm as she depressed the trigger. The steel cable followed expediently behind as the wheel holding the fibres unspooled rapidly. When the spear pierced the mountain, she hooked the spear gun into the frame on the other side of the cabin and pressed the recall switch to remove any slack that was remaining in the cable length.

Janus reached down to pick up her backpack, slinging it over her shoulders before collecting the climbing gear next to the pack. Now that she was only a few moments away from beginning, her heart started thrashing in her chest, flooding her body with anxiety and doubt.

She took a deep breath.

You can do this; you've made the climb plenty of times before . . .

She put on the spiked gloves and boots that would let her grip the ice wall properly, the ritual allowing her body and mind to relax a little. Checking that they were secured tightly to her extremities, Janus reached above the door on the inside of the cabin, and snatched a steel pulley before attaching it to the cord. She squeezed both sides of the pulley, locking it in place with a satisfying click. From where she stood, it seemed like the cord vanished into a swirling wind of white fog as fierce shards of ice whipped passed like razorblades.

"I'll see you in an hour!" she said, barely able to hear her own words over the raging wind.

"Good luck!" said Ducard. "If those transports don't work, or you get into trouble, let me know!"

Janus held onto the handle of the pulley as she let herself fall underneath the aircraft. As she dangled from the cable, she felt herself roll down, slowly but surely gliding over to the open hangar.

The noise of the tempest grew dark and frightening as she zipped through the malicious winds, the safety of the aircraft cabin now a distant memory as she steeled herself for what lay ahead. One moment she was looking at a thick cloud of wind and snow, then the cliff face appeared in front of her instantly as she released her grip on the pulley running purely on instinct. Janus sailed through the air for a few meters, her heart refusing to beat as she clenched her jaw, roaring with adrenaline as she smashed her hands into the cliff face with all her strength. It gave her the grip she needed, albeit at the cost of knocking the wind from her chest.

Coming to rest, she placed her head against the mountainside, relieved but terrified.

I made it, thank the Pioneers . . .

Taking a few moments to catch her breath, she laughed despite herself.

Seriously need to stop saying that . . . Especially if I'm going to be killing one of them soon . . .

Janus climbed the mountain, carefully pushing into the cliffside with her feet and hands, seeking purchase before grasping firmly to lift herself to the next section.

Focus on the climb.

Her vision was hindered by the storm, so she had to rely on how the grip felt before committing to it. The thermal suit was the only thing keeping her from freezing to death, and it helped her ascend much quicker compared to the thick wool jackets and underclothing she'd normally wear for such a climb.

Janus couldn't help but dwell on the differences between duties performed under orders from STARCOV and running private ones for her own purposes. The stark contrast was her focus, as when she was in the unit, it was easy to remain professional at all times. The training and mental conditioning that STARCOV administered prevented an operator from thinking; in time, everything had become habit, ingrained in one's instincts.

It wasn't an overnight process, however. If an operator were found to be doing something irrelevant to their work, that person would be reprimanded immediately. The punishment was harsh, even by military standards, so avoiding said punishment had been the initial motivation to remain focused on the job at hand. Each STARCOV operator obeyed without question, relying entirely on their instincts to bring them through duties. Thinking was reserved for officers, after all.

Now that she was running duties outside of the realm of STARCOV, she found it challenging to keep her emotions in check. Medications were available that could assist her with rogue thoughts; in fact, some of the more anxious operators were known to take something to take the edge off.

No . . . my mind needs to be at its sharpest . . . I can't rely on substances to keep me focused. My alcohol abuse may have been partly responsible for my failure at the National Park.

Regardless of her fatal miscalculations, she couldn't help but ponder each moment of her failed duty to rescue Oscar. Thanks to Grey, however, a second chance was within her grasp, and more importantly, Janus had a purpose again. It was a purpose that had come at the best possible time in her life after weeks of feeling emotionally displaced, and if successful, might be the first step in restoring normality to her life again.

Once Janus reached the hangar, she stopped to catch her breath.

Sighing with relief, Janus pulled herself up, leaning on the edge of the hangar with her elbows. Glancing around the airport pensively, she found that the staff here was minimal, with a handful of soldiers scattered around the hangar.

It would've been at least eighteen minutes since she took down the barrier. If all went according to plan, the support staff would've been evacuated deeper into the facility.

Her first step was to calculate which targets could be neutralised safely while avoiding detection and potentially alarming the rest of the facility.

She considered strategies as she reached for the weapon strapped to her back. The suppressor that was bolted onto the front was redundant in the current circumstances. The roaring tempest that grasped the edges of the hangar would be a greater noise suppressant for now.

Climbing over the edge, Janus raised the Surge Rifle with both arms extended and moved quickly to a pillar near the wall on the left. Pushing her back against the cold metal, Janus shouldered the rifle.

Sliding the bolt of the rifle back allowed her to load a Surge round into the chamber. Pushing the lever forward sent the bullet into the barrel with a satisfying click, confirming that the weapon was now ready to fire.

Need to make this slug count, it's going to take a while to reload.

Janus lifted the rifle to her eye, staring down the sights and taking deep breaths as she scanned the forward area for a target.

The woman enjoying a cigarette in the corner opposite her was utterly isolated from the other two. She was resting her back against one of the many airships, cursing aloud at each attempt to re-light the cigarette between her fingers.

After a few moments of patiently lining the crosshair of the scope over the woman's neck, Janus pressed the trigger. The slug soared across the hangar and passed through the open cabin of a helicopter before striking her throat. The woman raised her hand to the impact zone as she felt the hard plastic slug pumping its payload into her body, but it was already too late.

One down . . .

Janus moved her head away from the rifle as she observed the other two guards. They were near the large hallway on the far left-hand corner of the hangar having a conversation.

Need to wait until they look away.

After forty-six seconds, she found her moment as they turned around to look down the hallway they were guarding. She sprinted across the open space with ferocity, covering the distance between her position and the nearby gunship in less than three seconds, climbing up the rear engine and taking position on the top. She took one last look at the woman she'd shot with the Surge round. The body was frozen in place, her hand still resting over the slug embedded in her neck. Enough time had elapsed that the woman would've been dead by now.

She could see an engineer focused intently on the wall monitor next to the hangar entrance. His face glowed against the warmth of the monitor, tapping away anxiously on the keys underneath it. Staring at him while she moved, Janus stowed her climbing equipment into her backpack with care as he was far too close to her position.

Janus reached around to her lower back, unbuckling her ST-31s with haste and bringing it to her shoulder.

Stock extended, safety off, sights up.

Taking aim down the sights, she trained the gun at the back of the engineer's head. As she went to squeeze the trigger, something stopped her.

Does this man really deserve to die . . . ?

She sighed with irritation. The operator within battled with her logic, something that wouldn't have happened during a STARCOV duty.

Is he even armed . . . ?

She shifted the weapon's sight down slightly to check his waist and pockets for the familiar bulges and shapes of firearms. Janus noticed as she scanned down his profile that the man was wearing a wedding ring as he pulled the loose beanie back down over his head.

Janus swallowed dryly, lowering the sight as the squinted at the man in yellow overalls.

Sighing, she slung the weapon back to its holster before revising her approach.

Janus took one last peek at the two behind her before she dropped back down to the floor.

As she landed, the barrier that she'd neutralised before leaving Ducard's aircraft came online, restoring the silence of the hangar as it blocked out the raging tempest beyond, reducint it to a dull roar.

Janus clenched her jaw as panic began flooding through her system.

"There," said the engineer, as he began to turn around.

Not like this!

She dashed towards him with outstretched arms as she wrapped her arm around his neck and began choking him with all her strength. She clenched her jaw as she lifted him off his feet, pulling her arm tightly into his neck to reduce the noise of the strangling, gurgling noises that spurted from the engineer.

"Hey, Vanial, are you all right?"

A man was approaching from the left.

Damn it, where did you come from!?

The engineer was a civilian, and not a very fit one, so he couldn't resist her strength despite his flacid flailing at her arm and face. Once he was unconscious, she let the body go and swung the Surge Rifle around to her arms.

"Van? Are you—"

It was a guard. His eyes became wide with shock as he saw Janus pointing a rifle his way.

She fired.

The round pierced his throat as he clutched it with both hands. Janus watched him move slowly, as if in slow motion, as his head reeled back from the sheer force of the impact. He brought his head forward and stared at her in horror as his neck muscles tightened and his face became bright red. Then he didn't move at all.

I'm sorry. I can't risk the chance of you alerting your friends . . .

He would be dead in a few minutes, but in this state, there would be no sound of a man falling to the ground, nor a weapon clattering loudly across the floor.

Janus slipped the rifle behind her as it hung around her back by the shoulder strap, allowing her to use both her hands to drag the engineer inside the nearby gunship. She decided to climb inside the cabin, and as she flopped the unconscious man over the pilot's seat, Janus peered through the rear window. She could see the two other armed guards through the scratched bulletproof panels; they still hadn't noticed anything.

Either my timing is perfect, or these two are clueless . . .

Janus hopped out from the cabin through the left and brought the Surge Rifle around once more. Lying down on her stomach and crawling underneath the helicopter, Janus trained her weapon on one of her two foes. The cold concrete floor made her suit heat up considerably, relaxing her muscles and tempering the unavoidable trembling in her arms.

She decided to wait until the two men were finished talking. During this time, she focused only on her breathing, taking deep, quiet breaths until her moment came. Completely absorbed in the present, Janus concentrated intently on the guard who began to walk down the large hallway behind them, which would be one of two paths that seemingly went deeper into the facility. The other guard moved closer to the hangar exit, near the pillar on the side of the barrier where she'd first taken cover. Janus fired a slug at the one closest to her.

As he began to freeze up, she dashed towards the corner of the hallway the other man had walked down. After a few minutes, she heard him call out to the statue which used to be his colleague. Footsteps boomed down the corridor in a panic sprint.

Human nature was an interesting concept.

After a career filled with wet work, assassination, insurgency, and studying people from the shadows, the natural tendencies of humanity began to form patterns, detectable to those who specialised in finding ways to neutralise resistance. A great deal of information could be ascertained from how a person reacted to the situation she'd placed this man in.

The fact that he walked towards his friend and didn't check his left side as he entered the hangar told her the man was not a soldier.

The evident voice crack as he called out his name told her that they were close.

And lastly, the fact that he had not raised his weapon, or called for backup, told her he was terrified.

Clenching her jaw, she raced over to him with tenacity.

Within two heartbeats, she was right behind him. She kicked the back of the man's knee and wrapped her arms over his neck, squeezing him tightly to enhance his fear.

He raised his hands immediately, dropping the weapon.

"Where are the labs?" She asked with a firm tone.

"Who . . . who are you . . . ?"

She pulled her arm into his throat, choking him for a few seconds as she asked the same question, albeit fiercer than before.

He choked in protest as he pathetically tried to pry her hands away.

"They're past . . . the white doors . . . !" he gurgled. "But you won't . . . get far . . ."

She released him and spun him around so he faced her.

Janus kicked him in the gut, hard.

"Why!?" He coughed and wheezed as he fell to his knees. "It won't make a difference if you kill me. The power's out . . . so you can't . . . open the doors. I can give you the code, if you let me live."

He gasped as he stared up at her with a scowl.

She glanced away from him, looking at the white door on the right-hand wall with her peripheral vision. The entryway to the laboratory looked to be sealed by an octagonal door with a keypad on the side.

"Are you lying to me?" she asked mirthlessly.

"No . . . I—" She booted him in the face, knocking him on his back as he wailed in pain.

"Enter the code on the keypad," Said Janus. "Or I'll kill you, slowly."

She hefted him up by his shoulders, launching him towards the octagonal door with an impatient push. Stumbling over to the door, the soldier nervously punched in the code.

2 . . . 9 . . . 7 . . . 6 . . . 3299 . . .

Janus repeated the combination in her mind as the soldier turned around, holding his broken nose as it bled freely over his face. The white doors clicked ajar slightly, revealing a white hallway that lead down and to the left with no other adjoining doors in between. Due to the low power state of the facility, however, they didn't seem to have opened the entire way.

"Open it up," she barked, bringing around her ST-31s.

He grumbled as he turned around and placed his hands on either side of the door. Prying them apart, he pushed each piece into the doorframe as they rested inside with an audible tick.

"You won't—"

She punched him in the jaw with the stock of her gun as he turned, knocking him out cold as he fell into the hallway. Janus stepped inside as she unhooked her backpack straps and swung the pack around, sitting and crouching over it. She hooked the Surge Rifle into the thick straps on the back as she took out a small torch from the front pouch.

Taking a nervous breath, Janus flicked it on before strapping it to the frame of the ST-31s.

Hard to believe this hallway is a part of the same building.

When comparing the hangar to the laboratory, the contrast was stark. The hangar was built with cement and steel, standard fare for a place where aircraft and supplies would be unloaded. The hallway Janus stood in now, however, was reflective white, and while the floor had scruffs and some scratches, the walls were almost entirely untouched. The perfection of it made her skin crawl; she'd never seen anything quite like it.

The complete silence of the hallway was suffocating her calm.

Janus stood quietly for a few moments, as a primal part of her mind demanded she flee. The urge was powerful, but Janus moved through the darkness nonetheless.

Her boots were manufactured to be silent, but she could still hear them scuffling along as she moved through the white hallway, slowly and deliberately. As she approached the end of the hall, she stopped moving. Snapping around with her ST-31s at the ready, she saw only the incapacitated man lying on the floor at the end of the hallway.

Something's wrong . . . I should leave . . .

She exhaled slowly, as she lowered the gun.

It's the nerves talking.

Breathing in deeply, she returned to her original path, stepping around the bend with her weapon shouldered. There were no signs of life on this new stretch of hallway, so she soldiered on, the light cutting through the thick, dust-filled darkness.

Reaching the end, she had two paths to choose. To her left stretched another hallway with multiple connecting halls and doors on either side.

Janus stepped down the right path. She could see multiple doors and entryways here too, but unlike the other hallway, each of them had been sealed like the entry door she'd come through. Stepping over to the first door, Janus pried it open with her fingers. As she slid it open slowly—gritting her teeth at the strength required—she poked her ST-31s through. It was a storeroom with cleaning supplies, linen, and other items of similar nature.

The second room was a bunk room, which would've housed at least twenty people. Beds and other furnishings were decorated with personal effects like photos, jewellery, and clothing racks. Not one soul was in this room either, although she checked each cubby to make sure. They were relatively small yet contained a single bed and a work desk, along with a bookshelf built into the wall.

Janus was glad that she didn't have to deal with anyone, but the whisperings of doubt and fear were starting to gain traction in her mind. She expected a trap, and the further she moved into the facility, the more her mind nurtured the idea.

Don't jump to conclusions; stay focused and keep searching . . .

She returned to the dormitory entrance, quickening her pace down the hallway.

Continuing her search, Janus stumbled across a kitchen, showers, and bathrooms, along with a few more supply rooms and dormitories.

It was a safe bet that her insurgency had gone unnoticed to the greater facility so far. But healthy scepticism went a long way, especially for solo operations. No one would be coming here to save her if she got into trouble, after all.

Janus decided to go back the way she came and take the other path. Taking the first hallway on her right, it soon opened up into a sizeable surgical assembly. It was overwhelming at how many instruments and tools were spread across the tables within the room, and as Janus walked inside, she felt an uncomfortable tickling gnaw at her spinal cord.

Despite her logic reminding her it was most likely nerves, Janus still ran her fingers long her back, as far as she could reach, to feel for anything that might actually be crawling on her skin.

Shaking her head free of the thought, she looked over the implements with the light from her weapon, the metallic coating eerily reflecting the beam with a starry glint. The only noise inside the room was her suit and equipment jostling as she scanned each section. There were blades, pliers, glove dispensers, and plastic sheeting, each laid out with perfect spacing.

Must be for wounded soldiers . . .

She clenched her jaw, unsettled.

Why would they take wounded soldiers to Blue King . . . It doesn't make sense . . .

Janus continued her search. She would have time to ponder the specifics later.

Moving briskly along the hallway, her search resulted in some similar finds. She came across another operating room with a similar layout to the one she'd inspected earlier. A storeroom and another dormitory were found and examined before stumbling across what she was here for.

It was a weapons testing area.

As she entered the room, she heard someone screaming behind her.

Janus, startled and fearful, twisted her body and scanned the hallway as her heart beat like a drum. There was no one there.

What the hell was that!?

She leant around the corners of the hallway searching for threats. Janus preferred not to navigate the path yet in case someone was waiting for her to do so.

Then, she heard it again, louder than before. The scream echoed through the hallway, bouncing around the room behind her, chilling her blood as it rattled around her ears.

I have to find out who that is; they could attract attention my way if I let them carry on . . .

Entering the adjacent hallway, Janus moved with purpose. As she approached the end of the hall, she entered a room which seemed almost empty, then she noticed the two-way mirror which she inspected carefully. There was a woman's face, held in place by a black suit of armour, her eyes darted around manically in their sockets. She pleaded into the void for help.

Pioneers . . . She doesn't have any arms . . . or legs . . .

Janus lowered her weapon as she swallowed dryly.

What do I do . . . ?

Part of her wanted to leave.

Part of her wanted to help.

Shit. I can't just leave this woman here like this . . .

Janus sprinted into the room next, ignoring her professional instincts.

The woman began sobbing as her eyes locked onto Janus.

"Pioneers, save me!" she screamed. "I thought I was the only person here! Where am I? What is going on!?"

Janus slipped the ST-31s around to her back and held out both hands calmly.

"It's okay, I'm here to help."

"What are . . . who are you!?"

"My name is not important . . ." said Janus, inspecting the contraption the woman was trapped in.

The woman was encased in a black suit of armour, similar to the photos she'd seen of the black armoured soldiers Ducard had shown her a few days ago.

"Is my wife okay?" she pleaded. "What happened to Renai; tell me she's okay."

Janus stopped inspecting the armour and walked around to face the woman directly. Her pale skin, green eyes, and sharp nose were distinct, and on top of the accent, she knew from her appearance that the woman was not from Menilax. She had a bandaged skull, which was alarming, and it appeared as though she was bald underneath.

Did someone . . . shave her?

Janus sighed. She needed more information to assess the situation properly. "What's the last thing you remember?" She asked, trying to keep her voice gentle and calm.

"I remember . . . driving . . . We were leaving Kendelli on our way to Silver City to see my parents . . ."

Her eyes flicked from left to right as the woman tried to desperately recall her memories.

"There was . . . another car, which came into my lane. It hit us, and . . ."

She stared at Janus with fear-soaked eyes.

"I don't remember anything else, I woke up here, and you came in . . . Who are you?" she asked.

Why did they take her here? How did they . . . ?

The questions would serve no purpose now, and she didn't feel like probing this poor woman any further.

"Listen, try to take it easy," said Janus. "I'm going to see if I can—"

As she walked behind the woman, she found a clear vial of fluid on the bench the woman had been propped up on.

It's a vial of anaesthesia . . .

Janus looked at the back of the woman's head; she couldn't move it at all. Janus noticed the muscles in her neck shifting around, as if she was trying to move it despite the armour holding her in place.

"What are you going to do? Can you tell me what happened to Renai? Is she okay? Please . . ."

Damn it! I don't know what to do here . . .

Janus stared at the syringe.

I can't bring her with me. I still need to search the facility for Ducard and Grey . . .

"*I'm sorry,*" she whispered, as she picked up the syringe.

"What are you—"

The woman gasped as Janus slipped the thin needle into the back of her neck and plunged the clear fluid inside. She only injected a small amount before pulling it out.

"No . . . Please . . ."

The woman closed her eyes and lost consciousness.

Janus gasped as her eyes became red and tears began to well in her eyes.

I'm so sorry, but I just don't have time for this . . . Need to keep going . . .

She groaned as she shook her head and covered her mouth as she sobbed.

"*Please forgive me . . .*"

You are an operator, Janus Scitilliant! Get your shit together! Now!

Staring at the sleeping woman, Janus brought her ST-31s around to her hands and promptly left the room. The walk back to the weapons testing area was silent, although her mind felt frenzied and panicked.

How could you leave her there?

You're a monster!

You're seriously walking away from that poor woman? She needs help!

Janus shook her head.

There's nothing I can do for her. I'm here for Oscar. There is no one else; there is nothing more.

Slipping back inside the weapons testing room, she took an interest in the gun rack to her left, which was filled with many different weapons. Ahead was a shooting range preceded by a bench where various munitions had been placed. On the right of the room stood faceless black mannequins fitted with black armour plates of different varieties.

Looks lighter than the other variants I've seen, even compared the one that woman wore . . .

Janus focused on her breathing to try and relax, inspecting each plate, covered with scratches and marks earned from the extensive testing they must've endured.

On either side of the entrance were palettes supporting white crates, stacked on top of each other tied with orange plastic straps to keep them secure. The stacks were unevenly allocated for the palette; some had two boxes and others had five. Janus stepped over to one of the shorter piles.

Slipping her knife out from her belt sheath, she cut off the orange plastic straps before unsealing the lid of the crate, looking inside curiously.

A complete set of armour was held in place by a warm gel. She took the helmet out of the container with ease as the gel reformed, puffing out to its standard flat shape. Keeping it in her hands with a wrinkled brow, Janus turned it around in her hands, analysing it from multiple angles. Realising it was a helmet, she turned it so it was staring up at her.

The eyes looked a dull red and seemed opaque, like blood on the surface of water. Strangely enough, the right eye seemed slightly larger than the left, and on the top of the helmet, she found a word engraved into the metal.

ONYX . . . is this the manufacturer? Or the model of the helmet . . . ?

Flipping it over, she found a scrambling apparatus attached to the mouth, used to alter the voice of the speaker to help hide their identity. It protruded from the mouth as a short, stubby, cylindrical shape with a swappable filter coming out from the right side.

Must double as a breathing apparatus too . . .

Her hand glided over the black metal, which was cold to the touch. The front part of the mask looked to come away, but she couldn't find any switches as she ran her gloved fingers over the material. The rear section was thicker, clearly reinforced to provide greater durability.

I need to get some of this back to Grey and Ducard.

Janus pushed the helmet back into the gel. It gave way with relative ease before it settled back into its original position. As she scanned the container, she found the manifest of the palette stuck inside a plastic sleeve. She skimmed it before stashing it in her backpack.

This case is only for the armour pieces. Perhaps I can find a pallet jack and bring a few crates back to one of the helicopters.

After a minute of searching, she found a cupboard in the corner of the room which contained three foldable electric palette jacks. She took two and unfolded them before switching them on, causing the two forks to extend. With great exertion, she slid the crates off the pile and onto the jacks as they crashed down, causing the noise to echo through the empty labs. Due to the heavy weight, she was barely able to lift one crate at a time, but the jacks seemed to hold them up easily enough.

Endeavouring to secure a variety of equipment, she stashed one of each crate onto the jacks, securing eight in total before setting the controls on the pallet jacks to move forward automatically. She had to manually steer them to navigate the corners, but it made the task doable at least.

Returning to the hangar, Janus sealed the laboratory doors behind her, before she moved her loot to the helicopter in the middle of the garage. She found a button on the jacks to raise the forks, lifting them up to the cabin of the aircraft. One by one, she slid the crates inside and tied them against the safety bars inside the cabin with some heavy duty ropes she found in the rear of the cabin.

Once all twelve crates were tied down, Janus leapt down from the cabin to the cement floor, noticing too late that four soldiers had opened the lab doors and were currently checking the vitals of the man she'd knocked out earlier.

Shit!

Janus crouched down, hiding behind the wheels of the gunship before her. With her slender frame obfuscated by the landing gear, she was protected from the men who began to search the hangar. Three more soldiers stepped through the large door over to the right, one of which wore the black armour that she'd loaded into the helicopter. The black titan stomped ahead of the others as they began to split up.

She took a quick breath.

Time to go loud!

Wasting no time, Janus careened around the corner with her weapon raised and squeezed the trigger. After three seconds, the magazine was spent, and the seven unarmoured men had perished, leaving only the Onyx guard standing before her unscathed.

It turned to face her with red eyes staring her down maliciously, as Janus slid back behind her makeshift cover, reloading her weapon and listening intently for movement. The image of those misshapen eyes branded themselves onto her retina, unsettling her as she readied herself.

Janus raised her weapon for another volley as she peeked around the corner once more. Before the bullets could hit their target, thick metal plates slid out from the chassis, shunting into place with a stout snap to cover the vulnerabilities around the neck and joints, the rounds plinking off the armour plating as a result.

The ST-31s began to dryfire, letting the Onyx titan know she was out of ammunition. It raised its palms toward her as two spinning discs popped out from the wrists. Janus slid behind the relative safety of the gunship, and as she did so, hundreds of tiny needles peppered the area around her. She watched some of them zoom past as they pelted the helicopter she'd loaded the crates into, instilling fear in her throbbing heart.

That weapon is insane!

Looking down at the hangar floor, she could see thin metal needles rolling around, pooling in small piles around her. How the weapon was able to fire so many at once was incredible, a technology she didn't think existed.

That amount of ordinance is complete overkill for one target . . . Why would you need that much firepower?

The dense thuds of the Onyx guard stomping over to her reverberated through the floor as she heard the needle weapon spin back up with a machine-powered whir.

Janus pushed away from the corner, sprinting furiously to her helicopter.

By the time it fired again, she was already sliding underneath between the landing skids, continuing to navigate around the row of aircraft lining the hangar. Another barrage of needles pelted around her, barely missing her flesh as she dived for safety.

Need to get this thing away from my ride!

Hiding behind a row of crates at the far end of the hangar, she closed her eyes and focused on her situation. If she tried to leave with the helicopter, the needle weapon could potentially damage a critical flight system. Janus had to deal with the titan before she could escape.

I can't use the ST-31s or the Surge Rifle . . .

The guard unsheathed a black rectangular object from its back. Holding it with two hands, the guard twisted and pulled the handles, transforming the object into a high-powered rifle with a few quick motions. She turned around to look at the crates she'd taken cover behind, they looked similar to those she'd loaded into the helicopter.

Time to give this thing a taste of its own medicine.

Inside the top crate, Janus found a smooth black rectangle with a few buttons and levers around the unit. It appeared to be the same object the Onyx guard had unsheathed moments ago. It was a little larger than her ST-31s, but was sleek and polished, making it appear more like a showpiece item rather than a weapon.

The handle was in the middle of the object, and when she grasped it, the gun unfolded into her arms, pushing against her shoulder with an awkward jerk as she held it up. A sharp, eardrum piercing whine thrummed from inside the chassis, but it stopped after a moment. Tilting her head to the side, Janus inspected the weapon carefully, discovering a round hole the right side of the weapon. The instructional shapes seemed to insinuate that this socket was used for the loading mechanism. Shaking her head and rummaging through the crate, she found a metal cylinder with blue fluid floating inside. She slid it inside the socket, noting how warm it felt through her gloved fingertips. Janus slipped a few extras into her pockets. She was ready to fight back.

Climbing the side of the gunship, Janus positioned herself on the roof and aimed at the titan marching forward.

The weapon was fast; the muzzle pulsing a brilliant blue glare with each round, sending small concentrations of solar-like energy to her foe. Janus felt the heat of the rounds as if she was standing in front of a large flame, grimacing against the firey blaze.

Staring up at her curiously, the Onyx guard couldn't manoeuvre away from the volley as they pelted the armour, splashing over his body like liquid.

The Onyx Guard brought its armoured arms up to block the gunfire, preventing its head from being struck. Once her salvo was over, the weapon was scolding hot from continuous use, so she dropped it thinking it was of no use.

Lowering its arms, it raised what remained of the weapon it had taken out to deal with her, the metal now melting in a pile of claggy, blue metal on the ground.

The liquid flame burned angrily through the armour as smoke seeped from the gun holes. Janus ran forward, lowering herself from the roof of the gunship before sprinting ferociously at the reeling titan. As she got close, she flicked the handle of her knife, bringing it forward and gripping it tightly. As the guard looked up at her, she smashed the hilt of the blade into the face of the helmet. It fell back, dazed and confused at her dynamic offensive.

Damn, the neck is still covered by those armoured plates . . .

Gripping the shoulder plate with her left hand, Janus leapt on top of it and pushed her blade into the shoulder of the Onyx Guard, jamming it deep enough to puncture the flesh underneath. The deep screaming of the operator bellowed out around the hangar as she reached down and cut at the back of the knees to prevent the machine from moving anywhere quickly.

"We'll find you," it said, as she spun the blade around and stood before what sounded like a man's voice. "You think you can steal from us and just walk away? Because we're the new kids on the block?"

She slammed her boot into his face, but the titan grabbed her foot from the air and pulled her down to the floor.

Janus's fingers loosened in the scramble, causing her ST-31s and knife to clatter to the floor.

Shit!

The titan reached out to her with an armoured hand as he held her ankle in place, keeping her in range as she desperately tried to free herself.

She began to reach for her handgun.

The titan's hand wrapped over her face, but before he could close his hand, Janus pulled her head away. All that he managed to grab was her mask, compromising her identity as she slid her pistol out from the holster. As she raised it to fire, he let go of her ankle, causing her to push away from the scuffle. Wasting no time, she stood up and dashed away from his reach and raised the pistol at his head. Raising armoured hands before her in a surrendering gesture, she hoped that he wasn't going to fight any further.

Panting heavily, Janus used the time to try to catch her breath. His flesh hissed from the molten rounds she'd fired at him earlier, however it seemed the plating had absorbed most of it.

What the hell is this plating made from?

She shook her head, wiping the sweat from her brow.

And why did he let me go . . . ?

"Janus . . ." said the man.

He knows me . . .

A defeated tone reverberated through the voice filter. The fact that he knew her sent a shiver across her skin as goosebumps crept out from her flesh.

"You know me?" she said, tilting her head.

"Yes . . ." said the guard with a chuckle. "Of course I do . . ."

Janus turned her head towards the helicopter.

I should leave now before more come . . .

"Janus . . ."

The guard's jittery hands rose to his helmet, unclasping three braces around the base before lifting the front panel away and dropping it to the floor.

She looked down at him with anger and confusion, her jaw hanging loose.

"Morgan . . ." said Janus as her hands began to tremble.

Shame was smeared across his face, his dark eyes refusing to meet hers.

Her trembling became more and more intense until she started to clench her muscles to make it stop.

"I'm sorry," said Morgan. "I didn't realise it was you until . . . I took off your mask . . ."

Morgan's every breath was raspy and pained.

Maybe some of those rounds did penetrate after all . . .

"What are you doing here?" he said, shaking his head. "I thought you were still in the hospital . . . ?"

"What am *I* doing here?" mocked Janus. "What about you? *This* is the unit you joined? Do you have any idea who these people are?"

Anger and anxiety flooded her mind, as the tremor in her arm snaked out across her body, causing Janus to shake and stutter.

"We can talk about this later. Janus, this is a government facility . . ." said Morgan.

Government . . . ? So there is a councillor behind this . . .

"You'll be treated as a terrorist if they find you . . ."

Janus had scrambled the communications systems in this block of the facility, the EMP rounds made sure of that. However, Morgan could still identify her.

She raised her weapon and levied it at his face.

I've lost all of my family . . .

Her trembling worsened.

But this is necessary . . .

The little pieces of the gun rattled and shook, her arms refusing to stabilise.

I can't do this.

Her throat tightened.

If he identifies you to them, you'll be hunted . . .

Janus clenched her jaw.

I've lost so much already . . .

Janus started to depress the trigger as her eye began to twitch.

He's your enemy! He tried to kill you!

"Janus?" Morgan looked up at her with watery eyes, shaking his head slightly, unable to accept what she was about to do. "What are you doing?"

Janus lowered the weapon as she groaned exhaustively. Turning around in place, Janus put her hands behind her head as she cursed herself and the situation she inhabited. Opening her mouth to speak, Janus simply could not find the words, her body frozen with anxiety as she stared at Morgan and his broken body.

You were going to kill him . . .

As salty tears welled up in her eyes, she turned away, clenching her jaw as tight as she could.

"Janus?" he asked, "Please . . . tell me. Why are you here? Did you come here to hurt me?"

She heard scuffling down the hall.

Reinforcements . . .

She trained her weapon down the hallway to fire, but Morgan held his arm up to block her shot. He stood up despite the injuries she'd inflicted on him.

"Listen, we can meet up later," he said, gesturing to her mask on the floor.

She nodded, sheathing the weapon and picking up the mask before donning it quickly.

"I'll talk to them, I'll make something up . . . Just get out of here."

Janus nodded.

"I'll explain to—"

A beam of light scorched a hole in his face. Janus was turning towards the helicopter as the beam came through, inadvertently dodging the beam as it burnt the side of her face. The wound was not fatal and the intense pain that followed faded into the background as she watched as Morgan's head slump over, resting quietly in the suit which held up his corpse.

"Morgan . . . ?"

Small embers danced around the blackened ash where his face used to be, disintegrating the area from his chin to his eyes. Janus could see the soldiers running towards her through the hole.

Another beam of light scorched the air beside her head.

She gasped as the heat from the blast snapped her back to reality.

She took one last look at Morgan's face before she left, committing it to memory, unable to process the devastation and numbing sensation that consumed her body and mind. The inside of the wound was black and charred as if it had cauterised immediately, causing no blood to spill out over his body.

Morgan's life had vanished in the blink of an eye, leaving only this empty husk in a suit.

Janus crouched to avoid another shot as the round punched into the gunship behind her. Rolling out of the soldier's line of sight, she sprinted back to the helicopter, leaping inside the pilot's seat as she powered on the engines and the sonic blades on top of the aircraft. She had enough time to release the engine's safety mechanisms and take off before they entered the hangar proper.

Tears flowed freely across her face, spilling out from her eyes despite the lack of emotion she expressed with her neutral face. She blinked, sending fresh tears along her cheek as her tired eyes felt like they were burning from the inside.

Janus felt apathy replace every feeling she had as her arms seemed to move on their own, piloting the aircraft, and flying her to safety.

All she had left inside was complete emotional paralysis.

There were no thoughts, no feelings.

Only emptiness.

⌘

19: ARKWRIGHT

⌘

Dennis Arkwright was a known associate of Sinew, and perhaps the last Pioneer still residing within the walls of Menilax. Hiding in isolation for the better part of a decade in Sector Four, Grey hoped the immortal still had some semblance of sanity.

Strange that he's been under our noses this whole time.

Artemis thought it wise to wait until nightfall to investigate, citing the man's reputation as reason enough to avoid unnecessary attention. Grey remained sceptical about Artemis's findings; Sinew never remained in one place for more than a few weeks, and Dennis had been in the same place for many years now. If he really was an associate of the man, why would he be so reckless as to leave a trail behind like this? Perhaps he hadn't learned this particular habit from the man after all.

Regardless of his preconceptions, the lead was worth checking.

The sky was relatively clear tonight. The cobalt moonlight illuminated the usual darkness resting between the white street lamps, abolishing the thick darkness that was commonplace in Menilax of late.

The sounds of distant traffic were the only discernible ones apart from their footsteps, as Artemis walked briskly beside him. The typical attire he chose for most occasions—long black pants and a black shirt—weren't quite enough tonight, so he wore a black woollen jumper for the unseasonably cold night. Artemis wore a long, dark brown coat and a black bulletproof vest underneath. The light armour plating was stitched throughout the layers, offering protection at a low cost of mobility to the wearer's range of motion. His long black hair draped over the dusty jacket, giving him a rather distinct look.

Artemis had insisted on joining him during this duty; his skills as a scholar were legendary among the kindred, but what his students didn't know was that he was also one of the best Shifters Grey had ever seen. Curiosity got the better of his old friend, so he came along despite his irritation at Grey's impatience. Artemis had instilled a strong sense of caution about Dennis, who was apparently one of the more unstable Pioneers the kindred had documented. The only thing that perplexed Grey about the records on Dennis was why they hadn't taken him down yet.

Probably waiting until someone comes along to offer them cash . . .

It'd made him ill to use the kindred as a resource to get the information, but he couldn't think of any other options.

I've been searching for Sinew for my entire adult life . . .

He took a deep, stress-riddled breath.

I'm willing to do whatever it takes to find Sinew and end him. Even it means talking to a monster like Dennis, and using the kindred to find him.

"How confident are you that the information's still accurate?" asked Grey.

"We have Seekers keep tabs on potential targets."

"I thought the kindred didn't use Seekers after the debacle with Bertrude?" asked Grey.

The name of the Seeker brought back painful memories. Images of the Seeker cutting through the STARCOV team he'd worked with that night flittered across his eyes, awakening a restless, intense feeling of guilt and heartache.

"Indeed," said Artemis. "The blights were . . . let go."

"The Eminence trains a new generation of Seekers now, ones that *aren't* infected."

Artemis's choice of words made Grey's eye twitch, which tickled his scar as he scratched at it irritably. Not all of the sentient blights were like Bertrude, but the murderous Seeker had left enough of an impression that he understood where Artemis's bias came from. He wouldn't have employed the blights he came across all those years ago—looking for safety anywhere they could find it—if he didn't trust them, but he wasn't about to tell Artemis that. The Revenon infection typically transformed a healthy human into nothing more than a shrivelled up husk, with behaviour varying between staring at their pray blankly, and attacking like wild animals, biting and mauling their victims.

The only cure to the plague seemed to stem from a doctor who'd mysteriously vanished, but it wasn't a complete fix. While their bodies remained ravaged and permanently scarred, their minds were saved; their skinny, practically skeletal-like bodies were light, and they didn't need much food or water to survive, making them ideal spies and intel gatherers.

If I looked like that, I would probably want to stay away from people too.

They were almost there.

Time to focus up.

As they reached the end of Gesture Street and made the turn onto Yurning Road, Grey suddenly remembered the significance of this place. Some of the first buildings in Menilax were constructed along the landmark-riddled road, and after a few minutes of strolling along, gawking at the dated architecture of the apartment buildings and community centres, they found the gravesite. The plot seemed to span into the distance for at least two kilometres.

Gravesites in Menilax had very little maintenance, and as a result, they had become lonely and decrepit reminders of the way things were. One noteworthy ritual involved those close to the deceased digging the grave themselves, lowering the body into the cavity, and then climbing their way out. Needless to say, these archaic rituals were no longer practised; cremation had become the primary option to dispose of the dead in modern Menilax.

Both before and after the cremation, children and young adults were prohibited from attending, and were relegated to one of the Pioneer temples around the city, where Keepers would provide emotional support to the youths during proceedings.

Grey smirked. He'd considered the prohibition a challenge as a child.

He fondly recalled his late-night excursions to the many gravesites around Menilax, observing the behaviour of adults during such nights. Learning things he wished he hadn't on these excursions; such experiences had traumatised his young mind, giving an early glimpse into the evil that resided in the hearts of humanity.

I'm glad he's dead.

She was sleeping with my husband; I hope he follows her to the grave . . .

I was the one who told him to kill himself.

I'm responsible . . .

Reflecting on these words with an adult mind, Grey realised how much they'd affected him. He'd become convinced that the world was black and white, where one was either on the side of good or bad. Over time, he'd learned that things were not so simple.

If the world were black and white, I would be a monster . . .

Life had seemed so simple to him as a child. Having idealised the role of protecting people, he'd planned to enrol with Enforcement or perhaps even train to be a soldier. As fate would have it, that desire for justice was manipulated by those in positions of power, disguising their true motives and pushing their own agenda.

I've done terrible things thinking they were helping the world. Hard to believe how naïve I was not to question them for so long.

The black bitumen of the street lit up as a car drove behind them. Once the white sedan zoomed past, he and Artemis crossed the street. Grey peered through the rusted chain link fence, taking in the details of the old graveyard. Faded yellow lamp lights illuminated the yard, making the scenery eerie to observe. There were many manmade holes in the fencing, large enough to allow them to squeeze through if they so desired.

"I think we should walk along the perimeter a little more," said Grey after brushing his fingers against the rust coated fencing.

Artemis met Grey's gaze with a determined look on his face. "Indeed. That would be best."

Soon enough they made it to the main gate, where Grey's eyes were drawn to the cement stairs that snaked up the hill before them. Walking further wouldn't serve any purpose now as their visibility would be blocked by the overgrown grass and the sharp incline of the hill. They walked in silence through the gate as Grey took the lead, the dirt-encrusted stairs having just enough space for one person to step up at a time. Within a few moments, they reached the top of the hill as they both took out their weapons, scanning the area before them.

There was a forked path which weaved its way through the many gravestones around the site, and it appeared that not all routes between the resting dead were lit equally. Turning to speak with Artemis about their plan of attack, he stopped short as a sobbing cry echoed throughout the graveyard.

Grey held his handgun forward, smirking at Artemis knowingly.

"Just like old times, eh?"

Artemis sighed. "Not exactly . . ."

He slapped Grey on the shoulder before moving along the left while Grey jogged on the right.

Grey would approach the threat directly, while Artemis would position himself to fire from another angle in the low light. If lethal force was required and it was Dennis, an immortal demigod doing the weeping, he'd be happy to have someone ready to ambush him in case the conversation went south.

All augurs are susceptible to surprise attacks. Just need to take them out before they can use their abilities.

Taking a deep breath, Grey picked up the pace through the poorly lit graveyard as the voice grew increasingly decipherable. Focusing on tone, he realised that it was a single voice talking sparsely in a defeated way, reminiscent of the voices Grey overheard from patients in the hospital.

Grey glanced at Artemis, who was barely visible as he skulked behind the row of headstones near the fencing where the lamps were broken. Gesturing ahead with an open palm, Grey declared his intentions as he moved briskly towards the voice. He could finally see the man, who seemed to be praying before a particular stone. Feeling confident, Grey took a few steps toward the man, who was still muttering to himself. Gripping the pistol grip tightly and aiming it forward with his finger hovering over the trigger, Grey was ready to announce himself to the possible threat.

Sighing at his hostile behaviour, Grey felt a pang of guilt pulsate through his mind for walking into this hallowed ground ready for violence. He turned to shake his head at Artemis as he buckled his gun back into the holster.

His eyes lingered on Artemis's expression for a few moments, waiting for him to stand down. Instead, he noticed that he'd lost the colour on his face as he stared at something behind Grey. As he began to turn, he felt a steely hand grip the back of his neck, slamming him face first into the dirt with incredible power, holding him in place.

"*What* business does a kindred assassin and a Councillor have in a place like *this*?" said a hateful male voice.

Gritting his teeth, he yanked his neck away and rolled out from under the man's grip, coming out of the grapple in a crouch. On his knees, Grey swung a powered fist at the man's knee, but his foe was ready. The man stomped on his wrist, slamming his arm down into the dirt while he pushed a shotgun barrel against Grey's head.

He had a woeful, homeless stench, a bald head, and a pale, malnourished appearance.

Grey raised his other hand into the air.

"Hold up now," he said, spitting the dirt out of his mouth. "We're not here to hurt you. We just want to talk."

"Oh, is that right?" he said, nodding to Artemis. "I suppose your friend is also looking to talk?"

Grey looked over to Artemis, who'd broken his concealment and approached the two of them during all the commotion.

Gritting his teeth, Grey considered his options.

You've taken point-blank shots before from shotguns; just reach up and grab his throat. You need to gain control over the situation.

The man twisted the boot holding Grey's arm in place, causing him to grumble in frustration.

"Listen to me!" he growled. "We ain't lookin' for a fight!"

"I saw you getting ready to ambush that man. Explain yourselves!"

Grey looked over at the man who was sobbing. He was watching the confrontation, stunned and fearful for his own wellbeing.

"Let's cool off for a second, all right?" proposed Grey. "Artemis! Lower your damn gun already,"

Grey looked up at the man, clenching his jaw.

I'll have to neutralise him . . . Can't risk it.

As the man looked over at Artemis, Grey smashed his fist into the man's leg with his potential fuelled to its maximum. The bone crumbled under the superhuman power of the blow. As expected, the man squeezed the trigger as he fell pumping a deadly spray of buckshot into Grey's enhanced chest. Even with his ability peaked, it still felt like a train had careened into him, sending him sliding through the dirt before crashing into a gravestone.

Groaning to himself, Grey rose to his feet, brushing the shotgun pellets that were stuck in his chest, irritated that his shirt now had tiny little holes peppered across it.

This was my good shirt too . . .

The man was on the ground now, rolling around in a fit of screaming and cursing as he clutched at the limp and floppy leg, which looked to be completely shattered on the inside. Artemis was next to the man in moments, picking up the shotgun and tossing it aside, dismissing the praying man who yelped and bolted from the scene.

As Grey walked over and looked into the writhing man's eyes, he suddenly realised that it couldn't have been Dennis.

He's got green eyes . . .

Grey clicked his tongue in disappointment.

Guess it would've been too easy . . .

"Now," said Grey, crouching beside the wounded man. "There's no need for this to get any messier. Tell us where Dennis is." Grey gestured calmly, ignoring his throbbing chest. "We're looking to talk with the man, that's all."

The man's heavy breathing subsided for a moment as his attention was drawn behind Grey.

"I think this has gone on long enough . . ." spoke an elegant voice from the shadows.

The suddenness of it made Artemis jump as they both turned around, searching for the perpetrator with raised weapons.

"If you're looking to talk, then talk," said the voice.

Grey and Artemis glanced around, desperately searching for signs of the perpetrator.

"I knew you couldn't stay away from this place, kindred dogs! Do you think I don't see your little spies roaming my perimeter?" said Dennis, stepping out from behind a tall grave. "I am not hurting anyone. No one knows where I am, except for you and your kind. Am I going to have to kill you all before you leave me alone?"

He had scruffy black hair, an unkempt beard, and angry, determined features filled with disdain. The man's white eyes bore holes into Grey's, the Pioneer watching him like a predator as he stepped toward them.

"You are not welcome here," he continued. "Leave immediately, or I'll send your heads back to your masters." The man clenched his fists, holding them at his side as he walked. "That should serve as an appropriate message, I think."

Grey felt his body attempt to activate its "fight-or-flight" response, which he suppressed for now. The surge of adrenaline that came with the sensation could be used to significant effect if used correctly, so he decided to wait until the right time to unleash it.

Dennis wore a dark green, buttoned-up jacket and black pants, and he looked to be in his mid-thirties. This would not be a real indication of his age, however. Like the man with the broken leg, his pale complexion made him look ill, but he looked a lot worse compared to his compatriot. He had bags under his eyes like he hadn't slept in years, and his skin seemed slightly loose. His sinewy frame would've once supported a fit physique, but now made him look like he was malnourished. He looked like an addict, the combination of a Pioneer and an addict was something that he never thought he'd see, but it seemed they were capable of the same folly as their mortal counterparts. An augur's power was directly linked to one's physical attributes and mental stamina, meaning the strength of his abilities would be significantly diminished.

The tomes had not reported on what sort of augur Dennis was, so they would have to be cautious until they knew what they were dealing with.

"Listen to me, friend," said Grey. "We're not here to fight, we're only here to ask you a few questions, then we'll be on our way."

Dennis was having none of it.

"This is your final warning, kindred dog. This is hallowed ground, and I will not stand here and allow it to be desecrated by your filthy morals."

"I don't work for the kindred anymore," said Grey with conviction. "I'm here for my own reasons, just lookin' to talk."

"You use such words, and yet you still associate with *him*?" said Dennis, gesturing firmly to Artemis.

"You are in no position to speak of morals," said Artemis. "We are aware that you used to work with Sinew."

Their foe smiled broadly. "So *that's* why you've come? For revenge?"

"No!" said Grey, losing patience as he raised a palm to each of them. "We're not here to fight. We're here to talk!"

"We know what transpired, Dennis," said Artemis. "It wasn't documented in our reports, but I know why you won't leave this gravesite."

Dennis's lip twitched.

"I heard you got a wife out of your service to that creature of a man. Your wife Kristen was taken, tortured, and experimented on extensively by your compatriot. Was that part of the deal for you joining him? That he'd give you a beautiful, young, subservient girl who was too broken to know better? Or was she brainwashed? Manipulated into loving a cretin like you?"

Dennis started moving toward them, his eyes burning like hellfire.

"She loved you, regardless of the circumstances. Her letters to Sinew asking him to leave the two of you alone were recovered from her corpse all those years ago."

Dennis clenched his fist.

"And what did you do with her after she passed? You buried her here, a decrepit, dark pit in an isolated city miles away from her friends and family!"

A howling wind passed through the gravesite. It began slowly at first, whistling between the stonework and fencing, picking up dirt and dust as it whisked debris between the three men.

"You know nothing of what happened!" yelled the Pioneer as he raised his hands into the sky.

"Why'd you have to piss him off?" said Grey as he clenched his jaw.

Within moments, a monsoon enveloped the graveyard. The soil eroded away, carried into the sky with the mighty winds thundering around them violently with Dennis standing in the eye of the storm. The two men were thrown aside like toys, sliding across the ground helplessly as Grey reached out desperately for purchase.

What the hell just happened!?

Artemis entrapped himself in a cube of energy as he threw his hands out to his sides, forcing the gravity to normalise around him. He floated to the ground, standing with his weapon shouldered and waiting patiently for his moment. Grey enhanced his density to help him regain some footing, standing before the mighty fury that Dennis had summoned.

The time for discussion had ended as quickly as it had begun. Grey would have to subdue him fast, as there could be others near the gravesite in danger of getting swept up in the immortal man's fury.

Grey unstrapped Sithaleir from his back, holding the hilt firmly in his right hand as he grimaced against the wind. Squeezing the handle with supernatural strength, his body heat and augmented pressure summoned the mighty blade from the ether as plumes of smoke emerged with it. The black, ink-like smoke that spilled out of the edge was carried away by the storm as quickly as it came. Grey snarled against the force wishing to take him away along with the headstones, dirt and lamp lights flying around the graveyard.

Grey could no longer see Artemis. His vision had become wholly obfuscated by the gale as it picked up the soil of the gravesite, blinding him from everything except the ground beneath his feet.

Stay inside that barrier of yours, Arty; leave this one to me . . .

He had to be careful here. If Grey pushed his body too far he would lose consciousness. Doing so in a storm as massive as this would result in his doom, so he had to manage his strength wisely if he wanted to get out alive. Moving around in the monsoon was like trudging through mud, but he had no choice, focusing his ability on weight enhancement to keep himself on the ground. Grey stepped toward Dennis's last known location with his jaw clenched, stepping through the dust-filled tempest as he shielded his eyes from the dirt, while grass and debris whipped away at his body.

His skin began to sprout goosebumps, as the biting cold of the night combined with the storm chilled him to the bone. His ears felt like they were going to burst as the howling, ferocious winds refused to give him any latitude.

Eventually, he found Dennis, who still had his arms raised to the sky. The storm's fury had carved out a safe space for him to stand without suffering its wrath, and as Grey approached, Dennis snarled at him before the vague silhouette disappeared in a sea of dirt and refuse, swallowing the once safe space he'd stood in.

What have we gotten ourselves into?

Grey suddenly felt as though it was difficult to breathe. He began to gasp like a fish out of water, taking take large, panicked breaths in quick succession.

The storm . . . it's suffocating me . . .

Grey was out of options.

Sithaleir rose vigilantly amidst the endless storm as he held it high, the green runes on the blade shining maliciously through the muck. A chilling and ancient whispering became louder in his head, forcing its way into his mind and threatening to overwhelm him. Channelling the unmalleable power through sheer will, Grey brought the blade in front of his body, sealing his eyes shut as he redirected the surging energy through his every cell.

Within a moment, he felt as light as a feather.

He stood weightlessly as the storm moved around him like a cool breeze as he breathed in and breathed out with a supernatural calm. With renewed vigour, Grey began moving confidently over to the man in the centre of the storm. Within a moment, he stood before the Pioneer, Sithaleir at his side, ready to do what was necessary.

Thump. Thump. Thump.

The beat of his heart slowed as the whisperings of the blade dulled all sensation, removing all doubt and fear, replaced with focus and conviction. Bringing the edge forward with both arms in an attempt to cut into the Pioneer's shoulder with a vertical slash. Grey watched the immortal smile as he crossed his arms and leapt back into the storm, levitating effortlessly through his own creation.

Chasing him is not an option.

Grey channelled the darkness once again.

"You are . . . talented . . . You . . . do not need this . . ."

Grey's muscles tightened as he channelled his strength into the blade. He felt his body weakening quickly while his head began to pound as a throbbing pain suddenly sprouted in his skull.

"Such potential . . . Together . . . we are . . . special . . ."

Grey yelled as he opened his eyes, swinging the blade diagonally through the air. The runes distorted the air around him, discharging a billowing black wave of energy through the monsoon. The power that Sithaleir projected consumed anything it touched, completely removing it from existence. Hovering in the sky with his arms crossed, Arkwright darted aside effortlessly as he smirked at Grey's efforts to neutralise him. Screaming a frenzied, blood-curdling scream, Grey continued to slash with Sithaleir, sending out obsidian fissures towards his foe in a flurry of swings. The Pioneer moved around them quickly and sharply as Grey continued his assault, swinging the blade efficiently to summon as many projectiles as he could. Arkwright pushed downward with his arms, launching himself even further into the air, completely vanishing from sight.

Despite the toll it took from his mind and body, Grey continued to pitch the void strikes into the storm, although he had to guess at where the Pioneer may be, having lost sight of him.

"Submit . . . Let him be mine . . ."

Within moments of scanning the dust-filled sky, he saw the silhouette of a person tumbling around with the rest of the gravesite. Grey watched it in awed silence as it swept around and came spinning around to him. He brought Sithaleir back and prepared his other arm to grab the person out of the sky. Snatching his arm up, he clutched the throat of the man, but it didn't feel right. Squinting at the silhouette, Grey brought the body closer to inspect it.

It was a decomposed corpse.

He yelped as he let go of the body, allowing it to sail into the storm unceremoniously.

Slowly craning his neck up, he watched as numerous silhouettes floated around the sky.

Sweet Pioneers . . .

⌘

Artemis stood at the ready, surrounded by the gravity shifts that kept him on the ground and in one piece. He couldn't see anything beyond the blue energy he'd summoned, and yet he scanned the area around him with his rifle shouldered in case he saw Dennis.

I should not have let my emotions get the better of me.

He had no idea if Grey was still alive, and yet he couldn't lower the barriers to find out. If he did, he would be swept away along with everything else. The only activity he observed was the soil erode into the storm, which could prove troublesome considering what the cold earth kept beneath it.

As the thought struck his mind, Artemis watched the storm begin to subside. Within a few seconds, he could see Grey standing where Dennis was at the start of this mess; however, his eyes were fixated in the sky.

What is it that you are looking at . . . ?

A massive force slammed into his shields, causing them to rattle as the shimmering weakened for a brief moment.

What in the world!?

Glancing up, he watched a body roll over his barrier and slip down into the dirt. It was a skeleton, although it still had some black and orange flesh stuck on the bones.

Artemis threw up immediately. His compromised mindset destroying the barrier that kept him safe as he scowled and groaned.

"Arty!" yelled Grey.

Artemis held his arms up in fright, summoning another barrier in the nick of time as boulders crashed into the walls of energy, weakening his gravity-defying defensive wall.

As he glanced up to see if Grey was ok, he saw his old friend hold up Sithaleir in a defensive stance. In the blink of an eye, Artemis saw a massive torrent of power smash into Grey's position, sending dirt and stone clattering around the area. The Pioneer stood over Grey now, ready to finish him off.

No!

Artemis relaxed his arms, releasing his energy barrier as he charged toward Dennis with renewed fury. Readying his weapon, Artemis squeezed the trigger as a chatter of gunfire burst forth from the barrel. With an outstretched hand, Dennis threw a phantom gust of wind toward Artemis, scattering the bullets as they veered off course, peppering the bowl of soil created by the Pioneer.

Spending the remaining bullets in the magazine, Artemis held his weapon to the side as the autoloader arm ejected the old magazine and slapped a new one inside. Flicking his wrist, Artemis threw out gravity walls around Dennis, allowing the shots to bounce between him. The Pioneer showed his teeth angrily before throwing himself up into the air, propelled by a manmade cyclone with a suddenness that took Artemis by surprise. As he flew, Artemis saw flecks of blood drip down into the dirt as he allowed the gravity shifts to dissipate.

Artemis could barely make out what Dennis was doing in the sky as he ascended quickly out of sight.

He is probably going to try the same tactic that he attacked Grey with moments ago . . .

He shook his head.

I am still not used to calling him that . . .

Expecting an attack of some kind, he constructed a cube of energy, encircling himself with it as a precaution. Waiting patiently, the manipulated gravity fields shimmered a magnificent blue, distorting space as he peered through nervously.

Artemis watched as a grand tornado came roaring down from the heavens.

Prepare yourself.

Artemis threw up extra shifts, preparing for the incredible power coming directly at him.

Crashing into Artemis's barriers, the manoeuvre caused them to shatter completely as Dennis came down onto Artemis, pinning him into the dirt with his arm over his chest. Thankfully, his momentum had been slowed considerably by the barriers, otherwise, he would've been crushed like an insect under a boot.

I am in trouble . . . I need to delay him and hope Grey can assist.

Blood was dripping from the Pioneer's mouth, and judging from the large gash across his arm and the small bleeding holes in his shoulder, he'd suffered wounds from both Artemis and Grey during the fight.

"How . . . could you do that . . . to your partner . . ." said Artemis.

Gritting through the pain as he grappled the Pioneer, Artemis groaned. Both men were panting heavily, but Dennis had the advantage of course as

Artemis struggled to breathe after being completely winded by the Pioneer's attack.

Dennis swallowed dryly, raising a trembling fist back as he clenched his jaw angrily.

"You're a cruel monster . . ." said Artemis. "Far beyond your sinister master."

Grey suddenly appeared next to them as he drove his boot into Dennis's head, knocking him clear of Artemis.

⌘

Using the momentum from Grey's kick, Dennis rolled up into an upright position. While he did manage to stand, he was unsteady and confused, trying in vain to regain his composure. The Pioneer unsheathed a silver pole from under his jacket. Gripping both sides, he pulled them apart after a moment of struggling, extending it to create a long staff before spinning it around gracefully.

Grey recognised the weapon; it was an ancient Pioneer baton used to incapacitate targets. Blue and green bolts of energy swam around the long stick as Dennis activated it. It was as tall as a regular sized man with generous space in the middle for the wielder to safely grip it without electrocuting themselves. It was a nonlethal weapon in its original state, although Grey was unsure if that would hold true now. Dennis could have tampered with the voltage output, after all, as the electricity looked incredibly unstable.

"Wait a damn second!" said Grey. "We can talk—"

Dennis sprinted towards Grey with his baton at his side, screaming hysterically. Grey reached behind his back, summoning Sithaleir once more as he brought it above him to parry the strike. The smoke that plumed from the blade was ineffective as a tool of misdirection as Dennis continued his attacks through the smoke, unaffected like his usual foes were.

"You seek to use your artefact to distract me?" mocked Dennis. "You'll have to do better than that!"

Dennis Arkwright had been an immortal defender of Vale, a legendary Pioneer that most people considered to be gods. As a teenager training to fight, Grey had always wondered at how skilful they were. Perhaps others in the Pioneer order had a deft hand with a striking weapon, but this particular Immortal was a poor duellist. He was talented, but he was far from being formidable. The display made Grey realise that he had overestimated his opponent's skillset to a frightening degree.

Dennis overreached with his latest lunge, allowing Grey enough time to reach out and grab his wrist. Following up hastily, Grey rewarded the Pioneer's blunder with a vicious backhand, sending Dennis reeling away in a bloody spin. While Dennis stepped back clumsily, Grey leapt forward and kicked him in the chest as he stumbled back into the dirt.

Watching the immortal climb to his feet in his weakened state, he heard the voice whisper to him even stronger than before.

"Slow . . . Kill him slow . . ."

He could've quickly plunged Sithaleir into Dennis's gut, he thought, watching the panting Pioneer walk slowly toward him with anger plastered across his face.

"He . . . would be welcome . . . in this place . . ."

Grey launched himself at Dennis as his opponent unsheathed an automatic pistol, spraying at him wildly with a flurry of gunfire.

You're desperate . . .

Grey stalled his momentum as a stream of rounds sailed his way. Hardening his body, each bullet plinked off like they were flower petals before collapsing into the dirt. When the weapon was empty, Grey reached out to grab him. As he opened his hand and clamoured towards the Pioneer, Dennis summoned a mighty gale, pushing Grey clear of his position.

Grey's hold on Sithaleir had been weak, a potentially fatal mistake as the hilt sailed through the sky. Grey saw Dennis come at him with wind-powered velocity, launching himself into the air with the baton held high.

Accepting the fact that Sithaleir was out of reach, Grey raised his arms defensively.

Let's do this the old-fashioned way . . .

As Dennis blustered towards him, Grey stepped aside, allowing the Pioneer to crash into the dirt. Then Grey was on him quickly, slamming the side of his body with a right hook. The Pioneer kicked out from under the grapple, stumbling away and turning to deliver a blind haymaker with the baton. Grey punched at the Pioneer's wrist as he did so, causing Dennis to drop the stick with an easily inflicted wrist sprain. Stumbling around, Dennis grunted and panted as he unsheathed a small knife from his boot, careening towards Grey recklessly.

You don't have much left in you . . .

Grey drew his pistol and held it at his side, standing before the wounded immortal with vindication in his heart. He knew what had to be done.

As Dennis moved to stab at Grey with a growl, he grabbed his wrist.

Raising the handgun over Dennis' face, he gently held his finger over the trigger.

"We're not looking for bloodshed; we're looking to talk. If you feel the need to keep at it, by all means, you can try your luck. But I don't like your chances."

Artemis moved over to where Sithaleir lay in the dirt, picking up the oddity before joining them.

"Your old buddy Sinew's moving through Menilax kidnapping people again. We've got someone sayin' that one of your old boys is helping him out, and if it's not *you,* then we're looking for some help on who it might be."

Grey and Dennis stared at each other for a few quiet moments, both men panting and sweating.

"We *need* you to help us," said Grey. "I've been looking for this guy for far too long, and it's time we brought this monster to justice . . ."

He clenched his jaw.

"So you think you can start a fight, and then we can just talk it out?" Asked Dennis mockingly.

Grey released his grip on the Pioneer's wrist, allowing Dennis to start limping over to one of the many bodies littered across the remains of the graveyard.

"Don't suppose either of you has any medical training?"

He plucked up one of the bodies, lifting it over his shoulder. It was the man who'd initially ambushed them.

"I have a little," said Grey. "Do you have any medical supplies?"

Dennis shook his head. "No, I don't."

Grey nodded.

"We have some with us. If your buddy's still breathin', we can seal the wounds at least. Although that leg's going to need a proper doctor."

Artemis touched Grey's shoulder, handing over Sithaleir.

"You'll need to describe how to activate the blade component for me one of these days."

Grey chuckled as they all walked towards the guardhouse, which was still in one piece.

Must've been on the outskirts of this mess . . .

"I hope you are planning on reburying all of these cadavers!?" yelled Artemis.

"Don't worry," said Dennis. "I don't mind dealing with the dead . . ."

Grey carefully slid Sithaleir's hilt into the pouch on his back, before strapping it in securely.

"So i suppose we *can* start a fight, and talk it out afterwards," Said Grey mockingly.

Dennis turned to glare at him. "Don't push your luck, how about that?"

⌘

20: A DESIRE TO STAY

⌘

"The Pioneers kept many secrets from the world," said Dennis. "Do either of you even know how the Pioneer Order was formed?"

"We're not interested in Pioneer history," said Artemis in frustration. "We are interested in you, and how you came to work with that creature, Sinew."

"If you want information, I suggest you be more specific," said Dennis. "It's not as simple as you're making it out to be."

This "immortal" is getting on my nerves . . .

"Let's start with the basics then," said Artemis bluntly.

Grey turned to face him, sighing with frustration.

Artemis ignored him.

"When was the last time you showered? And is alcoholism a component of your *protection*?" Dennis turned to face him, his weathered features, bloodshot eyes, and grim stare did not intimidate him as he knew the truth behind the eyes. He'd dealt with plenty of alcoholics during his time.

"You talk about things you know nothing about," said Dennis. "You do not know what I have seen, and you *do not* know my side of the story when it comes to my involvement with Sinew and the rest of our order, let alone my beautiful wife . . ."

Grey nodded. "I suppose we don't . . . Arty," said Grey, gesturing gently to him, "don't piss off the immortal again, okay?"

Artemis sighed.

I will do what I must to get answers from this cretin.

The two of them waited for Dennis to open the door to the guardhouse at the edge of the gravesite. Within a few moments and after a handful of attempts fumbling with the keys, the door creaked open as Dennis limped inside. As they followed the Pioneer into the guardhouse, Artemis drew from his expectations on what they could expect from the interior.

I expect to see his home dishevelled and broken, identical to the exterior.

Following directly behind Dennis, Artemis quietly took in the details of the building, while the immortal muttered to himself about the mess around the house.

The floorboards creaked and groaned as they stepped through the hallway; empty bottles and food packaging had been stacked messily in no discernible order. They all had to tread carefully so as not to knock anything over. What was once a home for the caretaker of the gravesite was now home to a man with deep seeded emotional problems. Artemis surmised that the state of this place reflected the owner's mind in more ways than one.

It seems even immortals can be broken emotionally . . . Perhaps this is why he failed to take us down.

"I think your pal here's going to be okay," said Grey.

"I'm glad to hear it . . ."

"That monsoon o' yours could've done some serious damage," said Grey. "He's lucky to be alive . . ."

"Yes . . . I suppose he is . . ."

Dennis stopped in his tracks. He seemed to stare at the floor, becoming motionless before them.

Artemis shot Grey a look of concern; his old friend sighed as he placed his hand on the immortal's shoulder.

"Let me be clear," said Grey. "I didn't want to get into a tussle with you and your boy here. It shouldn't have gone down like that . . ."

Diplomacy first. Some things do not change.

Artemis made a thin line with his lips as Dennis nodded and continued to move through the house. Grey moved ahead of Artemis, knocking over a pile of bottles by accident.

It's hard to see you like this, old friend . . .

He'd watched Grey transition from a kindred assassin to a Councillor within the course of a few weeks, completely changing his identity. The transformation puzzled him extensively, for it seemed like two completely different skillsets.

How can a professional killer transition so cleanly to a politician?

Artemis had assumed that these roles wouldn't have any overlapping areas, but the man made it work somehow. Artemis exhaled through his nose, contemplating Grey's decisions.

As long as you are happy, I care not what you do with your life . . . Even if it is pretending to be someone you aren't . . .

"Don't mind the mess," said Dennis. "This place is getting knocked down soon anyway."

"I'm surprised you didn't knock it down with that little storm o' yours," said Grey.

Dennis sniggered. "Admittedly, I lost my composure when I called upon my gift. But I made sure not to let it branch out beyond the area of concentration."

"And the cadavers," stated Artemis. "Was that part of the area of concentration?"

Dennis shook his head. "I did not think the soil would give away so easily . . . My sincerest apologies to you both. I regret that you had to . . . see such horrors . . ." He turned around and gestured sorrowfully. "I will reconstruct their graves, even if it takes me years to do so." He shrugged. "I have the time, and I have the plots marked on a map by the old caretaker . . ."

"Let's focus on the present, shall we?" said Artemis as he gestured ahead.

Behind Dennis was a large area with a kitchenette, a table and chairs, and a pantry, as well as more piles of rubbish. The Pioneer turned to the right, heading down the hallway as Artemis followed along with Grey.

Hard to imagine this man as an immortal . . . He is a derelict!

Artemis's opinion of most people he ran into in the world was poor, although his standards for Pioneers had classically been rather high. Seeing this man served as a catastrophic disappointment and went against the records they'd left behind of their deeds and standards.

Perhaps this one is more damaged than the others . . .

The only people who had earned special considerations was his partner Chance, a handful of kindred students, and his friend walking behind him.

Artemis turned to face him.

Grey . . . The look does not suit you well, old friend.

The man had been through so much pain, and despite Artemis's attempts to try to help, he'd always stubbornly refused his assistance, insisting that the only way forward was to force his way through and turn a blind eye to everything around him. This stubbornness may have been the reason why he was the single kindred initiate to be fed lies about the sects true motivations; other students were told quite bluntly about the real purpose of the family. Factoring in his heritage and innocent view of the world, they had thought telling him the truth would've been too much for him to handle.

Perhaps they were right to deceive him . . . He had nowhere else to go . . .

So they'd lied to him as a boy, convincing him that he was taking the lives of evil people. The truth, however, was a lot simpler. The kindred were a cabal of killers, funded by those wealthy enough to pay their exorbitant price. Eventually, the truth came out, and he'd been allowed to leave, the details of which Artemis was still not privy to.

They were right about you, after all. You could not stomach the true intentions of the kindred.

Artemis squinted at Grey, wondering how to even approach a conversation about the man's mental health.

I wish there were a sentence I could mutter or a word I could say that would bring you back to what you were, flaws and all. I suppose I need to let go of that idea now. There's no going back, now that you've stepped into this new life.

"So, why humour us now?" asked Grey.

"Well, you didn't give me much of a choice; you were ready to kill me after all . . ."

This made Artemis twinge with annoyance.

"Defending ourselves from your poisonous anger was our only available option," said Artemis, throwing his hands up in frustration. "What sort of *man* throws his powers around without considerable provocation? You have no idea the fallout that the city would've taken from that storm of yours if it got out of hand! Not to mention the cadavers you tossed around like confetti."

Grey had caught up Artemis, placing his free hand on his shoulder.

"Let's just take it easy and get this guy healthy."

Artemis's eye twitched as he turned around and replied, "Very well."

Quelling his frustration, he unstrapped the medical satchel from his belt and held it at his side as the three of them walked inside the room on the right.

"You can place him there," said Dennis, gesturing to the messy bed.

The bedroom turned out to be as messy as the rest of the house. Grey and Artemis casually stepped around the piles of clothing and rubbish littering the room, as Grey planted the patient on the double bed and Artemis placed the medical satchel beside him.

"So who is this guy?" asked Grey as he opened the bag.

Dennis stumbled over to the desk in the room, sliding the office chair out from the table before spinning it around. He took a bottle of booze out from the desk drawer and fell into the chair lazily.

"He's a surrogate," said Dennis, taking a swig of the alcohol.

Grey frowned as he examined the patient. After a moment of quiet contemplation, he took the man's jacket and shirt off, carefully examining the wounds on his chest.

"For those of us who don't know what a surrogate is . . ." proposed Grey.

I have explained this to you before . . .

Artemis glanced to Dennis expectantly.

Perhaps I should let him explain. We might glean new information.

Arkwright took another sip as Grey unravelled a bandage from the satchel, using it to dab the wound. He looked to be removing as much dirt and dried blood as he could from the seeping, fleshy openings on the man's abdomen and leg.

"If we recognised a pure specimen among the population, we baptised them as surrogates of the order. If they were exceptional, we'd bless them with one of our gifts, or Augmentations, as you all refer to them. Most surrogates were encouraged to live mostly normal lives around their service; in fact, those who had children under our service were made into surrogates as well.

"Generally, those who were chosen were given stimulants and their genetics were altered accordingly. We wanted their offspring to be better than the parents, stands to reason. Surrogates were mostly used for Enforcement, Librarians, that sort of thing. This man—" Dennis gestured to the man on the bed, "was stationed at one of the temples we had near Menilax. He's a little set in his ways, but he's loyal."

He chortled. "It's always refreshing to have true loyalty . . ."

Taking a small incisor from the satchel, Grey used delicate flourishes to cut away some of the dirty flesh around the wound before readying the disinfectant. Handling the bandage, he turned to Artemis as he wiped the sweat from his forehead with the back of his hand.

"Arty, can you grab some water?" asked Grey. "I need to wash away some more of the dirt here."

Artemis sighed.

I am not your assistant . . .

Grey did seem rather busy with the man, and Artemis was merely standing as an observer at this stage.

"Very well . . ."

⌘

A grumbly Artemis left the room, leaving Grey and Dennis alone.

Dennis watched him leave, seemingly anxious for him to do so.

"Do you know which of your parents had abilities?" asked Dennis when he closed the door.

Grey looked over at Dennis; his eyes drifted to the alcohol in his hands.

"Mind if I have a drink?" he asked, raising an eyebrow.

Dennis tossed him the bottle with a smirk. Catching it out of the air, Grey unscrewed the lid from the bottle before taking a swig.

"My father, of course. Did you know him?"

Dennis stared at Grey intently.

"Your father . . . it's Gideon, isn't it?"

Grey nodded as he took another sip of the brown liquor.

"How did you know?"

The Pioneer nodded confidently.

"You have his eyes."

Grey chuckled, "Pretty sure I don't."

Dennis raised his hand as he cleared his throat, "Well, he had blue eyes before he went through the immortality ritual." He seemed lost in his thoughts for a few quiet moments, as he rubbed his dirt smeared face. "Hard to believe how long it's been since we started."

"Ritual? I thought you were all born that way?" replied Grey.

Dennis shook his head, "Not at all. When we woke up for the first time, we spent a few years learning and gathering our thoughts, figuring out what we could about the world around us. Eventually, we were given the gift of immortality through a ritual we discovered by those who came before. It was temperamental and inconsistent, but the end result was, well, what you see before you."

"Temperamental?" queried Grey, "In what way?"

"Well, we learned that we needed an augur of each discipline involved, but pioneers needed to be involved for everyone to come out in one piece. In the rare examples where we used an augur of human stock, it would usually result in the deaths of those involved."

Grey eyed him worriedly.

"We had to learn the hard way, unfortunately," Said Dennis. "We lost a lot of good people to that ridiculous ritual through our many failures."

"And my father, you knew him?" asked Grey.

He chortled. "We uh . . . worked together . . ."

Grey raised an eyebrow. "Doing what, exactly?"

The white eyes of the Pioneer did not waver from his, weighing his words carefully. "I'm sorry, but your father swore me to secrecy on his involvement . . ."

Grey squinted at him.

"I realise that raises quite a lot of questions, but if you know him, it won't surprise you . . ."

He tossed the alcohol back to Dennis. "I don't know him *that* well . . ."

Arkwright nodded as he snatched the booze from the air.

"And that's probably how he prefers it. If you want to know more about what your father, and what we did, then you should ask him."

Grey nodded as he looked away, churning the words around his mind.

"Fair enough, I'll make sure I do that. Now—" Grey went on to explain what Janus had told him about that night.

Dennis nodded to himself. "Keynan was the leader of our subdivision, and to be honest, I thought he was dead . . ." He shook his head. "It's surprising that he's working with Sinew; something drastic must've changed since the last time I saw him . . ."

Grey leaned forward. "Can you tell me anything about this guy?"

Dennis leant forward as he spoke. "He was the original Pioneer, although I use that term loosely. He never told us where he came from or what happened before we all woke up. Instead, he told us to look forward, to guide humanity as best we could on the challenges that would eventually rise."

He smiled. "Gideon and he were close. They shared the same views on what a fair world would look like. I suppose that's why they made him the vanguard of the Pioneers, to lead the rest of us on how true justice was to be fulfilled . . ."

True justice, huh . . . Wonder if it's an inherited value . . .

Dennis scoffed. "It was almost as if Gideon was made for the role, you know? He was always so obsessive about it . . . He could never seem to switch off that part of his mind . . ."

His eyes snapped back from the past as he tilted his head towards Grey.

"Now," said Dennis, "you must tell me where you got that blade of yours . . ."

Grey raised an eyebrow, shaking his head.

"Do you remember anything about it? How you came across it?"

Grey squinted at him, unsure on what angle he was taking here.

"Do you remember where you found it?"

"I don't remember much," said Grey. "But it's saved my skin more times than I can count . . ."

Dennis shifted his weight; the subject clearly made him uncomfortable.

"It's interesting that you can wield it so effectively . . ."

Artemis stepped in carrying a pot of water, moving quickly to place it on the bedside table next to the patient. He took a seat across from Dennis on the dresser table, crossing his arms.

"I had to let the water run for approximately three minutes before the dirt began to dissipate. Therefore, I cannot guarantee it will be sanitary."

Grey shrugged. "We don't have much of a choice."

Stepping around the bed, Grey picked up a fresh bandage and dipped it into the water before wringing it free of excess water.

"I have a few queries if you would not mind my asking?" asked Artemis. "It's important that we fill in the blanks in our own knowledge, even if they may come across as trivial to you. It might help us understand what we are dealing with."

Dennis shrugged. "Fire away . . . I've got all the time in the world . . . "

"In what capacity were you working with Sinew?"

Dennis rubbed his face with both hands, setting the bottle aside as he closed his eyes tightly.

"Initially, it was curiosity. Sinew was researching Augmentations from an early age, or so he said. He'd found a way to enhance his own ability, to an extent I'd previously thought was impossible. Somehow, he'd found a way to reach out to the bodies of other people and control them. It was subtle at first, making a person trip over or hurt themselves . . ."

He shook his head.

"His prowess went against the foundations we'd all established as limitations of the dredge Archetype, at least from that of an impure primal . . ."

He glanced at the two of them.

"That's . . . augurs . . . to you."

Dennis looked away, sighing deeply while Grey began to apply disinfectant to the wounds of the surrogate on the bed.

"I was so curious about how he managed to do it that I agreed to help him. I thought that through watching his methods that I'd learn the secret. Soon after, we began working together in his lab; we agreed that we needed live specimens; Augurs to study. We were going to try to figure out if we could enhance them in the same way that he enhanced himself."

The Pioneer opened his eyes, looking over at Artemis with tired eyes as he took another drink.

"We travelled around Vale, trying to learn what we could about the augur phenomena. We visited so many places, and we had so much fun. We had some good times during those early days; in fact, I didn't realise how much information I'd given him about the Pioneers then. In the end, we discovered quite a lot about Augmentations, and I learned so much more about myself."

Dennis leant back in his chair, his brow crinkled.

"We learned that descendants of the Pioneers didn't always show signs of being augmented through natural means, especially if those descendants were never exposed to conditions that would activate their ability. I suppose it's of no surprise to anyone that the concentration of augurs are the heaviest in Menilax's Broken Sector."

He chuckled. "I get stressed whenever I think about the place . . . Can't imagine what it's like for the people there. "

Dennis rubbed his chin with his right hand, staring into space as he continued to rant.

"We quietly inspected the population from the shadows, all the while trying to find a causality between the ones that had their abilities, and those that were still dormant. We'd come to the conclusion that we had to run experiments on those we'd identified as dormant to see if we could determine which person had what augmentation, and possibly force their abilities to come forth. It would be a few months until we had the facilities we needed to store them, but while we began gathering subjects, we caught the eyes of the remnant Pioneers."

"The rogue detachment of Pioneers who survived the war had started hunting us. I thought we were doing the right thing, so I helped Sinew fight against my own order. We hid, fought, and disobeyed them, all the while continuing the research. When we did gather a collection of subjects, Sinew tried to awaken their abilities, poking and prodding them to see if he could force them to summon their strength."

Dennis sighed, looking over at Artemis, who sat with his arms crossed.

"Sometimes their ability would awaken, and other times . . . well . . . he pushed too far . . ."

His eyes drifted over to the wounded surrogate.

"Once he put me in charge of keeping watch on the subjects during their resting period, my once frayed faith in him was shattered. I began to talk to them, get to know them. After a while, I got close to a woman I escorted to and from the cells to the lab. She later turned out to be my wife . . . and she . . ."

Artemis and Grey shared a brief look of understanding as Grey rubbed his scar, plucking a handful of bandages from the medical bag.

Dennis sighed, his eyes glistening.

"Well . . . Sinew tortured her, no way around that. The worst part about it all was that she was always so sweet to me . . . Even when I held her hand, escorting her to him . . ."

Silence filled the room for a few moments. The last sentence hung in the air as Grey thought on it. From the pained tone in his voice, the reason why he'd hidden away from the world in such an isolated place became evident. The guilt that this man felt was tangible in the air they shared.

I know that guilt very well . . .

"Sitting in her cell in her own filth, we'd talk about our lives and how we'd gotten to that place. She was completely blown away by what I was, an immortal man with the ability to manipulate the weather on our planet. Elise was such a gentle person, and I think that's why she never unlocked her potential after everything that happened. She had hope, hope that she would be saved and spared from a miserable death in that place."

Dennis cleared his throat, seemingly snapping back to reality as he glanced at the two men before settling back into his chair, drinking a startling amount of spirits from the bottle.

"Eventually, I couldn't take it any longer, so I escaped with her. We hid in Menilax, and our relationship formed during our time together in the following years. We were happy, enjoying a simple and quiet life."

Dennis chortled. "But of course, he found us eventually . . ."

"What did he do to her?" asked Artemis tenderly.

Dennis wiped his eyes with his sleeve

"He demonstrated his new power," he said, looking at Artemis with a pained smile.

"The true nature of his research and experimentation, the fruits of our labour . . ." Dennis mimicked the actions as he spoke of them. "He held out his hand, and threw me against the wall as if channelling the strength of Keynan himself. Then—" He gasped, sobbing quietly as he wiped the tears from his eyes. "The bastard broke her legs, then her arms . . .

"He did it all without laying a finger on her. Whenever I tried to intervene, he broke a limb, or tore out a rib . . ."

His lip quivered. "He tore her to pieces in front of me . . ."

Tears flowed quietly down his face. "He applied *just* enough pressure on my throat so I couldn't do anything, gasping for air while I watched him tear apart my precious, innocent wife . . ."

Dennis lit a cigarette, wiping his eyes again as his arm trembled terribly. "After she died, he told me that we were even. He'd warned not to intervene in his affairs again, or he'd come back."

He tittered nervously. His eyes stared into space with his mind miles away. "Sick bastard did it all with a smile on his face . . ."

Taking a deep breath, he held up the packet of cigarettes to the two men, offering them one.

Grey looked up at him and nodded as he walked over and slipped one out from the packet. He lit the cigarette before returning to the chair while Grey began smoking as he worked with his hands.

Artemis shook his head at the offer.

"I am sorry about the words I used, Dennis," said Artemis. "I should not have assumed . . ."

Dennis puffed on the cigarette leisurely. "Don't worry about it. I know the records don't say what really happened . . ."

"How does a man get so twisted?" asked Grey, shaking his head.

Dennis shrugged.

"Sinew was a surgeon before he awakened his ability . . . Or a doctor, one of the two. He didn't share much about how he became the way he is today, but then again, I never really asked about his past . . . I was always too frightened . . ."

Grey nodded to himself. "Come to think of it . . ." said Grey, "this Pioneer shared the same ability as Sinew, or so we've been told . . ."

Grey scratched his chin as he spoke. "He must've found a way to teach others how to do it after all."

Dennis shrugged. "It's possible. Although it's hard to believe that Keynan learned something from an augur . . ."

"What's his name, anyway?" asked Grey. "His real name?"

Dennis shook his head. "He never told me. He always referred to himself as Sinew. Such a strange fellow . . ."

Artemis looked over at Grey before rubbing his chin.

Dipping his hands in the water, Grey wiped the sweat from his forehead before lowering them again. He started to wonder if they would ever be able to find out any concrete information about Sinew's identity.

"Is my friend going to be okay?" asked Dennis as he ashed the cigarette on the floor and lit another.

Grey looked over at him warmly. "Yeah. He'll be fine."

Wiping his hands dry, Grey continued. "I suggest you take your friend to a proper surgeon. This is all temporary; don't rely on it to get him through."

Dennis nodded. "I appreciate your help."

Grey returned to the patient, nodding solemnly. He tossed the wet bandage aside and started to pack the extra medical supplies back into the satchel.

"I'm going to be honest here, gentleman," said Dennis, standing up.

Dennis put the bottle on the desk, sliding in the office chair underneath as he stood before them.

"Keynan is probably the most powerful Pioneer I've ever seen, and tracking him down might help you find Sinew by proxy—if they're working together—because we're all pretty predictable. Being immortals, the only thing left to most of us is our instincts, and we're desperate to find a place in this world that no longer has a use for us . . ."

Dennis swallowed, looking slightly rattled as he stared at Grey with concern.

"But make no mistake, it's not the Pioneer that you need to be concerned with. It's Sinew. You need to start preparing; construct a foolproof plan to take him down. He's killed all manner of people: Pioneers, Strin, armies, private mercenary crews, and even entire towns, all without a lasting scratch. He's probably the most dangerous individual I've ever met."

Grey and Artemis shared a concerned look.

"I wish I could help you more than just throwing words at you . . . but in the time I spent with him, he rarely spoke about himself. I hope you have something ready to deal with him, or you're both walking to your graves."

21: THE PARK

⌘

Magnificent rays of sun warmed her face.

The sky, uninterrupted by clouds, seemed as blue as the ocean, illuminating the brilliant bountiful green of nature, beckoning her return, promising that it wouldn't be the same as before.

A pleasant, soothing breeze cooled her skin as she opened the cabin door, blowing her hair back as she took in the sights, fighting the pain and pressure in her exhausted heart.

Facing the fear that plunged her into this nightmare, she hoped the effort to recover that which was lost would help her recover. Emotionally distraught, and thoroughly overwhelmed, Janus took a breath of fresh air, absorbing the atmosphere of the quiet park. That one simple breath seemed to cleanse her, allowing the serenity of the scene to lighten the load she weathered for far too long.

I've lost practically everything now . . .

Despite her internal distress, birds sung their sweet songs, insects chirped, and the scents of pine and grass danced around her sense of smell. Life here was unaffected by the terror that transpired over the last few months, she reminded herself. It seemed as if it was a different place compared to the park she'd visited previously; the dark overgrown forest from the duty serving as a hellish landscape that she'd stumbled onto by accident all those weeks ago.

Crouching under the blue Enforcement barricade, she saw a familiar stone tablet rising from the soil. Janus walked over and placed her hand on the warm sandstone.

While we strive to transform this land into the paradise it shall eventually be, let us not forget the flora and fauna of Menilax. We must find a way to share this bountiful land with them, for we cannot survive without these lifeforms we so easily dismiss from our minds.

With a promise made this day, we assume a responsibility to keep them protected from the elements, and ourselves.

With the divine blessing from our holy protectors, we bind ourselves to this oath.

May the Pioneers bless Menilax and the utopia that it shall one day become.

She saw a name at the bottom of the inscription, so she knelt down to get a closer look.

Councillor Decidus Randwick, 402 BGF.

Janus rubbed the back of her neck with her hands.

Just under three hundred years ago . . . Didn't realise how old this place was.

Craning her sore neck upwards, Janus observed the park office standing amidst the thick grass surrounding it. She could see the broken glass of the second floor, where Nathan had scaled the building and tried to save her. As her mind began to pull her back into that night, the calming breeze whisked the green blades of grass against her ankles, as they swayed along with the silent song of the wind.

Her eyes became drawn to the radio structure over to the right, towering above the tree line.

Mustering her courage from a withering reserve of emotional bandwidth, Janus continued along the path she'd once taken, quelling the incessant desires to leave and rest.

I can't leave it here. You spent too much time working on it . . .

As the thought of her father crept into her mind, so did the guilt and anguish she'd kept at bay for so long. Rather than push it away, as she'd done so for far too long, she let them in as the feelings caved through the mental barriers she'd stubbornly kept up. They flooded inside her skull without hesitation, filling her mind with grief, heartache, anger, and depression.

She closed her eyes and fell to her hands and knees, grimacing at the tightening of her throat and the ache inside her ribs as they threatened to break her completely.

I'm so tired . . . Tired of running away.

I'm tired of thinking that I'll become like my mother. And I am tired of pushing my emotions aside. It's time to deal with this, accept what has happened, and move on.

Oscar still needs me, and if I'm a crumbling mess, he has no chance of being saved.

Janus stood up slowly and untied her ponytail, flicking her shoulder-length hair aside. She resumed her journey in spite of the heavy, crushing fatigue, moving along at a slower pace than her anxiety demanded.

She looked around the National Park, observing the stark contrast between the peaceful, warm day before her eyes, and the horrible night she'd suffered through the last time she'd come.

Having been off the grid for more than two months now, Janus knew she'd been far too focused on earning Grey's favour in hopes that the augur would help her find Oscar. Her laser-focused attitude helped Janus excel during days past, but it had been a detriment for her emotional wellbeing since leaving the hospital.

If I didn't stop now . . . How far would I have gone on the same reckless path?

I need to be more mindful of what's going on with me; I can't afford to lose Oscar because of my short-sightedness . . . Not like Morgan, and not like Nathan.

The decision to proceed that night had plagued her mind with doubt and despair.

Having survived a career of dangerous duties and playing politics within STARCOV, Janus had felt accomplished with her time, yet weathered by the choices she'd made. The scars inflicted by such an active career still paled in comparison to the agony sustained from recent months.

Janus had approached every duty with the same level-headed professionalism she was known for, but it seemed like she was unable to do so when it came to her personal life.

She scoffed at the obviousness of it all.

I had family involved. There was a lot more to lose than my life or my career . . .

How could I have been so callous with their lives?

She meditated for a moment, standing before the thicket of trees where Nathan had slipped into after their first arrival that night. Memories of her mental state continued to trickle in, spurning her conscious thoughts with fear and anxiety.

She squeezed her hands as tightly as she could, taking a step forward.

The events around Oscar's disappearance flashed before her eyes like a picture show.

Janus tripped over a large rock, causing her to fall on her chest. She yelped, the impact leaving her breathless. Flipping herself over, Janus held her arms over her chest as she grimaced and took a laboured breath. The sensation brought her mind back to the first time Nathan had taken her out rock climbing.

Janus had only climbed a short way before falling; her stubborn nature refused to use the safety harness, to Nathan's dismay. He didn't seem surprised, and looking back, neither should he have.

"There's nothing wrong with falling," he'd said to her.

Morgan had laughed at her, of course.

It was a small fall, but at eleven years of age, she thought she was going to die.

"When we fail, we learn. Pay no attention to your silly brother up there—"

Her father's knowing smile coming down from the cliff side to help was a memory she'd always cherish. That smile had healing powers, the memory of him always helped her along the path, no matter what had come at her in the past.

"What did you learn today?"

Janus laughed aloud as a tear spilled out, running down her flushed cheek.

"Falling hurts like hell . . ." she whispered.

Her mind cascaded through memories as her breathing quickened. Closing her eyes, she revisited them all. Camping, hunting, fishing, she was always doing something with her family on the weekends, and they were consistently out and about on any number of adventurous activities. Venturing to a place they'd never been, seeking fun and challenge together across the globe; it was the only thing that had given her joy.

Another memory played before her eyes.

"Are you sure you're up for this?" said Nathan, presenting the dead animal.

She'd felt sick at the time, but she'd taken the knife to its skin nonetheless. *"Anything you can do; I can do . . ."* she whispered with an indulgent grin.

Janus had taken those peaceful times for granted. When she'd eventually left home to begin her career at STARCOV, she became a different person. At the time, Janus had never considered her regular days to be anything special. But now, those relaxing days with her family had become the happiest moments of her life. She relished the memories for the last few moments before getting up; her mind continued to play through them right up until she opened her eyes.

Suddenly, the world seemed colourless.

How did it all go to hell so quickly . . . ?

Blinking her eyes and breathing deeply, she began to stand.

Find the rifle . . . Bring him home . . .

Janus groaned as she stood, wiping her tear-stained cheek.

Exhaling elatedly, Janus stepped forward, crossing the threshold of the forest. The leafy underbrush crunched beneath her while the subtle aroma of soil incensed her. Glimmers of sunlight flashed across her face, shining through the gaps in the treetops, illuminating her path as she walked along the forest floor.

Once she reached the radio tower, she searched around it. After turning up nothing despite minutes of searching, Janus looked to the top of the tower, squinting to make out any rifle shaped objects. Unable to see much from where she stood, Janus knew she would have to make the climb. Beginning immediately, she leapt up to the first bar, the action puzzling her as she reached up to the next bar.

Do other people hesitate before doing things like this?

She did not have a safety harness or any climbing equipment, which meant there would be nothing to stop her from falling to her death if she made a mistake.

Everyone in my family is a little bit crazy and reckless, she mused, chuckling to herself.

All of us except Oscar; he would never do anything this risky or impulsive.

Janus felt relief flood through her system as she leapt up to the next set of bars. She was finally addressing some of the concerns that had plagued her mind recently. Being immensely thankful for the quiet time, Janus was glad for pushing herself to come back to the park, providing some sorely needed time to stop and address the mounting emotional trauma that nagged at her relentlessly. Introspection was an alien process to Janus, after all.

The steel bars of the tower felt hot on her hands, so she needed to climb quickly to avoid burning her skin. She felt immensely thankful for Nathan's consistent training during her childhood as he would drag her out of the house at four in the morning all kinds of physical training. When she'd been accepted by STARCOV, her lifestyle hadn't changed all that much. It was a natural fit, where practice and consistency were critical components of becoming a successful operator.

"A healthy body translates to a healthy mind, kid"

In the unit, every minute of every day was scheduled and premeditated by her superiors, priming their subordinates for maximum efficiency.

Procedure and policy, routine and conditioning . . .

Janus exhaled.

Strangely enough, I do miss the structure of it all . . .

She stopped climbing for a brief moment to mop the sweat from her face, swapping her hands quickly to avoid prolonged exposure to the heated bars. Lunging to the next metal bar with a steely grip, she thought on whom she'd spent most of her adult life talking to. Someone who was there whenever she needed him.

Blessed Pioneers . . . Morgan . . .

Her stepbrother was not perfect, but when she needed someone, he was there, even in the worst situations.

When an operation went the other way.

When people died.

When she'd taken a life.

Morgan was there for her through it all, rocking up at her apartment with a bottle of whiskey and an ear for her to chew on.

You were always there when I needed you . . .

I took you for granted the most out of everyone . . .

And you died, right in front of my eyes.

She closed her eyes for a moment as the image of his death flashed before her.

Janus sighed, shaking her head as tears spilled out over her cheeks.

"I won't stop now . . ." she whispered, leaping up to continue her climb.

Her pace quickened as she reached out to the next sun-bleached bar.

Feverishly climbing the tower with renewed energy, it seemed her grief and anger renewed her strength. As she scaled the last of the bars, Janus lifted herself up to a metal grate. She walked along to the edge overlooking the park office, and as she went to sit, she found the rifle as she reached her hand out to touch it. Her fingers rubbed the leather shoulder strap, tied to one of the bars where another smaller antenna stretched out further. The rifle shifted slightly against the wind as Janus watched it move on its own with reverence.

She fell to her knees.

"Versatility is your best weapon in the field . . .

"You can rely on your skill, your weapon, and your comrades, but the mission parameters can change at any time. Keep an eye on your environment; you never know what you could use."

She gripped the rifle with trembling hands as she swallowed dryly, crying bitter tears as she held it.

You were my hero . . .

Janus tried her hardest not to sob as her lips and chin quivered.

I tried to model myself after you, to make you proud, to become the best version of myself, the one that you always seem to see in me . . .

She held her head down, closing her eyes tightly. Janus focused on resisting the tightness building up in her chest and throat as she clenched her jaw as hard as she could.

I know you came that night to watch my back, which was more than enough of a reason for any father. But you knew you your limitations, you knew we weren't beyond reprisal, and yet you came anyway . . .

You were a soldier, a father . . .

You were the best person I knew.

And in an instant, you were taken away from me.

Now that I don't have you anymore, I don't know what to do, or who to be . . .

"I miss you so much, Dad . . ." she said aloud as she began to weep, brushing her hand over the rusted metal frame of the rifle.

"Your skills will be fine-tuned," he'd said to her once during her STARCOV training.

"You'll react to a situation without even thinking, which is exactly what they're training you for. But versatility . . .

"Keeping your mind open to possibilities can turn a bad situation into a good one. It can turn a toolbox into an armoury, a child's bedroom into an ambush position, or an empty magazine into an unanticipated opportunity.

"What sets you apart from others, Janus, is your versatility. That will be my gift to you, from one professional to another . . ."

Holding the weapon in her hands, Janus undid the shoulder strap from both ends of the gun before cradling it as if it were a child.

"I thought we were invincible . . ." She scoffed, shaking her head as a tear splashed on the weapon. "I shouldn't have been so reckless . . . "

Janus let her legs dangle over the side of the tower as she moved to the edge, watching the trees and grass sway against the breeze around the National park.

Nathan never seemed to let life's worries get the best of him. He would listen to her, hug her, talk to her, and kick her in the backside whenever she needed it; the man had never asked for anything in return. Nathan kept to himself and happily became the father that she needed him to be. She never had an opportunity to know him as a person, only as a father and mentor.

Janus smiled despite herself.

She could feel the weight from her shoulders lift mercifully as she pondered on what she had to do next.

"I'll find Oscar."

Her words fluttered off into the wind, floating into the sky along with her vow.

"Your sacrifice will not be in vain."

⌘

22: A PLACE TO CALL HOME

⌘

Grey sat at the only piece of furniture in the room.

The dark brown table had a scorch mark on the side with mismatched plastic chairs placed messily around it. Having come so far into the sector, Janus wasn't too surprised that the house was barren, but she'd hoped Grey would've had more to his name than what she saw here, especially considering how much of himself he'd poured into the role.

Their boots disturbed the thin layer of dust as they walked inside, irritating her sinuses as she held back the urge to sneeze. The faded brown floorboards creaked under their weight, each step sounding as if it might push through to the earth underneath.

"I thought I was clear . . ." said Grey, not looking up from his work.

Janus took a deep breath, composing herself.

I have no idea what to expect from this man . . . I need to stay calm if I'm going to convince him.

Glancing to Ducard with a raised brow, he met her gaze before nodding to her. She had her doubts that he would change his mind, but Ducard was confident.

"Grey," he said, "we have something you need to see . . ."

Her eyes were drawn to the gaping hole in the wall beyond the table. It looked as though an explosive of some kind had shredded the plaster wall; however, there were no scorch marks around the edges. Peering through, she observed the backyard, which hadn't seen any maintenance for quite some time. The area was stacked with litter, covered in dirt, and the grass had become a small forest, reminiscent of the National Park she'd visited yesterday.

I'm glad I went back there; I feel so clear headed now . . .

At the far end of the yard was an old shed, or at least the ruins of one. Scanning the rest of the yard, she noticed most of the fence palings around the property had fallen away, the other features in her field of vision showing the same desolate appearance.

As her eyes began to turn back to Grey, she saw the remains of a large, horizontal gas tank with the top completely blown open in the yard. Considering the size of it, she surmised that it must have had something to do with the state of the shed and the fence palings.

Looks as though the explosion must have taken the shed with it . . .

"You know how much I've got on," said Grey. "And to top it all off, I'm going to Silver City tomorrow. I don't have time for this right now."

His eyes glanced up to them for a moment before darting back down.

"Can we talk," proposed Ducard, "in private?"

Ducard gently placed his hand over Grey's before delicately taking the pen from his hands.

Grey looked up at him, trying to hide his anger as he slid the chair out, storming outside through the hole in the wall.

"Don't worry," said Ducard, tilting his head to Janus. "He's just under a lot of stress."

Ducard stepped outside with Grey and moved out of sight, the two of them talking in hushed tones.

Janus looked around the large room. To her left, she found a built-in kitchen counter on the wall with a cracked window overlooking the street. On the bench was a sink, surrounded with a row of appliances. On the opposite side of the room were two bedrooms and a bathroom, the doors of which were torn away, allowing her to peek inside. There was a crusty old mattress with no blankets or sheets, and the other room looked completely empty.

Scrunching her brow as she scratched the back of her neck, she suddenly felt sorry for Grey.

Is this how all people live in the sector . . . ?

It was no wonder he spent most of his time at the pub, this place didn't feel like a home to her at all. She'd been here a few minutes and already felt uncomfortable.

I can't imagine what it would be like to live in a place like this.

Janus reached up to her blue cap, fixing it over her head as she tucked her hair inside. Listening to the hushed murmurs of the two men outside, she slid out one of the chairs across from where Grey had been sitting, getting comfortable as she inspected the items on the surface. There was no discernible order to his workspace; he had food packaging, a couple of crusty glasses, and many food stained plates in between stacks of paper and stationery. The room stunk of cigarettes, but it seemed stronger now that she'd sat down. As she reluctantly slid away from the table, she tilted her head down to check what her foot rested on. It was a bucket of cigarette butts.

That's . . . . disgusting . . .

She slid back into the table, pressing her lips together as she pushed the bucket away with her boot. The awkward sound of the metal scraping against the wood caught Grey's attention as the two of them walked back in.

"Hey," he said with a chuckle. "Keep your toes off my bucket, little lady."

She cleared her throat as she straightened her back against the chair, unsure on what to say.

"Relax, darlin'," he said with a natural smile. "That thing's pretty nasty; I don't blame ya for not wantin' to be next to it. Been meaning to clean it up, but you know . . ."

The two of them joined her at the table, Ducard holding back a fit of laughter.

"We're going to have to make this quick," said Grey mirthlessly, placing his elbows on the table as he held his hands together. "Ducard tells me that you really helped us out recently, even went as far as to put your life at risk."

Grey pulled out a pack of cigarettes before continuing. "Don't know why you'd want to get back into the thick of it all after going through what you did, and I ain't going to pretend to know what's drivin' you . . .

"But regardless, It all comes down to this, kid. I appreciate any help I can get, I really do . . ." Grey lit the cigarette, smoking it leisurely. "But I made your mother a promise. And I'm a man of my word."

They were all silent for a few moments. "Your mother, she's done right by me, more than you know. So here it is; if you want to help me track down your brother and the bastard responsible for takin' him, I get that. But you need to clear it with her first."

Ducard nodded as he tilted his head sideways, rolling his wrist around with an open palm, gesturing for Grey to continue.

Grey smiled at him, blinking slowly before continuing. "I'm sorry for . . . sending you away a few nights ago . . ." He exhaled, breathing out smoke. "In my experience, operators aren't exactly the most trustworthy of people, which is why I was hesitant to trust you . . ."

She nodded, her eyes drifting to the objects on the table.

Can't say I blame him . . .

"But . . . you risked your life to get us that equipment. And if we didn't have you looking into it, it would've been months before I could've gone there myself."

He leaned back in the chair. "I appreciate what you did, darlin'; hell, I'm even a little impressed . . ." She met his smirk with one of her own. "If you can convince Adalia to let you do your thing, we'd be happy to have you aboard."

Janus took a deep breath before answering. "I've spoken with my mother about helping you find him," lied Janus. "And she understands. Oscar is the only thing we have left." She shook her head. "Nothing else matters now. All we want is for Oscar to come home."

The Councillor seemed sceptical.

Be honest for once in your life!

She took a moment to breathe, ignoring the tightening in her throat as she swallowed dryly.

"I can't move on until I know what happened to my brother. No matter what state we find him in. So I'm in until the end." She scoffed, trying to hide the anguish in her eyes. "Even if it all goes to shit again."

Grey slid his index finger over the scar tissue on his cheek before moving his hand down to palm the stubble on his chin.

Ducard took an exaggerated breath, slapping his hands together. "See?" he said, gesturing to them both. "She's got a personal stake in this, same as you." Placing a gloved hand on Grey's shoulder, Ducard tilted his head towards the door. "Shall we?"

"Yeah," said Grey. "Show me what you got."

"First of all," said Ducard, taking the manifest from his jacket pocket, "you might want to take a look at this."

They all walked out to the street as Grey handled the document. People in tattered clothes walked on the road and sidewalk, all of them turning their heads to watch the three of them leave Grey's house. The only audible noises on the street were the citizens' murmurings and the dull thumps of their footsteps as they came and went. It was off-putting not to hear any vehicles or aeroplanes above, making Janus feel as if something was missing.

They regarded Janus curiously with squinted eyes and whispers between each other, but they quickly turned away when Grey walked out behind her.

They must be a little cautious of him . . .

Shaking her head, Janus hoped that wasn't the case.

Perhaps they don't realise how much he helps them all . . .

"Janus went to take a look at one of their barracks, as it turned out," said Ducard. "Thought we might see if we could get some intel on these guys. We didn't expect to get so lucky with what we got, and let me tell you, It sure helps fill in a few blanks."

"Blanks . . . Such as?"

"They're being funded by Jone's company . . ." said Ducard.

Grey looked at him incredulously. "Lornan Futuristics? Those bastards. So *that* was the contract he'd gotten his grubby mitts on . . ."

"Yep," said Ducard, fiddling with the lever to open the truck. "I'm guessing these soldiers were part and parcel with the weapons they made."

Janus adjusted the brim of her hat to shield her eyes from the afternoon sun as she dismissed Ducard and operated the lever herself.

"Jone's company is funded by the kindred . . ." said Grey, anger overwhelming his face as he slipped the manifest in his pocket.

"What . . . ?" asked Ducard incredulously. "How do you know that?"

Grey shook his head. "I recognise the shell company they're usin' . . ."

"I knew they had something up their sleeves . . ." said Ducard. "Can't leave well enough alone, can they?"

Janus observed Grey's clenched hands and reddening face with concern.

"Hey," said Ducard. "They'll get theirs, don't you worry."

Grey looked to his friend, who hopped up to the rear of the truck.

"It's good news, man!" said Ducard. "We finally have a trail, something concrete on them. But we're going to need more if we want to get the council on board."

With his jaw clenched, fists curled into themselves, he shook his head.

"Should've dealt with 'em when I had the chance . . ."

"*Grey,*" said Ducard. "You're a *councillor* now, remember? Those days are behind you . . ."

As Ducard said the word "councillor," Grey seemed to snap back to reality.

He exhaled, nodding to his friend after a time.

"We'll get them," said Ducard. "Don't worry. Let's try to focus on one thing at a time, shall we?"

"You're right . . ."

"Now!" said Ducard, rubbing his hands together with glee. "Come inside and take a look at this stuff."

Grey nodded as he heaved himself inside with one hand. As he walked beyond Ducard, the pilot looked to Janus as he released a breath he'd been holding onto, visibly relieved.

Is he worried about what Grey will do?

She shrugged, hopping up to the truck cabin with the two of them.

With them until the end now, no looking back.

"Hey," said Grey as he pat Ducard on the back. "Thanks . . . for, well, everything . . ."

Ducard smiled broadly. "Don't worry about it."

Patting his friend on the shoulder, Grey lifted the lid effortlessly from one of the boxes.

"Well all right then," he said, lifting a black helmet with both hands. "This one definitely look similar . ." Turning it around in his hands, he sighed. "But it feels lighter than the others."

Janus cleared her throat as she lifted the lid on another box. "How about these ones?" she asked.

Leaning his head over to look inside, he nodded as he clicked his tongue. "Yep, that's them . . ."

"*And,*" said Janus as she lifted up the familiar helmet, "if you take a look at the logo . . ."

Grey chortled as he received it from her, placing the other back into the container.

"An Enforcement logo . . . those bastards!"

Ducard and Janus smiled, sharing a look of achievement as they glanced at each other.

"That explains why there were so many enforcers at Lornan Futuristics that night . . ."

Janus squinted at him for a moment.

Sounds like you had something to do with Jone's disappearance.

As she observed his behaviour, she thought now was probably not the best time to question him on it. She filed the query away for a later time.

Grey was smiling like a fool now, tossing the helmet up and catching it triumphantly.

He turned to Janus. "Thanks for the help, darlin'; your work here will help put this whole thing to rest."

She nodded gratefully.

"So," she said with a smile, "what's next?"

⌘

Grey had decided that an early night would be the best thing for him. Although sleep never came quickly, he thought he might try achieving the state of mind without any aid tonight, frivolous as it seemed.

It was after around three hours of lying in bed, unable to drift off, that he finally decided to get up for some water. It was then that he noticed two golden eyes peering at him from the lawn. Turning his head to glare at the presence outside, he smiled pleasantly.

"Hey, girl," he said as he bent down. "Haven't seen you in a while . . ."

A large wolf jumped through the hole in the wall and trotted over to him, the large, unkempt claws of the creature tapping away on the floorboards with each step. The old girl pushed her head into Grey's lap and allowed him to rub her matted fur.

"Phew," he said, shaking his head, "someone needs a bath."

The wolf groaned as it nudged him, before staring up into his eyes with a wagging, excited tail.

"I'll bet you've come back for food, right?"

It nodded.

Grey chuckled, standing up and putting his hand on his hips.

"If you're so smart, you should come up with a way to pay me some rent. It's about time you pulled your weight, wouldn't you say?"

The wolf raised its jaw into the air, howling and grumbling at Grey's incessant talking.

"Okay, I get it," he said, walking to the kitchen to open the refrigerator.

Fishing out the bag of meat he bought at the market, he opened it to show the contents to the old fur ball scuttling its way over to him. Placing the bag on the ground, Grey brushed his fingers through the sticky grey and white coat of the animal, smiling at the unexpected visit. "It's always good to have you back."

I hope one day you feel safe enough to stick around permanently.

Patting the wolf's head a few times, Grey turned around to fill a glass of water before downing it quickly.

Watching the empty street outside, he couldn't help but wonder what the wolf did in between her trips to the house.

"What *do* you get up to when you're away, hmm?"

Turning around to face her, he became anxious at her change of state. The wolf's tail was up, and she had her eyes pointing outside through the hole in the wall.

"What is it . . . ?"

Moving slowly towards the hole, Grey yelped as the wolf held its mouth over his leg as if to stop him from leaving the house. It released him from its jaw and leapt into the darkness without further delay, as he reached out to try and stop the animal from venturing out.

"Wait!" yelled Grey as he charged outside, clenching his jaw and preparing his muscles for a fight. But there was nothing, save for the sound of the wind howling through the alleys and the dew covered grass nipping at his legs.

The wolf began scouting around the yard, sniffing and trotting between the weeds as Grey looked around for any signs of life.

Sighing to himself, he felt anxious about what the wolf may have seen in the shadows. It wasn't the first time she'd seen something that he had not. Grey wasn't sure whether or not he was paranoid or if there really was someone stalking him during the night.

I suppose one of these days we'll find out . . .

"Come on, girl," said Grey. "It's warmer in the bedroom; come inside and get some rest."

23: DARKUS

⌘

Darkus ran.

Sprinting through an endless void of cold and crushing darkness, he felt utterly exhausted, overwhelmed and terrified. He could feel a presence waiting for him at the edge of his senses, demanding he cease resisting and embrace it. Moving as quickly as his body would allow, he knew that at any moment, it would consume him, suffocating his flesh and mind with everlasting dark.

A haunting silence engulfed his senses; he felt no breeze on his skin nor the ground beneath his bare feet. He was naked, but any sort of sensation on his skin was numbed. The only sensory thing he was able to discern were the crimson limbs, stretching out around him as he desperately tried to get away from it.

Don't look back!

It was stretching out to him. Demanding him.

Darkus knew in his bones that it was right behind him, tickling the hairs on his neck with a terrible appetite.

Suddenly, his body froze in place, refusing to obey his commands.

"Come . . . to me . . ."

Something forced him to turn, controlling his body like a puppet as his consciousness took on the position of an observer. Darkus could still feel his throbbing heartbeat, trouncing his ribcage as if it wanted to be free from his chest. Tensing and trembling, his muscles began to ache as he stared into the everlasting abyss, his eyes darting around searching for the presence. Darkus knew his eyes were deceiving him, but no matter where he looked, he couldn't see anything but black.

Then In his peripheral vision, he saw it.

Thousands of crimson tendrils stretched around his vision like spider limbs wrapping around the world. It snaked around his head and body, delicately yet firmly pulling him close for a final embrace. Following the trail of red from his outer vision to the centre, he saw nothing. Just darkness, nothing more.

I know it's there! It's staring at me!

He slowly turned his head, and like before, he saw the creature hiding in his peripherals.

His entire body seized as he gleaned the horrible truth. All of his muscles tensed to their breaking point, struggling and screaming without tone, his eyes clenched so hard they were about to burst.

Anguish enveloped him, as he felt his body being gnashed together and consumed by teeth and tongue.

Then he felt nothing.

⌘

"NO!" Darkus screamed out in horror as he woke up.

Trembling and sweating as he panted and gasped for air, Darkus fell from the cold metal table he was lying on a moment ago.

He looked around anxiously at the machines and other medical devices around the room, reporting on his vitals with screens filled with charts and statistics. Glancing down at his naked body, which was twitching horribly, Darkus began frantically tugging at the cables stuck to his body. They came away freely with frenzied swipes as he overswung, falling to the smooth white floor with a crash. There was no pain of any kind, and as he picked himself up Darkus looked around for an exit.

Free from his bonds and traumatised by the ghostly images of his nightmares, he sprinted down the only dark hallway before him, desperate to escape and find something familiar.

The only noise he could hear was his bare feet slapping against the floor beneath him, apart from his heart thumping in his ears.

Moving away from the light from where he'd woke and into the darkness with the frenzy of a scared animal, Darkus barely noticed the hallway open up into a large room. As he stopped moving, he began to squint, searching for the next route through the black.

Floodlights beamed in his face. He grunted as he shielded his eyes from the beams of light around him.

Darkus panted and gasped as he tried to angle his arm over the lights in an attempt to glean the faces of those who watched him from above.

"Do you know where you are, young man?" Asked a firm male voice.

"What's going on here?" he demanded. "Where am I?"

"Answer our questions, and we will answer yours . . ." said a young woman's voice.

Darkus could make out only sparse details through the glowing lights pointed at his face.

He was standing in the middle of a circular room. Before him was a grandstand where numerous people sat high above, protected by a bulletproof barrier with their faces obscured by the light. The room was sparse for detail, as the space around him was empty. No doors, windows, or furniture of any kind could be seen.

"Do you know your name?" Asked the same male voice from before.

His eyes returned to the silhouettes above, trying to discern details of any kind. He could make out at least eight silhouettes, all of them observing him thoughtfully.

"My name . . ." he muttered, his brain throbbing as he tried to remember. "Darkus . . . My name is Darkus."

"And your last name?"

"Maler . . . Malaroth . . . My name is Darkus Malaroth . . ."

One of the men scoffed.

"He's not going to remember his name, you say!?" mocked an older woman's voice. "What kind of conditioning have you put him through exactly?"

Another woman sitting across from her gestured dismissively. "This isn't a known science! We're doing our best, so you're going to have to be patient and work with us until we develop the right conditions."

"Tell me, Darkus," said the woman, turning her head to face him. "I'm going to have the man in the suit show you a photo."

The woman's voice was gentle, understanding. It made him feel relaxed.

A man stepped forward, heavily clad in protective armour. It was black metal, with misshapen red eyes beaming at him fiercely. He held out a photograph, the metal plates on his armour shifting audibly as he did so.

Darkus extended his hand, squinting against the intense light still on him.

"Do you know this person?" Asked the woman.

"That's . . . Darius . . . Darius Malaroth. My brother . . ."

Sweet Pioneers . . . Darius . . .

Darkus began to panic.

I told him I was going to come back straight away . . . !

He held his hands over his head, gasping audibly as he began to shake.

I have to get back to him . . . I promised I would take care of him!

"I'm sorry," he said. "I have to go! I need to see my brother!"

Glancing around the room nervously, Darkus searched for exits.

"I need to go! I need to find him!"

He heard a ringing in his ears as guilt and stress washed over him.

Darkus suddenly felt old, like a lot of time had passed since he went to sleep, the details of which were fuzzy and vague, confusing him. Darkus began to rub his face and body, searching for scars that were familiar to him. They were not there. Instead, he saw that his veins looked black, and his moon-white skin looked almost alien, as if he were inhabiting someone else's body.

"What the hell is going on here!?"

He shook his head as the black metal soldier stepped closer.

How I got here doesn't matter! I need to get back!

A cold sweat enveloped him as he felt a tingling sensation wash over him.

"This one is done," Said the man's voice. "Trooper?"

"Please!" He implored to the soldier. "Let me out of here! I need to find—"

The soldier lunged forward with a blade, piercing his heart.

He gasped.

A numb sensation washed over his body, rippling out from his chest like his body was falling asleep. Looking down frightfully, he tried to grab the blade that was sticking inside his chest, causing black blood to spill from the wound. His hand fell away as exhaustion began to consume his body.

His face became weak.

His eyes closed on their own accord.

Then he felt nothing.

⌘

24: CONSULTATION

⌘

"Hey there," said Grey. "I'm looking for John Westermann."

Squinting at him through wide-brimmed glasses, the receptionist raised her greying eyebrow at him curiously. "And who might you be?"

"The name's Grey; I'm a Councillor from Menilax, and I have an appointment with your boy here."

"*You're* a Councillor?" She chortled. "You look more like a *thug* to me."

Grey nodded curtly. "I get that a lot."

"One moment, 'Councillor,'" she said before tapping away on the keyboard.

She furrowed her wrinkled brow, clearly frustrated with the equipment as she shook her head.

"I know that face." Grey crossed his arms, peering down as he gestured to the computer. "Having computer troubles?"

She scoffed. "I *cannot* stand them! The young girl who does the computer work is sick today, so here I am, doing her job *for* her!" She gestured sharply at the screen. "Now it's stuck . . . !"

Grey chuckled. "I have trouble turning them on. You've gotten that far, at least."

"It's just so *slow*!" she said, gesturing accusingly. "I can never get any work done when I'm stuck on this *stupid* desk . . ."

Grey looked around the room as the old woman pattered away. It was carpeted, cramped, and had not aged well. The faded cream walls had patches where water leaks had been ignored, resulting in splits and cracks across the paint. The faint smell of mould was evident, masked slightly by the strong odours of cleaning products.

The stink of bleach makes my stomach turn . . .

Living in the Broken Sector, one became accustomed to such scents, but the intense cleaning aromas in the office seemed to make him a little lightheaded.

These guys need to open up a few windows . . .

The older woman looked up to say something, but the front door opened before she could speak. Grey turned around to see a familiar face, rattling his nerves.

"*Grim . . . ?*" he said under his breath.

"Hello . . . ?" said the man curiously as he walked over to the desk.

He'd aged considerably since he'd last seen him. His once thick salt and pepper hair had now receded, although he still retained his short, trimmed beard. His bulging eyes and hawk nose gave him a wise, experienced look, features that used to frighten him as a young man.

"Jim, it's been a while," said Grey as he rubbed his scar with his index finger.

"Greyson?" he asked, taking a moment to look him over.

Grey glanced back to the receptionist, who was ignoring them.

Turning back to face Jim, the man was looking him up and down curiously. Grey tried to hide the panic forming in his chest as the man observed his stature.

Come on . . . Don't do this to me . . .

"It's been a long time," Jim Grimmell's mouth curved at the edge as he spoke. That scar of yours . . ."

"Yeah," said Grey, chortling. "Complements of the boy you sent my way, all those years ago . . ."

"Darius did that to you?" he asked with a raised brow. Grimmell smiled as if he finally understood a joke that had been bouncing around his head for some time.

"I heard the two of you became quite close over the years," said Jim. "Guess I was mistaken . . ."

Grey shook his head. "Nah, you ain't mistaken." He crossed his arms. "We *were* close, but . . . Ah hell, it's a long story . . ."

"Now, don't you pay him any mind, Councillor!" said the receptionist with her rattling voice. "This man's a grumpy old thing . . . and certainly not the friendliest fellow!"

Seeing him after so much time and in his current state had thrown him off balance.

James Grimmell was an inspiration to him as a young man; in fact, Grey had adopted many of his tactical techniques and strategies into his own repertoire. Not to mention his lessons on human behaviour, which he'd absorbed like a sponge.

This was the last place he expected Jim to wind up after his time in Menilax.

Looking at the dark brown eyes of his old mentor, many happy memories flittered through his mind; however, now was not the time for diving into the nostalgic memories.

How in the world did you end up working with Westermann?

"So what brings you to us today?" asked Jim with a neutral expression.

"Councilman Greyson has an appointment with John," piped up the receptionist.

Grey gestured to the receptionist with his thumb extended. "Yeah," he said, "I called ahead."

You need to relax and take a breath.

"I see," said Grim. "And what business do you have with him?"

"I need some help looking for someone," said Grey.

"And which *side* of the law is this person on exactly?"

Haven't lost your touch, old man . . .

Grey smirked. "I suppose you could say he's on the *wrong* side."

Grim smiled with his yellow teeth. "Well, lucky for you, *those* sorts are our specialty."

Jim hailed the receptionist.

"We're going to go out for a bit," he said. "John's waiting for us at the duellin' ring."

"Take care, gentleman."

Jim gestured towards the door. "Right this way, *Councillor.*"

⌘

"You two are up there," said the usher, gesturing towards their seats.

"Thanks," said Grey as he and Grim walked beside each other.

The ring was quite packed. Hundreds of people were sitting around the circle, piled into rows of chairs that were wrapped around the centre stage.

Set in a large stadium, the ring itself was cased in bulletproof glass and held together by steel support beams. A large grandstand surrounded the centre, with at least three hundred seats bolted into the ascending platform. As they made their way to their places, Grey sipped his drink leisurely, enjoying the warm, thick black alchoholic brew famous in Silver City. As they slipped into their plastic seats, Grey was happy that they had a good view of the middle of the ring, which was shaped like a rectangle. Inside the glass were wooden chipboard panels and walls, as if it were an obstacle course of some kind.

Grey smiled in disbelief. "I can't believe he's competing . . ."

Grim nodded. "Aye, he's quite good."

"Yeah but, it's a bit unfair . . . isn't it?"

"Not at all," said Grim. "He's not using his ability. He competes as a primal to keep it fair."

He gestured towards the left side of the ring where Westermann sat hunched over with his eyes closed and his hands clasped together.

"It wouldn't be a true test of skill otherwise."

Looking carefully around the Pioneer, he saw the corner of a long table surrounded by mesh fencing and a small team of security officers beyond it.

"Well, let's not forget he's got lifetimes of—"

Grey stopped himself short, looking around to the other people around him.

I have no idea if they know he's a Pioneer . . .

Grim seemed to get the context.

"Well, there is *that*, it's true he's got a lot of experience. But experience isn't everything, and every person has their own unique slice of it. People can surprise you."

He looked at him with a smirk.

He knows . . . Of course, he knows . . .

"People of Silver City! May I present our two competitors!"

The announcer's voice boomed through the speakers built into the walls, each one a few meters apart. Some of the wall panels had posters advertising a few teams and players that were popular in the duelling ring.

"Competing for a place in the finals tomorrow, our two semi-final players will be duelling for a chance to fight Brandon Salvatia, our reigning champion!"

"Brandon must be good," said Grey.

Grim shrugged. "He's an up-and-comer. Not a fan of his attitude, but he's got good reflexes for an older fella."

The television screens above the ring came to life, the image displaying a split-screen, both showing metal doors that were sealed.

"On the north side of the ring; the man who watches our streets while we sleep. The champion who donates his winnings to charity, and the reigning winner of the burger devouring contest down at Benny's!"

The crowd chuckled, with a few clapping at the dueller's accomplishments.

"Our veteran gunslinger: John, J. Westermann!"

Cheering and clapping, Grey watched the sliding door open slowly. John wore light brown cargo pants, a dark blue shirt, and thick black boots. He was fairly average looking, but he had a smile that made the crowd cheer even louder. John had tanned skin, a few scars across his face, and dark blonde hair. He looked like a labourer; in fact, if Grey didn't know beforehand that he wasn't a Pioneer, he wouldn't be able to pick it. The fact that his eyes were blue—likely from wearing a lens—hid the man's true heritage.

On his belt was a large revolver resting in a brown holster.

"Aaaaand on the south side!" continued the announcer. "She's served in our armed forces and has served her country in many theatres, including Celeritus, Kadage and Sashiryu. A woman you do *not* want to get on the bad side of. Introducing, Useni Cerulius!"

The opening door revealed a woman with the skin colour of a dark night, with an average height, short, dark brown hair, hazelnut eyes, and full red lips. Her broad nose gave Grey the impression she was Kandellian.

Useni smiled and waved, looking like quite the showperson.

Grey felt tingles rise through his chest.

Wow . . . she's really something.

Her eyes reminded him of Ciril.

Pioneers . . . I miss you so much . . .

Grey closed his eyes, squinting as hard as he could, trying desperately to stop his mind from venturing down the torturous train of thought.

Ciril . . .

Saying her name, even in his head made his heart ache. After all of this time, her loss was still too much to bear.

"Are you okay?" asked Grim, touching his shoulder.

Opening his eyes, he saw flecks of static around his eyes, reminding him of how perpetually tired he was. Taking a deep and steady breath, he nodded to Grim.

"Gunslingers!" boomed the announcer. "Are *you* ready?"

The two competitors looked up to the camera and nodded.

Useni unsheathed her pistol. The black metal weapon had three roses painted on it, one of which was red, one blue, and the last one a light orange colour. Grey wondered how many of the competitors had their pistols customised, finding the decoration perplexing.

Never saw guns as anything more than a tool . . . But to each their own, I suppose . . .

"Let's duel!" barked the announcer as the crowd roared.

"So, Greyson," said Grim. "Tell me more about the person you're looking for."

The two duellists darted into the ring as the shutter slowly came down behind them, sealing them inside the ring.

"Looking for a Pioneer," he said. Grey felt safe enough to speak now; the roaring and clapping of the crowd would keep their conversation relatively private, so long as they kept their voices quieter than everyone else.

"A Pioneer, you say." He didn't seem too phased at the mention of a Pioneer.

"Can't say I know many who are still wanderin' around in the open. Most have changed identities or moved off-world. There are a handful still around, although they tend to stay off the grid, for obvious reasons . . ."

Westermann walked along the west side path with a casual, unworried gait.

Useni sprinted as hard as her body would carry her, darting around the corners as if her life depended on it. Grey assumed it would take thirty seconds or so for them to run into each other at this rate, judging on the size of the ring.

"We're also looking for a man who goes by the name of 'Sinew.'"

Grim clenched his brow, turning his head to Grey in disbelief.

"Sinew?"

I knew that'd get your attention . . .

Grey turned to nod at him, observing his unnerved expression.

"Yeah, you heard me."

"Well, that certainly changes things . . . What do you know about him?" asked Grim with a serious inflection.

Grey shrugged. "We know he's kidnapping augurs, working with a Pioneer, and he's practically invincible."

Grim nodded.

"I've been looking for him for a while now, but he's got no record or identification of any kind. Makes it hard to find him . . ." said Grey.

"I'm kinda hopin' that this Pioneer he's workin' with might be a bit more traceable. And considering *your* boy down there used to work with him, I'm guessing you really *are* the right people to help us out."

Telling Grim that he knew Westermann was a Pioneer was a gamble.

Hopefully, it moves things along. I have no interest in playing games.

"Well, what can I say, seems you've done your homework," said Grim. "We'll ask him about it when he's done."

Standing in the middle of a corridor, Westermann heard Useni's footsteps, so he walked behind a bulletproof panel and crouched behind it. The Pioneer unsheathed his pistol, holding it with both hands as he listened intently. His movements seemed too casual, too placid for the situation.

Useni stopped moving before the hallway he was hiding in, keeping her back flat against the wall.

Both of them waited patiently for the other for a few moments.

"Tell me," said Grey, "how did you two come to work together?"

"Aye, it's a bit of an unusual partnership. My way of dealin' with things is quite different to West's way, that's for sure, but I suppose you could say I wanted to tidy up my way o' livin'. Menilax was starting to eat away at me too much . . . You know how it is . . ."

Grey nodded.

"John runs a tight shop 'ere, meanin' we do everything by the book."

Grim crossed his arms.

"Never really had the opportunity to be a part of a community before. It's a nice change from the way things were in Menilax."

Useni purposefully rattled the panel she was hiding behind before peeking around the corridor carefully. She was hoping to bait some movement from John, although he didn't take the bait.

As she stepped out to sprint across to the other side. John reached over and fired a single shot at her. The electronic slug pelted the far wall, slightly missing her as she got into cover safely.

John held the angle with his gun trained on the corner she'd disappeared behind, waiting for her to try her luck a second time.

"That was close . . ." muttered Grim.

"Losing your touch, *lawman?*" she jested, the mic on her lapel picking up her commentary.

Westermann did not respond. He kept his focus down the sight of his pistol.

"No room for a bit of fun then . . . ?" she said under her breath.

Fun is an unusual way to phrase it . . .

"It seems so lively here," stated Grey. "Do you boys run into much trouble with the people here?"

"Aye, we did initially when we took over from the old team, but now it's pretty quiet. I don't mind it much, gives us plenty o' time to help the community, and be a part of the culture."

Grim gestured around him. "Where else in the world would you be able to come and enjoy good sport and not worry about someone knifin' ya."

It was true. The only security guards were at the entrances to the duelling ring. If it were Menilax, there would be security teams patrolling the walkways with weapons, some on the catwalks above, and possibly even some undercover as regular citizens.

"Must be nice . . ."

Grim stretched his arms behind his head. "It's a good way to live, Grey. Maybe when you're ready to retire, you can come out here and work for us."

Grey scoffed. "Don't think retirement's an option for me."

Confident that John wouldn't press her, Useni quietly walked away from the corridor, training her weapon on the corner as she backed away. Her movement had the desired effect; John remained stationary as she crept away and relocated.

After a few moments, John began to move away from the reinforced wall, keeping his pistol aimed down the corridor in case Useni peeked around.

"Do you have a family?" asked Grim.

I used to . . .

"I uh, had a daughter, once."

"Oh . . . I'm sorry to hear it," said Grim. "What was her name?"

Grey swallowed dryly.

"Ciril,"

"That's a beautiful name."

She was a beautiful woman . . . the woman of my dreams . . .

"What happened to her?" asked Grim.

"Darius happened to her . . ."

"Really? Didn't think the boy had it in him to hurt a woman . . ."

"It was an accident . . ."

Grey turned to face him with tears welling in his eyes. Grim sighed and nodded before meeting his gaze, pursing his lips as if he understood. Shaking his head, Grey crossed his arms.

"But, well . . . it is what it is."

"Sorry. I shouldn't be prying."

Grey sighed. "Even though it's been a few years, it still feels like it only happened yesterday . . . Things have never been the same since."

Grim nodded. "Aye, I do get that. Darius was like a son to me, and even though he was a mixed-up little lad, I miss 'em terribly. He had such potential . . ."

Didn't realise you had such strong feelings . . .

"I remember sending him to ya during his early days," said Grim. "I thought honest work would've straightened him out. Even though the kindred sent him to me as a punishment, of sorts, I figured it might not be too late to bring him around. Guess all that crap they stuffed in his noggin' turned out to be too much for him to deal with in the long run . . ."

Grey shrugged. "Yeah, I tried my best, but . . . hell, he was a stubborn kid."

Grim laughed fondly at that. "Aye, that he was . . ."

Useni had circled around to flank John, who had backed up around the corner to displace. As she fired her shot, he stepped back, narrowly avoiding defeat, visibly rattled by her sudden appearance on his flank.

She pressed her advantage, and instead of pushing toward him from the alley, she climbed up to the top of the ring with both arms, momentarily leaving herself open to attack. John picked up on this, but instead of risking a shot, he sprinted away, moving down the corridor to get some distance.

By the time she hoisted herself up, he was halfway down the hallway.

"Damn you, old man!" she barked as she trained her weapon at him. "Stop running and fight!"

Firing a shot down range, Useni narrowly missed the Pioneer as he darted around the corner. Shaking her head, she kept her weapon trained on his last seen location as she began to move along the top of the wooden panels. Slipping out from behind cover with his gun arm extended, John fired a shot before ducking back to safety. Useni saw it coming as she dropped to the floor, flicking sand into the air with her landing as she returned fire.

Jogging across to the other side of the corridor, Westermann fired another shot at her as she landed. As her feet hit the sand, Useni threw herself on her back, clenching her jaw as she fired two shots his way. John didn't break his stride as he reached the other side, hiding behind the wall and holding his weapon next to his head as he listened intently for Useni to make a move.

"It's going to be tough for her now," said Grim, watching her quickly stand.

She's on her last shot . . .

By Grey's count, John still had three shots remaining. His bold manoeuvre to the other side had drawn out Useni's ammunition, making Grey confident that it was the real purpose of his movement. It was a gamble, but it had worked out for him, it seemed.

John played the waiting game once more, listening for his opponent to make the first move, while Useni had her pistol trained on his position, ready to fire at a moment's notice.

As the camera panned on Westermann, Grey could make out the eye lenses clearer than before. However, if he wasn't looking for it, he wouldn't have noticed it.

"Does he ever take those lenses off?" asked Grey.

Grim shrugged. "Not so much. It wouldn't do him much good staying under the radar with those pearly whites of his. Most folks can spot 'em a mile away."

Of course. That makes sense.

Grey rubbed his chin.

I wonder how many people I've come across who were secretly Pioneers . . .

Useni began to sneak forward.

The crowd went silent.

John kept his ear around the corner, trying to listen carefully for movement.

Her footsteps were silent; in fact, not even the microphones could pick it up as her feet sunk delicately into the sand. She gained good ground, but after a few moments, John grew impatient, peeking the corner and catching Useni sneaking along the corridor.

The two of them locked eyes as Useni charged his position with a battle cry. John pulled away from the corner to safety. As she came around the corner, she dived into the sand, aiming her weapon at the intersection of where she last saw him.

"Oh, crap . . ." she muttered, not realising he'd climbed up at the last moment.

Standing on top of the wall, John fired a single bullet at her chest.

The slug pelted her stomach, sending electric shocks through her body for a brief moment as she spread out over the sand. Once the charge had finished punishing her hubris, she stayed, panting and chuckling to herself.

The crowd roared in excitement as they all stood and clapped.

Grey and Grim remained in their seats.

He couldn't hear what the competitors were saying to each other, but John helped her up as her body still spasmed a little, shaking her hand and nodding to her respectfully.

Good sportsmanship.

"Well," said Grim, "that's that!"

It was hard to make out the words over the applause.

"Let's go meet up with the old boy," said Grim as he stood. "Have you tried the coffee here in Silver City?"

⌘

"Did you have any trouble finding the place?" asked John as the waiter gestured for them to sit.

"Grim led the way, so no trouble at all," replied Grey.

"I'd be lost without this man," said John with delight. "It is a pleasure to make your acquaintance, councillor," said Westermann, extending an open palm his way.

"Likewise," replied Grey, gripping it tightly as they shook hands.

"And how are you finding Silver City so far?"

Sitting at a bench outside of a coffee shop, Grey sipped his lightly alcoholic coffee sparsely.

Don't want to get drunk in front of the immortal . . .

Sitting across from him, John traced his finger around the rim of the rustic, clay mug, waiting patiently for Grey's response with a smile.

"It's . . . different from what I'm used to," said Grey. "In a good way though," he continued hurriedly. "It's nice to enjoy a drink without having to keep my eyes on every person that walks past me."

John chuckled as he sipped the coffee. "Aye. It's quite the opposite to what *we've* come from," said Grim, flicking his chin Grey's way.

John nodded pleasantly. "I can't say I have ever been to the big city," he said.

Grey pursed his lips. "You ain't missin' much; besides, when you have it *this* good, why would you ever leave?"

John nodded politely. "We do our best to keep the peace, although it's not as perfect as it looks."

Grim nodded, the two of them sharing a look of concern.

"But *that's* not the subject of our discussion . . ."

"You boys mind if I smoke?" Asked Grey, slipping out the pack.

"Please," said John, "help yourself."

"You're quite the duellist," said Grey. "And your game plan looks pretty solid."

John chortled. "I try to play patiently. Sometimes it gets me into trouble, but for the most part, it works well for me."

"Salvatia's goin' to give you a run for ya money tomorrow," said Grim.

"Truth. He is a *patient* duellist too," replied Westermann, "which means I may need to adapt my strategy."

"So you do have a strategy in mind?" asked Grey, lighting the cigarette.

"Yes, indeed. I have fought with him in the past, so I'm reasonably certain I know what he is going to do. But you never know with these things." John smiled warmly. "When one knows the game as well as he does; strategies can be adapted and countered with enough study on your opponent. He's quite versatile when he needs to be. We'll have to wait and see how it all unfolds.

"Now," said John as he put his elbows on the polished stone table, "to the matter at hand." Clasping his hands together, he gestured towards Grey as he spoke. "Grim tells me you're looking for a *Pioneer.*"

Straight to the point. I like it.

"I do not wish to give you an incorrect impression here," said John, "but why do you think I'd tell you the location of someone who *obviously,* does not want to be found?" Even Grim was taken aback with his words.

"You know what I *really* am, Greyson," he said leaning forward. "So why do you think I'd risk the life of one of my compatriots? We've all spent a great deal of time making new lives for ourselves, after all," Retaining his focus on Grey, his smile faded.

"This is *not* a challenge, so please do not take it that way, but I would like to hear a good reason for your request. We are a dying breed, and I do not easily lend myself to the idea of giving out their locations."

Grey nodded. "I can respect that."

Placing his arms on the table and clenching his jaw, Grey searched the immortal's face for answers. "Let me tell you about the man that your *boy's* workin' with. Does the name Sinew mean anything to you?"

John's eyes darted to the upper left corner as he thought for a moment. "Sinew . . . ? The name does not ring a bell, I'm afraid." John raised an eyebrow as he looked to Grim, who crossed his arms, chuckling to himself.

"You know this person he speaks of?" asked John, as he leant back in his chair.

Grim nodded. "You have to trust me when I tell you," said Grim, "this man is quite possibly the most dangerous person I've ever known, and he rivals that of any terrible foe *you've* faced in the past, at least the ones you've told me about."

John rubbed his clean-shaven chin. "I find that hard to believe. Neither of you witnessed the horrors we faced, centuries—" Westermann looked around, forgetting himself for a moment. "Forgive me. Please, Greyson, tell me about this 'Sinew' character," he said, getting comfortable in his chair as he rubbed his chin.

"He's a dredge," said Grey, "but he's more evolved than your average one. Somehow, he's found a way to control the bodies of others, and none of us knows how he's done it . . ."

John shrugged. "That's nothing new."

Grim and Grey both looked at John quizzically.

"The ability to control another person is a demonstrated ability and is acquired through decades of practice," said the Pioneer. "It was performed by *many* a Pioneer, at least those of the 'dredge' variety, as you say. Although there aren't too many around that can still do so, perhaps he's found a way to study his augmentation enough to learn it, or maybe he even learned how through a Pioneer that could do it. Either way, the name is obviously an alias. I seriously doubt that 'Sinew' is his real name; it's far too ridiculous for the likes of us . . ."

Grim shook his head. "He's *not* a Pioneer. The man's on the senior side, and as far as I know, Pioneers do not age . . ."

"Truth. We do not age the same as primal humans. Although he could've gone through the ritual at an old age, which would explain it."

"Either way," said Grey. "He's able to regenerate fatal wounds in a matter of seconds. Don't suppose you've ever seen that?"

Say yes . . . Pioneers, say yes . . .

"No," said John. "No, that *is* unusual and frightening . . ." Westermann's brow clenched as he searched the table for his words.

"The man's a walkin' nightmare," said Grim. "I doubt even you'd stand a chance against *this* one."

John nodded to himself as he rubbed his chin. "Yes. I doubt that, as well." He looked up to Grey quizzically. "How is it that I've never heard about this man?" he asked. "If he's such a threat, I find it difficult to believe that I'm only hearing about him *now*."

"Aye, I should've told you about him before," said Grim.

Grey lit another smoke.

"Well now," said Grey, "are you willing to help us out? Your *boy's* workin' with that scumbag, and it ain't doing you or your kind any favours. We need to find these two, and we need to find 'em now before they take any others."

John nodded, his arms crossed.

"If what you say is true, then I will help you."

25: MOTHER DEAR

⌘

Janus watched her family home from the backseat of the car as the heavy rain set the scene for an event she was not looking forward to. The conditions were not the best to be running errands, but Janus had left this particular one by the wayside for far too long. She paid the driver and asked him to wait for her return before closing the door.

She would not be staying long.

Janus sprinted along the driveway to her family home as thick water droplets pelted her from the darkened dusk sky. Her jacket was saturated by the time she made it to the entrance.

Knocking on the smooth, wooden door brought with it a warm feeling of comfort, yet with it an undertone of oppression and fear. Not all of the memories she had there were positive ones.

Janus looked through the windowpane for activity, and after a minute of not seeing anyone, she knocked on the door again. Sliding her hand under her jacket, she rubbed her shoulder, sore from a rough night's sleep.

Hopefully, no surprises are waiting for me inside. I've had enough of those to last a lifetime.

Knocking on the door once more, she was struck with the realisation that her mother might be back at work, a possibility which she prayed was true.

Nodding to herself, she turned to make her way back down the driveway.

"Janus!" yelled her mother from the front door of the house as the door swung open.

Turning around, she saw Adalia standing in the open doorway sporting an old, white bathrobe that was frayed and stained in multiple places. Janus smiled artificially as she returned to the door, slowly discerning her mother's state. She looked terrible and smelled even worse.

"How are you?" asked Janus.

"I'm fine," she replied, gesturing for Janus to come inside. "Come on in!"

She's unusually chirpy.

Janus took off her shoes as she moved inside. Placing them on the white tiles, Janus watched her mother's slow gait to the loungeroom; un unmistakable sluggish stumbling that came from being inebriated, which brought back painful memories she'd made considerable effort to dismiss. The warmth she felt had dissipated, replaced by the sinking feeling of aversion and discomfort. Adalia's Caucasian complexion had tipped towards malnourished, and as she returned to the couch and slipped under a blanket, Janus saw the black bags under her eyes as Adalia looked up at her daughter and blinked at slowly.

"It slipped my mind before I made my way over, but it's budget week, isn't it?" asked Janus, already knowing the answer. "Is it as crazy as usual?"

"I rescheduled it to next month, so no! Not crazy at all!" Adalia rubbed her eyes with both hands as she tittered. "You can leave your coat there," she said, gesturing to the hanger as she tried to blink away her sore eyes.

Janus looked at the coat rack with a sigh; she was used to seeing the frame full of her family's clothing. Draping her wet jacket over the stand, Janus adjusted it for a moment before stepping over to her mother, underneath the plush carpet. Janus cringed upon getting close to her.

She really reeks!

As she sat, Janus felt something break underneath her, forcing her to stand up in a hurry.

"I think I broke something."

She shifted the couch cushions to find a wine glass, or what was left of it, sitting underneath. Picking up a small piece, she found wine residue around the glass, crusted and old, as if it had been there for a few days.

The sight worried Janus, bringing back feelings of fear, pain, and depression. The sight stunned her as she held the shard before her eyes, feeling anxiety flush through her body and freeze her in place.

"Oh, I'd forgotten about that; let me get a bag!" Adalia quickly got up from the couch, almost falling over before stumbling into the kitchen. "Don't worry about the glass!" she said, her voice echoing through the house. "I've got plenty of them!"

Once she disappeared from view, her eyes snapped back to the crushed glass.

It can't just be the one glass.

Placing her hands under the couch and heaving it up, Janus bent down to look at the carpet beneath. As she leant down, she counted thirteen wine bottles, all empty and rolled towards the back. Each bottle had small red stains on the carpet below the open mouths of the bottles.

"*Oh no . . .*" she said under her breath.

Hearing her mother's slippers clapping against the kitchen tiles, she gently lowered the couch before picking up the pieces of the glass, putting them in a pile on her hands as she carried them into the kitchen.

It makes sense that she'd be back here, I suppose . . .

Painful memories of her mother and father arguing, of bottles being thrown by her mother's drunken rage, it all came back to her at that moment, skimming by like a slideshow over her eyes.

Keep it together . . .

"I *said* not to worry about that!" said Adalia meeting her in the kitchen. "I shouldn't have left it there in the first place . . ."

Her mother held open the bag as Janus kept up the fake smile, pouring the shards into the white plastic.

"How are you?" asked her mother as she tied the bag. "How's Grey's investigation going? Has he had any luck finding Oscar?"

Janus shook her head, rubbing her index finger and thumb together. "We're still looking."

"That's nice . . ."

You probably would've said that regardless of how I'd answered . . .

Adalia took the bag to the bin, clearing her throat as she scuffled across the polished white tiles.

Janus looked around the room, noticing that the windows were down and the blinds drawn over.

Moving back to the lounge room and over to the television, she rubbed her hand over the back panel. It was sweltering, and her hand came away with a layer of thick, matted dust stuck to her skin. Guilt pressed down on her head and shoulders as she clapped the dirt away, watching it floating down to the discoloured, sticky carpet. The house hadn't been cleaned in a long time.

When her mother returned to the lounge room, Janus stood before her with her arms crossed.

"Are you okay?" asked Janus.

Her mouth curled into a smile, but her eyes didn't match the expression. "Yes, of course . . ."

Bloodshot eyes, dry lips, malnourished skin tone. The signs were all there. Adalia must've been pretty consistently out of it for a while now to be in this bad a shape.

Janus sighed, glancing to the bathrobe. "Where's *your* bathrobe?"

Her eyes were wet immediately. "I left mine at the hotel . . . Why does that matter?" Adalia looked at her incredulously.

Janus shrugged. "No reason. I just always liked your robe. Suits you better."

A tear flowed from Adalia's eye and down her cheek. She shook her head at her daughter, squinting and sniffling as she moved towards the lounge, plucking a box of tissues from beside it. "I miss your father . . ."

Adalia couldn't hide her grief any longer, wiping her face and nose with a handful of tissue as she sobbed quietly. The emotional rubberbanding between one extreme to another was another sign she couldn't ignore.

Janus swallowed dryly. "I'm going to get some water . . ."

As she walked into the kitchen, Adalia followed her. She sighed, hoping that the woman wouldn't throw anything at her as she walked behind her.

I don't need this right now . . .

Janus opened the fridge and picked up a glass of water, tearing the thin plastic seal from it as she tossed the seal in the bin, turning to find Adalia standing before her.

"A part of me blames you . . ." she said, squinting at Janus with a surly look on her face as she crossed her arms, hoping that Janus would take the bait.

Janus sighed. "I know you do . . ." Drinking the water, she realised only now how thirsty she'd been.

"You're just like your father; you lock away your emotions and refuse to deal with them!" Adalia began gesturing wildly. "If I hadn't sent *Grey* along after you, I would've lost everyone that night! If only you'd paid attention to what's going on in the world, you wouldn't have cost me your father's life with your stupid, immature attitude. You can't save the world on your own! You little brat!

"I know you've seen what these people can do, defying nature and science. The thing is, those people have been around for a lot longer than you and your stupid little unit, and if you'd have only told me what you were up to, we could've done it the *right way!*"

Adalia was hurting, that was clear. Janus felt pity for her mother, but the guilt that was building up as soon as she walked in the door melted away at seeing how pathetic she was.

"Are you going to say something to me . . . ?" said Adalia, shrugging pensively as tears rolled down her face.

Janus sighed. She didn't feel the need to say anything in reply to her mother's abusive ranting.

Biting back won't do any good; been down that road too many times not to learn . . .

"I could've sent any number of people after Oscar, but I didn't want to jeopardise my son's life. Don't you understand that? He was my *boy . . .*"

Janus closed her eyes.

"*My baby boy,*" whispered Adalia. "And you took him away from me . . ."

Janus took a deep breath before answering. "I know you're going through a lot," said Janus nodding assertively. "And I hope you understand that I am too." Janus ambled delicately towards Adalia. "I am *trying* to get through this the best way I can. Slowly and steadily," said Janus embracing her shocked mother.

She wasn't known for her affection, so Adalia stood stiff as a board, her arms trembling slightly.

"I need you to—"

Adalia shoved her away. Along with the sudden force came with it a feeling of hurt and rejection, which thrust its way deep into Janus's chest like a bullet. She glared at her mother with insecurity, embarrassment and anger flooding through her mind.

"You're going to try and find these people *again*, aren't you!?"

Janus sighed. "It's the best way to get—"

"Oscar is gone!" yelled Adalia, stepping forward to shove her again.

Janus allowed her mother to shove her, regaining her balance as she stumbled past the fridge before standing upright and watching her mother come at her again. When Adalia got like this, Janus would retreat inwards. She did the same now, holding on until the storm had passed.

"He's dead!" screamed Adalia. "Just like your father! And it's all *your* fault! They're dead because of you, you stupid little—" Adalia stepped forward to shove Janus again, this time knocking her to the floor as she slid onto her backside on the tiles. Janus didn't hide her defeated expression; she wore it as she stood up and looked into her mother's pained, weepy eyes with pity.

"And now you're going to throw yourself back into it? I don't remember raising a daughter this stupid!"

Janus tried to hide her anguish. This was not the first time her mother had assaulted her.

Rubbing her lower back, she remembered when she'd told her about signing up for STARCOV. The fight had ended with Janus sporting a swollen cheek, a loose tooth, and a kitchen knife being thrown at her as she ran away. It had required surgery, which Adalia had paid for privately. She'd never told Nathan about the abuse. Knowing her father well enough, she'd always assumed that Nathan would've left Adalia once he'd found out; her silence had ensured that had never happened.

You didn't raise me . . . She wanted to say. *My father raised me. And he was proud of the person I'd become.*

She thought about how Nathan could've gotten together with such a mess of a person as she squinted at her mother. Nathan was away from home a great deal, but to be totally ignorant of his wife's alcoholism was a stretch. She'd never known how Nathan felt about it and wasn't sure how to even approach a conversation with him about such matters. But he must've known, she thought, even if he wasn't present for most of the more serious episodes.

Adalia's mortified, grief-stricken face stared at her, panting and crying pathetically.

"Please . . ." she finally said, "don't leave me *alone* in this world . . ." She collapsed to the ground crying. "I need someone . . . to help me . . . I can't handle all of this on my own . . ."

Janus stood before her mother, staring at her wordlessly from across the kitchen. She watched her vulnerability with apathy, practically conditioned to react this way after seeing it so often. The sound of falling rain filled the silence for a few quiet moments, allowing Janus to return from her inner hiding place within her mind.

Janus took a deep, jittery breath before joining her mother on the floor.

"You hate me . . ." said Adalia, her voice cracking as she started sobbing.

"I know you do; I'm so sorry. I've never known how to be a mother. I don't know how to handle you kids; I never have."

She looked up at Janus, her mother's skinny, trembling fingers rubbing her daughter's warm, blushing cheeks. "What am I supposed to do without your father? He was the only good thing in my life, and now he's just . . . *gone . . . ?*"

Janus looked away for a moment, thinking about what she said. She genuinely believed it to be an undeniable truth in their relationship; Nathan was the rock of the family. Without Nathan, Adalia was perpetually lost in a storm, unable to stop thrashing about, coming apart at the seams with every wave. If she didn't get any support, Adalia would no doubt be devoured in depression and self-destruction.

"I've spent years trying to ignore everything about my childhood," said Janus, breaking her silence. She reached down to grasp her mother's face in her hands as he struggled to find the words, searching deep inside for an answer. "But that time is done now. What's happened has happened."

Janus kissed her mother on the forehead tenderly, returning to sit in front of her. "I forgive you." Janus forced a smile as a tear rolled down her cheek.

"I don't understand you," said Janus with a saddened laugh, "but I forgive you. I don't want to see you like this, lost and alone, drinking yourself to death. You've done bad things, and so have I, but if we keep wallowing in the past, we're never going to be able to move on with our lives."

I haven't cried for her in years . . . didn't think I had any tears left . . .

"I am an adult now," said Janus, taking a deep breath before continuing. "The time we had as a mother and daughter is over." Janus pulled her mother's face so she could look into her eyes up close. "We are *equals* now. Two adults trying to get by the only way we know how."

Janus helped her mother stand up. Adalia exhaled as she continued to sob, breathing as if a weight had suddenly lifted from her chest.

"I think you should take a break from work, officially," said Janus. "Speak with an Inquisitor and stay with Aunt Reeta. I know you have enough money now to live comfortably for the rest of your life, even if you never work again." Janus rubbed her shoulder. "Focus on yourself for once."

Adalia grinned as she picked up a box of tissues from the kitchen counter and held it up in offer. Pulling out a tissue from the crumpled box, Janus held it firmly for a moment, gesturing with the soft paper as she spoke.

"Try and get some proper, *sober* rest," said Janus as she dabbed her eyelids. "It's only us for now. But if I can find Oscar, that'll make three . . ."

Adalia nodded, hugging Janus sincerely for the first time in her life.

"I want Oscar to come home and see *you*, the woman he remembers . . ." Janus sighed.

Not the woman I remember . . .

Joel Thomas Cooke

26: PERCUSSION

⌘

"When we take these details into consideration, we've reached the conclusion that this was an offensive operation with no pretence of resolving the situation peacefully," said Grey. "It was terrorism on home turf. The actions of these soldiers are indefensible and despicable."

The other councillors were looking at the pictures of the crime scene, along with the written report Grey had prepared. The document included testimonies from Grey, the survivors from the assault, and stories of the families who were affected by the tragedy.

"What happened to the operators?" asked Leanna sitting at the head of the table.

"They were killed in action."

Leanna raised an eyebrow. "Was that necessary?"

Grey looked to her neutrally.

"Absolutely. Once these 'Onyx' soldiers opened fire, I had to put 'em down. Didn't want to risk anyone else getting hurt."

His delivery and word choice when discussing official business had become second nature. Interruptions were still something Grey was working on, so he was glad the other councillors were letting him finish. He didn't want to have to look at his cue cards more than necessary, questions and comments had the risk of throwing him off, and he struggled to jump back and forth between different points and discussions.

"You took down three of these bastards?" asked Marko.

He was looking at Grey incredulously from across the table, photo in hand. His white, collared shirt and no tie spoke of his humble upbringing. The faded colouring of his clothing and the fact that we wore it once a week said a lot about the dark-skinned, middle-aged man. He was in charge of the industrial sector of the city, boasting one of the larger tenures of any councillor, clocking in at twenty-six years of service.

"I did," retorted Grey with a neutral expression.

"Not a massive surprise," said Adalia Scitilliant. "None of you have witnessed Grey's aptitude in combat, and on *that* note, you should be thankful that you haven't. Things can get rather messy if you get on his *bad* side."

Grey and Adalia shared a knowing look as Grey nodded slightly.

Good to see you back on your feet, ma'am.

"I take it that you have—in fact—seen Greyson in action then?" asked Marko, raising a bushy eyebrow at her.

Adalia shrugged, staring at Marko with a mischievous smile. "I suppose you could say that." Gesturing to the chairwoman at the end of the table, Adalia continued. "But I believe I was called in to consult on how best to remediate the risks of this 'ONYX Project,' as a subject matter expert, not to squabble about Grey's competence with killing terrorists. I'm here tonight as a favour to Grey, after all, I'm *supposed* to be on personal leave."

"And we thank you for taking the time to be here with us tonight," said Leanna assertively.

The room was filled with a deafening silence. Grey hated moments like these. It wasn't the message he was trying to send when people dwelled on things like this, but he was slowly learning to accept that he couldn't change how people thought of him.

This whole charade may not have been required if people had the capacity to change their opinions about me . . .

"If these soldiers acted on orders from a superior," continued Grey as he pushed through the silence, "then I'd like to meet the person giving the orders. Sending unrecognised, privately governed soldiers to a sector without the approval of the appropriate sectors councillor, is a crime, and those responsible should face the consequences of their actions."

I'd love to go out tonight and find out who's involved here . . . Take things into my own hands and just get things done right . . .

He would have to ignore his instincts. The first raw feeling that would strike Grey involved developing plans for slipping through legalities and due process; he'd made a career out of doing so up until a few years ago. But that was not how a councillor behaved.

Do this one the right way; you can't be implicated any more than you already have.

He sighed, nodding to himself.

Killing those soldiers . . . they'll be watching you now, waiting for a mistake. Might need to wait until the spotlight drifts away before I try something again . . .

"I agree with Grey," said Adalia. "Transparency in these conditions is paramount, and if we do not agree on how to go about deployment and procedure, then these soldiers can go about the city as they please."

Adalia tilted her head toward Leanna, who smiled pleasantly at her. "If these suited thugs were to have invaded *any* other part of Menilax, you'd be thrown out onto the street for incompetence." Leanna's smile faded.

"Well," said Grey, cutting the awkward silence quickly, "we're not completely in the dark. I have information about the soldiers and their equipment. Mostly from analysis and observations from the items we recovered. Our equipment is outdated, and our resources are thin as we're working on the new Enforcement building at Cardinal Point."

Grey swivelled to face Leanna at the end of the table. "But here's the point. I think an official investigation is in order. No one should have the power to send in soldiers to any part of Menilax without coming through us first."

She nodded. "I appreciate your *transparency*," said Leanna smiling mockingly at Adalia. "I can assure you that if someone gave any such order to infiltrate your sector, we *will* find out."

Grey nodded, his eyes darting to his notes for a moment.

"I'm sure you've all read through Grey's official report and statement on the attack and his subsequent investigation," Said Leanna. "The signs point to 'Lornan Futuristics' being responsible for the manufacture of the components used by these soldiers, and now that Jone Lornan has vanished, I find it quite disarming that the project is left to the wind.

"Tell me," said Adalia, speaking before anyone else could comment, "Who was responsible for this project?"

Grey stood up abruptly. "If it's all the same with you, ma'am, I'd like to get to the more important part of this attack first. The victims . . ."

He waited for a moment, watching Adalia with a smile. She nodded, making herself comfortable on the leather chair. Scooping up a report on those who'd been injured or killed, he continued.

"I've calculated the compensation that the families require. If you'll take a look . . ." he said, sliding it over to Leanna. "You'll notice I've included a description of each cost, and I'm hoping for the following amounts."

Grey looked over at Jonathon's usual seat, finally deciding to bring up the Councillor's absence to everyone. "Where is Jonathon?" asked Grey, looking over at the chairwoman.

The chairwoman sighed. "Councilman Jonathon died in his sleep a few nights ago. We're investigating the circumstances carefully . . ."

Grey squinted, crossing his arms. "I wasn't aware . . ." stated Grey as he grimaced.

He was definitely involved in the project . . . Said so himself . . .

Rubbing his scar with his calloused index finger, he thought on this for a quiet moment.

Something doesn't feel right about this whole thing, looks like it might be a setup.

A thought struck him. Magdeline may be responsible. Looking over at her chair, he noticed that she too was absent.

Damn, I'm not with it tonight, need to catch up on sleep . . . He closed his eyes, rubbing them gently. *Which means I'll be drinking . . .*

"And Mag?" asked Grey. "Where is she?"

"She left Vale on the same night that Jonathon was found dead in his apartment.   Now," she said, clasping her hands together as she leant forward, "I'm aware of how it looks. Foul play is not being ruled out." Leanna gestured delicately. "It could be a coincidence . . . just as it could be a sign of guilt. But we need to belay our judgment for now and stay focused on performing our roles until the investigation is complete."

Her confident and neutral tone carried through the room succinctly as she looked at each councillor around the room.

"An Enforcement investigation is underway. In the meantime, please cooperate with any inquiries; they're just doing their jobs after all," said Leanna. "I've been assured that this case is their priority."

A lot can happen in the course of a few weeks, it seems . . .

Magdeline was a ruthless councillor, but Grey never thought she'd be capable of such a sloppy murder such as this. She was the first suspect, considering her involvement with the project, which made Grey think it was too obvious for her to be primarily responsible.

If I ever have an average week, I'll probably have a stroke from paranoia . . .

Each councillor nodded and muttered in agreement.

She raised a finger. "There will be two separate Enforcement teams working on the investigations. Grey, once the meeting has adjourned, if you'd like to hand over your information to Captain Travers so she can start investigating the attack."

Grey nodded, returning his gaze to the papers he'd prepared to sort them out for Alicia. Looking up to nod at her politely, she nodded back from the corner of the room respectfully. Her long blonde hair was tied behind her head in a ponytail, which draped over her navy suit. She was young for a captain, at thirty-three years of age, but she was wise beyond her years. Her oval face, pale complexion, and bulbous nose gave her a professional yet approachable vibe.

"Getting back to Jonathon and Magdeline," said Leanna. "While we're searching for applicants for their positions, I'll be handling their dealings and responsibilities. The damages will be coming from Jonathon's sector for your costs, Grey, due to some of the project responsibilities residing under his jurisdiction."

Leanna leant on the table, gesturing to Adalia. "Mrs.Scitilliant—" she started, before Adalia interrupted.

"It's . . . Ms . . . now, actually . . ."

Everyone in the room looked over to Leanna, who exhaled and nodded solemnly.

"My sincerest apologies, Ms Scitilliant. Captain Scitilliant was a great man, and the city will not be the same without his steadfast example." Leanna's eyes began to tear up frighteningly fast, as she tore a tissue free from the centre of the board room table before speaking.

"Thank you . . . Leanna . . ."

"Perhaps . . ." continued Leanna, "you'd be willing to participate on the board with us in a long term position, assuming that you're ready, of course . . ."

The room locked eyes with Adalia, who seemed vulnerable and distressed. But at that moment, she sat up straight, cleared her throat, and nodded like the professional she was.

"I'll consider it. Someone recently taught me that nothing is beyond repair, and it looks like you lot could use someone like me to push things forward a little bit."

Grey tapped his hand on the table, accentuating her statement. "Here, here," he said, smiling pleasantly with Adalia.

"Either way," said Leanna, "I'll ensure that this 'Onyx' project will be investigated thoroughly, and we'll make a point to validate its viability moving forward. Grey: I'll read over your proposition and get back to you at the next meeting, assuming we don't have any emergencies between here and there.

"If a decision needs to be made quickly without too much discussion, I'll reach out to you all individually. However considering the circumstances, an emergency meeting may be necessary, so please be ready just in case."

The other councillors shifted nervously, even Grey.

"What's going to happen with the Onyx Guard project?" asked Grey.

The chairwoman took a quick look around the room, meeting eyes for a brief moment with all of the councillors. "That hasn't come up for discussion, as of yet."

Grey leant into the desk, his body facing Leanna as he tapped his hand on the black leather finish across the middle of the table. He'd been struck with an idea.

"We can discuss it now, if you have some thoughts on the matter." Said Leanna.

If these soldiers can be formed into a proper military or enforcement unit, I might actually have a team that could patrol the Broken Sector safely.

He smiled. Adalia seemed content to sit back and assess the situation, regarding Grey with a raised eyebrow.

Regular people could safely patrol without worrying about being taken down by a crazed augur if they're sporting one of these things.

"If I may, chairwoman," he said, "I have a solution that could solve a few problems here."

He placed both hands on the desk, leaning in as he spoke.

A man in a mask kicked in the door of the boardroom, the double doors slamming against their hinges as everyone's attention snapped over to the source of the commotion.

Wearing a black long-sleeve shirt, with gloves and pants to match, his ghostly white neck was the only part of his flesh that was exposed. He looked to be average height, had a lean build, and was hunched over slightly. The mask on his face was seared onto the flesh of his face, evident due to the inflamed scar tissue that ran around the outside of the metal.

"Security!" yelled Leanna as the rest of the board stood up from their chairs.

Grey saw the masked man raise an automatic weapon to the councillors as Tobias and Alicia drew their pistols without hesitation.

"Get down!" screamed Grey.

Leaping across the desk towards the attacker with his ability ramped to its maximum, Grey covered the distance in a split second, although he was too slow to stop the man firing off at least fourty rounds with the high-powered weapon. Grey's momentum had pushed them both outside the boardroom and into the hallway outside, and as Grey pulled an empowered hand back to smash his face in, he realised that he wasn't holding onto him anymore. All he could see was a thin layer of smoke wisping menacingly between his fingertips.

"I'll deal with you in a moment," said the masked man, appearing inside the boardroom.

Grey snarled as he stood up while the masked man fired more rounds into the room. Unsheathing Sithaleir, the smoke plumed out as he dashed forward, roaring through the smoke like a wraith as it trailed around him.

The masked man turned to face him. Thrusting the blade a the man's back, he vanished into a plume of smoke once more as Sithaleir passed right through him. It was the same smoke Sithaleir created when he invoked its presence, he noticed.

Spinning in place with enhanced movement, he looked around with hyper focus, waiting for a sign of the masked man with his muscles primed to react in an instant. Instead of finding the assassin, Grey's eyes were drawn to the gruesome remains of the board members. Their bleeding corpses were strewn around the room amidst the blood and gore from their bullet riddled bodies.

"Grey!" yelled Adalia from under the desk, before standing up from her hiding place, holding her side as she gasped and limped towards him. He could see multiple gunshots on her body.

An intense panic surged through him upon seeing Janus' mother wounded. The implications of what happened creating chaos in his mind as he shook his head, unable to accept reality.

Leanna coughed from underneath the head of the table, causing Grey and Adalia to share a glance filled with shock as Grey sprinted to her and cradled her bleeding body in his arms. He searched her clothes and skin feverishly for wounds, finding a few bullet wounds across her leg and chest. Unlike Adalia who joined him a moment after, Leanna's wounds may prove fatal.

"Don't you die on me!" he said. "I'm going to get you to my hospital. You'll be okay, just hang on!"

"I have a question to ask of you, Greyson . . ."

Grey turned his head to find the masked assassin standing at the end of the table.

"Where is Darius Malaroth?"

That's what this is about . . . ?

"Who the hell is this *freak!?*" demanded Adalia as she coughed and backed away towards the glass.

"You murdered the leaders of this city . . . to ask about a dead man?" Grey's voice was filled with murderous rage, his muscles primed to seek retribution as he held Sithaleir forward.

The mask shifted from side to side. "No. Their lives were already forfeit. But yours?" The man unsheathed a sword of his own from his back. "You still have use. You know where Darius is hiding, I am sure of it, and I am done waiting for you to lead me to him. So I will force your hand."

Facing Adalia, Grey stared at her with concern, placing a hand gently on her trembling shoulder. "Stay here, " he said, as she nodded, her eyes wide with uncertainty.

With a clenched jaw and a stern grimace on his face, Grey saw nothing but red as he charged the assassin recklessly.

"No," muttered the assassin. "We're not done yet . . ."

Grey leapt forward, thrusting Sithaleir at the masked man's abdomen. As the blade passed through his foe who had already vaporised into smoke, Grey smirked, expecting him to do so again. Grey spun around, slashing behind him in a quick arc. The assassin stepped back as he appeared there, avoiding the attack by millimetres.

"The records indicate that your abilities should not be this advanced . . ." said the masked man as he dashed away. "How . . . interesting."

Grey reached out with his hand to snatch the assassins blade, but he was ready. Spinning it around and slashing at his palm, the man punished Grey for his grapple attempt, causing him to reel back with a pained yelp.

"Who in the hell are you!?" Barked Grey.

And why is your voice so familiar . . . ?

"You know who I am . . ." He held his blade in a defensive position. "And I know who *you* are . . ."

What's my next move here?

I could invoke Sithaleir's higher power, but it'd risk Adalia and Leanna.

I could take out my pistol, but again, can't risk their lives with a stray bullet, and he's surely going to be able to evade gunshots.

Grey smiled.

I know.

Enhancing his legs and arms, he flicked his wrist, tossing Sithaleir at his foe. The assassin reacted as he expected as his form began to wither into smoke. Grey channelled all of his power into his right side, from his shoulder to his fist.

Before the assassin vanished, he roared, turning and driving his fist into the air. As the assassin appeared before him, Grey was already in full swing, so the fist crunched through the masked man's chest with a wet, fleshy explosion. His body parted against the weight of Grey's fist as he roared, his mind frenzied and furious as he growled in the killer's drying mask.

Clenching his jaw, Grey grabbed the assassin by the throat, using the leverage to yank his fist from the gaping cavity he'd made. Holding the body up as he panted, he noticed black blood dripping from the wound; the assassin barely moved an inch or made a sound during the whole process. Grey's eyes flicked across the mask for a few quiet moments as he caught his breath, satisfied that he wasn't sensing any signs of life.

Tossing the dead body out of the boardroom like a sack of rubbish, Grey jogged over to check on Adalia, scooping up the hilt of Sithaleir on the way.

"She's still awake, but barely," said Adalia, sharing Grey's panic-stricken look.

"Are you all right?" he asked Leanna, reassessing her wounds.

She was breathing, if not faintly. Her eyes were flittering back and forth.

"I've . . . been better . . ." she said weakly.

"Let's get you to the hospital."

"I know just the one," said Adalia, "We'll go to the same one where Janus was treated, they—"

"No," said Grey firmly, lugging the chairwoman over his shoulder as she groaned. Grey looked around the room, inspecting the chaos around him with a shake of his head.

"We're going to the Broken Sector hospital; it's safe there, easy to defend . . ."

Clumps of blood and gore dribbled down the walls, and the rear glass that overlooked the city was peppered with bullet holes. The gold metal shell casings, ejected from the gunman's weapon, had a glint in them, reflected by the fluorescent lights on the ceiling. The once loud murmurings of his colleagues had been replaced by a cold, piercing silence, severely threatening his near-broken sanity.

"As you say, then," said Adalia, scrunching her face, "Let's just get the hell out of here."

He rubbed his hand over his face, trying to make sense of how it had all gone to shit so quickly.

What are we going to do now . . . ?

A loud snap rang out through the room.

Grey's eyes were drawn to the noise from the hallway, noticing too late that the man had an explosive launcher locked around his shoulder. The assassin stood up straight, unphased by the hole in his chest as the rune on his mask glowed bright green. As the assassin squeezed the trigger, Grey turned around and kicked a hole through the bullet-peppered glass behind them. Snatching Adalia and keeping the two women as close to his body as he could, Grey threw his back into the window, leaping with as much momentum as he could while keeping the two women safe from the impact of the glass.

As they cleared the building, the explosive detonated. A pulse of kinetic energy rang out, pushing Grey further into the air as he gasped, quickly moving Adalia and Leanna—who were screaming as loud as their lungs would allow—behind him to spare them the shrapnel that pelted his flesh. Screaming in agony as the hot metal burned his insides, he tried to push the pain away and focus on how he was going to land without killing himself and the two women that depended on him.

Grey's momentum from the push of the explosion had run out as the three of them began to fall.

⌘

27: A BRIEF REPRIEVE

⌘

"Is she going to be all right?" Asked Grey.

"I believe so," said the nurse. "Leanna's a fighter, that much is certain. The surgery went well, so we just have to wait until the anesthesia wears off so we can properly assess her."

The young nurse touched Grey's tense shoulder, leaving her cold fingers on him for a moment in an attempt to comfort him.

"If she gets worse . . ." He began to say as he turned to face her. "I want you to use the experimental cell regeneration procedure on her."

The nurse opened her mouth to protest, but he raised his hand before she started. "I know it's risky on non-augurs, but if she starts circlin' the drain, you do whatever it takes to keep her with us. We clear?"

"Ciril station hasn't cleared the treatment yet for regular humans, you know that," she said, her pale face crinkled with concern. "There are good reasons why it's not approved, and I-"

"Yeah, I know, but I pay the bills to keep everything churnin' here," he said, gesturing firmly. "And if this woman dies, *we* are screwed. So you do whatever it takes to keep her alive."

"As you wish, councillor," she said, crossing her arms. "You should let me assess you as well before you go. I don't know how you're still standing after what you went through."

"I'll be all right Darlin'," he said gently. "They took out the shrapnel pieces, so I'll heal just fine on my own now."

Although the way things seem to be headed, I'm starting to doubt that I will be okay.

He turned to regard Leanna with a sigh. The decision to take both women to the Broken Sector hospital was an easy one to make. Without any real clue on what else was hunting him, Grey knew this place was the safest place for them to heal. That, and no one else had access to the advanced healing tech that Ciril station had been working on from the safety of Vale's moon.

"What are we going to do now?" Asked Adalia, sitting up in her bed across from Leanna.

With a heavy sigh, Grey left Leanna's bedside to stand next to Adalia.

"*You're* going to rest up," he replied, patting her on the shoulder. "And you should consider yourself lucky, no one else made it out except for us."

The Nurse took some more notes, before leaving the dimly lit room without another word. He turned to regard her with respect as she walked down the hall.

I suppose they're used to me dismissing them by now. I might try to clean myself up a little before I leave, I promised to meet Ducard and Janus at the bar tonight. Last thing I want is them asking questions.

He rubbed his face as stress began to fill his insides, weighing Grey down as if concrete had settled in his stomach.

Pioneers deliver me . . . What am I going to tell Janus?

"Who was that man who attacked us?" Asked Adalia, interrupting his thought process. "Do you *know* him?"

It sounded like my brother. But it can't be . . . he died a long time ago.

"No," he lied. "But it doesn't matter. He's dead, ain't no one survivin' that blast."

"Well he sure seemed to know *you!*" Said Adalia incredulously. "What aren't you telling me, Grey?"

He sighed aloud, his frustration piercing his calm.

"I don't know who he was, okay? So stop askin'," said Grey, gesturing sharply. "All I know is the board was blown to hell by some psycho in a mask, same as you!"

Adalia shook her head, "Well you'd better figure it out fast, councillor. I need to get back to work, and I can't have some crazy assassin walking around threatening me or my family."

As I didn't have enough to worry about.

"Listen," said Grey, "I gotta go. Focus on getting better for now, and leave this whole mess to me."

He moved back to the end of Leanna's bed, gripping the cool metal handle at the foot of the frame. Her eyes were flittering back and forth, and her breathing seemed laboured.

"Is she okay?" Asked Adalia, leaning over the side of the bed to get a closer look.

"I think she's having a nightmare," said Grey with a sigh. "I'll send the nurse in on my way out, couldn't hurt to check on her again."

He watched her quietly for a moment.

You hang in there, chair woman. If you die here and now . . .

He rubbed his tired eyes, and shook his head.

Pioneers, I can't do this on my own Leanna. Menilax needs you. I need you.

Touching her leg through the thick blankets, Grey felt as though things were beginning to fall apart. The plans he'd made, and the beliefs he'd held onto to get him through the day to day repetition of his life, now felt fractured, blown to hell along with the rest of his colleagues on the board.

"Promise me you'll watch her?" Asked Grey as he regarded Adalia one last time.

"I will," she replied. "As long as you watch over my daughter. She's not as invincible as she thinks she is, and she's far too emotional to see things clearly."

Grey nodded. "I'll do whatever I can to make this right."

"Promise me," said Adalia as Grey began to turn away.

He scoffed, shaking his head.

She threw her arms up in the air, "I'm not an idiot, Greyson. I know there are plenty of things you keep from me, and the rest of the world for that matter. But I want you to promise me, that you'll put Janus above it all. She's risked so much for you, and I want your word that you'll keep her safe."

Adalia rubbed her water eyes, "She's all I have left."

He inhaled and exhaled slowly, crossing his arms as the two of them glared at each other. "I promise."

Without another word, Grey left the room in a hurry.

He was already late.

⌘

<u>END OF PART ONE</u>

⌘

ABOUT THE AUTHOR

Joel is an Australian author, perpetually fascinated by the storytelling process. He's spent the last eight years writing and perfecting his craft, and every day his passion for the development process grows.

When he's not in the office working on fiction, he's typically spending time with his wife, Carol, his loving family, and supportive friends. Not to mention he has a husky and a border collie, who keep him on his toes with their high energy.

He enjoys video games, television shows, movies and novels of all kinds. Anything that has a unique or immersive story to capture the imagination, serves as the inspiration that makes his fiction possible.

If you'd like to see more of Joel's work, you can check out the website, www.jtcooke.com. You're also more than welcome to look out for us on Facebook, Instagram or twitter, or sign up to our mailing list on the website to be first in line for updates.

www.ingramcontent.com/pod-product-compliance
Lightning Source LLC
Chambersburg PA
CBHW050032120726
47903CB00006B/2002